Acclaim for Catherine West

"A beautiful exploration of the bonds that tie us together as family and the secrets that sometimes unravel those threads. Catherine West builds a world worth entering and characters that linger long after the last page is turned."

—JULIE CANTRELL, NEW YORK TIMES AND USA TODAY
BESTSELLING AUTHOR OF THE FEATHERED BONE

"Smartly written and highly engaging, Catherine West's *The Things We Knew* dazzles, piercing the shadows of a family's tragedy with the light of love."

—BILLY COFFEY, AUTHOR OF THE CURSE OF CROW HOLLOW
AND WHEN MOCKINGBIRDS SING

"I began reading *The Things We Knew* with eager anticipation and reached the end with complete satisfaction. Displaying an understanding of the conflicting dynamics of family relationships, Cathy West deftly weaves together the tumultuous storylines of the Carlisle and Cooper families. In *The Things We Knew*, she wrestles with how secrets can hide the truth of the past and cloud the future, while asking the question: *Does knowing the truth always set you free?*"

—BETH K. VOGT, 2015 RITA FINALIST, AUTHOR OF
ALMOST LIKE BEING IN LOVE

"A poignant, multi-faceted novel that pulled me in deeper with every turned page, *The Things We Knew* so adeptly explores the power of truth and its ability to set us all free. I can't wait for readers to fall as hopelessly in love with Nick and the Carlisle family as I did. Well done, Catherine West!"

—KATIE GANSHERT, AWARD-WINNING AUTHOR OF
THE ART OF LOSING YOURSELF

"Catherine West's debut, *The Things We Knew,* is a beautifully readable exploration of family secrets and their continuing effects on both those who know and don't know them. But nothing is truly hidden from grace, and the offered redemption at novel's end is both satisfying and real. A celebration of love, resiliency, and the promises of forgiveness."

—CHRISTA PARRISH, AWARD-WINNING AUTHOR OF
STILL LIFE AND *STONES FOR BREAD*

"Catherine West creates a well-drawn portrait of a family in crisis. I laughed and cried and cheered as I read this lovely novel. I can't wait to see what's up next!"

—KATHRYN CUSHMAN, AUTHOR OF *FINDING ME*
AND *FADING STARLIGHT*

"*The Things We Knew* is a remarkable story, and author Catherine West is truly a wordsmith. Not only does West paint pictures that catch you up in their exquisite detail, but she also creates believable characters that will stay with you long after you've finished the last page. I can't encourage you enough to treat yourself to this exceptional and poignant escape to Nantucket and its varied inhabitants—and while you're at it, consider getting a copy for someone else. They will thank you for it."

—KATHI MACIAS, AWARD-WINNING AUTHOR OF *RED INK*

"In *The Things We Knew*, author Catherine West captures the nuances of deeply rooted familial pain and its impact on those in its wake. Intriguing setting, realistic characters with all-too-familiar tensions, and a tangle worth tracing to its source make *The Things We Knew* as satisfying as a Nantucket sunrise."

—CYNTHIA RUCHTI, AUTHOR OF *AS WATERS GONE BY*
AND *SONG OF SILENCE*

"Dynamic and lovely. This is a story that will capture your heart from the first page."

—ALICE J. WISLER, AUTHOR OF *RAIN SONG* AND
UNDER THE SILK HIBISCUS

"Integrally woven, fast-paced, and hard to put down. Loved the setting and loved the characters. Great book!"

—CELESTE FLETCHER MCHALE, AUTHOR OF
THE SECRET TO HUMMINGBIRD CAKE

"Winner! Cathy West's latest novel takes us on a journey into the heartache of aging parents, regrets, and sibling issues in ways that are both penetrating and infused with hope. Well-written, painted with emotional battles, addictions, and romance, West gives us poignant moments that stay long after the final page is turned."

—JAMES L. RUBART, BESTSELLING AUTHOR

The Things We Knew

Catherine West

THOMAS NELSON
Since 1798

Published in Nashville, Tennessee, by Thomas Nelson. Thomas Nelson is a registered trademark of HarperCollins Christian Publishing, Inc.

Published in association with the Books & Such Literary Management, 52 Mission Circle, Suite122, PMB 170, Santa Rosa, California 95409-5370, www.booksandsuch.com

Thomas Nelson titles may be purchased in bulk for educational, business, fund-raising, or sales promotional use. For information, please e-mail SpecialMarkets@ ThomasNelson.com.

Publisher's Note: This novel is a work of fiction. Names, characters, places, and incidents are either products of the author's imagination or used fictitiously. All characters are fictional, and any similarity to people living or dead is purely coincidental.

Library of Congress Cataloging-in-Publication Data

Names: West, Catherine (Catherine J.) author.
Title: The things we knew / Catherine West.
Description: Nashville: Thomas Nelson, 2016.
Identifiers: LCCN 2016002049 | ISBN 9780718078102 (paperback)
Subjects: LCSH: Family secrets—Fiction. | Nantucket (Mass.)—Fiction. |
   Domestic fiction.
Classification: LCC PR9680.B43 W478 2016 | DDC 813/.6—dc23 LC record available at https://lccn.loc.gov/2016002049

Printed in the United States of America

16 17 18 19 20 21 RRD 6 5 4 3 2 1

To all those in search of truth.
"… and you will know the truth, and
the truth will make you free."
—John 8:32 NASB

"You are braver than you believe, and stronger
than you seem, and smarter than you think."
—A.A. Milne

Chapter One

Sometimes in the dead of night, Lynette Carlisle heard her mother's voice. Sometimes it was easy to forget her mother had been dead twelve years.

Curled up in bed, covers pulled tight, she strained to hear the whisper over the wind. Some nights the voice was clear, like Mom was right there in the room, the faintest scent of light musk and lavender tickling Lynette's imagination. Other nights, all she heard was her own sigh of disappointment as angry waves crashed against the Nantucket cliffs beyond the garden wall.

Some nights she welcomed the voice. Some nights it made her wish for the impossible and remember life as it had been, before.

Some nights, like tonight, it kept her awake and rattled the cage of her memory. Tonight the voice came to her, as it so often did, in a dream.

The message was urgent, but she couldn't remember a word of it.

Dad.

That was it. She sat up in bed and rubbed her eyes.

Something about Dad.

A few sleepy moments later, Lynette stood in the doorway of her father's bedroom and stared at the empty bed. Red numbers glowed through the semidarkness. Four a.m. She checked the bathroom, but he wasn't there.

Thoughts of where he might be created a momentary state of

paralysis. Lynette waited a moment, listening for any sound, but the big house was silent.

She pushed her arms through the sleeves of her robe as she thundered down the stairs to the ground floor. Her two Labradors sat stationed by the front door, indicating he'd already made good his escape.

Panic pushed her forward. This served her right for staying up too late trying to finish that painting.

"Dad!" Lynette pulled open the heavy door and a gust of cold, salty wind smacked her face. Spring nights on the island still held a chill. A full moon lit her way as she raced across the white gravel in bare feet. No time to go back for shoes. She gritted her teeth and pressed on toward the road. Shouts came from the direction of the house next door.

Dread dragged her to a stop.

Diggory and Jasper began to growl as another shout punctuated the silence. She hoped they wouldn't start barking. "Shush, guys." Lynette picked up her pace again, grateful when her feet finally sank into the soft stretch of grass between the two estates. She squinted down the winding drive that led to their neighbor's home, the Cooperage, and scrambled for a viable excuse.

Perhaps Mr. Cooper was away for the weekend.

If he wasn't . . .

"I know you're in there, Cooper! Get out here this instant!" Her father's baritone voice punched through the night like a warhead honing in on its unsuspecting target. No stopping him now.

He stood on the front porch, swaying in the wind, his bathrobe flapping like dark wings, wild hair flying around his neck as he pounded on the double doors with both fists.

"Dad!" Lynette shot up the steps and grabbed his arm. "Stop it!" Perhaps it wasn't too late to just take him home. Perhaps, with a little luck, Mr. Cooper was indeed off the island.

The porch light came on and that hope washed out like the tide.

The lock turned, the door creaked open, and Nicholas Cooper peered around it.

"Nick." Lynette stepped back, fully expecting to be faced with an angry Anthony Cooper. Nick hadn't been back to Nantucket in years.

"Who . . . what?" He stepped forward, blinking under the glow of the carriage lantern above them. "Mr. Carlisle?"

"Aha," Dad bellowed as he lunged for the young man. "Where is she? Tell me where she is before I beat the tar out of you!"

"Whoa, Mr. Carlisle?" Nick disentangled himself, put up his hands, and ducked out of reach. Bleary blue eyes caught hers. "Lynette?"

Lynette made a frantic grab for her father's arm. "Dad, stop! You're confused. Let's go home." She pushed him, hard. "Daddy!" Her childlike cry stopped his flailing. "STOP." She met his eyes and saw them fill with murky confusion.

His anger slunk away like a punished dog. "I . . . I'm sorry. I . . . forgot myself."

Lynette glanced at Nick and patted her father's arm. Dad clamped his mouth shut and studied his slippers.

"Let's go, Dad. It's okay." Lynette shook her head. It wasn't okay. Not at all.

Dad trudged down the steps, sinking onto the last one. His shoulders heaved with a heavy sigh. The dogs settled by his feet, eyeing her for further instruction.

She wrestled with embarrassment and despair and forced herself to face Nick Cooper's questioning gaze.

"Is he all right?" Sleep still muddied his eyes. And apparently made him ask stupid questions.

"He'll be fine. Sorry about waking you." The quake in her voice betrayed her lack of confidence, but she refused to let tears escape.

Nick looked to where her father sat, rocking back and forth, humming. "Do you want me to call someone?"

Who would he call—the psych ward at the Cottage Hospital? She didn't think they even had one. "No." Lynette pulled the sash of her robe tight around her waist and shivered in the cool night air. She gathered up her scattered thoughts and put them away with her emotions. "I'm sorry about this, Nick. I'll just take him home." She turned toward the steps.

How could she explain something she didn't yet understand herself?

"Wait." Nick's hand rested on her shoulder, his unexpected touch comforting. "Can I drive you?"

That was so like Nick. Always trying to do the right thing. A smile tiptoed across her lips. "It's only next door. I think we can manage."

"Your feet." He pointed to her stinging soles, reminding her she'd have to endure more pain to get back home.

Lynette lifted her shoulders in resignation. Bruised feet she could deal with. It was the turmoil inside that tortured her.

"Hold up." He disappeared and returned with an old pair of boat shoes. "They're probably a bit big, but better than nothing."

She mumbled her thanks and slipped into the giant-sized loafers. Nick donned a pair of sneakers and helped her father up. His earlier outburst already forgotten, Dad chatted amicably with Nick as though he'd just happened over for a visit.

They took their time while the dogs ran ahead, sniffing the boxwoods and peeing on trees as though walks before dawn were commonplace. Lynette shuffled along behind Dad and Nick and wondered whether they would become so.

Once they reached home, she guided Dad in, turned to Nick, and handed over the borrowed shoes. "Thanks. Sorry about this."

"You don't need to keep apologizing." He hovered in the doorway, baggy pajama pants, T-shirt, and tousled hair giving him a boyish look. "Are you going to be okay?" He hesitated like he should come in but didn't want to.

She couldn't blame him.

"We'll be fine." Lynette nodded, more to convince herself, but her eyes stung as badly as her feet. "He won't remember it in the morning. I usually wake up, but—" A crash came from somewhere inside. "I have to go."

"Are you sure you'll be okay?"

"Yes. Welcome home, Nick." Lynette closed the door and leaned up against it.

Her heart thumped out unasked questions.

Once her older brother Gray's best friend and extra member of their family, Nick Cooper left Nantucket without warning, five years ago.

Left them.

She longed to know where he'd been, what he'd been doing, and why he'd returned. And whether he remembered that night so long ago—the night of her nineteenth birthday—the first, and only, time he'd kissed her.

The last time she'd seen him.

~

Lynette watched Dad more carefully over the next week. To her relief, he hadn't wandered off again and he was sleeping better. Which meant she could too. On Sunday afternoon, she put the finishing touches on a painting while he napped.

Up here in the art studio on the third floor of the house, things never seemed quite so terrible. She dropped her brush into a small jar of turpentine and stepped back from her latest creation. Dad had taught her to let the painting speak for itself.

This one certainly did.

Along a stretch of white Nantucket sand, families gathered for Fourth of July festivities. Kids played Frisbee, dogs raced after the flying disks, and toddlers poked chubby toes at the white foam waves while anxious mothers hovered over them. High on the hill behind the beach, a sprawling gray-shingled house presided over the holiday scene, a flagpole proudly sporting the red, white, and blue to celebrate the day. Gulls dotted the pale blue cloudless sky.

Off to the side of the organized chaos, a girl sat alone on the rocks. She hugged her knees to her chest, her gaze fixed on the wide expanse of Atlantic beyond the shore, her face half hidden by a mane of sun-kissed blond hair.

It would do.

Another painting rested on an easel across the room.

Lynette drew in a shaky breath, pulled toward it by an inexplicable force. This was the piece she'd stayed up so late working on the other night, the culprit, she was sure, behind the dream that had woken her.

She'd wanted to re-create the inside of the house as it had been that day all those years ago, but only a staircase floating in midair had emerged, the rest of the painting splattered in dark shades, burnt sienna, cobalt blue, and specks of black.

Memories hovered out of reach, hidden in the shadows of her mind.

She'd prayed for the memory of that day to be restored for years now, yet it remained as blank as a new canvas. Perhaps it was better this way. Perhaps it was time to let it go.

Lynette picked up a paint-splattered sheet and covered the evidence.

She shook off a shiver and went back to tidy up the area she'd been working in. Between her job at the day care and worrying about Dad, the days were long and tiring.

A sudden gust of wind whistled through an open window, melding pungent scents of oils and turpentine with sea air. A shutter banged against the side of the house and made her jump.

The floorboards squeaked as Lynette marched over them and pulled the window shut. The locks were rusty, but with a little effort, she secured them. Diggory gave her a mournful glance while Jasper slept on, oblivious. "Sorry, Diggs. We'll have to go out later. Looks like rain."

She retied her messy ponytail and surveyed the space designated as an art studio since before she was born. The long room was scattered with paintings, some on easels, some stacked against the walls, many completed, others left half done to taunt and jeer.

She and Dad used to spend hours up here. From the time she was very small, he encouraged her to paint, let her create a colorful mess and called it art.

She didn't know when he'd last set foot in here.

Drake Carlisle's greatest works languished under sheets, unseen and unappreciated. Banished.

Her mother had little interest in drawings and paintings; photography had been her passion. Capturing moments most would miss. She'd never been serious about it. A hobby, she'd called it. Lynette's gaze dragged to the door on the far side of the room. The darkroom—bolted shut and padlocked years ago. Her father's doing.

Everything in that room remained out of reach, locked away like the difficult things Lynette didn't like to think about.

Strains of Handel's Water Music suddenly filled the air and chased away the ghosts.

Lynette frowned and wondered where she'd tossed her cell phone. She found it hiding beneath a sketch pad. "Hello?"

"Hey, sweetie, it's Evy. How's that painting coming along?"

Lynette marveled at her friend's timing and dropped into the old rocker by the window. "The beach scene I told you about? I just finished it." She pushed off with her bare feet and began to rock.

"Wonderful. When can you bring it in?"

"Oh." She studied the paint flecks on her hands. Blue, yellow, red. Similar stains marked her jeans and shirt, probably her hair. She'd scrub them out later, but the red always remained. "I don't know."

Evy huffed. "I thought we had a deal. You promised me you would start selling your work on a regular basis, remember?"

"I remember. But honestly, Evy, it's not that good, and—"

"Nonsense. Honey, trust me, you're good. I sold your last two paintings for a much higher price than we anticipated, right? Listen, have you thought about doing a show? It's the beginning of May. Tourists will be coming in soon."

Lynette played with her necklace, a strand of wooden beads from Africa. Her brother Ryan sent them last year in the Christmas package for her and Dad. If only Ryan could have delivered them in person.

She thumped her head against the back of the rocker. "I won't do a show."

"So you've won the lottery?"

"No." Lynette scrunched her eyes and wished she'd never met Evy McIntyre. "I'll keep painting, but only if we stick to my rules."

"I know. I promise I won't use your real name." Evy let out a honk worthy of a Canada goose. "Honey, you can call yourself Attila the Hun for all I care. Just bring me your stuff. I'll get you cash, like you asked. How about Wednesday?"

Lynette poked at a hole in her jeans. Scraped at the red paint, pried it off with a fingernail. "I'm working."

"Wednesday is your day off."

"Fine, Evy. You win. I'll see you then. Happy?" Lynette imagined her friend's wide smile.

"Delirious." A throaty laugh crackled down the line and Lynette ended the call. Evy could talk her into anything, blast the woman. She should call her back, tell her she changed her mind. Tell her there would be no more paintings.

Tell her . . . what?

Evy was right.

To say they needed the money was an understatement.

Lynette left the studio by way of the rickety back stairs, the dogs at her heels. On the second floor she poked her head into Dad's bedroom. He should be up from his nap by now.

"Dad? You awake?"

The overpowering scent of Old Spice shot up her nose. A spilled bottle lay on top of his dresser. Clothes were strewn about the floor and falling out of the highboy's open drawers. His bed was empty, sheets rumpled and hanging off the side of the antique four-poster. The bathroom was vacant, water streaming from the tap. Lynette turned it off, gave the rusting spigot an extra twist just to be sure.

"Dad?" Her heart began to dance to the erratic beat that started up every time he did this. A draft from the open windows scattered pages of a newspaper on the round table, but the faded chintz curtains barely budged against the wind. Lynette pushed the curtains back and tied them in place with silky gold cords that were likely older than her. She fumbled with the heavy wood-framed windows, eventually latched them, and caught a glimpse of the sky, now dark and menacing.

"Dad?" She ran down the main stairs and into living room. *Calm, calm, calm.* He was probably in there reading. Lynette stopped in the doorway. "Dad?" Only the cat occupied her father's favorite chair by the window. Moxie rested on top of an open book, yellow eyes glinting as she flicked her tail and put her head back down.

"Oh, Dad, where did you go this time?"

Diggory and Jasper circled her legs, whining. Furious, frantic thoughts filled her head of what she would do when she found him. Would this be her life from now on? Chasing after the kids at the day care, chasing Dad during her time off?

She raced to the sliding glass door in the kitchen and slipped into her loafers. And then she saw him.

He stood by the stone wall at the edge of their property, facing the stormy sea. Monstrous black clouds loomed westward as drops of rain began to splash against the salt-stained glass.

Relief washed through her and doused out anger.

Lynette grabbed her Windbreaker from the coatrack and stepped onto the porch. A fierce wind tried to push her back, but she leaned into it and pulled her hood over her head. The dogs raced across the lawn, barking above the noise of the coming storm.

Dad didn't move.

Thunder rumbled off in the distance as Lynette ran over the already soggy lawn toward him, careful to avoid the anthills and patches of thistle. By the time she reached him, her breath came in spurts and rain stung her cheeks like tiny pinpricks.

"Dad, there's a storm coming!"

He startled when she took his arm. "Lynnie? What are you doing home? Shouldn't you be in school?"

Rain ran along the crevasses of his face. "No, Dad." School would be a welcome release, were she still the young girl he pictured in his muddled mind.

Lynette got him inside as quickly as he would allow. She sat him down and went for a towel. No use suggesting he go upstairs to change, too much effort. The dogs scattered water as they shook themselves and then settled under the kitchen table.

She worked to keep her voice steady. "Here, dry off. I'll make us some tea." Her heart rate slowly returned to normal. He could have gone anywhere, fallen, decided to climb the wall . . .

Somehow she'd have to figure out how to get him to the doctor again.

"Why were you out there in the rain, Dad?"

He grunted and wiped his brow. "I went for a walk. Is that a crime?" He patted his gnarled feet with the towel and pushed them into the worn leather mules she'd dropped beside him. His hair hung limply around his flushed face. He'd always worn it on the long side. Now that it was thinning on top, she might convince him to cut it.

She took the towel and dried his wet head. "You scared me. I didn't know where you were and—"

"Hush, child. I'm fine." Brown eyes twinkled and told her he was, but she'd been fooled before.

Lynette squelched a corrective response. At twenty-four, she was hardly a child, but Dad apparently still wasn't used to the idea of her being an adult.

At least he hadn't left the property this time.

~

Later that night Lynette put away the last of the supper dishes and went upstairs, ready for some downtime. She stopped outside her dad's room. The volume of the television was so high she'd heard it from the kitchen. She pushed the door open and looked in. A *MacGyver* rerun blared from the set, but Dad was snoring. She found the remote under some magazines and shut it off.

She stood over her father, watched his chest rise and fall. If only she knew for sure what was going on inside his mind. She leaned over and kissed his rough cheek. "'Night, Dad."

Whenever she mentioned the idea of him getting another checkup, he'd pitch a fit to rival some of the toddlers at Kiddie Kare. But dodging the inevitable was like pretending they didn't have to pay taxes. Sooner or later Uncle Sam would come calling. She would have to drag him to the doctor. Still, a diagnosis of dementia or Alzheimer's was not what she wanted to hear.

But what else could it be?

In her own room, she donned a cable-knit sweater and went onto the upstairs porch, as she did every night before bed. The cool night air refreshed and renewed her spirit; it was a temporary reprieve, but she welcomed the deceptive peace as it washed over her and stripped away the stress of the day.

Waves beat out their rhythm on the rocks as the moon slipped from behind the clouds and lit the garden below. The ocean's roar was hypnotic. Lulling her into believing things she knew weren't true. If she listened long enough, she might forget the strange dreams and shadowy figures that crept into her nighttime thoughts and hinted at things she didn't understand. Staying out here for any length of time often convinced her it was perfectly normal for someone her age to suffer gaps in memory.

It wasn't.

But she succumbed to the soothing sound and indulged in the illusion.

Nature's music also reminded her she was never quite alone.

Even in her moments of profound sadness and confusion, she still believed God would show her what to do. That somehow, some way, He'd provide the answers she needed.

If only He'd hurry up about it.

As the wind played with her hair, Lynette looked at the house next door. The Cooperage presided over the acreage abutting theirs, the long upper porch closest to her property. When they were kids, Nick and her brother Gray would hurl a baseball between the two porches, until they broke a window and their mothers put an end to it. Tonight the big house sat in lonely darkness.

But then a light came on, illuminating the porch. Lynette slid into the darkest part of her patio and let the shadows swallow her up. A door squeaked open and slammed shut. Nick Cooper stepped onto the deck, strode to the railing, and stood there, mirroring the position she'd held a moment ago.

He glanced her way and she almost bolted back inside, but something—curiosity mostly—made her stay.

Thanks to Evy, always abreast of town gossip, Lynette had learned Nick was now working for his father at the bank. Odd, considering Nick and his dad had never been close. And Nick had always talked about becoming an architect.

Since finding Dad at the Coopers' front door a week ago, she'd spied Nick huddled in a deck chair on the upper porch of his house more than once.

Some nights he sat in silence. Some nights he strummed on a guitar, lazy notes floating toward her across the inky sky. Some nights she wondered what he was thinking. Other nights she was glad she didn't know.

Distance and darkness hid his expression, but she could feel his melancholy. Maybe that was only her imagination. If they were to speak again, what would she say? How did one start over after years and time and circumstances muddied the waters?

If he knew she was there, on the other side of the estate, watching him, he never let on. And she preferred to stay in the shadows, unseen.

Suddenly he coughed, stretched, and moved as though heading back inside, but then he turned, slowly, perhaps deliberately, and looked straight at her.

Busted.

Chapter Two

Nick Cooper propelled his body through the lukewarm water, focused only on reaching the other end of the pool, arms pulsing as he pushed through the pain.

And it's Cooper in first position, in record-breaking time . . .

He slapped the warm brick with one hand, slid up his goggles, and reached for the stopwatch on the stone deck.

Take that, Phelps.

A grin stretched his stinging skin as water trickled down his face.

Nick rested his arms on the coping and his breathing slowed. After a moment, he concluded he wasn't going to have a heart attack. Since high school, all he'd ever wanted to do was swim. His coaches said he held great potential, and for a while Nick believed them. But now, at twenty-six, that aspiration had long since been stuffed into the box of things he'd stopped dreaming about.

He hoisted himself up, shook water out of his ears, hopping on one foot until he felt the warm release of liquid, and shuddered. In another month or so the ocean would be warm enough, but for now he'd settle for their heated pool.

Nick grabbed a thick green-striped towel he'd tossed across one of the lounge chairs, dried off, and took in the view of the Atlantic. Yesterday's storm gave way to better weather and the ocean glistened in momentary calm. Saturday provided a welcome break.

He'd survived a week at his new job, survived being home for two weeks.

Maybe he could do this.

Today might actually be a good day.

"How'd you do?" His father's voice floated toward him.

Or not.

Anthony Cooper picked his way over wet spots and pulled out a chair from around the patio table.

Nick gave his head a vigorous rub and wrapped the towel around his waist. He found a lounger a safe enough distance away and sank onto it. "Not great, but better than yesterday." The smile he attempted lasted as long as one of Michael Phelps's records in the 2012 Olympics.

His father brushed off the cushion of his chair before he sat. With the white sweater draped over his black polo, a pair of Ray-Bans nestled in the V of his shirt, and the silver Rolex around his wrist, he oozed East Coast aristocracy.

Nick hated that. Hated the awkward silence that always ran between them. Hated the way his dad looked at him without speaking. Scrutinizing.

Why bother timing yourself, Nick? You never were that good. Do you really think you're able to resurrect a lost cause?

Nick's pulse took off like he'd just heard the starting gun, and he leaned a little farther back in his chair. Maybe he was being unreasonable. Maybe Dad was actually making an effort.

And maybe they'd find a cure for cancer before the week was out.

Nick pulled a breath of sea air into his lungs. "You headed to the golf course?" Casual conversation he could do.

"Yes. I'll be gone most of the day, having dinner at Cliffside tonight."

"All right." Nick jiggled his left ear and dislodged more water. "I talked to Mom yesterday. The operation went well."

Dad's blue chips of ice seemed to melt a bit. "Oh, right, the knee surgery? You should go out to Arizona to visit when I get back. Take Mindy. I'm sure your mother would love to see her."

Nick wouldn't commit to that suggestion. And Mindy, his sometimes-when-it-suited-her girlfriend, would balk at the idea. "I'll think about it. How long will you be in Boston?"

"I'm not sure." His father glanced at his watch, as usual, after chatting for more than a minute. "I leave midweek. Are you settled in enough for me to go? Can you handle things on your own?"

A drop of water rolled down Nick's back and made him shiver. "I think I'll manage."

His father's thick brows slid together, relaying his lack of faith. "If all goes well, I'll be back in a week or so. I'm leaving the bank in your hands. You're in charge now, Nicholas."

"I know." Nick pressed his toes against the wet stone. He'd worked enough summers at the bank with Dad. And they'd gone over the new procedures a million times.

"You have my schedule," Dad continued. "Wanda will make sure you're prepared well in advance for any events that come up."

Nick stretched out on the lounger and closed his eyes. Pointless to debate whether he was responsible or not. In Dad's eyes, once a screw-up, always a screw-up. "I'll try not to stab anyone when I cut the ribbon on the new hospital wing."

His father cleared his throat a little too loudly. "I'm trusting you to be my representative, Nicholas. Your grandfather's legacy is nothing to joke about."

"Who's joking?" If he had to listen to Dad drone on about the Cooper legacy once more, he'd be stabbing himself with those scissors.

"Don't think for one minute that I'm not watching you, son. When you screw up, I'll know about it before you do."

Nick got to his feet. "Thanks for the support."

His father gave a slight shrug. "It's not that I don't appreciate your being here. But trust has to be earned, my boy."

Despite the sun on his bare shoulders, that thin smile left Nick chilled. "If you don't trust me, then don't leave me in charge. Tucker Watts can do my job."

"Tucker Watts is a moron."

"Then I guess you're stuck with me."

His father sighed and studied the ocean. "Must every conversation we have end in an argument?"

"Fine, Dad." Nick remembered the reason his father was leaving and mustered a smile. "I hope things go well for you."

Dad waved a hand and stood. "I don't want to be worrying the whole time I'm there."

"Then don't." Nick pulled on a pair of gray sweatpants. "I won't burn the house down, and I'll make sure the bank doesn't go under."

"Just . . . stay out of trouble." He placed a firm hand on Nick's shoulder. "I'm counting on you, Nicholas. Don't let me down. Again."

Nick held the granite-like gaze and pushed back his shoulders. "I'm going to shower. Have a good day."

Later, once he heard the front door slam and his father's Mercedes roll out of the driveway, Nick grabbed his car keys, slid into his sports car, and gunned the engine. Lunch at his favorite hole-in-the-wall would shake off the foul mood he was now in.

He turned off the sandy road onto Polpis and headed toward town. Despite his disgruntled spirit, the sight of the ocean was something he never tired of. An early spring brought calmer seas, and he spotted more than a few white sails out there. He might venture down to the yacht club later, see who was around.

Nick parked outside The Longshoreman, entered the bar, took a seat at his favorite booth, and counted. Soon the bar owner pushed an icy mug his way and dropped into the seat opposite him.

Nick chuckled. "Thirty seconds. You're slipping, Jed."

"Shut up, rich boy. I got customers." Jed Hagerman flicked a damp cloth, droplets of water flying.

"Really?" Nick scanned the almost empty establishment. The dark, dank walls gave the place a mysterious air. Posters of groups from the seventies and eighties still adorned the walls, and he'd bet the jukebox in the corner hadn't been updated in this decade. He took a swig of amber ale, wiped froth off his upper lip, and grinned. "You're counting Harry as a customer now? I thought he was part of the furniture."

Old Harry swiveled on his stool, wagged a finger in Nick's direction, and swayed a little dangerously. "Watch yer tongue, young Cooper."

Nick tipped his head. "Sorry, Harry."

Harry raised his glass and nodded before swiveling back around. Jed studied Nick. "So, how's it going, man? You happy to be back home or what?"

"Thrilled." Nick frowned as the ale settled on his empty stomach. "Can I get a burger?"

"Sure thing." Jed turned toward the woman behind the bar and bellowed, "Lila, burger up!" He scratched at the scruff on his jaw and tugged on the grimy white apron that barely covered his belly. "What brings you back to the island? Life in the real world too boring?"

"Not exactly." Nick leaned against the wooden bench and let some tension out of his shoulders. Familiarity—smoky air, fried food, and the smell of the sea—settled in through his senses. "My dad needed me at the bank." He'd leave it there.

"Least you've got a job, man. Lots of my buddies on the mainland are looking for work." Jed stood, wiped down the table, and picked at a dried-on piece of food with a dirty fingertip. "This is not the time to be unemployed."

"Can't argue with you there. But if any of your buddies want to give it a shot, they'd be welcome to."

"Still butting heads with the old man?"

His friend's laugh was infectious. "We tolerate each other."

Jed nodded like he figured as much. "Gotta say, I'm surprised to see you in here. Thought you'd be all up with the country club muck-mucks."

"Only when I have to be, Jed. You know that." Nick glanced toward the bar. The waitress was new. A Marilyn Monroe wannabe—platinum blond hair, too much makeup, and too top heavy. She'd noticed him and was doing her best to look busy and sexy at the same time.

Jed jingled change in the pocket of his apron. "Never got you, Cooper. If I had your stash, I'd be as far from this fish town as possible."

That had been the plan. "Well, Jed, if you hadn't quit high school . . ."

"Shaddup." Jed's grin was as wide as his girth. "Hey, you . . . uh, seen your neighbor yet?"

Nick fished his phone from the pocket of his jeans and checked his messages. Mindy. Mindy. Mindy . . . "Who? Miss Perkins? Thought the old battleaxe died."

Jed huffed and cleared his throat. "Lynette."

"Oh, Lynnie?" The memory of finding Drake Carlisle on his doorstep his first night home still rattled Nick. Something was definitely wrong with her father, but Lynette's frantic face bothered him more. "Yeah, why?"

Jed's smile widened. "Talked to her?"

Nick played with the handle of his mug and registered the interest in Jed's eyes. "Not exactly. Kind of surprised she's still here, actually."

"Yeah." Jed wagged his head. "She never really left. Not like the rest of them. Didn't last long at college. You know her old man got into some trouble a few years back. I heard he lost a chunk of change in the casinos." Jed drummed out an annoying beat on the table.

"Is he still drinking?" That had been Nick's first thought when he'd opened his front door to find Drake Carlisle standing there, ready to accost him.

Jed shrugged. "Don't think so. If he is, he's not doing it here. Used to be as regular as old Harry. So if you see Lynette, maybe you could mention me to her . . ."

Nick slugged his beer. "I haven't talked to any of them for a long time. They might prefer to keep it that way."

"But . . . you and Gray? You guys are still tight, right?"

"Wrong." Nick snapped a coaster in half and let it fall to the rough-hewn surface of the table. "If you're interested in Lynnie, just ask her out."

"I have." Jed looked away.

Even in the dim light, Nick saw Jed's cheeks darken. Somehow he couldn't see Lynette ever agreeing to date Jed. Oddly enough, the thought comforted him.

He smiled and smacked the big guy on the arm. "Well, if I see her again, maybe I'll mention you. Now, how long is that burger gonna take?"

Jed ambled off and Nick let out his breath. He hadn't considered what feelings might be evoked, being home, seeing the Carlisles again—the family he'd once been so much a part of. The family he still, even after all these years, felt strangely responsible for.

Chapter Three

Lynette pressed her back against the leather chair and tried to gauge the thoughts of the man seated on the other side of the wide mahogany desk. She'd debated coming here to see Nick at the bank. Surely Nick could help, at least advise her on what to do next.

Because she was all out of answers.

"So, Lynette." Nick sat forward, elbows propped, long fingers intertwined beneath his chin. "Good to see you again. How's your dad?"

"He's all right." Her cheeks began to prickle and she prayed he wouldn't dwell on the matter. Dad was nowhere near all right, but she didn't know how to explain that. And her father's health issues were not what she'd come here to discuss.

"He seemed a little . . . off that night."

"That's one way of putting it." She blew out a breath and shrugged. "You know he's always been a bit eccentric. He's fine, really."

"Okay." Nick's expression said he wasn't buying it, but he glanced down at a pile of papers, pushed them aside, then looked back at her. "I have to admit, I was a bit surprised to get your call. What can I do for you?"

Oh, nothing, just give me a million dollars. "Well, I was hoping for some advice." She tried to look confident. "Um. Financial advice. I think I might need to talk about a loan."

"Then you're in the right place." Nick's warm smile didn't put her at ease as much as it should have. He tapped a pencil against the folders in front of him. "I took a look at your files when I heard you were coming in." His knitted brows said their finances were in worse shape than she'd thought. "You have . . . let's see, a savings account in your name and a checking account in . . . oh . . . yours, your brother David, and Liz's names, correct?"

"Yeah. They usually deal with all this." She'd tried to reach Liz on the phone last night after David didn't pick up, but the call went straight to voice mail. Her two eldest siblings seemed to be MIA of late, and she couldn't wait any longer.

"And you had your father's signing privileges revoked on all accounts a couple of years ago. Why was that?"

Here we go again. "Because he was spending money unwisely." Lynette shifted, and the leather squeaked under her. "I don't think there's a whole lot left in the account, is there?"

Nick tipped his head and studied her through the startling blue eyes that had earned him a constant following of giggling girls in high school and college. "It does seem to be dwindling."

Lately, Lynette was shelling out more money than she was earning, and that terrified her. She curled her fingers around the seat bottom of her chair. "We had some unexpected expenses with the house last year." The big storm had knocked over a large oak in the backyard, clipped the roof of the back porch, and narrowly missed the rest of the house. She'd needed to hire a crew to fix the roof and remove the tree. "And with my dad not being . . . quite himself . . . there's health care down the road." A lump formed in her throat. This was harder than she'd anticipated.

Nick cleared his throat and looked like whatever he'd eaten for lunch had come back to bite him. He loosened his tie. "So your father's pension is your only source of income? Do you have a job?"

She crossed her legs, the white cotton skirt sticking to them.

The green silk blouse she rarely wore felt like a straitjacket. "I'm an assistant at a day care. The salary's not much. Covers groceries and gas, that's about it."

"And I gather your dad isn't working?"

"He hasn't sold any paintings recently." She didn't expound on what *recently* might mean.

Nick nodded, still wearing that serious expression. "I have to say there would be concerns with giving you a loan. How would you pay it back?" His mouth formed a thin line and he tapped his little finger against the back of his other hand.

Despite the cool air blowing through the vent above her, the elegant office with its potted palms and dark blinds was stifling. "I don't know." She'd suspected this was how the conversation would go, but hadn't prepared as well as she should have.

Nick shuffled through the papers on his desk. "So, you're working at . . . which day care?"

"Kiddie Kare. Over on Hinsdale. I've been there a couple years." But if she kept taking time off to deal with Dad, she might not be much longer. Joanne had called her in for a meeting, worried. Her boss was wonderful and caring, but she could only put up with so much.

Nick tapped at his keyboard. "The cost of upkeep on a house the size of Wyldewood is significant. How have you been managing?" His smooth brow wrinkled to match his cautionary tone.

The room lost a little more air.

It was a valid question, but she didn't need the reminder of the dire straits they were in. "We've closed up most of the bedrooms. We only use a few rooms in winter. We get by." Lynette didn't want to admit the truth. The old house was drafty, frigid in the colder months, and firewood wasn't cheap. The radiators worked when they wanted to, not often. With the price of oil today, she welcomed summer's approach.

"Who looks after your father when you're at work?"

"He doesn't need looking after." Lynette clamped her mouth shut and looked away.

Of course he did; any idiot would know that within minutes of meeting him. She faced Nick again and saw reality in his eyes. "I mean . . . he's okay most days. When he's having a bad patch, I call Mrs. Wilkinson down the road. She's pretty good about coming over and never takes any money."

Nick studied the files again. "David is the executor of your mother's estate, correct?"

"Doesn't it say that in there?" Lynette remembered the last real conversation she'd had with Nick Cooper and it hadn't been this difficult.

He sighed as though he was thinking the same thing. "Look, I'm sorry, but I'm just . . ."

Lynette nodded. "Trying to do your job. I know."

He lifted his chin. "And if we agree to a loan and you can't make the payments?"

She traced the floral pattern on her skirt and watched a shadow skip across the floor. "You're the banker, Nick. You tell me."

Nick drew his lips together. "You might qualify for a Chapter Thirteen. I can get you the name of a bankruptcy lawyer."

Bankruptcy. The word choked her, made her want to spit it back at him. "My father would never declare bankruptcy." Why had she said that? Dad wasn't in any shape to understand much of anything these days. And it wasn't up to him anymore.

"Have you and the family thought about selling the house?"

"Selling?" The question jolted her. It shouldn't have. In her darkest moments, the option loomed foremost in her mind, much as she loathed the idea. Liz had suggested it last year, but Lynette had shut her sister down.

The corners of his mouth twitched as he raised an eyebrow. "It is something you should seriously consider. You don't have a mortgage, but without substantial income—an old house that size—I don't see how you can live there much longer." He shook his head, his expression softening again. "I'm sorry."

Lynette pushed her sandaled feet against the fine Persian rug, pushed against his words. She inhaled and forced her eyes back to his. "The last few years have been difficult. I didn't think we'd get to this point."

He frowned and ran his fingers through his thick blond hair. "Sooner or later the money runs out."

Heat crept into her cheeks. Drake Carlisle's gambling habits and penchant for alcohol were no secret. Shame she'd lived with since she was twelve years old snaked around her, tightened its hold, and tried to squeeze the air from her lungs. "It's true my father incurred some rather large debts a few years back. We were able to pay those off." Just. And without that money to fall back on . . . Nick was right. How could they keep the house?

"Lynette, I need to ask . . . Does your dad still have those problems?"

"No. He got help. He's changed."

A smile inched up the corners of his mouth. "I believe you."

"Really?"

Dad hadn't touched a drop, hadn't been near the casinos on the mainland since she'd come home from college at the end of her freshman year, and with David and Liz's help, checked him into rehab. And that cost more money. But it had been worth it. He'd been doing so well until the spells started, even coming to church on occasion.

"Does he have any idea how bad things are?" Nick asked.

"No." She fiddled with the strap of her purse and studied him. "You really think selling is our only option?"

Nick placed his palms down on the desk. "The market is picking up. I doubt you'll get an offer right away, but you could always list it, see what happens. Like I said, without a steady source of income greater than what you're making, I'm not sure how you're going to manage."

Sudden tears stung and she blinked them back. "I can't imagine not having Wyldewood, Nick."

"I know." His eyes filled with concern as he leaned back in his chair. "How do you think the others would feel?"

"They'd probably jump at the idea." Lynette pressed two fingers against her forehead and tried to think. "My mother's will states that all decisions about the house have to be unanimous. So if I don't want to sell . . ." She wound her thumbs together. They had never all agreed on anything.

"Lynette, you're going to have to be reasonable." Nick moved across the office, poured water from a carafe at the bar, and offered her a tall glass. "Selling is a viable option."

She took a few sips and put the glass on the floor beside her chair. "I don't have to like it."

"No, but I'm afraid you do have to consider it." He sat again and took a long gulp from his own glass. "Wyldewood is one of the most beautiful estates on Nantucket. But everyone else has left. Why postpone the inevitable?"

"It's my mother's house. She'd hate this."

"She would, but . . ." Nick sighed. "Lynnie, maybe it's time to let go. Look, I know how you feel—"

She sucked in a breath. "You have no idea how I feel."

"Fair enough. I'm sorry." That look of pity settled over him again.

"So you've said."

A sudden chuckle lit his eyes. "I have to say I don't remember you being this stubborn."

The somber mood lifted a little and made her feel better. "You've been away too long, Nick. I'm a Carlisle. Arguments heard clear across the island ring a bell?"

"Right." His face cracked into the handsome smile she remembered. Actually, more handsome than she remembered, but she wouldn't go there.

"Well, we could have a problem," Lynette went on while she still had the nerve. "My mother also stipulated that all discussions would have to take place here, in person, before any plans to sell Wyldewood could be finalized."

"Seriously?" Another deep chuckle filled the room. "I always did like your mother."

She managed a smile. "The feeling was mutual, Nicholas. She used to say you were her favorite stray."

Nick stayed silent a minute. She missed those days, when he was just as much a part of the family as any of them.

"You don't think the others will come home?"

"Only if they have to." And only if something was in it for them.

"Well, I can tell you this, if you do sell, you should end up with a handsome profit. I'd say your property, the size of the house, acreage and waterfront combined, is worth more than a few million, even in today's market."

Lynette swatted at a fly. She should probably close her mouth before it flew right in. Millions? Sure, the house looked deceptively grand from the outside, but the place was falling down around them. The weight of the moment sat heavy on her shoulders. He was giving her the answers she'd come for, but now she wasn't so sure she wanted them.

Nick drummed his fingers on the desk. That smile came out again. "If I can be honest, this isn't exactly how I wanted our first real conversation in years to go."

"Me either." Lynette fiddled with the emerald solitaire on her right hand. Her mother's ring. Dad had given it to her on her nineteenth birthday, the last time she'd spent any time with Nick.

"Lynnie?"

She blinked, her cheeks growing warm too quickly. She reined in her vagrant thoughts. "Sorry. What were you saying?"

"Will you be all right talking to the others about this?"

"Sure." Lynette watched him grow silent. "What, Nick?" He shrugged and she rolled her eyes. "You've got that look. Like you need to say something but don't know how. So, what?"

Nick coughed and drank more water. "Well, if you did decide to sell . . ." He sighed and set his gaze on her. "There is a hotel chain scouting a couple properties in the area. My father has had a few meetings with them. I just thought—"

"Absolutely not." How could he even mention it? The very thought of the home she'd grown up in being bulldozed to the ground made her want to flee for the nearest bathroom.

"Keep it in mind." Nick stood and walked around the desk. "You've got a lot to absorb, plans to make. But you will need to make a decision. Soon."

She got to her feet, wanting to run, but manners kept her in place. "Thanks for seeing me, Nick. I appreciate your honesty."

He placed a hand under her elbow as they walked toward the door. "I'm sorry things are so rough right now."

And about to get a whole lot rougher. "We'll figure something out." Lynette dragged her eyes upward.

"I'm glad you came in," Nick said. "I wish I had better news for you."

She gave an involuntary shiver. "Yes, me too." She should leave, but his interested expression cemented her feet to the floor.

"How is . . . everyone?" Nick leaned against the doorframe.

"Fine, I guess. David and Josslyn have twins; they're two."

"Really?"

"I know. Ryan's over in Africa working with some mission I can never remember the name of. Liz is in New York. She's a corporate attorney."

"And you're still here. The only constant." His low laugh floated around her. A glimpse of the Nick she remembered sidled over and nudged Mr. Corporate America out of the way.

"I guess I've always been predictable." Lynette looked down at her painted toenails.

"Hey. That's not a bad thing." He gave her arm a light squeeze. A friendly gesture, but the touch of his fingers sent a strange energy zigzagging through her. "Will you let me know what they say about coming home? It'd be great to see everyone."

She shrugged, desperate now to end their conversation, escape the room, the memories. Him. "Sure."

"What do you hear from Gray these days?" Nick's smile disappeared.

Lynette frowned as she thought about her brother. "Not much. He's on tour. In Canada now, I think."

"He did good, huh?" His voice radiated warmth again and reminded her of happier times. "I used to laugh at his talk of becoming a famous rock star. We all had our dreams. His were just bigger than all of ours put together." It wasn't hard to catch the regret in his tone.

"He's hardly a famous rock star, Nick. Gray's got problems just like the rest of us."

"Is he okay?"

"I don't know. He says he is, but I've had this weird feeling for a while now. I can't shake it."

"I'm sure he's fine." He sounded confident. "Gray's tougher than he looks."

"I hope you're right."

It was strange seeing Nick here in such austere surroundings. She'd always pictured him on his yacht—shirtless, of course, the wind racing through his hair—sailing the world with beautiful women at his side. Not back in Nantucket, behind a desk pushing papers.

Working for his father.

Something he'd sworn he would never do.

"Well." His hand closed around hers in a brief squeeze. "Take care, Lynnie. If you need anything . . ."

"You've already said you can't give me a loan." She almost laughed, but shook her head instead. "I'll call you once I talk to everyone." She wanted to go home and crawl under the covers.

"And you'll mention the hotel chain? It could be a very lucrative decision."

Lynette sighed. Nick could rival any of them in the area of stubbornness. He'd always been the last to give in on any matter of contention. The fact that he and Gray hadn't spoken in years proved it. "Fine. I'll mention it."

"You know where I am if you need me."

"Yes. Good-bye, Nick." Lynette reached into her canvas bag for her sunglasses, lost her grip on the strap, and the whole thing fell to the floor. She bent to retrieve some of the contents and counted the seconds until she could escape further embarrassment.

"Pez?" Nick held the red plastic dispenser with the Winnie the Pooh head toward her, a sly grin playing at the corners of his mouth.

She grabbed it and pushed it deep inside her purse. "I work at a day care."

"Ah. Of course."

"I have to go." Lynette turned toward the door and wished she could fly.

"Lynnie." His forehead wrinkled with worry. "I really am sorry about all this, you know." The look he gave her was so familiar that she had to smile. That was the Nick she knew, always standing up for her. He'd never been afraid to speak up, to speak his mind.

Something she rarely did around her siblings.

"Well. Thanks again." Her voice caught in her throat as childhood memories tried their best to resurface. She had a sudden stupid urge to throw herself at him and sob, but quickly stifled that thought.

Nick studied her. "Are you going to be okay?"

Lynette nodded, but couldn't reply.

That was one question she didn't have an answer for.

Chapter Four

Nick decided to walk down Main after work to clear his head. Today's meeting with Lynette had been painful. The desperation on her face made his stomach clench, and he couldn't shake it. She was no longer the young, carefree girl who lived in his memory. Still beautiful, but her eyes told him more than he'd bet she wanted him to know. He'd seen something in them, something haunting, disturbing.

He'd wanted to whip out his checkbook and solve all her problems. But of course he couldn't. She'd never agree, for one thing, and his father would skin him alive.

Dad had called less than an hour after Lynette's appointment. Nick suspected Wanda, his dad's secretary, was keeping tabs on his every move. That didn't surprise him. But his father was more than interested in hearing about the possibility of the Carlisle home going on the market. And something about that bothered Nick.

He kicked at a pebble and watched it bounce over the worn cobblestones. If only problems could disappear so easily. The temperature was warmer today, the ocean breeze refreshing, and he tried to enjoy it. The foliage on the trees grew thicker, providing shade for the summer months to come. Flowers in bloom made him think of his mother. She loved this time of year on the island. Probably about the only thing here she had appreciated.

He yanked his tie loose and stopped walking as he passed the new art gallery, Timeless. A painting in the window caught his attention.

The colorful beach scene reminded him of lazy summer days when all he'd had to worry about was his tan and whether it would rain. He stepped closer, pushed up his sunglasses, and peered through the window.

It was typical Nantucket folk art, yet different, more whimsical.

His eyes landed on the girl on the rocks, set apart from the activity on the beach. Long honey-colored hair hid her face. She looked lonely.

A sense of déjà vu pulled him into the gallery.

A bell tinkled as he entered and paintings of varying sizes greeted him, displayed under recessed lighting. Thick rugs in muted shades covered the hardwood floor and soft jazz played from hidden speakers.

He could have been in New York.

"Good evening."

Nick turned toward the voice. A willowy woman rounded the desk and fairly floated toward him. Swathed in a caftan of emerald green, her silver hair was streaked with red—bright red—choppy to her shoulders. He wouldn't dare pin an age on her, but she was definitely up there. Still attractive, in an aging movie star kind of way.

"Just having a look," he told her. "I remember when this used to be a liquor store."

"Do you now?" Her black-rimmed glasses glittered. "That was several years ago. You would have been just a teenager, I'm sure."

Nick grinned and nodded toward the front of the gallery. "That painting in the window. Who's the artist?"

"Oh . . ." The woman fiddled with her many bracelets. "Yes. She's very good." She sailed across the floor, pressed a button on the wall, and the platform, which held the painting, rotated.

Nick stepped forward and nodded. "Something about it . . ." A memory, perhaps. "There's no signature."

"No. Verity prefers not to sign her work."

"Verity?" Latin. Meaning truth, if he recalled correctly. Nick scratched his chin. "Does she have a last name?"

The woman squinted. "Just Verity."

"Is she local?"

"You could say that." She smiled, relaxed again. "We don't see much of her. You like that painting, I can tell."

"Yes. It's quite . . . familiar." Nick admired the fine detail and shadows. "I grew up here. I know that particular beach very well."

"I see. Are you interested in making a purchase, Mister . . . ?"

"Cooper. Nicholas." He extended a hand and produced the smile he saved for good friends and his grandmother. Her confidence put him at ease.

"Ah, Mr. Cooper. I've been wondering when we might run into one another."

"Have you?"

She laughed as she moved to a long granite desk and busied herself with papers. Nick followed, catching a glimpse of the gold nameplate on the desk near the phone. Evy McIntyre.

"We haven't met before, have we, Evy?" He'd definitely remember if they had.

She waved a hand, flashy rings covering her fingers. "Oh, no, darling. But your return has been quite the talk at the spa. And it's Ev-ee, like Chevy."

"Okay." Nick rubbed the back of his neck. He tried not to laugh. "Well, Evy like Chevy, how much is that painting going for?"

Her eyes danced with certain mischief. "How much is it worth to you?"

~

After they finished an early supper that night, Dad wanted to sit outside. Lynette followed him down the wide hall, her bare feet treading carefully over worn spots in the wood floor that might send up a splinter. Most of the hardwood on this level needed repair or refinishing. Long rugs used to cover the floors. They were probably rolled up in the attic, being eaten by mice or moths.

She paused to pull a cobweb from the hanging brass lamp in the middle of the hall and noticed one of the three small bulbs had burnt out. A couple of the screws securing it to the wooden beam dangled rather dangerously out of place. She stood on tiptoe, tried to reach them, but couldn't. She'd need to drag a ladder out for the job.

Maybe tomorrow she'd get around to cleaning and doing the many chores she'd been putting off. If only Cecily hadn't quit, drat the woman. But Lynette could hardly blame her. She wouldn't be happy working and not getting paid either.

The array of framed photographs on the wall caught her eye, Cecily's round, cheery face jumping out at her, as though she'd been summoned somehow, to make her smile.

~

"Lynnie, child, ain't no reason to cry now. You're safe and sound."

Lynette choked back a sob and buried her head in Cecily's ample chest, comforted by the smell of fresh baked bread and talcum powder. "I hate those boys. They chased me and scared me and made me fall down."

"I know, baby." Cecily shifted from her cross-legged position on the floor and peeked under the wet paper towel she held over Lynette's scraped knee. "Looks like it's all better, see? No more blood."

Lynette scrunched her nose and studied the throbbing red spot, gave a little shiver, and then shrieked as the boys burst into the living room, whooping and hollering, racing around her, dirt and sand smeared across suntanned chests. Their game of cops and robbers was a favorite, but she always had to be the robber, and they always caught her.

"Go away!" she yelled, burrowing her face again, grateful for Cecily's warmth and the comforting arms that came around her.

"Hush, now." Her parents' friends called Cecily the housekeeper, but to Lynette and the rest of them, she was family.

"Baby, baby, Lynnie's just a baby!" Gray ran circles around them, Ryan hot on his heels, waving the long piece of rope he'd picked up on the beach that they'd threatened to tie her up with.

"Boys, that's enough!" Cecily used her I-mean-business voice. "Ryan, you throw that dirty thing outside right now. Y'all are soaking wet too."

"Storm's coming." Ryan tossed the rope out the open French doors and shook his head, drops of water flying as he flopped down beside them, propped on his elbows. Lynette chanced a look at her brother and tried to stop her sniffles. "Sorry, Shortstop," he said. "Sometimes I forget you're only six and can't keep up."

"I'm almost seven."

"Almost." Gray hung over Cecily's shoulders and wiggled his fingers in Lynette's face.

"Stop it, Gray!" She swatted them away and Cecily hushed her again.

"Shoo, you gonna get sand all over me, Grayson!" Cecily scolded.

Gray just laughed. He always laughed when he got in trouble. Getting in trouble was a bad thing. Lynette didn't know why he thought it wasn't.

"Where's Mom?" Gray rolled off Cecily and onto the rug, sticking his scrawny legs high in the air. "She better get back soon or she'll get stuck out in the storm."

Thunder crashed overhead and they all jumped. Fear pulled tight, and Lynette swiveled to look into Cecily's dark eyes. "Ce-ce? Where'd she go?"

Cecily shook her head, smiled, and cupped her warm hands around Lynette's cheeks. "Child, you worry too much. Anyone ever tell you that? Your mama knows that beach better than her own face.

And God's looking after her. She'll be back soon now. Don't invite trouble in 'til you have to."

"Yoo-hoo! Darlings, I'm home!" The front door slammed and their mother's voice sang through the hallway.

Cecily laughed and kissed the top of Lynette's head. "See there? Now, what I tell you?"

~

Some days Lynette missed Cecily Johnson more than she missed her own mother.

"Are you coming, Lynnie?" She heard Dad moving furniture around on the back porch and picked up her pace. At the end of the hall, she pushed open the wide screen door, stepped onto the patio that ran the length of the house, and took in Wyldewood's crowning glory.

It didn't matter how often she came out here, that expanse of blue surprised her. The ocean stretched as far as the eye could see. The water was calm this evening, gentle whitecapped waves rolling along toward the shore. But the sight of the dandelion-infested lawn chased off her happiness.

"I didn't realize the garden was such a mess." Winter had kept them inside, and spring somehow failed to capture her attention this year.

"A mess?" Dad's eyes crinkled with laughter. "It's beautiful."

Thick oak trees were positioned carefully on either side of the grounds so as not to obstruct the view of the Atlantic. Their weathered branches sprouted new leaves. Daffodils and crocuses came back year after year, and a few purple or red tulips joined the display.

"We sure had some fun, didn't we?" Dad mused. "The parties your mother used to throw . . ."

"I remember."

The once elaborate flowerbeds snaking around the house and along the boxwood hedges were overrun with weeds. The swimming pool had been drained and covered years ago. Rotting leaves and debris crusted the black tarp. Beyond the pool lay the tennis court, cracked and covered in grime, the old net twisted in a heap by one of the rusted poles that once held it in place.

Dad shuffled up beside her. "Isn't it as lovely as ever, Lynnie?"

"Yes." It was only half a lie.

Lynette balled her hands, her eyes burning. He saw it all as it had been—loved and cared for, with lilies and roses and exotic plants she couldn't begin to name, all in bloom. The pool provided a cool retreat, always overflowing with children, adults vying for space on the lounge chairs along the surrounding terrace.

She rubbed her nose, tipped her face to the setting sun, and tried to find comfort in the memory. Gulls circled the cliffs below the property. There was a well-worn path to her left, the wooden gate off its hinges, covered in wild rose brambles. The path led down to a stretch of white sand, the private beach they shared with the houses around them.

"Come, sit." Dad lowered himself onto the white wicker couch, the once navy-striped cushions now faded and spotted with mildew. "I'll have Cecily bring us some iced tea."

Lynette pulled her dark blue cardigan tight around her shoulders and slipped into the rocker opposite him. A breeze floated around her and cooled her cheeks. "Cecily doesn't work for us anymore, Dad."

"She doesn't?"

She hated that confused look. Hated that he was losing so much memory so quickly. And she especially hated that there wasn't a blessed thing she could do about it.

He raised an eyebrow, then chuckled, playing with the gold wedding band he still wore. "Of course she doesn't. Why is that again?"

"Because we couldn't pay her." Lynette spied the dogs poking around at the far end of the garden and whistled. "Diggory! Jasper!" They soon clattered up the steps toward her, clamoring for attention. She fussed over them a bit before turning back to Dad.

He gazed out at the ocean, his mind no doubt someplace far from here. Lynette spent most of her prayer time asking God to heal him. The last time she'd talked with Cecily over the phone, she'd voiced her frustration over God's silence.

"God speaks when He wants to, honey," her old friend had said. *"And could be sometimes you're not listening."*

Whatever that meant. Sometimes Cecily was as mysterious as God Himself.

It was possible Dad was just getting old. He was a few years from seventy, seemed healthy, but there was no telling what years of alcohol abuse had done to his body. Maybe Nick was right. Maybe it was time to talk about putting the house on the market.

"Would you ever think about living someplace else, Dad? Maybe something smaller?"

He looked her way, his face pinched, eyes void of their usual sparkle. "Someplace else? Why?"

"I don't know." Lynette wiggled her toes, choosing her words carefully. "This is a big place for just the two of us. We could buy a condo somewhere, maybe even around here, still on the ocean. I was talking to Nick Cooper, you remember Nick, from next door? Anyway, I thought—"

"Why were you talking to Nick Cooper, Lynette?" His eyes narrowed as anger flashed across his face.

Lynette blinked. "Well, I was just—"

"There's no reason to talk to him anymore. Is there?"

"I don't know, I . . ." Confusion covered her, thick and dense, taking her breath away and leaving her floundering.

"You will not discuss our business with that family!" Dad pushed out of his chair and stormed across the patio. "I won't have it. I'm telling you now, Diana, I want this to end!" He picked up an old conch shell and hurled it across the lawn.

Sometimes, in less lucid moments, he confused her for her mother. But she'd never seen him angry when that happened. Lynette ignored her fear, raced to him, and grabbed his arm. "Dad, stop! Dad . . ." Her throat clogged as he turned to look at her. "Dad, it's me. Lynette."

His gaunt cheeks were blotchy, his eyes wet. That bewildered look settled over him again. "Yes." He nodded and shuffled back to his chair. "Yes, of course it is."

Lynette returned to her seat and sat on her hands to stop them from shaking. "I didn't mean to upset you."

"We can't sell this house. I can't leave your mother." He pulled a thread on his khaki trousers, resolute as he watched the waves roll in, the last few minutes forgotten.

"Dad . . ." She patted one of the dogs, slowed her breathing. A few white sails dotted the water. Tears stung and she ran the back of her hand across her face. "Moving from here wouldn't mean leaving Mom. She'll still be with you, in your heart. In your memories."

Her dad looked at her, his face awash with pain. "That's just it, Lynnie," he whispered. "I'm starting to forget."

Lynette sent up a silent prayer and listened to the waves crash against the rocks. How could she even think it, forcing Dad from the place he'd shared with the love of his life?

He leaned back in his chair and closed his eyes. "Tell me what it was like, Lynnie." He dragged a hand across his trembling mouth. "Help me remember what I can't."

"Oh, Dad." Sorrow brought fresh tears.

It was as close as he'd come to admitting the truth.

That he was losing time. Losing the past.

While Dad was losing his memory, she wished she could get hers back.

What a pair they made.

Lynette inhaled, found a smile, and began. "Mother's great-grandfather, Tristan Wylde, always dreamed of a house on the ocean. He and his wife honeymooned here. He fell in love with the place, purchased land, and proceeded to build Wyldewood. The Wyldes lived here for generations, until the house passed to Mother, who was, of course by that time, a Carlisle." Lynette gave a sigh of satisfaction and retreated to the place in her mind where she went to pretend.

She'd been raised on tales of bygone eras that now mingled with the memories of her own idyllic childhood—weeks of doing nothing but sailing and swimming and tennis. Sweet scented summer nights spent dancing under the stars; bitterly cold winter days passed by the fire, playing Spit, Monopoly, or backgammon. Sometimes Dad would have her brothers haul out the large screen and projector, and they'd watch old family movies or their own reels, laughing at themselves until the tears rolled down their cheeks.

"Your mother loved this house." Dad's breathing was shallow, his head bobbing every now and then. "What about the parties?"

Lynette nodded. "Mom loved to entertain. She'd plan events for weeks, making sure everything was just so. Used to drive Cecily crazy. But it was always worth it. She'd make us dress up in winter, which I hated. I had this red velvet dress with a white collar that prickled my neck."

The house was always filled with laughter and heady conversation, people coming and going in a whirl of social activity. In its glory days, Wyldewood had been whatever one wanted it to be—a paradise, a sanctuary, or a playground. "I remember one year"—Lynette laughed a little—"Mom had a bet going with Mrs. Cooper that—"

Dad put up a hand. "I'm tired now, Lynnie. I think I'll go upstairs." He rose, steadied himself, and sent her a small smile.

She watched him head in, let out her breath, and closed her eyes. If only she could get those days back.

The life she remembered ended abruptly, twelve years ago, when all their dreams turned into siren-screeching nightmares. Nightmares she could only recall in flashes.

Flashes of the ferocious storm. Flashes of huddling in darkness, hands clapped over her ears. Flashes of long dresses hanging above her, perfume tickling her nose.

Then finally, David, reaching, pulling her from the depths of the closet where she'd hidden.

Hidden from what, exactly, she still didn't know.

Chapter Five

Lynette had an hour to kill before heading back to work on Tuesday afternoon. After running her errands, she walked toward the waterfront, relishing the fresh air.

More tourists milled about this week. Hydrangeas and wild roses colored the gardens of the houses she passed. With Memorial Day weekend approaching, the summer season would soon be in full swing. Nothing really changed on Nantucket. Shops changed hands, a few families moved away, but Lynette could always count on the familiarity of the island she'd grown up on. If only things at home would stop changing.

Her cell phone rang out while she contemplated lunch. She searched for it inside her purse and took a seat on a nearby bench. "Hello." Lynette stretched her legs and watched a young couple stroll by, helping a toddler navigate the sidewalk. The little girl looked her way and Lynette smiled.

"Lynette, this is your sister."

"I know. I felt the icy blast when I held the phone up to my ear."

"Tell me why you keep calling my cell phone and hanging up."

Lynette groaned inwardly. "Because I don't want to talk to your voice mail. I want to talk to you."

"Well, if you actually left a message, I'd know what it was you wanted to talk about." Liz's sigh of exasperation made Lynette grin.

"Well, if you actually called me back sooner, you'd find out."

"I happen to have a life, you know. I have a very demanding job, and I can't just drop everything when you decide you want to chat."

Lynette rolled her eyes. "Liz, I don't even remember the last time we 'chatted.' And in case you've forgotten, I also have a job. And I'm pretty sure I'm the one living in a house that might fall down any minute *and* running after Dad in the middle of the night."

An altercation with Liz the Lawyer was not what Lynette had in mind for lunch. She poked around in her purse, found her Pez dispenser, and popped a candy into her mouth.

"Lynette, what's going on over there?" Liz used her answer-me-right-now-or-I'll-slap-it-out-of-you tone.

She'd already explained the situation to her sister. "We need money."

"Please. What else is new?"

"Liz. Did you even look at the financial statements I e-mailed you the other day?"

"I haven't had a chance," Liz said. "As I told you, I'm rather busy."

"Of course you are. Well, here's the CliffsNotes version. We're broke."

"Oh, come on, Lynnie. I'm sure—"

"Liz. I went to see Nick Cooper at the bank yesterday. I don't think we can get a loan, and as much as I hate to say it, I think we need to talk about selling the house."

"Nick Cooper? What's he doing back there?"

"Working at the bank. I think I just said that." Lynette shook her head and prayed for patience.

"I thought you didn't want to sell the house."

For somebody with a law degree, Liz could be awfully stupid sometimes. "I don't. But the place needs so much work. The bills are ridiculous, even with just me and Dad there. It'd be nice for us to have something to live on into Dad's old age, but at this rate, unless you want to send me a million dollars, I don't see another option."

"Well, now you're making sense. Selling is the only way forward, although some repairs should be made before we list it. And why in the world are you just now telling me this? Have you spoken to David? Have you—" The long mournful blast of the ferry horn drowned out Liz's screeching.

"What, Liz? Didn't catch that." Tantalizing aromas from nearby restaurants reached her nose and her stomach began to growl. Lynette leaned over her knees and watched a trail of ants march by the tip of her Birkenstocks.

"We should have sold that tinderbox years ago, like I suggested," Liz grumbled. "The market has bottomed out now. We'll never get what it's really worth."

Lynette twisted her hair over one shoulder, her neck damp. "You'll have to come back if we want to talk about selling."

"Come back?"

"Mom's will." Lynette imagined the look of disgust on her sister's face. "She made the stipulation that—"

"I know what Mom's will says," her sister snapped. "I have some vacation time coming. Spending it on Nantucket wasn't what I had planned, but I'll suck it up."

"Don't rush over. I don't know what everyone else is up to yet and maybe selling isn't best."

"Of course it's best. Didn't you just say you were broke? Don't be stupid, Lynette."

Convincing Liz she was wrong was like chasing the dogs when they went after a strange cat. "Well. There's also this thing with Dad . . ."

"What about Dad?" Liz's voice shot up a notch. "Don't you dare tell me he's gambling again, Lynette, I swear I'll—"

"He's not. He's just . . . not himself lately."

"Sweetie, I'd count that as a blessing."

"Shut up, Liz." Lynette's eyes began to burn.

Her sister sighed deeply. "Sorry. What's going on with him?"

"I mentioned it before, but clearly you've forgotten." Lynette popped another candy into her mouth and crunched. Loudly.

"Lynette. Tell me, don't tell me, I'll find out anyway."

Lynette clapped her sandals together and startled a few birds pecking around a nearby garbage can. "He just . . . he wanders off sometimes. He sleeps weird hours; some nights he doesn't sleep at all. And . . ." She pinched the bridge of her nose with her thumb and forefinger. "Last night he thought I was Mom."

"Mom's dead."

"No, really? When did that happen?"

Liz swore and Lynette grinned. Her sister always brought out the worst in her.

"Lynette! Stop being a child and swear to me that you're telling the truth."

"I am telling the truth and nothing but, so help me God."

"Lynnie . . ."

"Why would I make this up, Liz?" Lynette waited through her sister's silence.

"So you're telling me you've got no money, Dad's off in la-la land, and who knows what else. Seriously, Lynnie! Your timing couldn't be worse. Work is crazy right now; I don't have the time for this."

"Forget it, Liz." Lynette shook her head. So much for her sister actually being helpful.

"Don't do that! Tell me what I'm supposed to do here."

"I was kind of hoping you'd tell me. I'm on my own out here, Liz. I need help."

"All right, settle down." Liz's tone softened. "I'll figure something out. Meanwhile, I can send a check this afternoon, just let me know how much."

On the other side of the street, a sleek, silver BMW slid up to the curb. Lynette watched Nick Cooper cross the street and quick-step it in her direction.

"Are you still there?" Liz did not care to be kept waiting.

"I thought that was you." Nick stood in front of her, hands on his hips, smiling, his eyes hidden under dark shades. "Oh, sorry, you're on the phone."

Lynette shrugged and made a face. "Just Liz."

"Who are you talking to?" In the next breath Liz let out a shriek that made Lynette pull the phone from her ear. "Is that the time? Oh, for heaven's sake! Listen, I need to get to a meeting. Call me tonight. And call David. Tell him everything, and be straight with us from now on. Got it?"

"Sure, Liz. Bye." She dropped her phone back into her purse. No need to call David. Liz was probably already texting their brother with one hand and hailing a cab with the other. She looked up at Nick. "If you want to talk about selling the house again, I'm not in the mood."

"Actually, I was going to get some lunch." Nick took off his shades. "I'm in the mood for chowder. Are you meeting someone?"

"Yeah, Chris Hemsworth." Lynette laughed at the way he scowled. "The movie star? I'm kidding. I'm on my lunch break, but I have to get back to work soon."

"Do you have time to join me?"

She tried to gauge his sincerity. He seemed serious. And she was starving. "Chowder sounds good."

They chose the closest restaurant and settled at a table. Crusty sailors sat at the bar telling tall tales, while sunburned tourists took in the nautical atmosphere. She made a mental note to bring Dad down here on the weekend for a lobster roll.

"I'm glad I ran into you," Nick said after they placed their order. "I hate to eat alone."

"Me too."

The food came quickly, and Lynette gave silent thanks before she began to eat.

Nick noticed. "You pray a lot?"

"A lot more than I used to." She lowered her gaze and studied the steam rising off the top of the thick white soup. It smelled delicious.

"So, you like working at Kiddie Kare?"

She glanced up and found him still watching her. "I do. I love kids. They're so full of life and excitement. You never know what they'll say or do next."

His eyes shimmered in the sunlight bouncing off the glass. "I remember you babysitting during the summers."

"You do?" Lynette tried not to stare. Tried not to search his face to find things he remembered that she didn't. Tried not to feel that sudden connection that came when he held her gaze for longer than he should have.

"Sure. I remember lots of things, Lynnie. Don't you?"

"Um." Lynette flushed under his easy grin. So not going to answer that question.

Nick got busy with his meal, shook salt and pepper into his chowder, and stuck his spoon in. "I'm surprised you stayed on the island. I thought you might have settled over on the mainland. Be married with a couple of kids by now."

"Nick, please." She rolled her eyes at the very idea. "I'm not anywhere near ready to get married. And unlike the rest of you, I happen to like Nantucket." Plus, there weren't exactly any eligible young men banging down her door.

The soup was hot, but she forced it down to keep her mouth busy.

He played with his straw. "I never said I didn't like Nantucket."

Lynette almost spat out her mouthful. "You so did! You and Gray were always talking about the day you were going to get off this rock, out into the real world."

"I guess." He turned his head slightly, surveying the room. "Sometimes the real world doesn't turn out to be all you think it is when you're eighteen." A sadness settled on him and Lynette swallowed any further comment. She turned her attention to her meal.

"Where'd you go the last five years?" she finally asked. Curiosity stepped over discretion. "You were at Princeton, right?" Last she'd heard he'd been on the swim team for the university.

"Yeah." Nick made slow work of pouring dressing over his salad. "I transferred. Spent some time in England."

"Oh." She hadn't heard that, but something told her not to ask.

"Hey, how's Cecily? Still here?" His swift change of subject said she'd been right.

"Yes. Still lives in the same house on Washington. She . . . doesn't work for us anymore, though. I see her at church mostly, when I'm able to go. You should give her a call. She'd love to see you."

"I will." His smile dimmed. "So do you feel any better about the idea of selling?"

"No." The chowder didn't taste as good as it had a minute ago. Liz and David would come up with a plan the minute they talked. Probably already had. The two of them would rally, pack Dad up and cart him off to some nursing home, and have the house sold before she could blink.

"Lynette? You seem distracted. Did your sister say something to upset you?" Nick took a gulp of his diet soda and pulled a slice of bread apart.

"She usually does." Lynette swallowed. "I told her I met with you. That we should talk about selling. And I told her things weren't good with my dad. She's ticked that I didn't call sooner."

Nick screwed up his nose and blew on his soup. "The wrath of Liz. Not a pleasant experience."

Lynette poked at her salad. "I've been thinking about it, Nick, about selling. I really wish we didn't have to. Not yet."

"Do you have a better plan?" He stopped eating, looked so

serious, like every word she spoke was important. It made her want to confide in him.

"Sort of." She sniffed and dabbed her lips with a napkin. "I'm going to call Gray first. I'll beg him if I have to, but he's the only one who has enough cash to get us out of this mess. We could at least make repairs, maybe buy some time. The thought of having to move my dad right now . . ." She shook her head, overwhelmed by the idea.

"You think Gray will help?" Nick's skeptical expression mirrored her feelings.

Lynette twirled her spoon around the bowl. "I don't know. He doesn't keep in touch like he used to."

They ate in silence for a while. Nick finished his meal before she was halfway through her own. Lynette eyed his empty dishes and grinned. "I guess you were hungry."

He returned the grin and mussed his hair. "I'm always hungry. You still eat like a bird."

"I suppose." She smiled and took a sip of her drink. "So you and Gray . . . you haven't talked at all?"

"Nope." He didn't have any food left or she was sure he would have scrambled to put something in his mouth.

"And I guess you don't want to tell me why?"

"Right." Nick leaned back in the captain's chair, ran a hand down his face, and gave a muted groan. "It's not worth getting into. Look, Lynnie, why don't you at least get in touch with a real estate agent. Get some hard figures so you've got something to go on."

Lynette folded her arms and studied what was left of her meal. "I suppose. But what if there was another way?" The idea had come to her awhile back, but she'd set it aside, convinced it wouldn't work. But now . . . "What if we converted part of the house, or most of it, into a bed-and-breakfast? That way Dad and I could stay there, and—"

Nick held up a hand. "Do you know how much work that would take? What that would cost?" He downed the rest of his soda and crunched ice. "And how would you convince the others to get on board with a plan like that? I mean, people are doing it, I'm not saying it's a terrible idea, but I'm not sure your brothers and Liz would agree."

"See, that's just it." Lynette clapped her hands together, a bubble of hope rising. "Once we're all back together, I could convince them. Make them see . . . remember all the good times."

There were good times. In spite of everything, they *had* all been happy.

"I think they might have different memories."

"What's that supposed to mean?" She clenched her fingers around a paper napkin and twisted.

His brow creased and he tried out a smile that didn't go anywhere. "Nothing. Just that, well, they haven't been around." Nick pushed his chair back a bit and looked like he was fighting a bad case of heartburn.

"That's not what you meant."

Raucous laughter floated over from the group at a large table across the room.

As much as she tried to remember what had happened the year her life catapulted into unimaginable tragedy, she couldn't. At twelve, she'd lived in a whirl of swimming, tennis, beach parties, and sailing regattas. And then one day her mother was dead, and Lynette's secure world became a scary place.

She pushed away the taunting thoughts.

Nick put a hand on her arm. "I'm sorry. I know how hard this is. I just don't want to see you get disappointed."

Lynette shrugged and met his eyes. "It's okay." She glanced at her watch. "I should get back to work. How much do I owe you?"

Nick shook his head. "Don't be silly. I asked you, remember?" A lock of hair hid one eye from view, his dimples deepening with his smile. If Chris Hemsworth had shown up, she would have passed him over.

Lynette's cheeks grew warm. "Thanks, Nick. It was great."

"Maybe we could have dinner next time? Give us more time to talk?" He sat back, totally at ease with the suggestion.

Years ago she would have agreed without a second thought. But now . . . spending time with Nick Cooper was not a great idea. Because she'd enjoy it too much, and, if she was honest, she wasn't altogether sure she'd gotten over the childhood crush she'd carried for longer than she cared to admit. She couldn't afford that kind of distraction. "No, really, I . . ." Lynette floundered for a quick refusal but her brain wouldn't work with her tongue.

"Well, if you'd rather we send smoke signals the next time we're out on our second-floor patios, I could do that."

If it was possible to die from utter embarrassment, she was about to find out. She pushed her chair back and got to her feet. Her legs threatened mutiny, and she took a moment to make sure she could stand. "I wasn't spying on you, if that's what you think."

"I never thought that." Nick paid the bill and stood up, his laughter rising above the noise in the restaurant.

He insisted on walking her to her car. "Thanks again for lunch, Nick," she mumbled, hurrying to find her keys before he brought it up again.

He leaned against the side of her old Toyota, his sparkling eyes matching the color of his blue shirt. "Next time you're outside alone, give me a shout. Sometimes company is nice. Don't you think?"

Lynette hoped her face wasn't as red as it felt. "Maybe. Bye, Nick." She opened her door and he moved off the vehicle. Once she'd pulled onto the street and he was out of sight, she gave a sigh of frustration.

Nick Cooper's company was more than nice. But she had enough to worry about.

She wasn't about to fall in love with the boy next door.

Not again.

Chapter Six

Gray Carlisle stretched out on the wooden bench in the park and watched the children on the swings. A guy with a hot dog cart sporting Montreal Canadien pennants pushed past him, the aroma a reminder of childhood, almost tempting enough to make him get one. Not that he'd be able to keep it down. He shoved his hands into the pockets of his leather jacket and shivered in the wind. If this was a Canadian spring, he definitely didn't want to be here in winter.

Happy shouts and childish squeals distracted him from the cold. Sitting here was self-inflicted punishment.

His eyes followed the little girl in the pink boots, with blond curls and a big smile. Last night's rain left its mark, and she was making a great show of jumping from puddle to puddle across the playground. He figured she was about three, maybe four.

"Daddy, watch! Watch me jump!"

Gray squeezed his eyes tight.

Laughter floated around him and he looked in time to see a burly man swing her around, high up in the air and down again.

Gray lit a cigarette and kicked a pebble across the grass, scaring a few pigeons.

"There you are." Marshall Gerome strode toward him with a grim glare that could have crumbled Mont Tremblant. Victoria followed close behind, carrying a cardboard cup tray from Starbucks. Gray was glad to see one of them.

"Here I am." He coughed, tried to get a handle on the wheeze that followed. "Hope one of those is for me." He smiled at Tori's scowl. Victoria Montgomery had been his manager since his career began. She knew practically everything about him, including how he liked his java.

"You're lucky I'm still talking to you," she said.

Gray remembered why Marshall was here and shot his lawyer a sidelong glance. "All sorted out?"

"We wrote them a check," Marshall told him. "You don't have much left in your account. But I guess you know that." The tall man's caramel cheeks got a shade darker. He sank onto the bench and took the coffee Victoria offered. He'd happened to be on business in Quebec this week. But he wasn't happy that Victoria had called him to sort out Gray's latest infraction. Not happy at all.

"Here." Victoria nudged Gray. "Move over." She sat beside him, handed him his coffee, and pointed at his cigarette. "One would think now would be an opportune time to quit, given the cause of the trouble you're in."

"One would think." Gray took a last drag, dropped his smoke to the ground, and stomped on it. "I didn't do it on purpose."

Marshall grunted, tapping the tops of his black leather shoes together. "Of course you didn't. Nothing is ever your fault, is it? Thankfully, they decided not to sue. What were you doing out in that barn in the middle of the night anyway, Gray? Singing to the cows?"

A chuckle snuck out of him. It wasn't funny. Not really. But how many places he'd stayed in had barns on their property? Hotel, guesthouse, B&B, or whatever they called it, it intrigued him. He'd just taken a night stroll, sat down for a smoke. He hadn't meant to send the barn up in flames.

Victoria aimed the pointy toe of her red boot at his ankle and fired.

"Ow. Physical violence is not necessary." Gray bent over and rubbed the sore spot. "Nobody got hurt. I thought I stubbed it out, okay?"

"We hear you." Victoria pulled on a pair of sunglasses and shuddered. "Wow, it's cold here. Good thing we're going home tomorrow."

Gray twisted to face her. "We're what?"

Marshall sighed. His hard stare made Gray squirm like a toddler put in time-out. "I talked to Neil this morning. You can't tell me you didn't see this coming. Two DUIs last summer, drunk and disorderly on New Year's. Where was that again?" He shook his head, disgusted. "Doesn't matter. And now you burn down a barn."

"Don't forget the past couple shows where you almost fell off the stage." Victoria wouldn't look at him.

She stared straight ahead.

Seeing the same things he saw.

Seeing their past. Their mistakes.

No. His mistakes.

Gray scratched his head and tried to ignore the ache in his chest. His agent wouldn't drop him. Unless Neil was finally so sick of all his crap. And could he blame him?

Gray stayed silent awhile, then forced out the questions. "Neil won't drop me, right? What about the new album? What about the gigs in Europe all summer?" His first record with Sony released last year and they said he had a chance. Said he could actually make it in this business.

He'd almost begun to believe it.

"No gigs." Marshall pulled on a pair of gloves and donned his shades. Gray half wondered if the dude had a double life working for the Feds. "They'll find someone else. The new album is on hold for now. Neil wants you to take some time off. He'll call you later. Get your head together. Get some rest and get yourself off whatever it is you're taking, Carlisle." Marshall stood, pitched his cup into a nearby garbage can, and nudged his dark glasses downward.

Looked at Gray through eyes that were a smidge softer. "You only get one go-round in this life. Make it count."

"Yeah." Gray cracked his knuckles and rubbed his hands to warm them. He took the hand Marshall extended and shook it. "Thanks for coming, man."

"Take care of yourself, Gray. You'll be in my prayers."

Figures. Of all the lawyers in New York City, he had to land a religious one.

He'd started out so well. He was young, but he had the drive and determination. And he'd been clean and sober. Playing gigs because they were fun, the fans were cool, and he loved hearing his stuff on the radio. Living the dream he'd had since high school.

He'd always hated the confines of the classroom. Always wanted to be someplace else. While his siblings studied, took courses for extra credit, and placed overly high expectations on themselves, all Gray ever wanted to do was sing.

And then he got scared.

Gray watched the tall man stride away, expelled a long breath, and bent over, head in his hands.

Victoria rubbed his back. "It's not the end of the world." The tremor in her voice told him it probably was.

"It's the end of my world." He didn't have to spell it out for her. She'd been working for him long enough to know how bad he wanted this. How hard he'd worked.

And how badly he'd screwed up.

"Is this it? It's all over, just like that?" He sat up, glad her eyes were hidden behind sunglasses.

"For now." She nodded, pushed her dark hair behind her ears, her mouth pinched. "Neil isn't dropping you. He just wants to be sure you really want this. But if you do, Gray, you need to make some major changes. It's fine playing in smoky bars and small stages, but if you want more than that, you're going to have to prove it."

"I know. I will." But he didn't have a clue how.

A huge Canadian flag flapped in the wind atop a building hidden by tall pines. Gray studied the overly large red maple leaf. Maybe he could just move here and start over. It might actually be worth considering if the country wasn't so cold. He put his cup down and pushed his trembling hands under his legs.

"Your sister called earlier. I told her you'd call her back."

Gray ground out a curse and scuffed his boots on the grass. "I don't want to talk to Liz." Their last conversation had escalated into a shouting match, after she'd suggested rehab . . . again. Like Liz's life was so perfect, living with that creepo boyfriend of hers. Gray suspected the guy was abusive. Couldn't prove it, and of course Liz would never confide in him. Or anyone.

"Not Liz. It was Lynette." Victoria stood and fished his cell out of her coat pocket. He was always leaving it somewhere. "I'm going inside. We're almost packed. But I guess now you need to let me know where we're going."

Gray nodded and took the phone. "Thanks." Another harsh cough overtook him, and he watched concern mar her expression.

Perhaps Liz had a point. Maybe it was time to give up the game he'd been playing the last few years, trying to convince them all that he was fine. That he wasn't falling apart.

He didn't even buy his own lies anymore.

His throat closed, his chest tight again. Gray couldn't remember when he'd last fallen asleep on his own. When he'd slept through the night without having to rush to the bathroom or remedy the urgent craving that robbed him of slumber and sent him back to the dark places he was desperate to avoid.

But maybe, just maybe, it was possible to start again.

He rubbed his nose and managed to look at Victoria. "A rehab center might be a good first stop?"

Tori took off her shades and wiped her eyes, reached for his hand, and held it a minute. Then she nodded and hid her eyes again. "Don't stay out here too long. It's ridiculously cold."

He waited until she was well out of sight before giving in to the wave of emotion that crested, crashed through him, and took his breath away. It wasn't like he tried to screw up. He was just really, really good at it.

Gray focused on the screen of his phone and dialed the familiar number. Didn't bother to check his watch, couldn't remember if there was a time difference anyway. The corners of his mouth lifted when he heard his baby sister's voice.

"Hey, Shortstop." He heard the dogs barking in the background, and Lynette shushed them. If he tried real hard, he could probably hear the ocean.

"Gray!" She pretty much screamed his name and he grinned.

"Yeah, it's me. Going deaf here, sweetheart."

"I've been trying to reach you for weeks." And clearly not thrilled that she hadn't been able to.

"Yeah. Sorry about that. I've been a little . . ." Strung out. "Busy."

"Well, never mind. It's so good to hear your voice. How are you? How is everything? Everyone keeps asking when you're coming out with a new album. Where are you now?"

Gray smiled. Sweet Lynnie. Always so quick to forgive and forget. Would she forgive him his sins this time, if she knew them?

"Montreal. Things are good. Just wrapping up here." He watched a flock of geese fly toward the city. "So, what's up with you? Everything okay at home?" He winced as she launched into a fast-paced, blow-by-blow account of everything he'd missed the past few months.

He inhaled, listened, and tried to make sense of it all. "Wait, what? Who said anything about selling the house?"

"We may not have a choice. Liz is all for it. And I think David will side with her. Maybe Ryan, I don't know. But, Gray, you remember all the good times, how much the place meant to Mom? You can stop this from happening. Can't you?"

Could he? His first thought was yes. Of course he could.

There was just that little matter of reality.

"Man, Lynnie." How could he tell his sister how badly he wanted to help her, and why he couldn't? Gray didn't have the words. Or the guts. "Maybe selling is best."

"Gray."

Traitor.

She didn't have to say it. He felt it right through to his bones, like the damp sea air that seeped through the floorboards of Wyldewood in winter.

"I'm sorry." More than she would ever know. "I . . . um . . . have to go away for a while. I'll be gone a few weeks. But when I get out . . . get back . . . what if I come home, huh? We can talk in person. Figure something out." That stupid cough overtook him again and gave an excuse for the moisture in his eyes.

"Gray. What's going on? You sound sick." Lynnie was a year and a bit younger, but she'd always felt older to him. Always the one he talked to first, before Liz or his brothers. The one who knew his secrets.

But now he had secrets he never wanted her to know.

"I'm fine." Or he would be.

"If you say so." She sighed. "Well, if the others want to sell, they're going to have to come home. Mom's will, remember? Nick says we might be able to—"

"Nick?" Gray curled his fingers around the bottom of the bench and felt his spine stiffen. "Nick Cooper? Why are you talking to him?"

"Because he's here, Gray."

When did his little sister get so feisty? "Cooper's a jerk, Lynnie. Stay away from him." He could hardly believe he'd just said that.

"Are you serious? Get over yourself, Gray. Look, Nick's working at the bank. I went to him for advice. It doesn't matter. The point is, I'm on my own out here, and I don't know what to do."

"All right, all right." He could hear the tears and desperation in her voice and he hated it. Hated that he was so far away, so messed up, and so not ready to go home. Even when he knew how much she needed him.

"Can you come home, Gray? Now?"

The truth sat at his heels like a stray pup. All he had to do was acknowledge it.

Tell his sister what a loser he had become.

"No, I can't come home. Not yet." He swore under his breath. "But I'll try and get there soon, okay?"

"Soon, then." She sounded satisfied with that. "You'll let me know?"

"Will do." Gray nodded. "See you, Shortstop." Gray pocketed his phone.

Home to Nantucket.

To the memories and the demons that lurked within them.

To Pops.

To the past.

It wouldn't be easy. Who was he kidding? None of this would be easy. The road he was about to traverse scared him even more than not quitting. But he had to. Knew it when he'd caught sight of that cute little girl with the big grin. Knew if there was ever a reason to start over . . .

Gray coughed again and concentrated on his breathing. He hadn't taken anything today. He wasn't dead, and despite the head-ache he already had—the nausea and the chills he knew would hit in an hour or so—the world hadn't stopped turning.

Perhaps, with some luck and a lot of prayer from the people in his life who had better connections with the big dude upstairs than he did, he could beat this thing.

He'd run out of options.

Chapter Seven

Nick found himself still thinking about Lynette the Saturday of Memorial Day weekend. He hadn't been prepared for the impact of seeing her again after so many years. He wondered if she felt the same . . . wondered if she remembered that night so long ago, when they'd walked the beach and talked—and he'd kissed her. He couldn't believe he'd done it at the time. Sometimes he still didn't.

Nick flopped onto his stomach, wishing for a couple more hours sleep, but he was wide-awake. He'd wanted to tell Lynette how he really felt that night. That he'd never thought of her like a kid sister the way the others did. But he'd lost his nerve. Then life got in the way.

And now? Now wasn't exactly the ideal time to rip the lid off any of his unresolved feelings. They both had more issues to deal with than the characters on those smarmy reality shows Mindy liked to watch.

Mindy . . . Nick groaned into his pillow and made a mental note to figure that one out ASAP.

Too quickly, his mind drifted back to the Carlisles. Something was definitely wrong with Drake. Alzheimer's was his best guess. Nick was no doctor, but he knew one thing for sure—in his befuddled mind, the man had come here that night looking for his wife.

Nick knew why.

He got up with the sun, slammed around the kitchen, and put together a quick breakfast. The overly toasted bagel didn't go down easily. After a couple of bites, he opted for just coffee.

Nick sat with his head in his hands, jackhammers drilling into his brain. For the thousandth time, he cursed the day his father had called requesting—no, demanding—his presence back here on Nantucket. He should have refused. Packed up his stuff and run as far as he could in the opposite direction. But he'd given in, for a good reason. Except now he was stuck, left to deal with a not-so-forgotten past and all its monsters.

His smartphone beeped with new messages. Nick scanned them and shook his head. Mindy Vanguard did not take no for an answer. He'd have to call her back eventually. If he didn't, she'd show up on his doorstep.

The early-morning sun rays shone through the bay window of the kitchen. He put his plate in the dishwasher and went upstairs to change.

Nick went for a swim, then jogged along the not-yet-crowded beach and let the sea air penetrate his lungs and purify his thoughts. He slowed his pace when he passed the steps that led to Wyldewood. The house still seemed grand, but the gray shingles were shaded with moss, more than a few missing. The roof looked in need of repair. A tattered flag hung limp from the rusted metal pole, white paint peeling off.

With all of them gone, and Lynnie managing the old man and working as well, it was no wonder the house was so rundown.

Back home, he showered, dressed, and made two phone calls. One to placate Mindy, the other, he hoped, to placate himself.

He pushed up the garage door and hopped into the old two-seater Jeep TJ he'd been driving since the day he was legal. He didn't drive her much anymore, but today the mood hit. She looked good, not a speck of dust on the shiny black paint. The engine came to life at once. Nick had Clyde, their groundskeeper, to thank for that. If his father knew the Jeep was still in working condition, he might have had it carted away. Dad didn't like to be reminded of Nick's rebellious youth.

He put the top down, pushed on his shades, and cranked the volume of the radio as he turned onto Polpis. Gray's latest Top 40 hit accosted him, and he pressed harder on the gas pedal. Everyone on Nantucket seemed to think Gray Carlisle was the next John Mayer.

Nick drummed on the wheel and listened to the gravelly voice belt out an unfamiliar tune. Something about pain, heartache, and addiction. Typical. *Write what you know, Gray.*

He whizzed by the dunes and watched kids race toward the water. The wind tugged at his hair and shook off sleep as he wound along the coastal road, through town, past Brant Point Lighthouse off in the distance.

He slowed to overtake a couple on pedal bikes. The sun warmed his skin and almost had him believing life was good. Nick checked out the water and thought about hauling his Sunfish overboard later. He hadn't been for a sail in a while.

Once he reached Jetties Beach, he spun the Jeep around and headed back toward town.

It was time.

He turned down Washington and coasted to a stop when a memory kicked in. He wasn't sure he would remember the place, hadn't been here since he was a kid, but there it was. The small gray-shingled house with blue shutters sat pretty in a neat little garden, boxed in by a white picket fence. Pink roses were in bloom, filling the air with heady perfume. Nick parked and got out, stood a moment, debating with himself.

"Nicholas Cooper, get on up here!" Cecily Johnson stood in the doorway before he reached it, her gleaming smile taking over half her dark face. "Shoot! Look at you. It's been an age." She opened her arms and Nick slipped into them with a grin. It had been years since he'd seen her, but when she'd worked for the Carlisles, she'd looked after him like he was family.

"Hey, Cecily." Her hugs always made him feel like a million bucks.

"I nearly fell off my stool when you called. Well, come on in." She pulled him inside, and the aroma of coffee and something baking wafted through the tiny hall.

Banana bread if his nose was any good. He followed her through to a warm kitchen and sat at an old oak table. "Lynnie said I should come see you. I mean . . . I was planning on it anyway."

"Sure you were." She chuckled good-naturedly. "Spending time with an old woman like me probably isn't all that high on your to-do list."

"Ce-ce, you're hardly old. Lynnie says you're keeping busy, huh?"

"Oh, yes. Always busy." Cecily bustled around, throwing questions at him as she poured the coffee. "You been home long? Seems like you've found your way back to the house next door."

Nick shoved his car keys into his pocket. "Not exactly. Lynette came to see me at the bank."

She set a steaming banana-cranberry loaf in front of him, cut into generous buttered slices, along with a cup of strong coffee. Nick reached for a slice and munched, giving a long groan of appreciation.

Cecily beamed and handed him a paper napkin. "Better than you remembered?"

"It's amazing."

"Good. Don't wait so long between visits next time."

"Sorry." Nick finished his piece of heaven and sat back, waiting for the coffee to cool. He glanced around the small room. A child's artwork decorated the refrigerator and a box of toys sat in one corner. "Guess your grandson must be getting big?"

"You wouldn't believe the size of him. He's off to kindergarten in the fall. Out fishing with his granddaddy today. The two of them are like peas in a pod."

"Can't believe you're a grandmother. You're looking younger and more beautiful than ever." Nick winked and grabbed another piece of the warm loaf.

Cecily shook with laughter. "You always were a charmer, Nicholas. I can't complain. The good Lord keeps me healthy and busy. We get by."

"I heard you're not with the Carlisles anymore."

"No." A sigh rumbled through her as she drank her coffee. "I stayed as long as I could, but my husband, he wouldn't have it. Said I had to make some money or may as well stay home and look after young Tyson for my daughter." Her brow furrowed. "How they getting on over there?"

Nick relayed the events of the past few weeks and shared his concern over Drake.

Cecily dabbed at her eyes and shook her head. "I guess Lynnie still can't get him to the doctor. What happens when she's at work?" Her eyes formed thin slits, her lips pinched in disapproval.

"Gets help where she can, I suppose. She mentioned a neighbor popping in."

"That poor man hasn't been the same since Mrs. Diana passed on, that's for sure."

"Lynette said he's not drinking anymore. Is that true?"

Cecily nodded, her dark eyes serious. "True as the Bible. At least it was when I was there. But it's something else now, isn't it?"

Nick played with a gold signet ring on his right hand. "Was he acting strange before you left? Forgetting stuff, wandering off?"

"In mind and body." Cecily picked a few dead bits from a purple violet plant in the middle of the table. "Started end of last year. I tried saying something, but you know Lynnie, don't want to admit when something's wrong. I just let her be."

She pushed the plate toward him and Nick gave in. "Cecily, do you know if they ever come over, David or anyone? It's a lot for Lynnie to manage on her own."

"It is. Too much. Far as I know, none of them have been back in years. Much as I'd hate to see them go, they should sell that old place and be done with it."

"That's what I've been telling her." Nick frowned and ran a finger around the flower design on his mug.

"You been seeing a lot of Lynette?" Cecily's eyes twinkled with mischief and Nick raised a brow.

"Don't start."

Her shoulders shook with subdued laughter. "Ooo, I think you're still sweet on that girl, aren't you?"

Much to his chagrin, Nick felt his face flush. "Cut it out, Cece. Anyway, I did talk to her about selling—she hates the idea. I get it, but honestly, I don't think they have a choice. And the rest of them will probably agree. I was thinking I might . . . I don't know. I want to help, I'm just not sure how."

Cecily gave him the honest look he remembered well and reached for his hand. "If you want my advice, don't take that on, Nicholas. You might still feel a part of them, but I'm not so sure they feel the same. 'Specially Gray."

It would have come up eventually.

Nick didn't know what to say so he looked out the window instead. A couple jogged along the street. Somewhere off in the distance a dog howled at a passing ambulance and the sea gulls chimed in, screeching piteous protests.

"Had a feeling you heard us that night."

She nodded. "You were outside, but he was yelling pretty loud. And I know you and Gray haven't talked since."

"Five years." Nick rubbed his jaw, surprised at how vivid the memory still was. Gray had slugged him there, good and hard. It was the first time they'd ever disagreed on anything. The first time his friend had ever hit him.

Regret he'd learned to live with pressed against his temples. "I thought I was doing the right thing, telling him."

Cecily squeezed his hand. "Honey, sometimes people don't want the truth."

Nick set his jaw. "I didn't ask for it either."

Cecily's dark eyes shone. "You've got a good heart, son. You always did. But they weren't your choices to make. You were just a boy. What could you have done?"

"Nothing, I guess." He shrugged, all that good baking threatening a hasty exit. "I knew for a long time. I only told Gray that night because he was being a jerk to Drake. They all blamed their dad, you know, after Diana died. And I was tired of carrying it around."

Cecily touched the gold cross around her neck. Folded up today's newspaper and stacked it atop a pile of magazines. A pained expression froze her face. "You got something else to get off your chest, don't you? That's why you came today?"

Maybe he shouldn't have come. Maybe it was better to leave the ghosts undisturbed.

"Why are you really here, Nicholas? Back on this island?" The voice he remembered, vibrant and true, pulled open a long forgotten door Nick knew he must step through.

"My dad. He . . . well, I guess you could say it's where I need to be right now."

"Go on. I'm listening."

It was what he'd come here to do. Nick knew it, accepted it, and told her everything.

If there was anyone in the world he trusted, it was Cecily Johnson. Whatever he shared in here would go no further. And once the words were out, he felt a little lighter.

They talked awhile longer, and then, for some reason he couldn't explain, he let Cecily pray for him.

Chapter Eight

B y the second week in June, Lynette felt more hopeful. Her paintings were selling, and things at home were bearable, for now.

She parked outside Evy's gallery after work that Friday with another painting. Flowers cascaded from the ancient water trough in the middle of the street—blue and white lobelia and other summer blooms on glorious display.

"Spectacular," Evy crowed, clapping her hands at Lynette's latest offering.

"Thanks." Lynette poked around the gallery, checked out the new work hanging rather than studying her own. "I can't believe my stuff is selling. Jamison is much better. His pieces haven't moved."

Evy laughed and went behind the desk. "Jamison is fantastic. But he's Matisse. You're more like Norman Rockwell. People like that. They can lose themselves in your story."

"Who's buying my paintings?" Lynette faced her friend, suddenly curious. She hadn't bothered to ask before, but she wanted to know now, having seen her competition.

"Here's your cash, sweets." Evy handed over an envelope.

Lynette did a quick count and gaped. "Seriously?"

"Four paintings. I think I'll raise the price on these. We are in high season, after all."

"Evy." Lynette dropped the envelope into her purse. "Some poor old lady doesn't realize she's throwing her money down the toilet. You're probably committing a thousand sins here, you know."

"The only sin is you not selling your work before now." Evy peered over the rim of her spectacles. "If you must know, our buyer is hardly a poor old lady. He's young. And very easy on the eyes. Although he's not my type." Wheezy laughter rang through the gallery as Evy reached for a black Chanel clutch and produced a gold lipstick case.

"So the same person is buying all my paintings?"

"Well, not all of them. But a few, yes."

Lynette watched Evy apply a generous amount of fuchsia to her lips. "Somebody from the city? That figures." She shook her head. It didn't matter. The cash would cover the next month's round of bills. Mr. City Slicker was welcome to her paintings.

"You look tired, hon." Evy leaned over the counter and studied her with the all-knowing look Lynette had learned not to dodge.

"I am, I guess." She dragged her fingers through her hair, lack of sleep doing a smackdown. "Things are getting worse with my dad."

"I'm sorry to hear that. Medical care is expensive." Evy pushed up her glasses with the top of a pencil. "I should know. Took about every cent I had paying off my first husband's medical bills. Thankfully husband number two had more money than Solomon."

"What happened to him?" Lynette wasn't so sure she wanted to know.

"Oh, nothing." Evy gave a throaty chuckle. "He was old. Passed away peacefully in his sleep."

"And left you a fortune."

Evy nodded and perused the gallery. "He did indeed. I sometimes wonder why I'm still here on this island instead of traveling the world."

"You told me you hated to fly."

"I suppose that would be one reason." Evy laughed, then took on a pensive look. "Sometimes, though, it's good to face your fears, isn't it?"

"Not always." Lynette reached for a chocolate from the bowl

on the counter, unwrapped the foil, and popped it in her mouth. "I just found out my father let the medical insurance slide. Everyone is pressuring me to put the house on the market. Even Nick."

"Nick?"

Lynette scrunched up her nose. "Nick Cooper. He's our neighbor. He works at the bank. You know, those Coopers? I went to see him a couple weeks ago. He was kind enough to tell me we're about ready for an extended stay in the poorhouse."

She sank into one of Evy's round leather objects that passed for a chair, leaned against the soft cushion, and closed her eyes. She could sleep for a thousand days, but when she woke, things would still be the same.

Evy walked through the gallery, pulling down the shades and locking the front door. Then her friend positioned herself in the chair opposite hers and passed the bowl of chocolates.

"Sometimes life just sneaks up and bites you in the butt, doesn't it, honey?"

Lynette stared a moment, then exploded into laughter. A moment later she wiped the tears from her eyes. "Thanks, Evy. You always make me feel better."

"I'm glad an old lady can be useful." Evy batted her mascara-heavy eyelashes, examining her a little too carefully. "Can I ask you something?"

"You will anyway."

"True." Evy played with the colorful glass beads around her neck. "Listen, can we reconsider the pseudonym? You're so good, hon. Why not take credit for your talent?"

Lynette hesitated. It wasn't that she hadn't thought about it. "I don't know really. I . . . I think I did it because of my father."

"You don't think he would like the idea of you selling your work?"

"No, it's not that. I just feel like I've stolen something from him. If he were well, he'd still be painting. I don't want to ride any coattails, and I don't really want my family to know I'm selling my paintings."

"That's why you want to be paid in cash?"

"They have access to our account. If I deposited checks, they'd wonder where the extra money was coming from."

Evy frowned. "Well, all right. It's up to you. I also wanted to ask, have you got any of your father's older pieces? You might think about selling those. I'd be more than happy to help with that. Just say the word."

Unexpected tears formed and Lynette blinked them back. Selling the house, selling Dad's paintings . . . She drew in a breath and wiped her eyes. How much more would she be asked to give up?

"I don't know, Evy. Those paintings are so special . . . especially now." She couldn't say it. Especially now, when his mind would never be the same.

Evy reached across the gap between their two chairs and squeezed Lynette's hand. "So this Nick . . . Is he cute?"

"Cute? No." Puppies were cute. Babies were cute. Nick Cooper was . . . so much more. Lynette concentrated on her toes. Her sandals had endured another go-round with the dogs and were looking a little worse for wear. Nick was also persistent. Kept calling to see if she needed anything. She'd finally agreed to another lunch, just yesterday, but vowed not to get carried away. Nick was just looking out for her, concerned, in a big brother sort of way.

"How well do you know this Mr. Cooper?"

A flash of heat raced up her cheeks. "Don't get any ideas. Nick grew up with us. He's like the extra brother I don't need. He'd never be interested in me romantically, even if I . . ." Drat. Evy could make her say anything.

"Even if you what?" Evy tipped her head slightly, eyes gleaming.

"Never mind." The look of amusement her friend wore made Lynette scowl. "Why are you laughing at me?"

"Sweetie, I'm not laughing at you. I'm just wondering when you're going to stop hauling that steamer trunk of worry around."

"What trunk?"

Evy's smile was kind. "We all have our problems, dear. Why pretend you don't?"

"My problems are apparently no secret to anyone." Lynette rose, slung her bag over her shoulder, and narrowed her eyes. "Nick means well, but he's got better things to do than worry about me."

"Maybe he likes worrying about you."

Okay, definitely time to go. "We're not talking about Nick Cooper again. If you bring him up, I'll take my paintings elsewhere. You did want an exclusive, didn't you?"

"Indeed." Evy walked her to the door. She patted Lynette's back. "All right, my dear, I won't tease. Off you go. I'll call you next week."

"I'm sure you will." Lynette pecked her on the cheek, gave in to impulse and hugged her friend's bony frame. "You drive me crazy, you know that?"

"Sounds like I've got competition in that department."

"Good night, Evy." She made a point of slamming the door behind her.

After picking up a few groceries, Lynette pulled into the driveway, dreading what she would find today. She needed to get to the hardware store and put a chain or something on the outside of Dad's bedroom door, to give her peace of mind at night, but the thought was too ghastly.

The past week had been uneventful, and she was grateful for that. Lynette entered the kitchen from the garage, the screen door squeaking shut. She stopped in her tracks. Déjà vu settled over her, and she was a kid, coming home from school. When coming home had been something she looked forward to.

Gospel music floated from the radio on the counter by the phone. Cecily stood over the stove, stirring a pot, singing along to the music. Mouth-watering smells filled the air.

Lynette clutched the grocery bag to her chest and blinked.

Cecily didn't work for them anymore.

Dad wasn't the only one around here losing his mind.

"Cecily?" Lynette blinked a couple more times, but Cecily stayed right where she was.

"Hi, honey. How was your day?" The older woman put down her spoon, crossed the room, and took the bag from Lynette. She plopped it on the counter and proceeded to unpack. Lynette stared.

"Cat got your tongue, missy?" Cecily's kind eyes sparked with mischief.

The kitchen was spotless. The windows shone, no sign of the salty film that had covered them this morning. The clean scent of pine said the floor had been mopped, something she'd been putting off for weeks.

"Wha . . . what are you doing here? Is my dad okay?"

"Your daddy's fine, honey, taking a nap in the living room. Hush, now." Cecily pressed a sack of potatoes into her hands. "Put these in the pantry. I'm back, and all taken care of, nothing for you to worry about. Would have started up sooner, but I had to get my grandson sorted. Nicholas came by earlier and put an alarm on your daddy's bedroom door. Said you'd know what it was for."

"Nick was here?" Lynette squeezed her eyes shut and tried to summon a thought that made sense.

She put the potatoes away instead.

David must have called Cecily, asked her to come back. Lynette hadn't talked to him since he'd called after Liz's interrogation. He'd apologized profusely for not knowing how bad things were. Didn't get mad at her like Liz had. She'd have to remember to thank him next time they spoke.

"I got the kettle on. You could make us some tea." Cecily threw a pile of peels in the garbage and washed her hands. Lynette fumbled with cups and tea bags, still in a trance, but salivating at the sight of Cecily's banana bread on the counter.

A few minutes later they sat at the table.

"Are you really back?" She stirred her tea, afraid to hear the answer. She'd been having some weird dreams lately.

The older woman smiled and nodded. "Yes. I'm back. Going to look after your daddy and take care of the house, just like always."

Lynette could only stare. "That's . . . amazing. I can't believe it."

"I can see that." Familiar laughter rang through the room. "How've you been, girl? You look tired."

"Ha. I've heard that a lot lately." Tears formed and Lynette didn't bother to brush them away. She managed to recount the important bits, how Dad was doing, the fact that they'd probably be putting the house on the market, which meant everyone would have to come home, and . . . Nick.

"I don't even know how to deal with that," Lynette admitted. "He's just so . . . you know, Nick. He needs to make sure I'm looked after."

Cecily gave a knowing smile. "Maybe there's a little more to it than that."

Lynette rolled her eyes but laughed. "Whatever, Ce-ce. I can't even think about it right now. My life is crazy."

They shared a few more stories, then Cecily grew serious and reached for Lynette's hand. "Baby, I got something to tell you, and it's not pleasant." She exhaled and dabbed her eyes. "It's about your brother Gray."

~

Nick wandered through the house to grab a soda from the kitchen. Another Friday night with nothing to do. His sixty-year-old father enjoyed a better social life than he did. Still, Nick was alone by choice. Dad was back on the island and entertaining, which meant Nick would disappear. Somewhere.

Soraya bustled around, preparing dinner, the radio blaring. The housekeeper nodded his way and continued carving a large rack of lamb. She loved classical music and the local news. Nick couldn't care less about island gossip, but as he crossed the large kitchen to the refrigerator, he stopped when he heard Gray Carlisle's name.

"What was that?"

"Sorry, too loud? You want me to turn it off?" Soraya reached for the dial.

"No. Turn it up." Nick leaned over the granite counter top.

"He's trouble, that Gray," Soraya muttered, clucking her tongue. "All mixed up with drugs and who knows what else. Used to be such a nice boy."

Nick shook his head and waved for her to be quiet while he listened to the broadcaster's account of the last few chaotic months of Gray Carlisle's life.

And two weeks ago, Gray had canceled his tour and checked into a rehab clinic.

Now the rumor was that he'd checked out.

Why hadn't Lynette told him? Unless she didn't know . . .

Nick stared down at the stone counter top, then grabbed a beer from the fridge. He popped it open and took two long gulps. His mind raced ahead, tossing images at him that he wasn't ready for.

Oh, Gray.

Soraya made irritating clucking noises and wagged her head. "See what happens when you go chasing after stardom, Mister Nick? You good to stay here, home where you belong."

The muscles in his neck began to pinch with the start of a headache. "Everyone makes mistakes, Soraya. At least he went to rehab, right? That means he's trying to start over." Strangely, Nick felt defensive, as if proving a point.

Soraya harrumphed and chopped up a carrot with vengeance. "That's what they all say. Those poor people got enough trouble already, with this to add to it. Lord, have mercy." She blessed him with her I-know-you're-my-boss's-kid-but-you're-an-idiot expression. "What his family got to say?"

Nick massaged his neck, his empty stomach churning. "No idea." Not that he'd believed Lynette would tell him everything, but they'd had more than a few conversations the past couple weeks, and he thought they were growing closer.

If she did know, this would be killing her.

"I'll see you, Soraya." He put the can on the counter, marched to the back door, slipped into his loafers, and flung open the door.

"What about dinner? Your father expecting you?"

"I doubt it. Tell him I had other plans." Nick slammed the door, ran down the drive and onto the main road, then turned into the gates of Wyldewood. He didn't stop running until he stood at the foot of the front steps.

Chapter Nine

Nick stared up at the place where he'd spent so much of his life and acknowledged an odd sensation of standing between two worlds. Even in darkness, the house had a magical feel. A long forgotten ache stirred within him.

Years slipped away and he was a kid again. A part of the family he'd wished had been his own. Nick remembered the feeling of belonging. Remembered how it felt to be loved without condition. Remembered . . . everything.

Times he felt so at home here he never wanted to leave. Times he wished he could freeze-frame so they'd never end. Times he didn't want to think about again, actually believed he'd banished from his brain.

Memories tumbled over one another like puppies playing on the sand.

Tree forts and sailing lessons, tennis matches and first kisses. Clambakes and tug-of-wars. Fourth of July parades and regattas. Parties that went on through the night, well into morning. Back then, his biggest worry was getting caught sneaking home past curfew.

Two long windows shed a soft glow onto the driveway, but the rest of the house remained dark. Dogs barked from inside and he heard Lynnie calling them as he walked up the front steps.

The heavy door opened before he could press the bell.

"Oh, it's you. Thank goodness." Cecily practically pulled him inside. The dogs rushed him, and Nick held out his hands so they could investigate. "Come on, she's on the phone." She hustled him through the house before he could get a word out.

"So it's true then? The news about Gray?" He stopped her in the hallway. Cecily nodded and drew him into a quick hug.

"We only heard today. Thank God my husband's out fishing. Gonna be gone about a week, so I can stay over. She can't be alone with this nonsense going on."

"Is she okay?" Nick gripped the back of his neck, feeling like he was about to walk into an end-of-year final he hadn't studied for.

"Of course she's not okay. David and Liz keep calling. Seems to me they should just get on over here, but that's my opinion. Oh, that boy . . ." Cecily clucked her tongue and ushered him into the living room. Lynette stood there, a cordless phone to her ear.

She nodded a silent greeting, her face pale and drawn. "It's David." Lynette pointed to the phone. "No . . . sorry, Nick just got here. Nick Cooper. Yes. Oh, somebody else is coming." The sound of tires crunching on gravel alerted the dogs and they began to bark again.

"Are you expecting anyone?" Nick went to the window and squinted through the darkness at the car idling just outside the open gates.

"Shoot, could be anyone out there." Cecily stood beside him. "We should call the police."

Lynette shook her head. "David says it could be local press. To keep the gates locked."

Too late for that. Nick shooed the dogs back. "I'll take care of it."

He stepped onto the long front porch again and shut the door behind him. The car parked halfway up the drive. Nick watched the driver jump out, camera in hand.

"*Inquirer and Mirror.* Can we get a statement from the family? Who are you? Can you tell us where Gray is? Is he coming home?"

Nick went down the steps to where the guy stood, put his hand over the lens. "Get lost, pal, or I'm calling the cops." The reporter yanked back his camera, returned to his car, and took off. Nick strode down the drive and struggled to push the heavy metal gates closed as the car peeled away into the night. They were rusted and stuck in the ground, but eventually they swung shut. If this kept up, he'd have to find a padlock. He jogged back to the house and found Lynette still on the phone.

Cecily hovered nearby, hands on hips. "Well?"

"Some reporter. I got rid of him. Where's Drake?"

"Up in his room. Whoo-wee, Nicholas, what in the world is this madness? I don't need to watch my stories with all this going on."

She was clearly enjoying the drama, disturbing as it was. Nick grinned and wagged a finger in her direction. "You shouldn't be watching that garbage anyway, Ce-ce. It'll rot your brain."

"Oh, hush, my brain does just fine." She bustled off toward the kitchen, her laughter making him feel a bit better.

The dogs ran back to him, tails wagging. Nick dropped to one knee, patted and scratched them behind the ears. After a while he rose, and they wandered off to settle around Lynnie's feet.

Nick exhaled, rocked on his heels, and waited.

"Okay. No, I won't. No, David. I don't know. I haven't talked to him. No. Okay. Thanks. Bye." She put the phone down and faced Nick. "Have you heard about Gray? Cecily says it's all over the local news." Her eyes were red-rimmed, her cheeks blotchy.

Nick nodded, his heart twisting. "I just heard it on the radio. I'm sorry, Lynnie. I would have come before now, called or—"

"We didn't know either." Defeat and desperation evicted her usual smile. "He didn't tell me, Nick. He lied to me. I thought he was still touring, not in some rehab center!" Her eyes filled and she drew in a shaky breath. "I can't believe it."

Nick didn't have a whole lot of experience with crying women. But she needed someone. So he crossed the room and held out his arms. Lynette slipped into his embrace, and the dam broke.

He let her get it out, patted her back, and struggled for something sensible to say. "Maybe it's not that bad, Lynnie. You know the press, exaggerating everything." He meant to comfort, but the words sounded hollow and insincere.

"I think it's bad." She stepped back, brushing dog hair off her multicolored T-shirt. As usual, she was barefoot. "I want to talk to him, Nick. Nobody can reach him. We don't know what to do."

Nick took her trembling hand and led her to the couch. He spied a discarded cardigan flung over a chair, grabbed it, and pulled it around her. "Do you think he'll come here?"

Lynette twisted a ring on her finger, meeting his eyes as he sat on the far end of the couch. "He told me he would try to come home soon, the last we talked. I guess if the local newspaper believes it, he's probably on his way." Lynette looked at the floor, like all the answers were written in invisible code on the old rug. "I can't believe he's been using drugs." She clenched her hands in her lap. "From what David said, he's in pretty bad shape."

Nick suspected as much, but it was still hard hearing it. "Maybe he won't come back then." He gave a hopeful smile.

Lynette arched a light brow. "If he does?"

"We'll just deal with it." They needed a plan. He wasn't sure how much publicity Gray might create, but he didn't want Lynnie coping alone. Didn't want her dealing with Gray either, but there wasn't much he could do about that.

"Gray swore he never would, you know. Come back," she whispered. "That year when the two of you had that awful fight . . ." She blinked back tears. "What happened, Nick? What did you fight about?"

Nick ran a hand down his face. No. Confiding in Cecily was one thing. But Lynette could never know. "Can't talk about it." His curt response cut through the air, surprising them both.

She went to stand by one of the long windows that faced the ocean.

Crickets chirped in casual cadence while waves crashed in unison with the methodical tick of the grandfather clock in the hall. Not that it ever told the right time. Memories flooded back again. A breeze played on the chimes strung from a beam on the back porch. The smell of old leather and musty books mingled with potpourri and pipe tobacco. If he tried hard enough, he could conjure up the lingering scent of Coppertone.

Nothing about the large, comfortable room had changed. The paint on the walls remained the same—robin's egg blue—Diana's favorite color. The old chintz-covered couches sat where they had always been, inviting company with their overstuffed cushions and chenille throws for when the nights grew cold. Antique mahogany coffee tables were covered with picture books of every description. Drake's paintings hung around the room. And the photographs . . .

Diana Carlisle had loved photography. She was forever chasing the kids around, capturing every moment of their lives on film. Gold-, silver-, and wood-framed images of all of them, him included, were everywhere—on the bookshelves and the tables and the top of the baby grand in the far corner of the room.

Nick pushed to his feet, feeling pulled to an old photograph of himself and Gray at about twelve, maybe thirteen, perched in their fitted dinghy after winning a regatta. He smiled at the pink freckled noses, sun-bleached hair, and mile-long grins.

"Lynnie, why didn't you say we had company?"

Drake's voice froze Nick in place. He tamped the urge to make a quick exit, turned on his heel, and tried to look as though he wasn't expecting to be verbally assaulted again.

Surprise shuddered through him. He hadn't really taken in Drake's appearance the night he'd last seen him, given the hour.

The man who'd once been like a father to him had aged considerably.

New lines creased his face. The thick moustache he'd taken such pride in was gone. His pajamas looked about two sizes too big and he seemed almost swallowed up in a ratty brown bathrobe. His long hair was streaked with gray and touched his shoulders. But his brown eyes held a familiar sparkle.

"Dad." Lynette cast a nervous glance at Nick. "I thought you'd gone to bed. Were you watching television?"

"Well, I . . ." The old man scratched his head and chuckled. "I don't rightly know. I may have been, but I dozed off." He faced Nick with a blank stare. "Who are you, then? Don't just stand there, boy, introduce yourself."

Lynette cleared her throat and took her father by the arm. "This is Nick, Dad. You remember."

Nick prepared to head for the door.

Drake's face split into a smile, and he let out a deep laugh. "Of course, Nicholas. Gracious, are you home from college already? Studying architecture, is it? Doing very well too, I hear. How's your mother?"

"Sir?" Nick caught Lynette's eye in question, but she glared at him so fiercely that he slapped on a smile and nodded. "She's just fine, sir, thank you."

"Good, good. Tell her I'll be calling her about my roses soon. Got that blasted black spot again. She's got all the tricks, your mother."

Nick scrambled for words, the vacant look in Drake's eyes more than worrying. "Yes. She . . . uh . . . sure loves her roses."

"Well, Gray isn't home yet, if that's why you're here. That boy can never keep a curfew. Looks like I'm going to have to ground him again." Drake gave an affable smile and turned to Lynette. "I can't find the sugar. I want tea, but you know I can't stand it unsweetened."

"Mr. Carlisle!" Cecily rushed into the room and let out a disgruntled sigh. "I thought you were up in bed."

"I want tea." Drake's exasperated expression matched Cecily's, and they engaged in a stare down Nick might have found comical any other night.

"It's all right, Dad," Lynette said, nodding toward Cecily. "You go on back up to bed and we'll bring you some tea. Okay?" Lynette smiled, but the tremor in her voice said the effort pushed her toward tears.

Drake shuffled away, Cecily following after him in a flurry. Nick and Lynette were left alone. He tried to process the last few minutes, and the weight of it sent him to a chair.

"Nick?"

"What?" He jerked up his head and found Lynette watching him.

She drew in a breath and folded her arms, recovering quicker than he did. "I'm going into the kitchen. To make the tea. Will you stay?"

Common sense told him he should go. Go before this place and all its memories sucked him in again. Go before it was too late. Go now, and never look back.

But Lynette's anxious tone and the way she pulled her arms over her chest like she was trying to shut out the world made it impossible.

"Yeah. I'll stay." He thought he caught a flash of relief in her eyes.

"Good. Take the dogs out back for me, would you? I'll put the kettle on."

Nick did as she asked, grateful for the fresh air as he paced the lawn and thought about Gray, who might well be on his way back to Nantucket.

Maybe his coming home would be a good thing. Maybe they'd be able to talk.

Put the past where it belonged and start over.

Nick kicked at a rock and shook his head.

There was little chance of that, but it didn't hurt to hope.

The sound of the ocean soothed him as the breeze blew through his hair. The moon slid out from behind the clouds and lit the old tennis court on the far side of the house. It was long abandoned, the net a tangled mess of leaves and moss. He stomped over a clump of dandelions and scanned the rest of the garden as best he could in the evening light. The straggly grounds were not as he remembered.

Nothing was as he remembered, really.

The magic he'd felt when he'd first arrived tonight had only been a lost memory trying to find its way home. There was no magic here anymore.

Only desolation.

Nick whistled for the dogs and went up the back steps, noting the peeling paint on the doorframe. He kicked a pile of rotting wood and leaves. Shingles were falling off the house. He shook his head. Lynnie's dreams of saving Wyldewood were too far-fetched for his liking.

By the looks of it, there was little left to save.

Nick found her in the kitchen, on the phone again. He straddled a stool and reached for the steaming mug she pushed his way.

"No, Liz. I'm fine," she said, sounding anything but, a frantic edge to her voice. "No. Why do you automatically assume I'm going to fall apart the minute something terrible happens?" She rounded the counter and walked toward the bay window. "I'm not a child, so stop treating me like one." Lynette lowered her voice, but he could still hear the tremor. "Do you know when? Okay. No. Yes, of course I'll call you. Next weekend is fine." Her short laugh sounded bitter. "What plans would I have?"

Her bare feet slapped the terra-cotta tiles as she paced. She fiddled with a long strand of beads around her neck. Nick couldn't stop a grin as he followed her with his eyes. Her parents' artistic nature manifested itself through her tenfold. She'd always reminded him of a throwback flower child of the seventies, even when she was younger. Never cared what she wore or what the latest fashion was. Lynette simply created her own.

Nick watched her move lithely across the room. She tossed her head, her long hair swinging just below her shoulders. What might it feel like to run his fingers through that hair? How would she fit into his embrace, if she ever allowed him to do more than simply hug her?

Nick drew in a quick breath and took a sip of tea.

Being back in this house was making him insane.

Making him think about things that were best left alone.

He studied the painting on the wall across the room. The oil on canvas was one of Drake's. *Safe Harbors.* The sleek navy sloop with the red stripe he'd helped paint himself, sailed across choppy waters, white sails billowing. He and Gray had sailed her many times.

The house must have quite a collection of artwork. Years ago, Drake's work had been popular, in high demand. If the family could be persuaded to sell them . . .

"Sorry about that." Lynette's soft voice startled him. She put the receiver back in the cradle on the yellowed Corian counter top and pulled up a stool next to him.

Nick smiled and gave himself permission to study her.

Honey-blond hair fell in waves around her oval face, and a slight smattering of freckles still played across her nose. He'd never seen her wear makeup. She didn't need it. Tonight her blue eyes mirrored that stormy ocean, wide and full of life and adventure.

"How's the tea?" Her full mouth turned upward in the beginnings of a smile. "Do you want milk? I couldn't remember how you take it."

Nick shook his head and took another sip. "No. It's good, thanks."

She nodded, stretched her arms over her head, and gave a frustrated groan. "Gray is on his way. Liz talked to him an hour ago. She doesn't think I'll be able to handle it. And she and David will be here next weekend."

"Well, that's good, I guess." He wasn't sure if it was or wasn't, and she didn't seem to know either. "I'm glad they agreed to come."

Lynette smiled in a way that caused him to suck in another breath of air. She was beautiful. Even in tears and dressed like a hippie. A sudden intense attraction almost made him bolt from the room. He couldn't deny the feelings that seemed determined to have their way.

"Well, it'll certainly be interesting." She gave a small sigh. "I don't think we've all been under the same roof since my mother died. Of course Ryan's still roaming Africa. Not sure if he'll show up, which will throw a wrench in things."

Nick noted the hopeful gleam in her eyes. "Your mother's will did say the decision to sell the house had to be unanimous. But—"

"Oh, I know." She waved a hand and rolled her eyes. "I'm prepared for the reality that we will have to sell, don't worry. But now this thing with Gray . . . Wow." She pushed her hair back, close to tears again. Her half laugh sounded more like a muted cry. "Do you ever wonder how life got so complicated?"

Nick nodded slowly, a thin smile about all he could muster. "All the time."

"Really?" Her eyes lit again, warming him in a way he hadn't thought possible. "And here I thought you were the one who had it all together."

"Nope." Nick chuckled and rubbed the strap of his watch. "Just trying to muddle through, same as everyone else."

She leveled her gaze and got serious. "What are you doing back here, Nick? You still haven't told me. I thought you were going to study architecture, like my father said."

He wasn't prepared for this conversation. "That didn't work out." Nick put down his mug and looked around the kitchen. It was exactly as it had been when he was a kid. The same butter-colored walls displaying all the kids' preschool artwork, each painting framed and labeled. Same old photographs, now yellowed with age, stuck to the refrigerator with the tacky tourist magnets Diana used to collect. Even the pencil marks on the doorway where Diana measured their heights at the end of every summer were still visible. He hopped off his stool and found his name.

"Nick, age 7."

Nick ran his fingers over the scratched letters and allowed the memories to have their way.

~

"Come on, Nick. Your turn." Diana waved him over from where she crouched in the doorway, yellow pencil in hand. Nick shook his head, inched farther back against the wall at the far end of the banquet. The others were waiting, anxious to be done and get back outside.

Nick had turned seven that summer. Just moved into the house next door. Almost at once they'd found him, laid claim to him, and made him one of their own.

Diana was the prettiest mom he'd ever met. He'd tried to call her Mrs. Carlisle, but she'd threatened to paddle him with Cecily's biggest wooden spoon if he insisted.

"Let's go, Cooper. We've got to get another sail in today if we want to win that regatta." David, the oldest, was the boss at almost fourteen. Nobody dared defy him.

Nick glanced at Gray and wondered what to do. His new friend shrugged and rolled his eyes. "It's only a measurement. Won't hurt."

"But it's just for you," he half whispered, catching Diana's twinkling eyes. "For the family."

"Well, of course it is, sweetheart." Diana smiled and held out her hand. "So what are you waiting for?"

~

Nick squeezed his eyes, got rid of the moisture in them, and returned to his stool.

"I did want to be an architect, you know." She'd pulled the confession from him with no effort at all.

"Why didn't you?" The question was full of sympathy and more than a little curiosity.

He shrugged and felt like that seven-year-old all over again. "My father convinced me a business degree was more practical."

Her expression said she understood, was sorry, and meant it. "You always do everything your dad tells you?"

"Pretty much." It was an old wound, still gaping. And he didn't care to exacerbate it further. "Do you know what's wrong with your father yet, Lynnie? Is it Alzheimer's?" He couldn't shake the look on Drake's face. He regretted the question at once, because her eyes got too bright again. Nick cursed his insensitivity and reached for her hand. "Sorry. You don't need to answer that. It's none of my business."

"Of course it's your business. You're still here, aren't you?"

Still a part of us.

She didn't say it, but he hoped that's what she meant.

Lynette slipped her hand from his too soon. "I think it has to be Alzheimer's. Last time I managed to get him to the doctor, that's what they feared was coming. He started acting weird last year. Forgetting things. Not knowing what day it was. He seems to have lost chunks of memory. Some days he's fine, other days . . . well, you've seen."

"Isn't there medicine, something that can slow down the progression?" Why had none of her siblings come? Leaving her all alone here, to deal with everything, it wasn't right.

"He throws a fit whenever I mention another checkup. I've talked to Dr. Miller and we're going to try to get him in again, once David and Liz are here. In the meantime, he prescribed some sleeping pills. I've just given him one now." She stopped talking and looked down at her hands. "I keep thinking one day he'll get up and be back to normal, you know? Liz is right, I guess. I don't handle things very well."

"They haven't exactly rushed here to help." The words were out before he could stop them.

"They all gave up on Dad a long time ago." Lynette set her tea down. "None of them really see how much he's hurting." She ran a finger over the rim of her mug, tracing the emblem of the Nantucket Yacht Club. "I was the only one left at home after Mom died. David and Liz were already in college, Gray and Ryan at boarding school. I knew it would be hard on Dad when I finally left. I didn't even want to go to college, but Liz and David forced me."

"I remember." Nick sat back and folded his arms. That was the last time he'd been over here, that Christmas after her first semester, right around her birthday. The last time he'd seen any of them.

"When I came home for the summer, his drinking was worse than ever." Lynette swallowed. "I knew he'd been taking trips over to the mainland. Cecily told me about the gambling. David arranged for him to go to a treatment center, and I . . . I stayed here with him when he came home."

"You quit college?" Nick tried to keep surprise and judgment out of his voice, but the look she tossed him told him he hadn't managed it. "I thought you had a scholarship."

"What was I supposed to do, Nick? Leave him all alone?" She balled her hands, her eyes flashing. "I think they blame him for what happened to my mom. But there's . . ." She veered her gaze.

Nick rubbed his jaw, tilted his head, and tried to make sense of her. "What is it, Lynnie? You can tell me anything, you know. You can trust me."

She let out a long groan and covered her face with her hands. "Never mind. It's not important." Her smile returned, but the shadows under her eyes stayed. "I have to wonder if this is all God's plan, you know? For everyone to come back. So we can get rid of all the junk between us and somehow find peace in all of this."

"Maybe." Nick hadn't given much thought to God over the years.

He'd gone to church with them when Diana had been on her religion kick, but when his father found out, Sundays with the Carlisles stopped. The faith he'd found there stuck, though. Once, when he was about eleven, Nick dared to question his family's attending every Christmas and Easter service and ignoring the place the rest of the year, but his parents refused to engage in the discussion. Through high school and college, he'd let that faith slide. In recent weeks, he'd found himself returning to the things he'd learned as a child. Asking God to help him make sense of things he didn't understand.

Nick scanned the coupons, scrawled out lists and postcards on the old bulletin board by the phone. "Remember that awful Sunday school teacher we had, what was her name?"

"Mrs. Bradbury." Lynette giggled, the sound a welcome reprieve. "You and Gray spent most of the time sitting in the corner, if I recall."

Nick turned her way and enjoyed the amusement that danced in her eyes. "You still go? To church, I mean."

"Yes. Well . . ." She shifted in her seat, certain sadness swallowing her smile. "I try to, when I can get someone to watch my dad. He's not always keen on going, so . . ."

"Right." He watched the dogs pace the room, then settle close to her chair. "Sometimes I wish I had more faith. I haven't made much time for God."

"It's never too late, Nick."

"You think?"

"Sure. Anyone can change, if they want to." She gave him the once-over, and he caught another glimpse of the woman she'd become. Heat raced up his neck, and he pulled at the collar of his shirt. Blindsided was an understatement. He'd been looked at by a lot of women over the years, but Lynette Carlisle's gaze turned his insides to jelly.

And suddenly talking about God didn't seem appropriate.

"Do you ever get a break, just go out, have fun with friends or . . ." Oh, what the heck. "Anyone special in the picture?"

Surprise widened her eyes. "Like a boyfriend? When would I have time?"

"Okay." His smile faded as he saw the next question coming.

"I hear you're seeing Mindy Vanguard." And there it was.

Thank you, small town gossip. Nick thrummed his fingers on the table. "Yeah, well, that's sort of complicated."

"Sort of complicated?" A bit of spark returned to her eyes. "How?"

"It's hard to explain. We go out sometimes. She and I are friends, and . . . Well, just don't believe everything you hear, okay?" Suddenly he wanted to tell her everything, but the words wouldn't come.

Maybe they should start talking about church again.

"Well, as long as you're happy, Nick. That's as much as any of us deserve, don't you think?"

Nick caught the flash of sorrow on her face. He could lay it all out on the table right then and there. Tell her the truth, and let the chips fall where they may.

Suddenly the dogs scrambled from the kitchen, barking like mad as the sound of tires on the driveway filtered through one of the open windows. Lynette swiveled on her stool, their conversation shut down.

The dogs went ballistic at the front door. Nick got to his feet. "That better not be the same guy—"

"Don't punch him." Lynette followed close behind.

Nick placed a hand on her arm. "You stay here."

He shut the door before the dogs could follow and stepped into the cool night air. A van, a cab actually, sat in the driveway, head-lights still on. He could just make out the shadows of two people in the backseat. The driver slid open the door, helped a petite woman out, then went around to the back of the van.

"Hey." She nodded his way. Nick watched as bags were tossed onto the grass, followed by three guitar cases carefully placed beside the growing pile of luggage.

"What's going on?" Lynette appeared beside him. The dogs raced past her, barking, then whining and jumping around the van. "Is it Gray?"

Cecily joined them outside and gave a low whistle. "Well, I'll be."

Realization prickled the back of his neck as the passenger door opened and a man appeared. He paid the driver and the cab drove off, then he bent over the dogs. Nick heard a familiar chuckle.

The guy's hair was long and stringy, his jaw covered in a straggly beard. Dressed in a baggy white cotton shirt and jeans that looked a couple sizes too big, his body was emaciated. He glanced their way and coughed, a deep, hacking sound that shook his thin frame and made Nick's heart lurch.

Lynette gasped, and Cecily let out a little cry. "Oh, my poor sweet boy." Tears shone on her dark cheeks.

Nick shook his head, feeling a little sick. "Poor sweet boy, my—"

"Grace, Nicholas." Cecily slipped an arm through his and pulled tight. "We don't know where he's been, and surely only the good Lord knows where he's going. But as long as he's here, for as long as he stays, it's our job to show him grace."

Nick bit back his next remark and stared at the man who was once his best friend, and the ground shifted under him.

Gray Carlisle was home.

Chapter Ten

"Gray!" Lynette flew down the porch steps toward her brother. She stopped a foot away. His gaunt cheeks and bleary eyes chased away her excitement. "Gray."

"Hey, Lynnie." He sniffed and thrust his hands into his leather jacket. "Bad time to drop in?" The barest of grins came and went, but it was enough.

She closed the gap between them and took him in her arms. Her heart pounded as she hugged his thin, trembling frame. He smelled of tobacco and spicy cologne. "Welcome home, Gray." After a moment, his stiff body relaxed and he hugged back.

"I've missed you, Shortstop," he whispered, his voice hard and gruff, not like she remembered.

"I'm so glad you're home." Lynette stepped back, trying not to stare. Or cry. Or smack him. But Gray wasn't paying attention to her anymore.

"What is he doing here?" He ground out the words like he had dirt in his mouth. Nick came down the steps and Lynette bit her tongue, tempted to tell him to get back inside. Where it was safe.

Although they'd always stood shoulder to shoulder, Nick seemed bigger than Gray, dwarfing him in bulk. Any muscle Gray once had was long gone. His hair needed a good wash and cut. Dark circles framed his eyes, his lips cracked and blistering.

Nick crossed his arms. "You look like crap."

Gray let out a ragged sigh and pushed his hair back with one hand. "Great to see you too." He gave a wheezing cough, his body shaking with the effort it took to stop it.

"Um, hi." The woman hovering around Gray spoke up, darting glances between them. "I'm sure you're happy to see each other and all, but let's take the party inside. Don't want any pictures hitting tomorrow's rag-mags, right, Gray?"

"Whatever. Nobody cares that much, Tor." The slow grin Lynette remembered slid out of hiding. "I'm not Justin Bieber, for cryin' out loud."

"And why in the world would you want to be?" The small woman stalked past him with a dramatic eye roll.

Lynette watched their sparring with veiled curiosity.

Gray cleared his throat, spat over his shoulder, then looked her way. "This is Tori. She's with me."

The younger woman sighed and shook her head. "I'm Gray's manager. And he doesn't pay me nearly enough." She walked back to Lynette and extended a hand. "Victoria Montgomery. You must be Lynette."

Lynette hoped she didn't look as overwhelmed as she felt. "Yes. Thank you for bringing him home."

"Well, he gives the orders." Victoria nodded toward the bunch of suitcases and guitars. "And we don't travel light. Sorry."

"Let's get you all inside." Cecily took over, shooing Nick toward the pile of luggage.

"Gotta barf." Gray clutched his stomach and took off toward the boxwood hedge.

"He caught a bug a few days ago. Like he needed another reason to puke." Victoria rolled her eyes again and muttered something under her breath. "So, where should we put everything?"

Nick placed a hand on Lynnette's shoulder. "You want them on the second floor?"

"Sure. The second floor." She forced her eyes away from where Gray huddled. Nick's touch and concerned expression tempted her to crumble to the ground and sob. And she didn't dare look at Cecily. She tried to switch off the sound of Gray's retching, still absorbing his appearance.

He resembled one of those zombies in the horror flicks her brothers used to watch. She hadn't known what to expect, but this . . . this was too much.

She couldn't fall apart. Not yet. There were sheets to find, beds to make. "Gray can have his room, and you . . . uh . . ."

"Oh, please. No, hon." Victoria widened her dark eyes, waved a hand. "I work for Gray, but I'm not sleeping with him. He'd have to be the last man on earth for that to happen. And probably not even then."

"Don't believe a word she says. She's madly in love with me." Gray shuffled past them, still coughing. He hoisted a duffel bag onto his shoulder and picked up a guitar. "I'm going inside. Where's Pops, Lynnie?"

Lynette wondered how to stall him as she cast about for an answer. "He's uh . . . he's in the—"

"I think he went to bed," Nick interjected. "Had a headache or something."

Gray accepted Nick's answer and made his way to the front steps, whistling for the dogs. "Looks like we're all set here. Take a hike, Cooper."

"Oh, go on now, get yourselves inside," Cecily chided, clearly not about to put up with any nonsense tonight. She clapped her hands behind them, and Gray and Victoria marched toward the house like obedient children.

Lynette almost grinned, made a half turn, and found Nick still with her. "Well, I guess he's home." She rubbed her arms as a cool breeze wove around them. "I'd better go check on my dad. I know he took that sleeping pill, but still, I hope all the commotion didn't wake him." She reached for what she hoped was a light carry-on and yanked. Not light.

"Leave that. I'll bring in the rest." Nick took the bag and gave her a sidelong glance. "You okay?"

Lynette bit her bottom lip and shook her head. "I'm not sure I know what okay means anymore, Nick."

He paused, moved toward her, then backed up. His eyes flashed, his face shadowed in the glow of the large carriage lamps that lit the front porch. "If you want me to go, just say. I don't want to cause trouble."

"You won't." She pulled her hair into a ponytail, secured it with an elastic band. "Did you see him? He couldn't argue with a slug."

Nick shifted the last guitar case to his other hand. "He doesn't look good."

"I didn't expect it."

"He probably looked worse a few weeks ago."

"I guess they'll need food." Lynette glanced upward, but the stars were few and far between. "Do you know what time it is?"

"About eight thirty. They must have caught the last ferry. Let me take this in."

Lynette hesitated, lost in the way Nick's eyes seemed to dance in the darkness. "Unless you have somewhere to be."

"Nowhere to be. And I'd rather be here."

And the way he looked at her, it was like . . . like he meant it. She couldn't deny there was comfort in that thought.

Yet years of silence still stood sentry between them.

He had lines beneath his eyes that hadn't been there all those years ago, a sense of melancholy that seemed to follow him around like a silent shadow.

"Are *you* okay, Nick?"

He smiled and lifted his shoulders. "I'm not sure I know what okay means anymore, Lynnie."

～

Victoria entered the kitchen where Lynette and Nick were preparing a quick dinner, scanned the room, and scowled. "Welcome to the seventies."

"Sorry?"

"This kitchen." Victoria swept the air with one arm. "No Viking? Sub-Zero? This looks like the set of *The Brady Bunch*. I can't cook in here."

Lynette raised an eyebrow, thankful Cecily was upstairs getting the rooms ready. She didn't need any more drama tonight. "Nobody's asking you to."

"But I do all of Gray's cooking. He's on a strict diet."

Nick glanced over his shoulder from his position at the counter. "Of what? Jack Daniels and a little blow?"

Victoria's five-foot-nothing frame got a bit taller, her face taking on a pit-bull scowl. "I resent that, mister. Gray hasn't touched anything in weeks. As you can probably tell, he's in bad shape. I'm trying to get him back on track. So back off."

"Maybe he should have stayed in rehab." Nick brought down the knife and split a red pepper in half.

"Yeah, well, he didn't. But maybe you should mind— Who are you anyway?"

"This is Nick. He's a family friend." Lynette sighed and indicated the fridge. "I think there might be fixings for a salad. I . . . wasn't expecting company. We can go to the store tomorrow." As long as Gray was paying.

She and Nick worked mostly in silence and managed to scrape together what would pass for dinner. The pasta boiled while Nick sliced the last of the peppers for the marinara sauce. Tantalizing aromas soon wafted around the room. Lynette found a fairly fresh loaf of bread and searched the cluttered drawers for another chopping board.

"Is there garlic in there?" Victoria peered into the pot of bubbling sauce. "He's allergic."

"Since when?" One side of Lynette's mouth lifted. "He may not like it, but he's not allergic."

"Oh, fine." Victoria turned to face her, a frown creasing her pale forehead. Her dark hair was cut short and kind of spiky, probably some celebrity style. Her small ears were covered with silver in places Lynette didn't know could be pierced. And she wore a lot of makeup.

"Did he tell you he's allergic to carrots too?" Nick asked. "He actually is. They make him swell up like the Hindenburg. It's kind of funny, really. We used to make him do it when his parents had company— Ow!" He dropped the knife and popped his finger in his mouth.

Lynette grabbed a paper towel and crossed the room. "Let me see." It was just a graze, barely bleeding. "Don't be a baby, you're fine. Keep chopping."

"I hate blood," he grumbled, sticking out his lower lip. "Got a Band-Aid?"

"Nick." She sighed and pointed to the cupboard above the sink. "They're where they've always been." She pushed up the sleeves of her sweater and stepped back. Victoria was scrubbing down the counter. "It's not dirty. You don't need to do that."

Gray's girlfriend, assistant, or whatever she was, stopped, cloth poised in midair, her face barely masking disgust. "But . . . there are . . . marks, see?"

"Those marks have been there since I was five. But hey, scrub away." Lynette sucked in her breath and prayed for patience. The woman had been in the house for less than two hours, had bleached the toilets upstairs, swept out Gray's room, and put the sheets back in the dryer because they felt damp. Cecily was not impressed.

"Whoa!"

She turned in time to see Nick scramble to catch the cupboard door as it fell out of place. A giggle stuck in her throat. "The hinges rusted out. I forgot to tell you."

"Thanks. Just about knocked myself out."

"Omigosh!" Victoria screamed and jumped back three feet. "Okay, there are bugs!" Her scream brought the dogs running and she jumped back another foot. Clearly animals were not on her list of favorite things either.

Lynette squinted, stared in the direction she pointed. "It's an ant. Just one."

Nick came up behind her and gave a low chuckle, his breath tickling her neck. "Well, you can't be too careful, Lynnie. You know those killer ants we have here in Nantucket."

"Dude. Seriously?" Victoria's eyes widened as she played with a thick silver chain around her neck, a chunky ornate-looking cross hanging from it. Lynette wondered if it meant anything or whether the pixie used it as a weapon in dark alleys.

"Do you want some bug spray?"

"Uh, no. You know what kind of toxins they put in that stuff?"

"Okay then." Lynette sent Nick a despairing look and went to check the pasta. Victoria was definitely going to be a challenge. And Liz was coming next week.

"Spaghetti? Haven't had that in years." Gray's rumbling tenor took charge of the kitchen before he did. Lynette reached for a dishcloth. She might need to stuff it in Nick's mouth.

The dogs brushed against Gray's legs and he bent over them. He looked a little better. His damp hair was combed back off his face, and a shave revealed the gaunt cheeks that had been hiding beneath the scruff.

Dressed in faded jeans and an old Harvard rugby jersey, he hardly resembled the popular singer she'd kept track of over the years. If she turned back the clock, this could have been any old weekend with the boys home from college.

But it wasn't. Gray's soulless eyes reminded her of that.

Her brother glanced her way and she managed a smile. "You look good, Gray."

Gray snorted. "You always were the worst liar. I showered. I think you might need to get the pipes looked at. Sounds like a choir of dying cats. And the water was a bit cold."

"I'm sorry." She offered him a raw carrot. "You hungry?"

"Funny." A grin came and went as he wagged a finger at her. "I puke everything right back up again anyway. 'Course, if you insist on letting Cooper hang out here, I might just puke for the fun of it. Still got that wicked gag reflex, Coop?"

Nick swiveled, knife in hand, his eyes glinting in a way that made Lynette step between them.

"Done with the peppers, Nick?" She pried the potential weapon from his hand, put it down, and lifted the chopping board. Tried to hum a tune and act calm as she scraped the green and red wedges into the sauce.

"Why are you here anyway, Cooper?"

"Um . . . want to come upstairs and help me sort out your stuff, Gray?" Victoria pushed aside the large bowl of salad she was working on.

Finally, common ground.

Lynette smiled her thanks when Gray wasn't looking. "Good idea. If you need any more hangers, just yell."

"I'm not going upstairs. I want to know what he's doing here." Gray's voice rose as he shuffled toward Nick.

"Your sister invited me." Nick cleared his throat and crossed his arms, but stayed where he was.

Lynette prayed for a sudden hurricane, earthquake . . . anything.

"Well, I'm uninviting you," Gray growled. "Get out."

"Make me."

"Stop!" She turned to her brother. "You haven't been home in years, Gray Carlisle. You don't have the right to give orders around here. And you, Nicholas, are just egging him on. Don't think for one minute I've forgotten the games the two of you played. Stop acting like children. Whatever went on between you, get over it. Or you can both get out."

"Hallelujah!" Victoria clapped her hands and gave Lynette a wide smile. "I think I'm going to like you."

"I'm not going anywhere," Gray barked. "It's my house. Make him leave." Another coughing fit paralyzed him and Lynette breathed a guilty sigh of relief.

"I'll go. It's fine." Nick wiped his hands on his jeans and looked her way.

"No, Nick, really—"

"Let him go," Gray growled between coughs. "At least that way I might be able to eat."

Lynette reached past Nick for a glass and filled it at the tap. She handed it to Gray but he started coughing again, lost his grip, and it fell to the floor, splintering into a million pieces.

They all stared at the mess and she wondered who would move first.

"What's all the noise?"

Lynette pulled up short at the sound of her father's voice, glanced at Gray and the broken glass all around them.

Okay, God, so not fair.

She'd prayed for a hurricane, not the Apocalypse.

Chapter Eleven

G ray stopped coughing and stared at his father.

Had he really been gone that long? Pops looked a hundred years old. He straightened, met his eyes, and battled a weird combination of anger and sorrow.

"Well, you finally decided to show up!" Pops bellowed, hands on his hips. His thick brows almost touched as his eyes narrowed. "Do you have any idea what time it is, Grayson John? Your mother's been worried sick. Where've you been? You look like something the dogs dragged in."

Gray leaned against the counter and gripped the edge so he wouldn't fall over. He tried to shift his weight, but his bare feet stuck to the kitchen floor. His throat tightened as his gaze slid to where Lynette stood.

Glass was everywhere.

Neither of them could move even if they wanted to.

Finally Nick went for a broom and began sweeping. Tori crouched beside him with the dustpan and a wad of paper towels.

"Stay over there, Dad," Lynette half whispered. "I dropped a glass. You forgot to put your slippers on." Her wide eyes brimmed with unshed tears. "Gray isn't that late. You . . . you've just lost track of time."

Gray clamped his mouth shut, clamped emotions, and clamped down the urge to demand answers. He took shallow breaths and studied his sister, still looking after Pops all these years, and his guilty heart surrendered to feelings he hadn't tapped into for a while. She looked like a waif off the street, long hair all over the place, wearing clothes she'd probably owned in high school.

He forced his gaze back to his father. His stomach rolled in protest as memories, medication, and misinformation melded together, pressed hard against his gut. "Didn't realize you were waiting up for me, Pops. Sorry."

"Sorry? That's all you have to say? Hope you filled up the car." Pops rubbed his jaw and Gray peered a little closer, taking in the vacant look in his eyes.

This was worse than coming off a bad trip.

Gray backed up when Nick got too close with the broom, its soft bristles tickling his toes. "Yo, dude. Take it easy there."

"Sorry." Nick glanced up and stopped sweeping. "If you take two steps that way, I can get those pieces behind you."

Gray sidestepped the shards. If it'd been him, he might have let Nick step on them.

Lynette rounded the counter and put her arm through their father's. "Dinner's almost ready. Since you're awake, would you like to join us?"

"Why are we eating at this ungodly hour?" Pops shook his head and smirked. "You kids and your wild parties. Well, I suppose I could have a bite. Gray, go get your brothers. It's time to eat."

"Mr. Carlisle!" Cecily ran into the room, out of breath. She put her hands on her hips and glared at Pops, then shot Lynette a harried look. "Lawdy, girl, I can't keep track of him. Man needs a cowbell or something. There he goes again!" She hurried after Pops as he headed to the dining room.

Gray scratched his head. He tried to dislodge the rock in his throat and managed to get Lynette's attention. "Lynnie, what the—"

"Stop." She looked back over her shoulder and shook her head. "Not now."

"I need a drink," Gray muttered as he watched her take their father into the dining room.

"I'll get you some water." Tori's glare shot through him.

"That's what I meant." She never did appreciate his humor.

Tori found another glass, miraculously produced a bottle of Evian from somewhere, plopped in two ice cubes, and handed it to him. Gray downed the cool liquid too fast. Bright spots flashed in his eyes and he bent over his knees.

Nick grabbed his elbow and jerked him up before he hit the floor.

"Gray!" Lynnie was back, bending to look at him. She took the empty glass from his trembling hand before he could drop another one. "Are you okay?"

"Peachy." Gray straightened and wriggled out of Nick's grasp. "What's wrong with him, Lynnie? He's not still drinking?"

"No! He hasn't had a drink in years, Gray, I promise you." She kept her voice low, her eyes frantic, willing him to believe her.

"Then what is it? And why didn't you tell me? And if you say you don't know, I swear I'll—"

"Stop shouting at me!" She whirled and stood with her back to him.

"Who's shouting? You want shouting?"

Cooper made a noise like he was choking on something and marched past them with a large bowl of pasta. His piercing gaze jacked up Gray's blood pressure again.

His stomach was doing a number on him. He should have taken Tori's advice. Because all this? A longer stint in rehab would have been a much better idea.

"Gray, chill." Tori scowled at him.

Lynette picked up a handful of cutlery and headed for the dining room.

Gray stared at her retreating figure. "Did she just leave? I asked her a question and she ignored me?"

Nick stalked past him again and poured thick red sauce into a white serving dish. He turned to Gray, bowl in hand. "Mind taking this out to the table while I get the bread?"

"Yes, I mind," Gray spluttered. "I want somebody to give me some answers!"

"Give it to me." Tori took the bowl from Nick and looked at Gray. "Go sit down and zip it. Please."

Gray couldn't make his head stop spinning. He blinked a couple times, took some deep breaths, and filled his glass with more water.

Tori was ordering him around, his baby sister was giving him the cold shoulder, his dad was going mental, and Cooper was treating him like the help.

This is what he got for deciding to get sober.

~

Gray hunched over the toilet and waited. Maybe he was really done this time. He'd tried to be quiet, but that was pretty much impossible when his entire body was being ripped apart from the inside out.

The bathroom door creaked open and somebody crouched behind him. Gray couldn't move to see who, could barely lift his head.

A cold cloth was placed on his forehead. "Your mother always said a little ginger ale and an ice pack could fix anything."

Gray blanched at the sound of his father's voice and pushed back on his heels before hitting the cold tile with his butt. "Thanks." He took the plastic tumbler and sipped. Fizz shot up his nose and made him cough. Pops reached for the cup and placed it on the counter.

He extended a hand, his face masked with worry as he looked down at Gray. "You want to go back to bed?"

Gray grabbed hold and let his father haul him to his feet. The old man wasn't so frail after all. "Sorry I woke you, Pops." He picked up the soda and shuffled back toward his bedroom.

"I was awake anyway." His father followed him into the room. "I don't sleep much these days."

Gray got back into bed and pulled up the blankets. The house was freezing. Damp, musty, and filled with the salty smell that infiltrated his dreams—hadn't left him even when he'd left the place.

"What time is it?" His throat felt clogged with cotton but he knew if he tried to clear it, he'd be running for the bathroom again.

"Must be around five. Sun should be up soon." Pops stood by the window, peering through the gap in the plaid curtains.

Gray smothered a yawn and closed his eyes.

"The first few months are the hardest." Pops thumped down on the edge of his bed.

Gray's eyes flew open. "What?"

"When you're trying to quit."

His father's expression was kind, soft even. Maybe he really had gone nuts.

Maybe they both had.

Because from what he'd witnessed last night, Gray had no clue how they were even having this conversation. But he'd take it.

"That's what I hear." Gray heaved a sigh and ignored the rattle in his chest. "Lynnie says you're on the wagon."

Pops played with the sash of his robe. "Been a few years now. I stopped counting the exact days. Actually . . . I have a little trouble keeping track of time lately." Slow laughter rumbled out of him.

"Oh." No kidding. "That's great, Pops. I mean, that you quit. Way to go." Gray rubbed his eyes and wondered if the rest of them knew about this and why he didn't. Then again, maybe if he'd bothered to call once in a while.

Pops crossed a pajama-clad leg over his knee and looked Gray straight in the eye, the way he used to when a lecture was coming on. Gray felt sixteen again.

"My mind plays tricks on me sometimes, son, but not all the time. I have eyes and ears. Know what I'm saying?"

Shame smacked his cheeks, and Gray studied the trophies on the shelf across the room. Posters of baseball players and rock bands still stuck to the walls. Faded Red Sox and Patriots pennants wedged between the Rolling Stones, U2, and the Stop sign he and Nick had stolen in tenth grade.

Everything in his bedroom was exactly the way he'd left it that last summer, the year he'd turned twenty, told them he was quitting college and heading to California.

"I screwed up, Pops."

His dad moved up the bed and placed his hand on Gray's arm. "I know."

Gray pressed his teeth into his bottom lip and met his father's eyes once more.

"We all make mistakes, Gray. I've made my fair share. But I don't need to tell you that. Your mother and I were always proud of you, no matter what."

"I don't think Mom would be too proud of me right now." Gray dragged a hand across his face and sniffed.

"She was a very forgiving person. I wish I had been."

Gray pushed up and took a sip of the cold drink. Glanced at the digital clock and reached for his pills. He saw his father's face and scowled. "Antibiotics. I had pneumonia."

Pops squinted at the label and put the bottle back on the bed-side table. "I'm glad you decided to come home."

Gray hadn't been sure. That year before he left, they'd had some wicked arguments. Gray squished his head against the soft feather pillows and tried to read his father. The room got a little lighter. Birds began to chirp outside, their morning song mingling with the ocean's serenade. "For real?"

Pops nodded, his face cracking with a rare smile. "Don't tell Lynnie. She thinks I'm still mad at you for totaling the car on your sixteenth birthday."

"So you're not?" That little joyride across Sankaty Head Golf Course in the middle of the night hadn't been such a great idea. His laugh brought on more coughing, his lungs practically evicting themselves from his body. If the sun came out today, he'd spend all day just sitting in it.

"I've decided to let it go." Pops rose and pulled the covers tight around Gray's shoulders, like he used to every night. Before.

"Sweet."

His father scratched his nose, tipped his head. "What's that supposed to mean?"

More laughter tickled Gray's sore throat. "It means cool. Good. Sweet."

"Oh. Okay then. Sweet."

Gray returned his wink and marveled at what was going on inside of him. An emotion he barely recognized worked its way upward. Pushed through all the muck and mire and the clouded judgment and lit the tiniest of sparks.

Hope.

Pops reached over and tousled his hair. "Go back to sleep. I'll tell Lynnie not to wake you."

Gray drew in a deep breath as his father shut the door. Despite everything, Gray knew he was exactly where he was meant to be. It wouldn't be easy, but there were things here he needed to take care of.

He pushed his forefingers into the corners of his eyes and cursed at the wetness. No matter. He'd survive this. Somehow.

He wasn't sure of much at the moment, but he did know one thing.

It was good to be home.

Chapter Twelve

Lynette backed off and studied the piece she'd created just before dawn.

The scene still didn't make any sense.

The painting took her mind places she didn't want to go. Pushed questions toward her she could neither comprehend nor contemplate.

She reached for the bedsheet with a trembling hand and covered it up.

Trying to remember the past through her paintings wasn't doing any good. It was only giving her more nightmares, more to worry about.

She left the art studio and took the dogs for a walk. As she trudged along the beach, she thanked God the week was over. It had been a long one, dealing with Gray and Victoria, playing referee when Cecily was around. Gray's friend was hardly amenable, and Cecily had already voiced strong opinions about her being here.

Lynette picked her way around patches of brown seaweed, discarded rope, and the odd dead fish. The dogs raced ahead, chasing sea gulls and each other, stopping now and again when they picked up a scent. Off in the distance a long white coast guard ship made its way around the island. Their beach was private, tourist free, providing the peace she needed.

Peace that never lasted long.

She hoped the sea air would rid her mind of last night's dream.

It was like all the others, but more intense. And vivid. Her mother was trying to tell her something, but as usual, Lynette woke before she heard the words.

A shell poked out of the sand, and she wandered over to retrieve it. The top was green and slimy and covered in moss, but when she flipped it over, a kaleidoscope of pearly pink, blue, and gray shimmered in the sunshine and spoke of hope. But that feeling never lasted. Even now, dark clouds gathered along the horizon, threatening to put the sun back to bed.

"Good morning, Lynette."

Lynette pocketed the shell and looked up. Anthony Cooper strode down the beach toward her. She stiffened, but waved a hand in greeting. "Hi, Mr. Cooper."

The dogs circled her legs and began to growl. "Stop that." She pushed them off, but they wouldn't budge. They stopped growling at least and sat at her feet.

"Doesn't look like we're going to see much of that sun today." He took off his sunglasses, tipped his head toward the mass of dark clouds.

"I guess not." A rainy day might afford more time for another painting. One she could actually sell this time. Lynette shrugged. "At least it's Saturday. Don't have to worry about going anywhere." In summer she rarely left the house unless she had to.

"True." His blue eyes were so like Nick's, but without the warmth. His smile seemed plastered on, no life behind it. And he looked thin, almost gaunt. "I thought I heard some noise last weekend over at your place. Cars coming and going, dogs barking? I hope there wasn't trouble."

Nerves pelted the pit of her stomach but she managed to meet his inquiring gaze. "No trouble. Gray's home. We had some local press poking around." Sudden fear seized her. "If they come to you . . ."

He gave a small smile. "Gray who?"

Lynette smiled back, but his expression made her uneasy.

Anthony fiddled with his watch, one corner of his mouth lifting. "I hear you're putting the house on the market. I think it's a sound decision, Lynette, under the circumstances."

She watched the wind whip up the waves, white surf churning. Her stomach was starting to do the same. "Circumstances?"

"Financial of course. And then there's your father . . ."

His air of nonchalance rankled her. "My father will—" What? Be fine?

He drew thick brows together and stroked his chin. "I'm sorry. It must be difficult. Alzheimer's, is it?"

Defeat gained a little more ground. "We haven't made a decision about the house yet. My brother and sister arrive today." Part of her wasn't ready to face Liz or David and all their questions.

Wasn't ready to accept the truth.

"I realize this must be overwhelming for you, dear, but I really think selling is—"

"I already talked to Nick. I know." She almost wanted to apologize for her sharp reply. "My family and I will figure it out."

"You know . . ." He turned to look at the ocean. "I happen to know some very influential people, investors. They've been looking at property in the area. If you want to—"

"Nick told me that too." Lynette tried to keep her voice steady.

He glanced her way, stone-faced. "Don't take too much time. Tell David to come to see me, won't you? We can discuss things. I'd love to help."

The lack of sincerity in his eyes scared her a little. The darkening sky threw down the first few drops of rain. "Thanks, Mr. Cooper." She wasn't sure he deserved her thanks, but didn't know what else to say.

"Best find shelter before it gets any worse." He gave her arm a squeeze, turned, and strode off toward his house. Lynette had to grab both dogs to prevent them from chasing after him. Her heart thudded as she caught sight of Nick charging down the steps that led up to the Cooperage.

Their raised voices were captured by the wind and tossed into the stormy sea. Lynette turned and headed home. She didn't want to know what they argued over. She had enough trouble of her own.

"Lynette, wait!" Nick's voice caught up with her just before he did. The dogs changed direction and greeted him with excited barks, tails wagging. Lynette pressed on against the wind, blowing sand and rain.

Nick jogged beside her and grabbed her arm. "Hey, wait up."

"Leave me alone, Nick." She shook him off and kept walking, wet sand infiltrating the tops of her worn sneakers. He moved around her, and she had no choice but to come to a standstill as he put his hands around her wrists.

"What did he say to you?" The concern on his face and the intensity of his gaze rendered her motionless. But anger won out and she struggled free from his grip.

"Nothing you haven't already. Oh, and thanks for spreading the news. Who else have you told?"

Nick's eyes narrowed, tinged with confusion. "Told what?"

"That my father has Alzheimer's. He's forgetting his life, but he doesn't need everyone knowing it." She pushed past him and stalked toward the set of rickety wooden stairs that led up to their house.

"Lynette!" Nick blocked her path again. "I never said anything to my dad about your father. Maybe he heard it somewhere else, but it wasn't from me."

Lynette clutched her elbows and shivered. Thunder rumbled in the distance and lightning slashed through the sky. Fear pushed her toward the house. "I'm going inside."

Nick put his hands on her shoulders. "Not until you say you believe me."

"What does it matter?" Salt stung her eyes and cheeks as the wind slapped her hair around her face.

"It matters to me."

His eyes pierced her and she couldn't look away.

"I'm on your side. I need you to believe that."

"Nick . . ." She gave up the fight and let the tears come. "I don't know if I can do this. I don't think I can cope anymore." The words choked her, bringing with them inexplicable sorrow and grief she'd never acknowledged.

Not out loud.

"Oh, Lynnie." Nick moved closer and slid his hands around her face. The warmth of his touch penetrated her cold skin; she shivered. "What can I do?"

"I don't know," she whispered. The thing she feared most stepped out of the shadows, looming bigger and darker than the clouds above them, daring her to pay it homage.

"You're shaking." Nick rubbed her arms and pulled her closer.

"I don't like storms." It was impossible to explain such an irrational fear so she didn't bother. Lynette met Nick's eyes and knew she had to trust him. There was no one else. "If I tell you something . . . will you just . . . don't think I'm crazy."

"I don't think you're crazy." He looked like he meant it, but he'd be taking back those words.

"I . . . have these dreams. Well, just one. It's always the same. About my mother. She's trying to tell me something. I think . . . about the day she died . . . because I can't remember."

"What do you mean?" He stared at her as though trying to unlock all her secrets.

"I mean . . . I can't remember what happened that day. I wish I could."

"You don't remember?" He gently brushed her wet hair off her face. "Anything?"

"Only bits and pieces, but they're so hazy it doesn't feel like they're really memories at all."

He squeezed her hands, the corners of his mouth taking a

downward detour. "You were just a kid. They said her death was an accident, right?"

"What if it wasn't? What if there's more to it?"

His eyes widened and clouded over. "Like what?"

Silence stretched between them, broken by another rumble of thunder that made her pulse skip several beats.

"I don't know." Tears stung as last night's vision played out in her mind. And the sound of her mother's scream still rang in her ears. "I'm scared, Nick."

He folded her against him and held tight, like he could squeeze out all the pain. Like he could get rid of all the mysteries from the past, waiting to strike.

"It's okay, Lynnie." Nick's words hummed in her ear. "You're not alone. I'm here. I want to help you."

She pulled back and shook her head. "Why?"

Nick's smile hinted at things she didn't dare hope were real. "Because I always have."

"Yes. You have." Lynette felt a sweet sensation pool in the pit of her stomach.

She'd been in this place before, wrapped in his arms, wishing for the impossible. It had happened once, on that night so many years ago.

It wasn't likely to happen twice.

Something in his eyes—confusion, temptation, she didn't know what—stalled the moment. A sigh slipped from his lips. He ran the back of his hand down her cheek, cupped her chin, and brought his face inches from hers. And as insane as it was, Lynette swore he was about to kiss her.

Nick hesitated, as though he hadn't quite made up his mind. What was even more insane was that she wanted him to. Maybe even more than she had the first time it happened.

"Oh, please." Her sister's voice sliced the air and pushed them apart.

Nick stepped back, looking a little stunned.

There was nothing she could do, no way to stop time and turn back the clock to see how the moment might have played out.

She moved away from Nick and looked upward.

Gray stood at the top of the steps, Liz and David behind him.

"You're early!" Lynette waved, tried to smile.

"We wanted to get here before the storm," David called down, yanking the zip of his yellow Helly Hanson slicker. "They're stopping the ferries for a bit. Come on up here!"

"I'm coming!" Rain fell harder, accompanied by another round of thunder.

Nick put a hand on her shoulder. "I'll call you later. I should go."

"Get your hands off my sister, Cooper." Gray moved toward them, but David grabbed his arm.

"Grayson, not now." He spoke in the same tone she'd heard Dad use a million times.

Gray shook free of David's grasp, his mouth twisted in a sneer. "What? Don't you want to protect your little sister from the likes of him? He'll use her and toss her out like yesterday's newspaper. Trust me, I—"

"All right, that's it." Nick let out a muted curse and took the stairs two at a time.

"Nick, don't." Lynette tried to stop him but he was too fast.

"Oh, here we go. Now we're cooking with gas." Gray shuffled down two more steps, looking anything but menacing huddled under the old Patriots blanket that had covered his bed for decades. "Coming after me, Coop? Come on then."

Another round of thunder boomed, closer this time, and the dogs ran for the house. Lynette wished she could go with them.

David sidestepped Gray and put out a hand. "Nick, stay where you are." He looked back over his shoulder at Gray. "Knock it off. What's wrong with you?"

"He's asking for it, he—" The rest of whatever Gray said got drowned out by another shriek from Liz.

"Save it, you idiots. I'm getting soaked! Lynette, get your butt up here!"

Lynette pulled her hood over her head and ran past Nick. "Why are you all outside anyway?"

"Looking for you!" Liz shivered and pulled her jacket around her shoulders. "Dad's gone mental and locked us out of the house!"

"He what?" Lynette shouted above the storm as they all ran toward the back patio, racing around rocks and the squishy patches that formed on the lawn whenever it rained. They huddled together as she tried the sliding glass door outside the kitchen. Sure enough, it was locked. All the doors were. "Where is he? What happened?"

David sighed and shook his head, sending water everywhere. "We let ourselves in. He was in the living room. I guess we scared him. He shot out of his chair and started threatening us. He . . . uh . . ." His dark eyes grew misty and his voice got thick. "He didn't know who we were, Lynnie."

"So why are *you* out here?" Lynette focused on Gray, who was still watching Nick, eyes filled with venom. A snake about to strike. Victoria had borrowed her car earlier to go into town; she had thought Gray was with her.

"I was having a smoke. I heard the ruckus, went around front, and there they were. Pops wouldn't listen to me either. You . . . don't think he saved any ammunition for those old guns he has, do you?"

"Oh wonderful." Liz shook her head and tapped a pointy-toed boot. "Lynette, don't just stand there gaping, do something!"

"Stop yelling at me, Liz." Typical. Home less than ten minutes and Lynette was already annoyed with her. "I'll go around and see if he's still in the front room." And bash the door down if she had to.

"Do you want me to call someone?" Nick asked, mussing his wet hair.

"Oh, could you?" Gray widened his eyes. "Get the cops out here and fire up the press for an exclusive, okay? Seriously, Cooper, that's a great idea."

"Just trying to help." Nick's fight seemed to have left him.

"Okay. Why don't we all just take it down a notch?" David took charge, like always. "Guess we should at least say hello first." He lifted an eyebrow and opened his arms. "How are you, Shortstop?"

"Hi, Davy." Lynette moved into her eldest brother's embrace, gave him a hug, and stepped back. He was thinner than she remembered, his almost black hair sporting some gray at the temples. But his smile said everything would be okay. Somehow.

"Don't you have a spare key under the urns by the front door, Lynnie?" Gray asked. "That's where Mom used to . . ." His voice trailed off and he looked away.

"I forgot about that." Liz clapped her hands like she was commanding the dogs. "Now, can we get on with unlocking the door before we get blown away?"

Lynette couldn't move, paralyzed by another clap of thunder. "I don't know if it's there anymore."

"Helpful, Lynnie." Liz pursed her lips and finally threw up her hands. "Okay, why don't we go find out?"

"I can look," Nick offered.

"A brilliant idea, Nicholas." Liz gave a conciliatory smile and flicked water off her black leather jacket.

Lynette caught Nick's sympathetic glance and sucked in a breath. "It's all right, Nick. We can manage. You should probably go." Not that she wanted him to, but with the way Gray was acting, having him here wasn't helping.

"That's the first intelligent thing I've heard you say since I got home." Gray lit a cigarette and blew smoke high into the air.

Nick rolled his eyes, but kept his gaze on her. "Call me when you get inside."

"She'll be fine," Gray growled. "She doesn't need to call you."

"Shut up, Gray." Lynette glared at her brother. He'd tested her patience to the max. "Thanks, Nick."

"Okay, well, I'll see you guys."

Nobody acknowledged his departure. And apparently nobody really wanted to go see if there was a key out front or not. Liz was too busy checking her smartphone, Gray was trying to jimmy the lock on the screen door with a hairpin Liz produced, and David stood with his back to them, staring out at the waves. Lynette watched Nick jog across the back lawn and disappear down the steps, and a little of her hope went with him.

"Not working." Gray tossed the pin to the ground a minute later and took another cigarette out from the pack in his shirt pocket.

"Gray, you just finished one." Lynette had asked him a hundred times already not to smoke around her. The last thing she needed was her asthma kicking in.

Liz hurled a few choice words their way and flung her purse onto the patio table. "Since nobody seems to care whether we all catch pneumonia, I will risk life and limb to see if I can find the key." As her sister tromped down the steps, Lynette caught sight of Dad in the kitchen. She went to the door and rapped on the glass.

"Dad! Let us in, it's Lynnie!"

He turned toward her, eyebrows raised. In another moment he slid the door open and peered out at them. "Good heavens, you're a bunch of drowned rats! What are you doing outside in this weather?"

"Getting a sunburn," Gray muttered, pushing past them to get inside.

"David, come on." Lynette waited for her brother to move, but he didn't. Just stood, staring out at the churning waves.

"David?" Dad cleared his throat. "Is that you?" He blinked a couple of times, definite recognition in his eyes as he raised a trembling hand to his mouth.

David slowly turned and settled his gaze on their father. "Hi, Dad." He walked toward him, stopped, gave a smile that didn't hold much warmth, then hurried into the kitchen.

Dad's face registered surprise and confusion, but he said nothing. Lynette was almost grateful when she heard the sound of banging on the front door and Liz screeching for someone to let her in.

Guess there hadn't been a key out there after all.

Chapter Thirteen

Nick pulled his wet sweatshirt over his head and dropped it in the laundry room on his way through the house. Lynette texted to say they were inside, and he breathed a little easier. The storm now raged, rain beating against the windows.

He'd come so close to actually kissing her—if the others hadn't shown up, he totally would have. He'd been dreaming about it for days. Still, part of him said he was asking for trouble. That he'd only be further complicating his life. Another part of him said Lynette Carlisle might be the best thing that ever happened to him.

Nick toweled off and grabbed a fresh T-shirt before going in search of his father. He found him in his study, standing in front of the window nursing a drink.

"Not quite noon yet, Dad. Something bothering you?"

"Yes. You. You are bothering me." His father swiveled on his heel and settled a cool gaze on Nick. "I thought you were going to talk her into selling, Nicholas."

Nick fended off the blazing arrows that shot from his father's eyes. "I told you, she doesn't want to. But I'm sure with the others here now, she won't have a choice."

"I want that house, Nicholas. As soon as possible."

Nick felt rooted to the rug beneath his feet. "You want to buy Wyldewood? Since when?"

"Nicholas." Silence said the rest.

"Drake will never agree to that." It was the first thought that came into his head, but his father's snide expression forced him to acknowledge the absurdity of it.

"Drake doesn't have a say anymore. And from what I hear, he's not always on the same planet as the rest of us." Dad drained the dark liquid from his glass and strode across the room to the cedar bar. Ice clinked against fine Baccarat.

"I thought you weren't supposed to be drinking." Correcting his father was never smart, but Nick seemed to be sailing on the wrong side of stupid these days.

Dad walked back to his desk and sat, holding up his glass in silent salute. "Do you think I care what a few doctors say?"

"Obviously not." Dark shadows lay under his father's eyes. Once again, Nick reminded himself why he'd come home. "But don't you think that you should—"

"What I think, Nicholas, is that you should mind your own business. I've told you, we don't need to talk about it."

"Dad—"

"When do you anticipate them putting the house on the market?" His father's glare muted Nick's concern.

"I don't know." Nick forced his thoughts back to the future of Wyldewood. "What's the latest with that hotel chain—Loxton?" He took a seat, his mind blurring. "Why bring that up if you want to buy the house for yourself?"

"Who do you think happens to be a major shareholder in Loxton, Nicholas?"

Ah, truth. "Let me guess. Oh, you. And your best friend, Senator Vanguard, no doubt." Of course Mindy's father would be involved. Dad often depended on Maurice's deep pockets for business deals.

"I stand to make a fortune if this deal goes through."

"You already have a fortune."

"Don't be smart." His father's thin smirk chilled him.

Nick began to feel a little ill.

"A small boutique hotel on this side of the island would be lucrative." Dad swirled ice cubes around the bottom of the glass. "Can't you see it?"

Nick wound his thumbs together, his throat dry. "This is about Drake, isn't it? About you finally getting something from him."

Veiled amusement played over Dad's face. "They'll get their money. And I'll get the house." His chuckle bounced off the walls and made Nick shiver.

Nick sat forward. "Don't you think you've done enough?"

"Excuse me?"

"Never mind." He searched his father's ice-blue eyes for the slightest hint of humanity and came up wanting. Fear worked its way into his already hurting heart. "Stay away from Lynette. I won't let you hurt her. Not again."

Dad cursed and downed the rest of his drink. "The past is dead and buried, Nicholas. Let it stay there."

That was exactly what Nick intended. "I'll talk to David. Just leave Lynnie out of it."

Dad leaned over the desk and nailed him with a pointed look. "You're awfully protective all of a sudden."

Nick stared down at his feet. He looked up again at the sound of his father's laughter.

"Please don't tell me you still have feelings for that girl. Your loyalties lie elsewhere. Don't get involved with those people again." He waved a hand in dismissal. "Now, I have some calls to make. Get packed. We're flying to New York in two hours, weather permitting."

"What?"

Anthony tossed him his classic I-can't-believe-this-imbecile-is-my-son look. "We arranged this last week. The banquet? Miss Vanguard is anticipating your arrival. It's formal, bring your tux."

Nick stood, shoved his hands in his pockets. "Make up some

excuse for me. I don't want to go." Spending an evening with Mindy and her parents was the last thing he wanted to do.

"That's too bad. We need Mindy happy. When Mindy is happy, Maurice is happy." His father rounded the desk and came to stand in front of him. "And when Maurice is happy, we're all happy." He patted Nick on the cheek. "Two hours, or the next time I talk with Miss Carlisle, I might tell her why you really left Princeton." A flicker of warning flashed over his father's face.

"That was a long time ago, Dad. And I was innocent."

"So you say."

"Forget it." Nick refused to argue. He was a marionette, and his father pulled the strings.

Dad nodded, his eyes hinting of victory.

~

Lynette woke Monday morning to the sound of hammering. Somehow her father was still sleeping soundly, so she got ready for work and went downstairs to investigate.

David was at the front of the house, perched on a ladder, fixing a shutter that had come lose during the storm. He pounded on a nail like his life depended on it. Since his arrival, he'd gone through every room, making a mile-long list of repairs. Dressed in old jeans, a tattered muscle T-shirt, and a red bandana tied around his head, he looked like he was actually enjoying himself.

Lynette had to yell to get his attention.

When he finally turned around, she laughed at his startled expression. "You'll have a few more people yelling at you in a minute if you don't keep it down." Lynette smoothed her khaki shorts and tipped her face to the sun. The weather had cleared and the forecast predicted a warm week. Perhaps they could take the kids to the park.

David clambered down the ladder. Dirt smeared his flushed

face and beads of perspiration dotted the dark stubble above his upper lip. "Gray up yet?"

"That was a joke, right?"

They shared a smile, and David took a drink from a water bottle perched on the front steps. "Who's that Victoria chick anyway?"

Lynette grinned. Gray hadn't welcomed his older siblings with open arms. In fact, he'd spent most of the weekend in his room. Hiding.

"Apparently she's his manager. Seems more to it, since she's here. But she's in her own room, so . . ."

"With Gray, who knows, right?" David rolled his eyes. Lynette followed his gaze to the shutters, blue paint peeling off them. "The place is falling apart. I had no idea things were this bad."

"How would you?"

If her comment meant anything, he didn't show it. "I've made a preliminary list, but I'm sure there'll be more to do. We can manage the minor repairs ourselves. Gray can help. Maybe we can find some kids looking for work. Are those twins still down the road? Oh, have you heard from Ryan?"

"No." Lynette marveled at the way her brother's brain seemed stuck on overdrive. "Mail takes awhile. I don't have a phone number. He moves around a lot. Africa's a big place—he could be anywhere."

David squinted in the sunlight, put up a hand to shade his eyes. "What if we can't reach him?"

"I don't know." She glanced at the house again, then back at David. "Did you know Gray was taking drugs? I mean, before it all came out." Lynette watched her brother's eyes narrow.

David shrugged and rocked back on his heels. "I heard something from Liz."

As usual, she was the last to know. "And nobody thought to tell me?"

"Lynnie, Gray has to sort this out on his own. I don't know what got him started, but you can't fix this for him."

"I'm not trying to fix it. I'm trying to understand it." She worked to keep the anger out of her voice. "He was doing so well. I mean, it's not like he was super famous or anything, but—"

"But maybe he wanted to be." David's eyes clouded over. "I don't know. From what I hear, that business is the toughest out there. Maybe our definition of 'doing well' doesn't come anywhere close to his."

"I guess."

"Well, he's home now. Let's try to support him. And if you really want to know his story, why don't you ask?" He squeezed her shoulder and smiled. "I guess we've never been all that good at talking, have we, Shortstop?"

Lynette blinked and gave a shrug. "I always felt like nobody wanted to hear what I had to say."

"That's not true. And before you say it, I know I've been avoiding your calls. Things haven't been so great for me lately."

"What do you mean?"

David tossed his hammer onto the grass and wandered around the perimeter of the rose garden. The bushes were overgrown, the ground around them hard and weed-infested, yet every year they stubbornly produced a riotous display that perfumed the air for weeks. New buds formed on every bush.

He stopped to pick off the deadheads, tossing them toward the old sycamore at the side of the driveway. "Josslyn and I have been having problems." David dropped his voice and kept his back to her.

"Davy?" Lynette went to him, took hold of his arm, and pulled him around.

"We're taking some time apart. We've been to counseling and . . . I think we can get through this, but . . ." He rubbed his face. "Life is never what you think it'll be, huh?"

"Davy, I'm so sorry." She thought of the two little faces she'd squealed over in the photos he'd shown her.

"We still love each other. But the past year . . . well, I've also been let go." His shrug said it had been unexpected. "The company changed hands. We knew there would be casualties. I didn't think I'd be one of them."

"Oh no." Lynette rubbed his arm. "You'll find something else."

"Hopefully. The comp package was decent. We'll get by for a while." He shook his head, clasping his hands behind his head. "I'm thirty-two. Not exactly ready for retirement."

Nothing she could say would make things better. "I appreciate you coming home, Davy. If I'd known . . ."

"What?" He flung an arm toward the house. "This has to be dealt with. We have to make a decision about the house, you know that. Then there's Dad . . . What are we going to do with him?"

"I don't know." Lynette kicked at the white stones beneath her feet. "I've been asking that for a long time." And haven't gotten any answers.

He sucked in a breath. "What were you thinking, keeping it to yourself? You should have said something before now."

"I tried! And each time I called, you were too busy to talk." Lynette's temper started to simmer. "Like you said, you've got your own problems." She turned back toward the house.

"Lynnie, stop." David blocked her path. "I'm sorry. I just . . . It's a lot to take in, okay? He needs a doctor."

"You think I don't know that?"

"Then . . ."

Lynette fiddled with a bracelet around her wrist. Counted to ten. Twice. "You'll have to figure out how to get him there, David, because I'm fresh out of ideas. You seem to have all the answers. You deal with it." She swiped at her cheeks and hated the animosity she felt toward her siblings since they'd come home.

"What are you mad at me for?"

Lynette stared, openmouthed. "Are you kidding? I'm doing my best. I've been doing my best, alone, for years. But I can't fix any of this—the house, Dad, all our issues." She blinked and lowered her voice. "I hate the thought of selling our home. And I hate that it's the *only* reason you're all here now."

David was the most even tempered of her siblings; she'd never talked to him that way. Never had to. Her oldest brother had always been her protector. Someone she went to first when things were desperate. He hadn't been there for her this past year.

"You let me down, Davy." Tears slid down her cheeks. "I needed you a long time ago. It's a little late to ride in and try to save the day now."

For a moment she thought he would walk away.

He let out a ragged breath and stared at her through glassy eyes. "I hear you. I'm sorry. I'm a jerk, okay? You can punch me if you want."

Their old camaraderie chased off her anger. He'd only just arrived, and she didn't want to fight. "It's good to have you home. But don't use being here as an excuse not to work on your marriage. Talk to Josslyn. Maybe she and the kids can come over."

He rolled his eyes, but grinned. "All right, I'll talk to her."

"Pinkie swear?" She held up her little finger.

"Come here, you." David pulled her into a sweaty hug.

"Ick. You're stinky." She pushed him back with a laugh.

"Now are you gonna tell me what's going on with you and Cooper?"

Lynette groaned and tugged on her hair. "Nothing's going on."

"Didn't look like nothing to me the other day. He was holding you pretty close."

"I was scared of the storm."

"Still scared of storms?" David's brow furrowed.

"Sort of." Sort of a lot.

Nick hadn't called and she hadn't seen him since Saturday. And she didn't want to talk about it.

"Why's he working at the bank? Thought he was going to be an architect."

"He said his dad needed him back here, but I think there's more to it." She watched a flock of birds disappear behind the house. "He's been helpful, Davy. You know Nick, he's not happy unless he's saving the world."

"Yeah, well. We don't need his help." David crossed the lawn and retrieved his hammer. Lynette heard the gates creak, turned as Cecily pushed through them, latched them shut, and marched down the driveway.

"Girl, you still here?" She tapped the watch on her wrist. "You gonna be late."

"Shoot." She turned to David before heading inside. "I wanted to thank you," she whispered. "For getting Cecily back. She's such a huge help."

David frowned, looked from her to Cecily, then gave a shrug. "Wasn't me. See you later, Shortstop."

Chapter Fourteen

Gray wandered through the big house in search of something to do. After a rude awakening by someone banging something to death, he gave up on sleep, showered, shaved, and ventured downstairs.

Tori stood in the kitchen, peeling, chopping, and taking vengeance on a very large eggplant.

Gray grinned. "Wow. Where'd you get that thing?"

She glanced his way, knife in hand. "There's a farm about a mile from here. Sweet old guy. We haggled over pricing, but I think he likes me. Told me to come back anytime."

"Old Jenkins likes 'em young. Heard he murdered his last wife." Gray ducked out of reach and went in search of food. He found bagels, popped one in the toaster, and peered a little dubiously into the coffeepot.

"It's decaf."

"I figured." He poured a cup anyway, leaned up against the counter, and watched her work.

"I'll do a shake for you in a minute."

"Yeah?" He raised an eyebrow. "I'll look forward to that."

"Keep that up and I'll put spinach in it again."

Gray made a gagging noise. Spinach, eggplant. He was afraid to ask what else she'd bought to force on him.

Tori laughed and dumped the vegetable refuse into a plastic container. She'd already given Lynnie a lecture on composting, and the other day they'd gone out together and returned with a big black industrial plastic container, now sitting somewhere in the yard.

Since coming here, Tori had discarded the chunky jewelry, stopped using a bottle of hair gel a day, and lightened up on the makeup. It took some getting used to, but as he looked at her now, he realized what she'd been hiding.

Natural beauty.

Gray tried to look away, but couldn't.

It was happening again.

And the feelings he'd locked up and banished could not return.

"You're staring." She met his eyes with a scowl. "Is my shirt on backward?"

"Nope." He reached into his back pocket. "Almost forgot. Brought you a present." Gray placed the half empty pack of cigarettes in front of her.

She turned up her nose and poked the cardboard box with the tip of her knife. "How sweet. I don't smoke."

"Yeah, I know. Neither do I. Anymore."

"Seriously?"

Gray nodded. He'd made the right decision. "Figure if I'm going cold turkey, may as well get rid of everything."

"All right. Good for you." She lowered her head and started chopping again, but her smile stayed put. "I made some calls. Apparently there's a new doctor in town who's very good. You have an appointment tomorrow morning."

"Tor, please. No more doctors." He'd talked to enough doctors and shrinks to last a lifetime.

She pointed the knife in his direction. "You really want to argue with me, Gray? You're the one who insisted on leaving the clinic after two weeks against your doctor's advice, so . . ."

"Okay, okay. I hear you." He eyed the pile of chopped vegetables. And he'd seen her carve a turkey. "Tomorrow it is."

Gray fixed his bagel and sat at the banquet in the kitchen. Lynnie had gone to work, and his father was comfortably settled on the back patio, watching David mow the lawn. Gray was still trying to get his head around the change in Pops. If the situation weren't so sad, it would be funny.

Every now and then Pops barked instructions at David over the noise of the mower, like he was trying to teach him how to play croquet. Pops loved that game. His cronies would come over on the weekends and they'd spend hours out back, arguing with each other and drinking Bloody Marys. This morning Pops was drinking Tori's lame excuse for coffee.

Gray flicked through today's paper, didn't find his name anywhere, finished eating, and tipped the rest of Tori's shake into the dogs' dish when she wasn't looking. Then he stood at the window and watched his brother work.

He should probably get out there and offer to do something.

But he wasn't up to any real conversation with David. Or any of them.

Not yet.

The lawn rose and fell in anthills and patches of thistle. Hardly the smooth stretch of green he remembered. Somehow, in the locked drawers of his memory, everything remained the same. He'd half expected his mother to appear the night he'd arrived, give her usual exuberant shout of greeting, and fly down the steps to meet him.

But she hadn't.

And his memory had deceived him.

Gray left Tori to her culinary experiments and went exploring. Cecily was in the living room, dusting away, humming to herself. Gray backpedaled, not ready for a run-in with the woman who'd practically raised him, but she turned too fast.

"Where you going?"

"Uh, nowhere." He tried out the smile that always worked on her. This time it didn't.

Cecily crossed the room and stood before him, more serious than he'd ever seen her. Gray had little choice but to stay put as she eyed him up and down.

"Ce-ce, whatever you're about to say, I've probably already heard it."

She narrowed her eyes, fiddled with the cross around her neck, and sighed. "You think so?"

Gray shrugged. "You don't need to tell me what a mess I've made of my life."

"Oh, I figured that." Lines around her eyes crinkled as she patted his cheek with a sad smile, and suddenly he felt like a kid again. "If you're waiting for judgment to jump out at you behind every corner, honey, you're in the wrong house."

He rolled his eyes, his throat tight. "Yeah?"

Her mouth formed a thin line. "Seems to me, the only one throwing judgment around here might be you." She brushed some dog fur off his shirt and placed her hands on his shoulders, her teary eyes reaching right through to his soul. "Home is where you come to heal, baby."

"That's ironic."

Cecily shook her head, studied him for a long moment. "Sometimes, Gray, you find hope in the last place you think to look." She drew him into a hug, then stood back with a smile that lit her face and patched one of the holes in his heart.

Cecily returned to her work, leaving him standing there, stupid tears in his eyes.

Gray moved to the round table by the piano and scanned the array of photographs on display. He ran his tongue over his bottom lip and picked up a picture.

His throat tightened again as he studied it.

He and Cooper sat in their Sunfish, arms thrown around each other's skinny shoulders. Midgets. Full of themselves and brazen enough to make sure the world knew it. Life had been pretty simple back then. They'd even ended up being sent away to school together. Managed to make more trouble there, something their parents hadn't banked on.

They used to talk about anything. Argue over everything and nothing, just to see who would back down first. Got into more than a few scrapes over the years and sent their parents into conniptions too many times to count.

While he was wild and often out of control, Nick was centered. The only one who could rein Gray in, make him take a breath and actually use the brain God had mistakenly blessed him with. Gray hadn't put it to much use over the past five years.

He'd always figured Nick would be around forever. His touchstone.

But he'd chased his best friend out of his life and made sure he stayed out.

And since then Gray had been lonely.

Gray put the picture back in place.

He left the living room and went into the next one. They called it the study, although it was more like a library. It was the only place Mom had allowed Pops to smoke. The dark wood-paneled walls still shone, built-in bookcases filled to overflowing with everything from Dr. Seuss to Aristotle.

Never much of a reader, Gray avoided the room, but the others could spend hours in here, perched on thick cushions in the window boxes on a rainy day, their noses buried between musty bindings. Gray preferred to be outside whatever the weather. Nothing like ducking a little lightning now and again.

But sooner or later you get hit.

"Did you need something?"

Gray startled and turned toward his sister's voice. Liz sat

behind the desk at the far corner of the room, laptop open. She stared expectantly.

"You scared the crap out of me." He scrubbed his face and waited for his pulse to slow down. "Didn't know you were in here."

"So I gathered." She studied him through black-rimmed glasses. Her blond hair was swept into a tight bun and large diamonds sparkled from her ears. She looked ready for a day at the office.

Gray struggled for something sensible to say. After their last telephone conversation, he'd avoided her. Liz was far too intimidating for his liking. Always had been.

"You look busy. I'll leave you alone."

She waved a hand, like she was swatting a fly. Or him. "I was just catching up on some work. The Internet connection is appalling." Her horrified expression amused him.

He cleared his throat and ventured across the faded Persian rug. "I don't think Lynnie gets online much. Kind of nice not to be tied to it, really." He'd steered clear of computers and television for weeks.

"I've already called someone. They should be over this afternoon to get us hooked up with high-speed."

"Sweet. You paying?"

"Of course I am. Some of us have work to do, Gray. I can't jog into town every time I need to send a file."

"I guess not." Not that he could imagine Liz jogging anywhere, but some fresh air might help her attitude some. He shoved his hands into the pockets of his jeans and stared at the portrait above the fireplace.

His mother looked down at him, lips curled in her usual half smile, blond hair shimmering under a setting sun. She was probably in her twenties when the painting had been done. Pops had captured her spirit in its entirety. It was possibly his best work. He'd even managed to give her that air of mystery Diana Carlisle had been famous for. Vibrant blue eyes hinted at secrets they would never know.

He rubbed his throbbing temples. "I still miss her. That's crazy, huh?"

Gray turned to Liz and caught a glimmer of tears. Surprise crept over him, followed by guilt.

Liz closed her laptop and gave a small shrug. "Hard to believe it's been twelve years. Being back here makes it feel like yesterday."

"Yeah." Gray slumped into a chair and fiddled with the chain around his neck. "I'll never forget it. Principal Wiggs came into the classroom and just looked at me. I thought I was about to be expelled." He could still picture old Wiggy's face. "That would have been the better news." One of these days, his heart might stop hurting. He wasn't counting on it, but it sure would be nice.

Liz stretched her arms above her head, a faint purple line of a bruise just visible on the underside, above her elbow. "I was in the middle of finals. Had to write all my exams late. I wasn't sure they would let me graduate."

He tried to see past the stone wall surrounding her, sighed and gave up. "Your life was hardly ruined, Liz. You got into Harvard. Got your law degree."

"Yes." She returned his stare, lips pulled tight. "Hardly ruined at all. Not compared to some, I suppose."

Gray swore and pushed out of his chair. "Nice chatting with you."

"Sit down, Gray." She was queen of the courtroom, deluded in believing he was under her control. But the slight tremor in her voice pulled him back down.

Liz put her head in her hands for a moment. The action made him uncomfortable. Like she was plotting his swift conviction. Or worse.

When she faced him again, her cheeks were blotchy, her eyes glistening. "We all have our issues, Gray. I don't know how you ended up on drugs, and frankly, I don't care. If you're really serious about quitting, then I want you to know I'm behind you. I'll help you however I can. But . . . could you just tell me, what in heaven's name made you think you had the right to shut us all out of your life? Because I'd really like to know." She pressed her palms down on the desk and pinned him with a desperate look. "Tell me why I had to hear about the mess you've made of your life from a friend who happens to be one of your fans and not from you."

Gray clenched his hands together to keep them from shaking. "I already had a lawyer."

"I didn't want to be your lawyer, Gray." Her anger fizzled as a new inflection crept in. One he hardly recognized. "I wanted to be your sister."

He studied the holes in his jeans, picked up a long-ago scent of the pipe tobacco that used to fill the room. It was hard to breathe again. He'd been struggling for weeks. Drowning under accusations of failure, floundering in the murky waters of regret.

He looked up and shook his head. "I was ashamed."

"Did you honestly think I would judge you?" Her compassionate expression made his eyes burn again.

Maybe Cecily had a point.

He'd been running from the truth so long he wasn't sure what it looked like anymore.

"I don't know." The admission settled heavily, pushing down his shoulders. "I deserved it. I didn't want to let you guys see what a loser I've become."

"Oh, Gray." Liz ran a hand over her face. "You're not a loser."

He shrugged and glanced around the room. "My so-called career is in the toilet. I wasn't exactly frugal with my money; I didn't have a savings plan. I don't know what the future looks like for me, Liz. That's a little terrifying."

She picked up a pen and twirled it between her fingers. "What does your agent say?"

"He, uh . . . thinks I should lay low for a while. He's too nice to get rid of me, but I doubt he'll be calling anytime soon."

"Are you broke?"

Gray leaned forward and stared at his toes, the reality of his situation as nauseating as Tori's spinach shakes. He let out a breath and sat up. "Pretty much."

Liz didn't smile and he was grateful. She tapped her pen against the desk and shook her head. "That's unfortunate. I think Lynnie was hoping you might . . . Well, never mind. The sooner we can sell this mausoleum, the better. You should get enough from the sale to pull you through. Get you on your feet again."

"Maybe." They were always hiring at Walmart. "Lynnie doesn't want to sell, does she?" Since he'd been back, his little sister seemed to be giving him a wide berth. He wasn't sure why, whether it had to do with everything he'd been through or his reaction to seeing Cooper. He suspected it was the latter.

Liz snorted and threw the pen down. It bounced off the desk and landed near his feet. "Lynette is thinking with her heart, not her head. She doesn't see the big picture, Gray. She has no concept of reality."

"Must be nice."

"Going through life wearing rose-colored glasses? I don't think so."

A hollow laugh escaped. "Seems to work for her. I'm willing to give it a shot." His eyes came to rest on the large family Bible in the bookcase. Passed down through generations, he wondered when any of them had last looked at it. "Lynnie's got more faith than the rest of us put together. Well, except maybe Ryan. Could be they're onto something with this Jesus thing, huh?"

Lately, in the early hours when he couldn't sleep, his thoughts drifted toward things he'd learned as a child. Faith. Mercy. Grace. Things he'd forgotten until recently. He wasn't entirely sure he was a candidate for forgiveness from the Almighty, but he'd been contemplating asking for it.

Liz's sigh scratched close to irritation. "Religion is a crutch, Gray.

Do you really believe there's some higher being up there controlling all this? Someone who actually cares what we do?"

"I hope so." If God wasn't real, he didn't have a whole lot left to hold on to. "Lynnie sure believes it. Why are you so hard on her?"

His sister swiveled the leather wingback to face their mother's portrait. "I don't know. I suppose I feel responsible for her."

"She's not a kid anymore, Liz. You need to lighten up."

"I need to lighten up? You haven't exactly been Mr. Congeniality lately."

Liz was right, as usual.

"I know. But I'm feeling better today." Gray flexed his stiff shoulders. A two-hour massage would be heaven. He could just imagine Tori's face if he asked for one. "For the first time in a long while, I feel almost . . . normal."

Liz laughed. She really was quite pretty when she wasn't scowling. "Should I alert the press?"

"Let's keep it between us for now." He rubbed the ring on his thumb and pondered his next question. "Did you ever wonder . . . what really happened the day Mom died?"

She snapped her head up and stared. "We know what happened. Dad told us."

Gray gnawed his bottom lip and shook his head. "He said they were arguing and she tripped and fell down the stairs. But what were they arguing about?"

"I don't know." Her voice got a little squeaky. "Why don't you go ask Dad? I'm sure he'd love to chat about it."

Gray had thought about it—thought about coming out here and confronting the old man—many times over the last few years. And now it was too late. "Does David know? He was home from college that weekend, right?"

"He had the flu. He was sound asleep at the other end of the third floor."

"What about Lynnie?"

Liz sat forward and glared. "Lynnie was twelve years old. She doesn't know anything."

"Didn't you think it was strange, though . . . I mean, she was so quiet after the funeral and everything. Didn't really speak for a long time. She—"

"She was in shock! We all were. Do I need to remind you what Dad was like? He was probably in one of his drunken rages and pushed Mom down the stairs for all we know."

A shiver raced through him, made him a little dizzy. "Is that what you believe? You and David? Really?" He'd mulled over that scenario as well, but it didn't make sense. For all his faults, Pops never got physical with anyone, and he never would have done a thing to hurt their mother.

Liz pressed her fingers down on the desk. "Leave it alone, Gray. And don't you dare go asking Lynnie about it."

"Yeah, okay." He would leave it alone. For now. "Well, I guess we'll get on with things. Think I'll paint the shutters today."

"Good. You and Davy knock yourselves out." Liz fired up her laptop again and put on her business face. "If you want to be useful, Grayson, go make us a pot of coffee. Real coffee, please. Not that stuff your girlfriend was serving this morning."

"She's not my girlfriend."

"No?" Liz raised a thin eyebrow. "That statement smacks of regret, baby brother."

"Life's full of regrets, Liz."

Liz smiled then. A real smile, the one she rarely used. At least when he was around.

"What?" He almost didn't want to know.

"Oh, nothing." Her gaze returned to the screen. "You'll figure it all out, Gray. You're smarter than you look."

Chapter Fifteen

After that last altercation with his father on the weekend, Nick took Monday off and went to New York. It was time he confronted Mindy.

He pushed his hands into the pockets of his jeans and waited for the crosswalk light to change. The city hummed in the summer heat. Sweat slid down his neck, and he batted away a waft of cigarette smoke from the woman in front of him. A couple of guys on the corner passed out fliers advertising a concert, reggae music blasting from the speakers of their stereo. Horns blared in a tune of their own, impatient drivers stuck in slow-moving traffic. After spending so much time on Nantucket, the crowded streets, noise, and city smog bothered him.

He crossed the busy intersection and headed toward Broadway. A few blocks later he took the elevator up to the photographer's studio. Two girls standing near the door recognized him and nodded in greeting. The loft was a beehive of activity, lit with studio lights, loud music shaking the floor.

Nick stood against the wall and watched Miranda Vanguard strut her stuff.

She was beautiful, no denying that. Not too tall, but in possession of a body most women would kill for. And boy, did she know how to use it.

No denying that either.

Her long, dark hair spread around her shoulders like silk. Tanned skin glowed under the bright lights as she flashed the smile that was growing more expensive by the hour.

Nick waited for the feeling—the one he knew so well now—of being sucked in, pulled under, and captured so completely by her.

It didn't come.

Instead, he felt something closer to relief.

Once upon a time, he'd found her exotic beauty appealing. Been drawn to her mysterious smile and elusive nature. Fallen for her many times. Maybe even loved her a little.

Today she was just Mindy.

"Nick!" She waved a hand and struck another pose. The photographer swore and barked instructions that she happily ignored.

Nick tried not to laugh. The shimmering blue evening gown that hugged all the right curves probably cost more than a small car. At least she was decent this time. The last unexpected visit he'd paid her, he'd found her modeling negligees.

"Miranda, dah-ling, this way please . . ." The guy was built like a Mack Truck and spoke with a thick accent, German maybe. He glanced at Nick, irritated.

Nick took a couple steps forward and caught Mindy's eye. "Are you almost done? We need to talk."

"Do you mind?" The photographer lowered his camera and glared. "We are working here."

Mindy laughed. "Oh, Horst, don't be such a grump. We've been at this for hours."

Nick pulled his gaze up in a hurry. This grandpa was the guy Mindy claimed to be in love with? No wonder she wanted to hide the relationship from her parents.

Mindy flounced across the floor toward them, her dress swishing behind her. The hulk practically melted as she placed a hand on his arm and stood on her toes to kiss him. "Can we call it a day, Horst? I'm exhausted."

"All right, my sweet. We're still on for dinner?"

"Eight o'clock. Don't be late." Mindy blew him a kiss and skipped over to Nick. "What are you doing in the city?" She put her arms around him and squeezed.

"Took a day off. Didn't know it was a crime to stop in and see my 'girlfriend.'" Nick shot her a wink and enjoyed the growl that came from the direction of the big guy. He had his back to them, packing up his gear.

Mindy rolled her eyes. "Stop it. Are you in a rush? It'll take me about ten minutes to get changed."

"More like twenty." Nick eyed a leather sofa in one corner of the long room. "I'll go take a nap. Unless Horse wants to buy me a drink."

"I am busy." Horst pushed a fistful of fingers through thick, almost yellow, hair as he strode over to them. He wasn't that ugly. Kind of rugged, in a Hulk Hogan sort of way. He tried on a tiny smile Nick figured was supposed to put him at ease. "You must be Nicholas."

"We meet at last." Nick took the beefy hand extended to him. "Go, Mind. Time's a ticking."

"So rude, Nicky. Honestly." She pranced off, leaving a whiff of heady perfume floating on the air.

Nick shoved his hands back in his pockets, checked out the girls on the far side of the room, and made sure nobody was in earshot. "You do realize how insane this is?" he asked the hulk.

"You don't have to tell me. But there's no reasoning with that one, as I am sure you know."

"Yeah. I do know." Nick exhaled. "But I'm gonna give it a shot."

"Good luck." Horst looked toward the door Mindy disappeared through. "Do you really think that her father would disown her?"

"Obviously Mindy does." Nick tried to guess his age. He had at least fifteen years or more on them.

Horst glanced at his watch. "I must go. Nice to meet you,

Nicholas. Perhaps we talk longer next time." He strode past him, stopped when he reached the door, and turned back, unsmiling. "And thanks."

~

Mindy sipped her Cosmo and tried to play dumb.

Nick prayed for patience as he stared her down across the table in the crowded Manhattan restaurant. It was so loud he could hardly hear himself think. "Can you listen to me for once, please?"

"I am listening to you. But I'm still mad at you for blowing me off last weekend. You were supposed to be at that party. My parents were not impressed." She gave him her best little girl pout.

Nick picked up the menu the waiter had forgotten on the table and wondered how much of a scene it would cause if he swatted her over the head with it. "I was sailing. I gave your mother my regrets. Look, I'm done playing games, Mind. I don't want to do this anymore."

Her big eyes filled as her bottom lip began to quiver. A well-practiced ploy she played to the point of perfection. Old Maurice might still fall for the crocodile tears, but Nick's days of playing Mindy's games were over.

"Daddy will kill me." She sniffed and took a huge gulp of her red drink. Coughed and took a moment to compose herself. "He hates Horst."

"Well, the guy did cheat on you. Twice. It's possible your father has a point."

Mindy's pout pulled into a scowl. "He's sorry. I wasn't exactly being faithful either, if you must know."

Nick raised his eyes to the ceiling. "TMI, Mind." He leaned closer. "This may come as a shock to you, but I actually do have a life. I'd like to start living it." He downed the rest of his beer and picked up the other half of his Philly steak. Mindy hadn't touched her salad. "Eat. Anorexia doesn't become you."

"Shut up." She picked up her fork and shoved a pile of green stuff in her mouth. "I don't know why we couldn't have gone for sushi," she mumbled. "That"—she pointed her fork at his monstrosity of deliciousness—"is disgusting."

Their waiter refilled their water glasses and smiled at Mindy like a love-sick sixth grader. Nick wondered how many restaurants Miranda Vanguard managed to take complete control over the minute she walked through the door.

She'd always possessed a power he found impossible to define.

Dressed in a simple T-shirt and skinny jeans, she looked more like a teenager than a top model. He'd known her since they were kids. Their families moved in the same circles and went on ski trips and cruises together. Mindy was a natural leader; their crowd went along with her suggestions, some of them outrageous. But her parents clung to the notion that she ranked right up there with the Virgin Mary. Amongst her many other questionable qualities, Miranda Vanguard had mastered the act of deception. The past few years, he'd gone along.

No more.

"What's up, Nick?" She sat back and folded her arms. "As much as I'd love to believe you came all the way here to take me to lunch, I'm not that stupid."

"I want this to be over." He'd actually said it. He'd thought about it, written it down a few times, but never voiced it. Until now. "I didn't mind providing your parents a distraction for a while, pretending we were dating, but it's getting out of hand. The parties, the dinners. Your mother actually said the *W* word the other night—did you hear that?"

Mindy giggled. "I thought you were going to choke on your clams."

"I didn't sign up for this, Mind."

"Nicky." Mindy's full lips parted in a half smile and she put a hand on his arm. Long scarlet fingernails shimmered under the small glass light hanging above them. "What's her name?"

Nick gauged her expression. Maybe he should have been a little nicer to her the past couple of months. They were still friends, after all. "Does it matter?"

"I guess not." She finished her drink and played with the rings on her fingers. "What am I supposed to tell Daddy?"

He sat forward, met her eyes, and saw fear in them. "Tell him the truth, Mind. You're almost twenty-five. You have your own money."

Thin eyebrows shot skyward. "Do you have any idea how much a decent condo costs in this city? Who do you think owns that penthouse on Fifth? Not me. He'll be so angry with me. He'll cut me off."

Did she really believe that? Maurice would step in front of an oncoming tractor trailer to avoid the slightest bit of harm coming to his beautiful daughter. Surely he wouldn't wash his hands of her for falling in love with the wrong guy.

Nick shrugged. "I think you're wrong. But so what if he does? Don't you want to live your own life for a change?"

"You're a fine one to talk." Mindy dabbed at her eyes with her napkin. Real tears this time, it seemed. "You're stuck on that boring little island, pushing papers. Yes-sir-ing your father left, right, and center."

"You know why I went back." The sandwich sat heavy in his stomach and he pushed his plate to one side. A couple across the room caught his attention. They were deep in conversation, intently looking at each other.

Nick watched the way the man reached across the small table and tucked a strand of the woman's hair behind her ear. A simple movement, yet filled with such affection. Watched the way she returned his smile and said he was her world without words.

He'd never felt that way about anybody.

But he wanted to. Wanted it bad.

Nick blinked and turned back to Mindy. "I like Nantucket. It actually feels like home."

"Oh boy." She laughed and gave a knowing look. "I bet it's that girl who lives next door. What's her name, Gray's sister? She was always making googly eyes at you."

"She was not." He lowered his gaze and cursed the heat prickling his cheeks.

"Oh, I'm right! Linda? Lynn?"

"Lynette." A smile spread before he could stop it. "Happy now?"

"You do look good, Nick. More at peace. Well, Miss Carlisle is one lucky woman. You're a first-class act, Mr. Cooper."

"Thanks, Mind." Nick allowed a little relief to settle in. "So let's figure this thing out."

Lynette walked past The Longshoreman on Wednesday after work. Jed Hagerman was outside taping a notice to the window.

"Hey, Lynnie," he said and she stopped walking. They'd gone to high school together, until he dropped out. He came by the day care to pick up his sister's little girl once in a while, and he'd asked her out enough times.

"Hi, Jed." She scanned the notice as he stepped away from it. "Looking for help, huh?"

"Yeah. Had a gal quit on me last week."

An idea pricked Lynette's mind. Art supplies were expensive. She had been putting the money she'd earned from her paintings right back into the house, skimming off the top of her salary to pay for her materials. She couldn't come out and ask David or Liz for extra cash. She wasn't ready for anyone to know about the paintings she was selling. Not yet.

She followed Jed into the dimly lit bar and waited for her eyes to adjust. The place was empty except for an old guy sitting at the counter. Jed rounded the counter and gave her the once-over.

"What can I get you?"

"Um." Lynette pushed her hair over her shoulders. "I'd like to apply for the job."

The word that shot out of his mouth wasn't the answer she wanted.

"Really, Jed?"

"Sorry." Jed cleared his throat. "But, really, Lynnie? You gotta be freakin' kidding me." He busied himself pouring what she hoped was Coke into a tall glass and set it down before her.

"Not kidding." She sniffed, checked out the bubbles, and took a sip. "What are you looking for?"

Jed leaned forward and grinned. "Now, darlin', you know what I'm looking for."

"Cut it out, Jed." Lynette frowned, already having second thoughts.

He straightened and picked up another glass. "Thought you worked at the day care."

"I do." She swallowed the fizzy liquid along with what little pride she had left. "But I could use the extra cash. So what's the deal?"

"Well . . ." He scratched his jaw, his beefy face brightening. "Serving, mostly. Can you cook? Need a hand with that too. No gourmet stuff. Just burgers, fries, straight up."

"Sounds okay. What are the hours?"

"Three nights a week, some Fridays. A little over minimum wage, but you get tips."

"Nights?"

"This is a bar, hon. I don't do much business during the day."

Maybe with everyone home now . . . Her stomach churned at the smell of beer and grease, but she concentrated on a painting on the wall. Her father's classic bold strokes and attention to detail gave her cause to smile. He and old Mr. Hagerman had been friends. "You've still got that painting."

Jed glanced over his shoulder and heaved up his pants. "Sure. My old man left it to me, along with this place and the mold and the cockroaches to go with it. Heckuva legacy, huh?"

"I can't imagine anyone else managing the place, Jed." She wiped her moist palms against her skirt and met his eyes. "When can I start?"

He hesitated, probably coming up with a thousand reasons to say no. But then he smiled. "Tonight?"

Chapter Sixteen

The painting was different. Darker. The house on the hill sat under threatening gray clouds, the roof shingles wet and glistening. Lightning slashed the sky and reached down to the sand on the deserted beach as whitecaps rolled into shore.

At first glance, Nick thought the house was Wyldewood. But a few details were different. Not as many windows, no flagpole, and the steps leading up from the beach were in the wrong place.

"You like it?" Evy stood beside him, head tipped to one side as she studied the artwork. "She has other pieces, brighter. Happier. I've already sold one today."

"Yeah, I saw. I like those too." Nick tried to make sense of the trepidation he felt. "But this one . . . the detail is fascinating." He could almost step right into it. Soft yellow light shone from one upstairs window, the rest of the house swathed in darkness.

"I'm not sure I like it as much," Evy mused. "There's something eerie about it."

Two bicycles leaned against the steps of the back porch. A curly-headed doll lay discarded a few feet away, red mouth open in protest, unmoving eyes staring up at him.

Nick shivered, searched his memory, then shook his head. He retrieved his wallet and took out his credit card.

"You've become her biggest fan, Nicholas." Evy rang up the bill.

"Why doesn't she do a show? You should arrange something." Nick wondered at the older woman's contrite smile.

"Verity is very private."

"There's a big charity auction coming up in August. I'm helping arrange it. If she was interested in putting a couple of paintings in—"

"I know about the auction." Evy studied the many rings on her fingers. "I've asked, but she doesn't want to participate."

Nick handed Evy a business card. "Have her call me."

Evy held up a hand and refused to take it. "She won't. Shall I have this delivered to the usual place?"

"Yeah." Nick ran a hand down his face and shoved off his disappointment. "Look, if she—" He sighed and shook his head. "Never mind. Actually . . ." May as well jump right in with both feet.

"Yes?"

"I have this friend . . . we're neighbors. Her father is a well-known local artist."

"Drake Carlisle?"

Nick nodded. "You've seen his work?"

"Of course. Hard to come by these days. How is he?" Evy busied herself behind her desk, pushing papers from one spot to the next.

"He's not too well, unfortunately. But I thought if the family would part with some of his paintings, would you be interested in selling them?"

She studied him, long fingernails tapping out a tune on the counter. "Of course I would, but I might advise them to go to the mainland. Bigger market, people willing to pay more. Or I could broker the paintings on the Internet."

"I suppose." Nick shoved his wallet into his back pocket. "Maybe I should mind my own business."

"Sorry?"

He'd said that out loud? "Lynette, Drake's daughter, isn't partial to accepting help when it's offered."

"I see." Evy bobbed her head, light dancing behind her spectacles. "Something tells me perhaps you can be a little too persistent, Mr. Cooper."

"Ouch." He put a hand over his heart. "I can't help it. I don't know why—this is going to sound stupid—but I feel responsible for her in a way."

Evy nodded, but stayed quiet.

"Everything gets left up to her; her brothers and sister treat her like a child." He shut his mouth. She'd already accused him of blabbing her business to half the island. "Well, I just think it'd be a good idea if we could sell those paintings."

"Yes, indeed." Evy clasped her hands together. "Perhaps Miss Carlisle might be persuaded over a nice dinner. It sounds like the poor dear might need an evening off."

Nick laughed at her suggestive tone. "She might. We'll see." He glanced around the gallery. He'd been chewing on an idea lately, something a person in Evy's position might be interested in. According to his father, Evy McIntyre was old money, Nantucket royalty of sorts. She'd disappeared for a while, gone through several husbands, but now made the island her home again. "I was wondering if we could talk sometime. I have a business proposition I'd like to discuss with you."

The immediate interest in her eyes didn't disappoint. "Do tell, dear boy."

~

Nick left the gallery, walked along the cobbled streets, and wondered how to juggle everything going on in his life right now. He'd bet he was the only one on the island who, on Friday afternoon, was not looking forward to the weekend.

His father had taken to spending the week in the city and coming back here on weekends. Nick intended to stay out of his way.

As he strolled past the various shops, he came to a halt when he spied the toy store.

A few minutes later he exited the shop and walked with

purpose until he reached the small house with the big colorful rainbow-shaped sign out front, Kiddie Kare painted in bold red letters.

It was pickup time. He grinned as he watched a little girl run into her mother's arms. A guy around his age came out holding a small boy by the hand. As they hit the sidewalk, the man hoisted the boy up onto his shoulders. The kid's shout of glee and the man's resounding chuckle tore Nick's gut. A visceral reminder of the kind of father he wished he'd had.

If he reached back into the musty pages of his memory, he'd come up short. Missed games. Missed birthdays.

Even missed his high school graduation.

Eventually Nick got tired of waiting, tired of hoping.

"Hello, Mr. Cooper. Something we can do for you today?" Joanne Harper walked toward him from the far side of the yard.

Nick gripped the paper bag in one hand and raised the other in greeting. "Afternoon, Joanne. How are you?"

"Can't complain. But I'll be a lot better when you stop sending me those notices."

Nick loosened his tie, her words biting. Another reminder of how much he hated his job. "Sorry."

She put a hand on his arm. "It's not your fault. I made a deposit yesterday, so we should be good this month."

He nodded, sudden regret making him want to turn and run. "Is Lynnie around?"

"Lynette? Yeah, she's inside." Joanne waved at two more kids as they left with their parents.

Nick shifted from one foot to the other, his heart doing the cha-cha.

What did he think he was doing here?

Since their encounter on the beach last Saturday, he'd gone MIA. He knew it, wasn't proud of it, and she probably thought he was the world's biggest jerk.

"You can go in, you know." Joanne nodded toward the house. "Unless you'd rather stand out here looking like a stalker."

He mumbled his thanks and strode past her before she decided to say anything else.

Nick moved through the brightly decorated rooms, taking in the colorful artwork on the walls, the toys, the small tables and chairs. The place smelled like kids and Crayola. Lego towers and abacuses lured him back to his own childhood.

Nick bent to examine a few finger paintings left to dry on one of the small tables. When he raised his head, he saw her.

She sat in a rocker at the far end of the room where they obviously did their reading; a small boy snuggled on her lap. Low bookshelves lined the walls, and a rug in bright primary colors covered the floor.

Nick watched as she and the kid read *The Cat in the Hat*. Lynette's voice was strong, full of inflection, her face alight with the joy of the moment. Her hair was pinned off her face, a few stray curls touching her cheeks. She wore a simple black T-shirt and jeans, sandals on her feet.

"Hi, mister." The kid saw him first, greeted him with a toothy grin and a wave.

Lynette stared a moment, her eyes wide, full of things she didn't say. "What are you doing here?"

Nick smiled at the logical question. But he wasn't sure how to answer it. Instead, he shrugged and held the bag toward her. "Got you something."

Lynette lifted the child onto the floor. "Tyler, go play on the swings. I'll come out in a minute, and then we'll go."

"For pizza?" The kid's eyes practically bugged out of his head.

She nodded and pushed him toward the door. "Yes. Five minutes. Tell Miss Joanne I'll be right out."

Nick managed to walk toward her in a way he hoped gave off confidence. In truth, he was having difficulty focusing on anything other than the scintillating shimmer in her eyes. "I thought you said you didn't have a boyfriend. Have you been holding out on me?" Her blush sent shock waves blistering through him, shredding his self-confidence.

"I'm looking after him this evening." She picked up a few books and put them away. "What's in the bag? Did you rob the bank?"

"Ha." He found his voice a few octaves above middle C. "That's not a bad idea, though. You could drive the getaway car."

"I think your dad would figure it out pretty quickly." She took the bag he offered and peeked inside. "Nick." Her grin was wider than the little boy's as she pulled out two brand-new Pez dispensers.

Goofy and Dumbo. He'd always been a fan of the flying elephant, and he felt both goofy and dumb right now.

He smiled at her surprise and the red hue in her cheeks. "You do realize those are practically collectors' items? I had no idea candy was so expensive. That lady in the toy store cleaned me out."

"Totally worth it." Lynette winked, popped a candy in her mouth, and held Dumbo toward him.

"Oh. No . . . really."

"Really?" Her smirk did nothing to soothe his already rattled disposition. "You know you want to."

He wanted to all right, but doubted they were talking about the same thing.

Now his cheeks burned like he'd spent a day on the beach. "Careful there, Shortstop." Nick cleared his throat and held out a hand. She dropped a white rectangle onto his palm and he threw it into his mouth. The sweet and sour taste was a blast from the past.

"You know, I hated that name."

"You did?" She was awfully good at hiding her true feelings sometimes. "I never knew that. Sorry."

"Forget it." She turned on her heel and made for a long cupboard at the far end of the room, slung her bag over her shoulder, and deposited her presents into it. He figured she had her own personal Pez collection stashed away someplace, but it had been a gamble just the same.

"I hope you don't have those already. I mean, they have a ton in there. I could always go—" Her quiet laugh cut off his rambling.

"I'm sure you didn't come here to talk about Pez dispensers, did you, Nick?" Lynette crossed the room again and stood in front of him, staring at him through clear eyes.

Nick held her gaze and wondered how she managed to pull it off.

Innocence wed with wisdom that went beyond her years.

Everything about her exuded radiance, a goodness he wasn't worthy of. Her undefined beauty took him by surprise each time he saw her now. She was the girl next door in so many ways—her long honey-colored hair, cute upturned nose, the sparkle in her eyes when she smiled—she didn't have Mindy's supermodel looks; there was nothing ravishing about her. Some may call her plain.

He would call her beautiful.

"Nick? Are you okay?"

Once again he found himself at a loss for words

This was getting tiresome.

"Uh. Sure."

"Well." She gave a half smile and shrugged. "I don't like these kinds of conversations, so I'll just get on with it. Just so we're both on the same page . . . Last weekend, on the beach . . . Was it my imagination or did you almost kiss me?"

She might as well have smacked him. "Wow, Lynnie."

"Wow, Lynnie?" She put one hand on her hip and frowned. "That's all you have to say? Because I'm pretty sure you told me you had a girlfriend. And I'm not about to get tangled up in that kind of mess, Nick. I have way more important things to worry about. Do you get what I'm saying?"

"Yes. I get it." He thanked God she didn't expound further. He already knew he was an idiot. "Can I apologize?"

"If you think you need to." Her smile returned and he couldn't tell whether she was teasing or not. The back of his neck tingled and he cursed this vixen who'd come out of nowhere and replaced his sweet, innocent Lynnie.

"Look"—he raked his fingers through his hair—"I'm sorry, but I'm not. I mean, I am, but . . . uh, I have no idea how to say this."

"I never would have guessed."

That smile was brutal—a volleyball slamming into his gut and knocking the wind out of him. Nick almost wanted to lean over and suck in air until he got his brain back. "Okay. The girlfriend thing . . . it's sort of a non-issue."

"Define non-issue."

"It's complicated." He reached for her hand, but she took a step back. "I'm not involved with Mindy Vanguard. Not in that way."

She rolled her eyes with an I've-heard-it-all-before expression. She wasn't the first woman to use it on him, but it made him doubt she'd put much stock in anything he'd come here to say. "Whatever, Nick. I've got enough to worry about right now."

"I know." He blinked and wished for words to prove he wasn't a complete moron. "And I know I sound like an idiot, but—"

"Let's just forget it." She glanced at her watch, then back at him. "I don't want to be rude, but I really have to go. Joanne needs to lock up." She was definitely annoyed, and he couldn't blame her.

Dark shadows under her eyes and the listless way she moved across the room gave him cause for concern. Nick wasn't ready to let her out of his sight yet. "How about I buy you and the midget some pizza?"

"The midget's name is Tyler." Her sigh said she still wasn't sure. "Okay. He doesn't have a dad around, so he'll latch onto you like a leech. But if you're up for it . . ."

Nick held out a hand. "Let's do it."

~

After dinner, they went to the park and sat on a bench while Tyler played.

"Thanks, Nick. This was nice." Lynette seemed more relaxed, so he took a chance and reached for her hand. To his relief, she didn't pull away, and they sat quietly for a while. Finally he let out a long breath.

"My dad has cancer." The whispered words hung on the air in a soundless echo.

"Oh, Nick." Lynette swiveled to face him at once. "That's why you came back."

He ran a hand across his eyes and nodded. "He . . . uh . . . came to see me last year when I was working in New York. Asked if I would consider coming back here, taking over from him. Of course he wouldn't tell me why, so I said no. A month later the company I was working for went under. I stayed in the city, hoping to find a new position, but nothing came up. And something kept tugging me back here."

Lynette covered his hand with hers. "Sometimes God talks like that, Nick. That weird feeling you just can't shake."

"I guess. I couldn't figure out why he wanted me back here so badly. Then I got a call from a hospital in Boston. He'd started radiation and had an adverse reaction. They almost lost him." Nick shuddered. "That's how I found out."

"Why wouldn't he just tell you?"

He gave a short laugh. "I have no idea what makes my father tick. He still won't talk to me about it. But he must be scared. For the first time in his life, he has to deal with something he can't control."

"But you're here. Surely that means something to him."

"Who knows?" Nick shrugged. He'd given up trying to figure out Anthony Cooper years ago. "I'd like to improve our relationship, I'm just not sure how. Whenever I feel like I'm up to the challenge, he opens his mouth and says something that makes me want to pin him against the wall."

"How bad is it, the cancer?"

"Bad." He gave a small groan. "But knowing him, he'll beat the odds and live to be a hundred, just to spite me."

"Nick." She sat close and held his hand tighter. "Thank you for telling me."

"I . . . needed to." He couldn't explain it. But he knew, outside of Cecily, she was the only person who really understood the complicated relationship he had with his father. He slid his hand from hers and gently pulled her toward him. And then he risked it all.

His lips moved over hers in a tentative question.

Lynette's answer was an almost silent groan that died in her throat as her arms came around his neck. She wove her fingers through his hair and allowed him to kiss her like he'd wanted to for weeks. Her response validated his own feelings, frightened him a little, but finally gave him the freedom to acknowledge just how much she meant to him.

"Gross." Tyler stood a few feet away, staring in disgust.

They broke away from each other, laughing.

"Okay, okay." Lynette smiled and got to her feet. "I'm glad you came home, Nick."

"Me too, Lynnie." He leaned forward for another brief kiss. "For a lot of reasons."

Chapter Seventeen

Lynette let herself in to the darkened house just after one in the morning. Saturday again. She hadn't seen Nick since their pizza dinner with Tyler last Friday. Working at The Longshoreman, combined with her day job and the extra babysitting she was doing, was proving to be exhausting. She might sleep in if David didn't have so much around the house to take his frustrations out on. Perhaps she should suggest he work on getting the gardens tidied up. Although knowing David, he'd start with a chain saw to a couple of the overgrown trees.

The dogs greeted her in the hall and she whispered her hellos to them, stopped when she spied a light on in the living room.

"Liz?" Lynette entered the room and allowed her eyes to adjust. "Hi, I'm home."

Her sister sat on the couch, twirling a wine glass between her fingers. A half-empty bottle sat on the floor beside her. Liz jerked her head up as though she'd almost been asleep. She put the glass down and pushed hair out of her eyes. "How was babysitting?"

"Fine." Lynette smothered a yawn. "Was Dad okay?"

"He was good. We actually played backgammon." Liz's tearful laugh echoed through the semidarkness. "He beat me."

"He was always the best at that game." Lynette kicked off her shoes and sank into a chair. Liz looked relaxed in a pair of yoga pants and baggy T-shirt, her hair tied in a messy ponytail. She'd probably die if anyone from the city saw her. "How did he seem, otherwise? Was he talkative?"

Liz pinched the bridge of her nose and sniffed. "He was, actually. It was almost like . . . old times." She reached for a tissue from the box on the round table beside the couch and wiped her eyes.

Lynette nodded, her throat tight. Dad's moments of lucidity were growing increasingly rare, but when they came, she embraced them for all they were worth. She was glad for her sister.

"Why do you smell like you've been working in a diner?" Liz screwed up her nose and reached for the pair of glasses on the couch beside her.

"I grilled burgers for the kids." *God, forgive me.* Never the best liar, she was glad for the dimness of the room.

"This babysitting job seems a lot for you to take on, Lynnie. Three nights a week, plus working at the day care and taking care of Dad?"

As always, Liz was right. It was too much. But Lynette bristled, indignation scratching at old wounds. "If you can't manage Dad, just say so. It's only for a few weeks."

"I can manage Dad just fine." Liz pushed herself up, her eyes narrowing. "You're not the only one who can look after him, you know. He's my father too."

Lynette folded her arms, heat rushing to her cheeks. "Since when do you care?"

"Excuse me?"

"You've never bothered to hide your feelings about Dad. All you can say is what a no-good drunk he used to be, what a rotten father he was, a terrible husband, a—"

"Lynnie, stop." Liz put up a hand and shook her head. "Where is this coming from?"

"It's true." She drew her knees to her chest. She'd opened the vault to her feelings now. "Ever since Mom died. You made up excuses not to come home on weekends and holidays. You hated talking to him on the phone. You—"

"He *was* a drunk, Lynnie."

"I'm well aware, Liz. I lived with him." Something all of them seemed to have conveniently forgotten. "You guys were all off doing your own things. I was the one who had to put up with it! So don't tell me what Dad was."

"I'm sorry." Liz's expression softened. "It wasn't always that way. Back before you were born . . . he was different. I was his favorite, you know. We'd go everywhere together. He used to call me his little princess. Oh, he loved the boys, too, but I was special. And then you came along, and suddenly I wasn't all that important anymore."

"That's not true." Lynette could give a hundred excuses. It was the alcohol talking. The late hour. But Liz's acrid tone could not be ignored.

Her sister's jealousy ran deep. Always had. It was the elephant in the room that Liz fed and Lynette did her best to sidestep, ignore, and hoped eventually would go away.

It never did.

And now it faced her head-on, ears back, threatening to plow her down.

"I don't remember things like you do, Liz. Maybe I wasn't old enough." Moxie jumped onto her lap and she ran her fingers over the soft fur. "The first time I realized how much Dad drank was after Mom's funeral."

"Then you were lucky." Liz pulled her hair out of the elastic band, tied it up again, and shook her head with a look of disgust. "He drank all the time when you were little. They both did."

"That's not true." She was starting to sound like a broken record.

Liz sat forward, rare emotion standing in her eyes. "Do you know what a functional alcoholic is?"

"Not really."

"It's someone who drinks more than average amounts, yet still manages to cope like they don't, holds down a job, appears fine to people who don't know any better." Liz swiped a hand across her flushed face. "I can't remember a day when they weren't mixing something or other in the blender or sipping champagne on the porch. I didn't know that wasn't normal until I went away to school and started visiting my friends' homes. I'm not saying they were bad parents, because they weren't. They just . . . they were different. After Mom died, Dad stopped caring how much he drank."

Memories remained out of reach. Safely packed away and hidden under a blanket of self-preservation. And, for once, Lynette willed them to stay there. "All I remember is the dancing, the laughter. We had so much fun, Liz. They were always so happy."

Her sister tipped her head, an almost amused smile perched on her lips. "So you don't remember the time Mom tried to clock Dad in the head with a frozen leg of lamb?"

"What?"

Liz took off her glasses and wiped them with the bottom of her T-shirt. "Well, I guess you were around nine. I forget what they were fighting about—they were both so dramatic. It could have been about a load of laundry for all I know. Dad ducked and it went right through the kitchen window."

Lynette swallowed a giggle. "I do remember the time he was supposed to go to an art show or something in New York. Mom didn't want him to go. She paid Gray and Nick to let the air out of his tires. We ran off down the beach once the yelling started."

Liz laughed and nodded. "Do you remember the way Mom looked when she'd get all dressed up, ready for a night of entertaining? She was so beautiful. I used to wonder if I'd ever be half as pretty as she was."

"I think you are, Liz. You're just as beautiful as she was." Lynette smiled at the tears in her sister's eyes.

"Thanks, Lynnie." Liz smiled back, a real smile. One Lynette hadn't seen for a long time.

She closed her eyes for a moment. "Remember that song Dad would always sing to Mom . . . What was it? . . . 'Hey, did you happen to see . . .'"

"'The most beautiful girl in the world . . .'" Liz cleared her throat and played with the collection of silver bangles on her wrist. She stayed quiet for a bit. Then she looked up and met Lynette's eyes. "He told me once, one of the few times I came home after she died, that he always knew she'd find somebody else."

The temperature in the room seemed to drop. The dogs paced and the wind blew against the windowpanes. Something Lynette couldn't explain, fear or foreboding or something worse, took hold. "What do you think he meant by that?"

"I don't know." Liz's genuine smile was replaced with the one she used whenever anybody got too close. The one that held up a hand and said, *That's enough, back up.* "He was pretty out of it when he said it." She waved a hand. "Don't listen to me. It's late. I've had too much wine. I don't know what I'm talking about."

"It is late." Lynette didn't want to press the point. A yawn escaped her on cue. "I'm sorry, you know, if I ever did anything that made you think Dad liked me best."

"Forget it. I shouldn't have said that." Liz wrinkled her nose. "You really do stink. That must have been some heavy-duty barbe-que you had going."

"Yeah." Lynette didn't have to lie this time. "You wouldn't believe it if you saw it."

"I'm sure." Her sister tossed a magazine in her direction. "Saved this for you."

It was one of those gossip publications, the ones Lynette only scanned while waiting in line at the grocery store. She picked it up a little warily. "If it's about Gray . . ."

"Oh, it's not." Liz lifted a thin eyebrow. "I thought you might be interested in checking out your competition. Miss Vanguard, and I quote, 'the sometimes-girlfriend of Nantucket's own version of celebrity-style hotness, Mr. Nicholas Cooper,' appears on page fifteen."

"Oh." Lynette scanned the article while sudden, unwanted tears filled her eyes. "But he . . . It's just . . ." It couldn't be true. What about that kiss last Friday night? Maybe Nick and Mindy really were dating. Did she know for sure Nick was telling her the truth? "This is just gossip, Liz." It had to be.

It better be.

Liz moved closer and nudged her shoulder. "Hey. We all know you had a crush on him when you were a kid. But I suspect it's a bit more than that now, isn't it?"

Lynette stared at her sister and struggled for words. "I was beginning to believe the feeling was mutual. But I suppose I can't compete with her." She dropped the magazine to the floor and wiped her eyes.

"Oh, sweetie." Liz ran a finger over Lynette's wet cheek. "You have so much more going for you than that ditz. And if Nick Cooper doesn't see that, then he's not worth it."

Chapter Eighteen

Nick sat on the dock at the yacht club that Sunday afternoon, watched the boats come and go, and wondered how long he could stand the status quo. He'd met up with a couple of buddies earlier for a sail, but hadn't stayed out long. His heart wasn't in it.

Lynette Carlisle had infiltrated a part of him he'd long believed impenetrable.

The more time he spent with her, the easier it became to forget where he'd been, what he'd done.

He was even beginning to believe in second chances.

A blast of U2 rang out from the pocket of his shorts and he fished out his phone.

"I miss you. When are you coming back to the city?" Mindy's voice crooned in his ear. Nick scratched his head and tried to muffle a sigh.

"You're up early for a Sunday."

"I couldn't sleep, Nicky. I was dreaming about you."

"Mindy, seriously, stop." Nick cut off her laughter. "Have you talked to your folks? Are we done with this stupid game of yours?"

"Not yet." She gave an irritating sigh. "I'm just reminding you about the party next weekend. Your father says you're coming."

"Oh, come on." The upcoming shindig at the Vanguard's Cape Cod estate was the last place he wanted to be. Mindy was in no apparent hurry to make any rash moves.

"I told you I want out of this, Mindy. I wasn't making that up."

"I know, Nicholas. You've been perfectly clear." The chill in her voice reminded him of the frosty margaritas she liked so much.

"Do you really think this is fair to me?"

"Like you care what I think. As I said, I need time to sort things out. Daddy isn't in a good mood that often. I can't just spring this on him."

Nick swatted at a fly. "It's not rocket science. 'Dad, I'm in love with Horse. We're getting married.' I don't see the problem."

"It's Horst, Nick."

"Really?" He was glad she couldn't see his face, but he kind of wanted to see hers. He heard her shaky intake of breath. "Okay, sorry. Just don't take too long with this, please?"

"You know your father isn't going to be happy either."

That he did. "Yeah. But you know what? I really don't care anymore."

"I hope she's worth it." She clicked off and Nick let out a groan, stared at his phone, and contemplated hurling it into the sea.

"Thought that was you, Cooper."

Nick looked up and saw David Carlisle walking toward him. "Hey, David."

"Been out on the water?"

"For a bit this morning." Usually a few hours out there remedied all his problems. Not today.

"You sailing in Race Week?"

"Maybe. Jordy Cox is putting a crew together. What've you been up to?"

"Had lunch with a couple of friends."

Nick didn't mask surprise when David lowered himself onto the bench beside him. "Sure you want to risk that? Gray might never talk to you again."

David whipped off his cap and pushed fingers through his hair. "Some days that would be a blessing."

"How's he doing?"

"Who knows?" David shrugged. A few days' worth of stubble covered his lower jaw. "He's been seeing a doctor. Seems to be serious about quitting."

"You think he needs more rehab?" Some intensive psychotherapy might be advisable, too, but Nick wouldn't go there.

"Doesn't matter much what I think." David pulled a stray thread at the bottom of his madras shorts. "Why don't you put your own crew together, Coop? I'll sail with you. Be like old times. We can drag Gray along too."

Nick laughed at that. "Last time I saw your brother he could barely stand. Are you sure he can find his sea legs?"

"He'd have to find his brain first, but yeah." David rolled his eyes. "Be good to get him out of the house, give him something to do."

"Sure." Nick doubted Gray would give the suggestion a second thought. He also doubted any of them would still be here next month. "You've been working pretty hard over there. The front looks good."

On his way to work every morning Nick saw David up a ladder, repairing shutters, painting, and who knows what else. A couple mornings Gray had been outside as well, shuffling around, coffee in hand, trying to look busy. Nick was always half tempted to stop in, but never did.

"It's a money pit is what it is." David leaned forward and scratched his leg. "Can't wait to get rid of it."

Nick shoved down a sigh. "You're really going to sell?"

"You got a better idea?" Shadows underlined his eyes and made Nick wonder how much sleep the man was getting.

Had Lynette told her siblings about the bed-and-breakfast idea? He'd have to talk to her about that again. The idea wasn't totally ludicrous. And he hated the thought of Wyldewood falling into his father's hands. "What if I did?"

David's quizzical expression almost made Nick think he was talking to Drake. While Liz, Gray, and Lynnie had inherited Diana's fair hair and blue eyes, David and Ryan were all Drake.

"What, Nick? Just say what's on your mind."

Nick shrugged. "Let me talk to Lynnie first. She had an idea. There might be another option."

David didn't seem enthused. "Well, we still can't get hold of Ryan. I don't know if we can sidestep that stupid stipulation in my mother's will if he doesn't show up." He pulled out his phone, studied it a minute, and shoved it back into his pocket.

Nick nodded. "Look, I know Gray doesn't want me hanging around, but if there's anything I can do . . ."

David stretched and let out a long groan. "Maybe Gray needs to let it go." He stared Nick down, unsmiling. "I need to ask you something."

"Okay." Nick wiped damp palms on his shorts, tapped his Docksiders together, and waited.

David twisted the gold band on his finger. "Gray came to see me. The week after you guys had that fight over Christmas, when was it . . . a few years ago."

"Five." Nick knew what was coming, no time to prepare.

"I need to know if what you told him is true." Something flickered in the other man's eyes—doubt, hesitation, Nick didn't know. But he sensed David already knew the answer to the question.

"Gray was my best friend." Nick worked to keep emotion out of his voice. "Why would I make something like that up?"

David pushed at a small mound of sand with the tip of his sneaker and swore. "How did you find out?"

Sea gulls swooped around the masts of the yachts in berth. Music blared from a couple of the boats as crews swabbed down decks and polished brass. A group of grade-schoolers walked past wearing orange life jackets, heading toward the Sunfishes, and reminded him of happier days.

Nick's chest rose and fell as he struggled for the right words.

"I saw them. The first time, I was twelve. The summer my folks divorced and my mother left. They were in the pool house. I was supposed to be with a friend, but I wasn't feeling well so I came home."

"There were other times?" David's voice hitched and he cleared his throat. He didn't look at Nick.

"Yes. She . . . your mom, uh . . . she would come over . . . to the house. My dad didn't care at that point. I don't think she thought I'd think twice about it." His throat closed, further explanation impossible. Unnecessary.

Nick leaned back, inhaled salty air and sun block, and remembered.

~

Diana Carlisle appeared in his doorway, unannounced, unexpected. "What are you working on, Nick?" She wandered into his bedroom like she had every reason to be there. A thin cotton dress hugged her slender frame. At thirteen, Nick was just beginning to appreciate her beauty. What he didn't appreciate or understand was the way she flaunted it in front of his father.

He was so surprised to see her, he didn't attempt to hide the drawings spread out across his desk. She scanned his sketches of buildings and houses and tilted her head, a smile sitting pretty on her lips. "These are wonderful, sweetheart. I didn't know you were so talented." She rested a light hand on his back, the heat of her touch making him want to jump from his chair.

He stayed put, pushed hair out of his eyes, and squinted up at her. "I want to be an architect. My father wants me to be a lawyer. Or work at the bank."

Her eyes were bloodshot, her cheeks flushed. A hint of rum mingled with her sweet perfume. She crouched before him, held his wrists, and stared at him through sad eyes. "You listen to me, Nicholas. Don't let him control you. You're too good for that, you hear me? You can do whatever you want. Follow your heart, darling. Promise me?"

"Sure." Nick swallowed down a weird lump in his throat and forgot about asking why she was here.

"I have to go." She smiled, stood, and pressed her warm cheek to his. "Don't tell anyone you saw me, okay, Nick?"

~

Nick clasped his hands behind his head, his stomach churning. "She didn't think I would know what was going on."

"Guess she underestimated you." David batted his cap against the palm of his hand. "My mother was pretty naïve. A free spirit. Did her own thing most of the time, didn't care what anyone thought."

"I'm sure she never intended to hurt any of . . . you." He'd almost said *us*. But he didn't have the right to include himself anymore.

David lifted his shoulders, his eyes too bright. "I was already away at school when my parents started having problems. I didn't realize how bad it was. How much my dad was drinking. Or how she must have hated it."

Nick pinched the bridge of his nose. "I don't think anyone else knew. After your mom died, I tried not to think about it. Until that day during Christmas break. Gray was so angry with your dad. I just . . . I didn't want him blaming Drake. I should have kept my mouth shut."

"Did my father know about the affair?"

Nick pondered the question. "Yeah, I'm pretty sure he did."

"So wouldn't that have given him reason to . . . I mean . . . I don't know." David smacked his cap again and stared at his feet. "I wish I would have woken up that day. Heard something earlier."

A ripple of fear made its way down Nick's spine. "David, your dad would never have—"

"I don't know what he was capable of, Nick. When he was drunk . . . well . . ."

"But the police didn't take it any further; there wasn't an investigation. It was an accident."

"Yeah. That's what they said." David's voice dropped. "You haven't spoken to Lynnie about any of this, have you?"

Nick was quick to shake his head. "No. I don't intend to."

"Good." David pulled his cap back on. "She's stressed enough with working and worrying about Dad. And now she's got this babysitting job."

Lynette was going to land herself in the hospital if she wasn't careful. "How long is she doing that for?"

"I didn't ask. Well." David gave a half laugh. "I have a meeting with your father next week. Wants to talk to me about some hotel chain that might be interested in the house. That'll be fun."

"He'd never tell Lynnie about the affair, if that's what you're worried about."

"How do you know that?" David's eyes scrunched together.

Nick watched a long navy sloop head out to sea, white sails billowing as it picked up speed. Wondered if Gray would actually consider sailing with him again. "He just wouldn't." Somehow he had to believe that.

"If you say so." David cracked his knuckles and gave him a sidelong glance. "What's up with you and my sister, Cooper?"

Nick allowed a smile and crossed one leg over his knee. "Not much." Not as much as he wanted.

David nailed him with a look Nick recognized all too well. "Like I said, Lynnie has enough to worry about. You'll answer to me if you hurt her. I'm sure you understand."

"Yeah, I understand. Your sister isn't a kid anymore. You can't order her around. Me either, by the way."

"Look . . ."

Nick pushed to his feet. "Trust me, Lynnie is the last person in the world I want to see hurt. She's been through enough."

"Yes, she has." David stood shoulder to shoulder with him. "What are your intentions?"

Nick tried not to laugh and wondered if the guy knew how eighteenth century he sounded. "Uh, I don't exactly have any. I mean, I'm not about to propose or anything, if that's what you're asking."

"Do I have your word that you won't hurt her?"

Nick rolled his eyes, pushed his arms high over his head, and stretched. "Relax. Lynnie and I are friends. That's all there is to it right now." But as soon as Mindy got her act together, he hoped that would change in a hurry.

"Fine." David pulled on a pair of shades and jangled his keys. "There's something else."

"What?"

"It's about Cecily. Lynnie thanked me for getting her to come back. The thing is, I didn't. Neither did Liz or Gray. Did you hire her to come back and work at the house?"

Nick ran his tongue over his sunburned lips and stared at his shoes.

"Nick, we can't pay—"

"I'm not asking you to." He jerked his head up, indignation taking him by surprise.

"You don't owe us anything." David gave a wan smile. "You know that, right?"

Nick shrugged and tried to look convinced.

"Well, thanks." David smiled. "Anyway. Guess I better head home. Going to start replacing the shingles around back this afternoon."

Nick nodded, checked his watch for no particular reason. "Need a hand?"

David raised an eyebrow. "Sure, if you've got nothing else to do."

"Nope."

Nick followed David up to the club. He felt drained from the morning's sun, sea air, and David's questions.

Maybe he should stop kidding himself. What he really wanted was so far out of reach, so far beyond reason, it bordered on the ridiculous. And were she to ever learn the truth about their parents . . . the whole situation was far too sticky for his liking.

Maybe the sooner the Carlisles fixed up the place, sold it, and moved out, the better.

Chapter Nineteen

L ynnie, you're killing me!"
  Lynette squeezed the brakes, stopped her bike, and turned.
Gray pedaled up behind her, red-faced and none too happy about
it. She smothered a laugh. "Come on, slowpoke. The windmill is
just around the corner." It had taken some convincing, but eventually he'd agreed to a bike ride.

Gray stopped next to her, panting. "You do know CPR, right?"
He took off his shades and reached for his water bottle. "I'm so out
of shape it's not even funny."

She let him rest a minute, then pushed forward. "Let's go.
You'll feel better when we get there." The Prospect Street bike path
was one of her favorite jaunts, but it had been some time since she'd
enjoyed a bike ride.

They soon pulled off the road and sat on the grassy embankment
by the old windmill. Lynette smiled as she watched Gray stretch out.
She'd kept an eye on him the whole way, in case he passed out on her,
but despite his complaints to the contrary, he looked okay.

"Here." She pulled out a couple of granola bars wrapped in
clear plastic from her backpack and tossed one his way. "Victoria
made these. They're really good."

Gray opened one eye. "Any spinach in them?"

"Not that I know of." If there was, she'd never tell.

She drank from her own water bottle and flexed her feet. A

breeze cooled her face and she relaxed to the creaking of the blades as the windmill turned.

"This place is old as dirt, huh?" Gray sat up and adjusted the blue bandana around his head. The past few weeks seemed to have worked some magic on her brother. The sun gave color to his nose and cheeks, his eyes starting to sparkle the way they used to. He looked a little less like a Tim Burton character.

Lynette stared at the gray structure with its red lattice arms and nodded. "It was built in 1746. Pretty old."

"How do you remember this stuff, Shortstop?" Gray laughed and threw some water in her direction.

"I don't know." But it was a good question. Why did she remember facts and figures of no real importance and not her own past? She bent over and undid the laces of her sneakers and freed her feet.

He stretched out again, one arm flung over his eyes.

"Gray?"

"Yeah?"

Lynette tapped sand out of her sneakers. "Is there a story between you and Victoria?"

A muted sigh slipped out. "You could say that."

"Is it a sad one?"

Gray folded his arms across his chest. "Very sad."

"Oh." She was almost sorry she'd asked. "Well. I like her, Gray."

The corner of his mouth curled upward. "Me too, Lynnie."

Lynette bent over her legs and pulled back on her toes, feeling her spine loosen. "Thanks for coming with me today."

"Did I have a choice? You know I'd still be asleep, right?"

"At three in the afternoon?" She nudged him with her foot. "I sure hope not."

"Hey, I work nights." He struggled up with a dramatic groan. "Used to."

So did she, but he didn't need to know it.

Lynette wondered what to say next. Since he'd come home

they hadn't had a sincere conversation about anything. Just argued mainly, about Nick, the house, and Dad's failing health.

Gray took a long swig from his water bottle, put it down, and smothered a belch a little late. "I owe you an apology."

"For that?"

"Not for that." He held her gaze for a moment. "You know what I'm talking about."

"Probably." Lynette wrestled with upended emotions. "Where would you like to start?"

He narrowed his eyes and fiddled with the thin silver hoop in his ear. "Where do you want me to start?"

Old grief settled in again.

The question was impossible to answer.

Years ago he'd never have complained about coming on a bike ride. She and Gray spent hours outside, exploring the garden, roaming the beach, riding the path they'd come down today. They were closest in age, and he never seemed to mind spending time with her. She could tell him anything without fear of judgment or teasing. Yet somehow she'd always known he'd go—known he would one day leave the place he'd come to loathe—but she never believed he would leave her behind.

~

"I'm going to get out of here one day, Lynnie."

They sat on the wall at the end of the garden facing the ocean, feet dangling over the side. The practice was strictly forbidden, which made it all the more exciting. Gray tossed pebbles onto the rocks below and they watched them disappear into the white foam of the waves. Lynette glanced back over her shoulder. If Mom or Dad found them sitting on the wall, they'd be locked inside for a year.

"Why do you want to leave so bad?" Life was pretty good as far as she could tell. Parties, barbeques, staying up late all summer, sometimes even on school nights in the fall, before it got too cold. And on days when Mom's headaches were too bad for her to drive, they got to stay home from school.

Gray pulled his arm back and released another fistful of pebbles, and they waited to see if any of them would hit the water. "You're only nine. You wouldn't understand."

Lynette rolled her eyes. She hated when he acted all superior. "Well, you're not so grown up. You're not even twelve yet."

"Almost. And when I get out of here, I'm going to make my own rules. Nobody's ever going to tell me what to do."

"Who tells you what to do anyways? You get away with everything."

"Yeah. Maybe." He nudged her with his elbow and she gripped the edge of the wall, just in case.

"What were Mom and Dad yelling about this afternoon, Gray?"

"Who cares? They're always yelling." But he moved a little closer until their legs were touching. His were starting to get prickly with thicker blond hairs.

"They always yell after parties, like when the Coopers are over." Lynette rubbed her sunburned nose, pulled at a piece of skin. Mr. Cooper and Daddy were supposed to be friends, but they sure knew how to argue like worst enemies.

"That's grown-ups for you."

"I don't like it." She turned her head a bit, just to make sure he wouldn't laugh. "I get scared, Gray."

"You don't need to be scared." Her brother put an arm around her shoulder. This was so unexpected and surprising that her fears suddenly didn't seem so stupid. "Whatever happens, I won't leave you. You don't need to worry about that. You can come with me, okay?"

~

Lynette wiped her eyes without Gray seeing and watched a couple of cars go by. A few other bikers passed. White strips of clouds crossed the sky, spread out toward the sun.

Finally she found her voice. "I want to know why you left. Why you cut me out of your life." It was almost a whisper. A thought she'd wrapped up and put away some time ago. But he'd given her permission to open it.

Gray's blue eyes settled on her. He raised a trembling hand and pulled the bandana off his head, swatted it against his knees, and sighed. "I had a lot of reasons for leaving. None of them had anything to do with you."

Moisture pushed over the rims of her lids. "That summer you were going to work at the yacht club and head back to college in the fall, the next minute you were off to California. You walked out of our lives. A phone call once in a blue moon doesn't qualify as making an effort to maintain a relationship. I was still in high school. I . . . I needed you."

"I couldn't take it anymore."

"What does that even mean?"

"You know what Dad was like."

Lynette sniffed but refused to look away. "Yeah. I do. Probably better than any of you."

Gray reached for her hand. "Lynnie, did he ever—"

"No." She snatched her hand back. "He was never violent. Never abusive. Usually all he wanted to do was sleep. We'd have dinner, he'd pretend to eat, then he'd go into the den, drink, and pass out in front of the television. And you have no right to judge him, Gray. Look in the mirror."

His silence hinted that she might have crossed the line.

But she didn't care anymore.

"You're right," he said after a few uneasy moments. "I know I can't make it up to you. I can apologize a hundred times over, but it won't change a thing. Could we just maybe . . . start over?"

She stared at the windmill again. Hundreds of years old, it withstood the test of time, weathered island storms, and still held firm. She wasn't that strong.

All the long, lonely nights missing her family. Wondering where Gray was, if he was okay. Getting the odd phone call now and then at all hours, hardly being able to understand the slurred words.

"Lynnie, I'm trying here."

"I know you are." There was still so much pain she couldn't push past. "I don't understand, Gray." She remembered the young jock, the sailor. "You were always so gung ho on staying healthy. Eating right. I know you liked to party but . . . I don't get it. Why drugs?"

"I don't know. Most addicts can't answer that question." Gray rubbed his chin. "Pressure, I guess. When things started to pick up with my career, part of me was scared I wasn't going to make it. Wouldn't be able to live up to the expectations everyone was putting on me." He pulled his knees to his chest and locked his arms around them. "At first it was fun, something everyone around me was doing. So I figured once or twice at parties wouldn't hurt. I never believed I'd become addicted, but then I got sucked in. Ended up in the School of Doing Things the Hard Way, got my degree in Stupid."

Lynette managed a weak smile. "Hope you didn't pay too much for that."

"I paid enough." His jaw twitched the way it always did when he was hiding something.

But she couldn't force it from him.

Wouldn't.

She moved closer and put an arm around his shoulders. "I love you, you know. But I need to know you're going to be honest with me, Gray. No calling and telling me everything's fine when it's not. If you want me in your life, I need to know what's going on with you."

He shrugged out of her embrace and inched away. The wall went back up. "You wanted me to tell you I was a junkie? That I was in rehab? You really wanted to hear that?"

"I would have preferred to hear it from you instead of Cecily."

He drummed out a beat on the side of his water bottle. "I didn't want you to know. I don't like what I've become. The look you're giving me right now is exactly the one I wanted to avoid."

"I would never judge you. I hope you know that. And whether it means anything to you or not, I'm praying. I really believe you can do this, Gray."

"Thanks, Lynnie. Seems you've got lots to pray about these days, huh?" He gave a short laugh. "What do you think God would do with someone like me?"

A lump pressed against her throat and she wiped her eyes. "Love you. There isn't anything you could do to make Him stop, Gray."

His faraway look said it was too much, too soon. "I haven't had a whole lot of faith lately. Not like you."

She gave a shaky sigh and met his eyes. "I haven't had a whole lot of faith lately either, but I'm trying to. I have to believe God's going to work all this out."

Gray nodded. "I'm sorry I can't help with the house. I don't have the kind of money needed to get the place back in shape. I know you don't want to sell."

She'd figured as much, but the truth of it squeezed her heart. "It's all right."

Gray scooched closer and took her hand. "But it's not, is it?"

Lynette lifted her shoulders. "I'll deal with it. At least we've all been able to spend some time together."

"And lived to tell the tale." His sly look hinted at old mischief. "So far."

If only Ryan would show up. And perhaps she could get the others on board with her idea before he did.

The very thought now seemed silly—but something made her forge ahead anyway. "I thought maybe, if we could afford it or get a loan somehow, we could renovate. Turn the place into a bed-and-breakfast. Lots of people around here have done that the past few years."

"Yeah?" A new light flickered in his eyes. "That's not a bad idea."

"That's what Nick said too. He thought that with the right investors, people really interested in saving the property, instead of just handing it over to a hotel chain, the idea might fly."

Gray rubbed his face, groaned low, and nailed her with his eyes again. "I wish you hadn't—"

"What, Gray? You wish I hadn't talked to Nick?" Sudden anger came out of nowhere. "At least he listened. There wasn't anyone else to talk to."

"I don't trust him."

"I don't believe that." The uncomfortable knot in her stomach pulled in on itself. "What's with the two of you? Can't you just get past it?"

"Nope. And I'm not telling you, so quit asking." Gray turned his attention to the windmill. "Why is he hanging around all the time, anyway?"

"Maybe because it's better than being at home with his father."

Gray knew Nick's history better than anyone.

She saw a spark of recognition in his eyes. "Did you ever think he might have regrets too, Gray? That he might want to work things out with you?"

Her brother pouted like a two-year-old.

"If you're going to make changes in your life, you should start with a big one. It's called forgiveness."

"Are you just saying this because you think he's hot?"

"Shut up." She smacked his arm. "I'm saying it because it's true. Nick's like part of the family, Gray. He was your best friend. At least think about it."

He raised his hands and glowered. "Enough already. I'll think about it." He pulled the bandana back over his damp hair and flexed his arms. "So do you like him? I mean, like him, like him."

Lynette stared at her hands and willed away the heat that rushed to her cheeks. "It doesn't matter if I do, I guess. Apparently he's seeing Mindy Vanguard." She was going to confront Nick about that kiss. The moment his lips had touched hers, her entire being lit with a warmth she couldn't explain. Being in Nick's arms felt like the most natural thing in the world. She could quite happily have allowed him to kiss her all night. And now she wondered if it would ever happen again.

"So he's just messing with you? Because from what I've seen, he seems to be interested in more than just friendship with you. And you want me to trust him?"

"We are friends, Gray. That's it." She couldn't mask her irritation. A car honking pulled their attention toward the road. Lynette watched Nick's Jeep pull up. "Speak of the devil."

"And he always shows up." Gray moaned like a dying cow and flopped back on the grass.

"Search and rescue at your service." Nick jogged across the road to where they sat. He wore baggy beige shorts and a Stones T-shirt that had seen better days. His blond hair was tousled and dirt streaked his face.

"What in the world have you been up to?" Lynette almost didn't want to know.

"Helping David replace shingles on the house. They said you'd been out awhile. Liz was about ready to call the police, so I offered to come look for you."

"We haven't been gone that long." Lynette hated the way her pulse picked up the minute he met her eyes.

Nick nodded toward Gray. "I think Liz thought this one might not make it home."

Gray sat up and yawned, rubbing the small of his back. "She

thought right. Please tell me that is a bike rack on the back of your Jeep."

"That is a bike rack on the back of my Jeep." Nick brushed sand off his shorts and pulled on the brim of his Yankees cap.

"Praise the Lord." Gray struggled to his feet. "Don't get too excited, Coop, but I do have to say that for once, I'm actually glad to see you."

Chapter Twenty

Lynette organized a barbeque that night. Jed didn't need her, so she fully intended to enjoy the evening off, even if it was spent grilling more burgers. Nick stayed, under protest from Gray, but Lynette informed her brother that if he wished to eat, he'd keep his opinions to himself. So far they'd survived the evening without war breaking out.

After dinner, once she'd settled Dad in front of the television, Nick found her in the kitchen, fixing coffee.

She glanced at him and tension crept across her shoulders.

He raised a brow, grabbed a dishcloth, and began to dry the stack of dishes she'd washed. "Is it my imagination or have you been avoiding me all night?"

She blew out a breath and put her back to him, watching dark liquid drip into the carafe. "Not avoiding you."

"Well, you haven't said two words to me. Did I do something to upset you, Lynnie?"

"Fine." She turned his way with a scowl. "Yes. You told me there was nothing going on with you and Mindy. So why do I see some stupid magazine article my sister showed me, all about you and her? Seriously, Nick. I told you, I'm not going to—"

"Lynnie, stop." Nick was beside her in two strides, his hands on her arms. "It's not what you think."

"How is it not what I think? I'm not an idiot, Nick, and I don't really care. But I don't want to be played for a fool." She blinked hot tears and rolled her eyes at her traitorous emotions.

"You don't care, huh?" He cupped her face and wiped her tears with the base of his thumbs. His touch sent a shiver through her.

"Shut up." A sigh slipped out as she grabbed his wrists and pulled his hands away. "I might care a little."

Nick's eyes sparkled under the glow of the overhead lights. "Do you trust me?"

"Nope. And I wouldn't trust any guy in this situation. No offense." Lynette studied his now serious expression and wished her heart had some sense. "And even if you're not in a relationship, I don't think I'm in a good place for any kind of involvement right now, Nick," she said quietly. "Maybe this is for the best."

"Lynnie, don't say that." He ran the back of his hand down her face. "I promise you, I'm not involved with Mindy. And I know what I want. But if you don't feel the same . . ."

Oh, could he make this any harder? She shook her head and moved away. "I have to get the coffee."

"Can we talk about this later?"

She shrugged. "David told me you're the one who hired Cecily back." She couldn't be angry with him for that. She'd tried.

"I wanted to do something to help."

Lynette nodded, close to tears. "Well, thanks."

She didn't want to discuss Mindy anymore and he didn't press the issue, so they worked in silence.

"Hey, before we go back out there . . ." Nick hesitated, catching her eye. "I've been thinking about your idea, you know, to convert the house into a B&B? I think you need to tell the others. Tonight."

"Really?" Lynette's pulse picked up. "I don't know. They'll think it's stupid."

"Lynnie, do it. I'll support you. Promise."

Apprehension almost made her refuse, but then she nodded. "Okay. I guess it's worth a shot."

Nick carried the tray of steaming mugs out to the back lawn where the others sat on blankets around the fire pit.

"Well, it's about time," Liz complained. "What were you two doing in there? Never mind, I don't want to know."

Laughter rose up from the circle.

Lynette was glad for the dim light as she passed out coffee and cake and then took a seat beside Gray.

David cleared his throat and stretched his legs, kicking his deck shoes together. "Since we're all here, and nobody's killing anyone, I say we talk about the house." His words sliced through the night, through Lynette's heart. "I've met with Anthony Cooper. There's a boutique hotel chain interested in the property. The price they're willing to pay is astounding. I don't see how we can refuse. So, I vote to sell."

"I second it." Liz brushed offending objects off her shirt and slid her legs beneath her like a gymnast. "Gray?"

"Whatever."

Of course her brother's answer would be noncommittal. Lynette glanced at Nick, but he was studying his hands.

"Lynnie?" Liz turned to her.

Lynette knew she had no choice. "Ryan's not here." It was a final attempt at stalling. "We can't vote on anything without Ryan. And I think I might have a better idea." She caught the flash of Nick's smile through the semidarkness. "Do any of you understand what you're deciding?" She swept an arm toward the house. "This is our *home*! We grew up here. Our lives are here . . . all our memories . . . We can't just sign on the dotted line and let it go. Have you thought of what they're going to do to it?"

She pulled in air and felt her chest tighten. "They'll bulldoze it to the ground. Everything we ever loved and cared about will be gone. Everything!" A cry closed her throat and she stared at them. "I think we should consider something else."

Nobody spoke. Waves crashed on the rocks below. The moon

slid out from behind the clouds once more and lit their small gathering.

"Go on." Nick's voice was soft and barely audible, but she clung to it like a life preserver. "Tell them your idea."

"What idea?" Liz was on the verge of a hissy fit. "Let me guess, you want to turn the place into a commune or a homeless shelter or something."

"Liz, let her speak." David sat beside Lynette, squeezed her shoulder, and gave a smile. "What's the idea?"

"The guesthouse thing?" Gray asked. Lynette nodded and filled the others in.

"I think it's brilliant." Victoria spoke first. "I've checked out the hotels around here and they're not cheap. If you could provide a nice alternative, a chance for people to really experience Nantucket the way it once was, to get a glimpse into the past, preserve a bit of history." She clapped her hands together and smiled. "I love it."

"Thanks." Lynette allowed a tiny seed of hope to sprout. Maybe it wasn't so crazy.

"In principle, the idea has merit." Liz nodded, but then shook her head. "The house hasn't been touched since Mom went slap-happy with a paintbrush when I was seven. And when did you last see a mustard-color refrigerator? You'd need to have a first-class kitchen, remodel all the bathrooms, redo the plumbing and the electric, and who knows what else. I shudder to think what that would cost. We'd never get a loan."

David held up a hand. "It's a nice idea, but I agree with Liz. Our relationship with the bank is pretty much shot. Would you agree, Nick?"

Nick looked thoughtful. "Yeah. And I know my dad really wants you to sell. But I've been thinking a lot about this. What if you had a few private investors? People with a vested interest in the property, willing to come on board with the money to back the project?"

"Sure." David looked at Liz. "That could work, right?"

"I suppose." She tapped her chin. "We'd all need to agree to this. And there's still the question of feasibility. Even with the right investors." Liz gave a nervous laugh. "You're really suggesting this? That we attempt to renovate a house that's practically falling down around us? Do I need to remind you how much money we'd get if we sold Wyldewood?"

Gray lifted his head and smiled. "Shortstop, I think you're grasping at straws."

"No, I'm not! And I don't care about the money!" Lynette couldn't let it go now. Somehow she had to convince them. "I know you all want to sell, but I actually care more about Dad and what happens to him."

"Lynnie, come on, that's not fair," David said.

She shook her head. "No. I've put up with all of you telling me what to do my whole life. For once, I'm telling you how I feel. This was Mom's house. Dad loves it as much as she did, and I want him to live here as long as possible. If I can keep him here, with the help he's going to need, he'll be so much happier. It's not right to take him from his home. Not after everything he's been through. So I'm not going to agree to sell. If you won't at least look into the idea, I'll do it on my own. And you'll have to go to court to contest the will, because my mind is made up."

They all stared at her, silent. Nick shot her a wink, but she looked away, her chest pounding. Never in her life had she dared raise her voice against her siblings.

She didn't know whether to cheer or cry.

Gray gave a low whistle. "Well, it's about freaking time you found your voice." He slipped an arm around her shoulders. "Hey, my life's in that compost bin you've got going out back. I don't have anywhere to go. I'll stay and help. What about the rest of you? We could cut costs by doing the preliminary work ourselves, couldn't we?"

"Probably." David gripped the back of his neck and let out his breath. "I'd have to make some calls. See what we're really looking at. What do you think, Liz?"

"I think it's a terrible idea. I have a job to get back to. I can't stay here and play Bob the Builder. I do actually have a life."

"A life?" Gray snorted. "Going back for another round of abuse a la Lorenzo or whatever his name is?"

"Gray!" Lynette clapped a hand to her mouth as Liz swore and got to her feet. "Liz, what's he talking about?"

"Nothing." Her eyes shone through the night like lasers, ready to make short work of slicing Gray in half. "His name is Laurence. He's English, not Italian. And I don't care for your insinuations."

"If the shoe fits, babe." Gray shook his head.

"Liz, sit." David took charge again. He shrugged and cleared his throat. "I sure don't have anywhere to go."

"What does that mean?" Liz gaped.

Lynette felt sorry for her brother, but the truth had to come out sooner or later.

"Joss and I . . . Well, she didn't exactly protest my coming here. We've had a bad patch. We're working on things; I'm pretty sure we'll get through it. But it's been hard. And as of last month, I'm currently unemployed."

"Sucks, man. Sorry." Gray shot him a sympathetic look. "Well, work things out with your wife and get that family of yours out here, now that I'm sober enough to remember them. You still have just two kids, right?"

"Funny." David laughed. "I can't guarantee she'd jump at the idea of coming over right now, but you never know." He looked around the group. "Liz? Will you at least consider Lynnie's idea? Let us look into it?"

"I've got some preliminary plans drawn," Nick said. "They're not great, but it would give you a sense of what I think could be done."

Lynette sent him a grateful smile, feeling more hopeful than she had in months.

"Why doesn't that surprise me? Well, Nicholas—" Liz glared. "Since you and Lynette seem to be in cahoots with this harebrained scheme, let's talk about investors. Any ideas?"

"Yeah." Nick gave a slow nod and a hesitant smile that told Lynette what was coming before he spoke. "Me."

~

Nick glanced around the group and gauged the mood. The moon came out from behind the clouds again and allowed him to see their faces.

David looked skeptical as always. Liz, astounded, probably itching to get to her laptop and start digging into his financial history. Tori stared at him through those big eyes that said nothing and everything. And Lynnie . . . He couldn't quite look her way. Didn't want to know what she was thinking. But it was Gray he was worried about.

"Forget it." Gray pointed a shaking hand at him. "No." He let lose a few words that cleared any doubt as to his thoughts on the matter, turned, and marched toward the house.

Nick sighed and rubbed his jaw.

"Where would you get that kind of money, Nick? Certainly not from your father." Pragmatic Liz. Cut to the chase. Take no prisoners.

"No. Please don't involve your father in this." David. Wary. Maybe even a little scared. With the secrets between them, he didn't blame him.

"I, uh . . . I'm going for a walk." Tori, taking the quick way out. He nodded and let her go. She didn't need to be here anyway.

"Nick." Lynette's voice trembled. "I know you mean well, but it's too much. We can't let you put money into Wyldewood."

"Hear me out." He summoned his courage and went on. "First of all, my father will not be involved. On that, you have my word. In fact, I'd have to ask you to keep this between us, if you all agree to it. I received a substantial inheritance from my grandfather a few years ago. And I've talked to another potential investor who's very interested. Liz, I'm sure we can work out a suitable agreement, but I love the idea of being a part of this, turning Wyldewood into a guesthouse. If you're all onboard, I'm in."

"Well"—Liz nodded toward the house—"we're not quite *all onboard*, are we?"

"I'll go talk to him." Lynette's sigh said she really wasn't up to the challenge.

Nick shook his head and got to his feet. "No. This is between Gray and me."

"Yell if you need backup." David gave him the thumbs-up sign. Nick glanced back at Lynette. She hadn't moved, still studying him like she wasn't quite sure what to make of it all.

Neither was he, really.

He began walking to the steps.

"Nick." Lynette caught up to him, slipped an arm through his, and forced him to stop and look at her. "You really don't have to do this."

If they'd been the only ones outside, he would have given up the fight. Taken her in his arms and shown her exactly why he'd made the offer. But David and Liz were five feet away, watching them like protective parents. "Yes, I do." It was all he could say.

Chapter Twenty-One

Nick followed the sound of the piano.

Gray sat behind the old baby grand in the living room. Nick stepped into the room and pulled the double doors shut.

Several instruments still lay in their cases near the piano. He shifted them aside until he found the case he was looking for, lifted the lid, and stared at the guitar.

Memories hid in the shadows around him.

Drake's old Taylor didn't look any worse for wear. Probably hadn't been used since the last time Nick had played it, Christmas, five years ago. Nick dislodged the instrument from its red velvet casing, kicked a nearby ottoman toward the piano, and sat.

Gray continued to play as though he wasn't there.

Nick took his time tuning, even though it sounded pretty good to his ear, drew in a breath, and gradually caught up to the rhythm of the music. It might have been his paranoid imagination, but Gray seemed to play a little harder. Faster.

Finally he slowed his pace.

And then he began to sing.

Nick knew the song. It was an old one they'd written together. He remembered the words, but couldn't force them from his tongue. Instead, he played along, pressed his lips together, and made peace with years of regret and hard feelings.

Gray finished, shut the lid of the piano with a thud, and turned toward him. Neither of them spoke. Finally Gray gave a resigned shrug. "What, Nick?"

Nick stilled the strings on the guitar and prayed for the right words.

"I want us to talk." Nick placed the guitar on the floor and sat forward. "This has gone on too long."

Gray pushed to his feet and began to pace the room. Nick watched him come to a standstill in front of the table that held images from a life Nick had once been part of.

"You don't know what she meant to me." Gray picked up a black-and-white photograph of his mother, held it toward Nick with shaking hands.

"You know better than that." Nick ran a hand down his face, unable to move. "When my parents were hightailing it out to New York every weekend for some social event, your parents took me in. They made me a part of this family. Don't tell me you don't remember that."

"Yeah. So, why?" Gray shook the picture at him, and Nick half feared he would hurl it across the room. "Why would you make up such a ridiculous story about our parents having an affair and expect me to believe you?"

So there it was.

After all the years, distance, and hate that Gray had put between them, he still wasn't willing to face the truth.

"Ask yourself the same question." Nick folded his arms and set his jaw. "Outside of the last five years, there's not a lot you don't know about me. Why do you think I'd make something like that up? What would I possibly have to gain?"

Gray put the picture down, flopped onto the couch, and flung one arm across his face. "I don't know." The muffled words were barely discernable.

"You don't know because I wouldn't. I've never lied to you, Gray. You know that."

"If you're talking about that stupid blood brother thing . . ." Gray's cough sounded more like choked laughter.

Nick grinned at the memory.

~

Do we have to?" Nick eyed the Swiss Army knife in Gray's hand, feeling like he wanted to puke and there wasn't even any blood yet.

"Yes, we have to. Do you want to be blood brothers or not?" Gray pulled out a blade and touched the tip of it with his finger. He kept an eye on Nick, probably thinking he might make a run for it. The blade looked sharp. It wouldn't take much, but . . .

"This is dumb. We're already best friends. Why do we need to do this?"

Gray sighed and drew his knees up to his chest. Crickets chirped outside their tent. His friend's face glowed yellow in the light of the Coleman lamp and Nick felt sicker by the second.

Gray tapped out a couple of Chiclets from the pack and popped them in his mouth. "Because right now, we're ten. If we don't do it, by the time we're twenty, we might forget the promise."

"I'm not going to forget the promise." Nick squared his shoulders and stuck out his bottom lip. "I don't need to cut myself with some stupid knife. What if it gets infected? My mom will kill me."

Gray cackled and grabbed Nick's hand. Before Nick could fight him off, he'd slashed a small gash across his palm. Gray did the same to his own and pressed their palms together. "Say it."

Gray's eyes took on a certain glow, filled with excitement and a little disbelief. And Nick smiled. "I will stand by my brother through thick and thin, under any and all circumstances. I will never lie to my brother, no matter what, and I will defend him to the death."

"So help you, God."

"So help me, God." Nick squeezed Gray's hand. "Your turn."

~

"I know we were just kids, Gray, but it meant something to me."

Gray swore, pushed himself up, and sat with his head in his hands for a long time. "You take things way too seriously, Cooper." A slow smile inched upward and put the sparkle back in his eyes. "Yeah, okay." He scratched at the stubble on his chin. "David told me he talked to you."

"Yes."

"Who else knows?"

"Nobody. Well, Cecily." Nick wished for the thousandth time he had the power to change the past. "But I don't want Lynnie to know."

"No kidding. She'd have a cow." Gray raised an eyebrow. "What's up with you and my sister, Coop?"

Nick shrugged. If he had the answer to that, he'd be a happy man. "When we figure it out, you'll be the first to know."

Gray gave a low laugh and shook his head. "Dang. Didn't see that one coming."

"Neither did I."

"I was being sarcastic."

Gray sat forward and studied him. "So what's the deal? You with Mindy or not? Because if you are—"

"I know, Gray." He held up a hand in defense. "It's not what you think, okay? The thing with Mindy is nothing."

"Yeah? Because if you hurt Lynnie, I have friends who can hurt you."

"I'm sure you do." Nick tried not to smile and had to look at his feet to manage it.

When he looked up, Gray had his game face back on. "About the house. I don't have a whole lot of cash left, but I could probably squeeze out a couple of grand for starters. You really think it'll fly?" He glanced around the room and made a face like he'd just sucked on a lemon. "I don't know the first thing about home improvement, but the place needs work."

Work or a wrecking ball. The wallpaper was faded, peeling in places. The floorboards throughout had long lost their luster; he'd bet some were rotting. But it wasn't impossible.

Nick nodded. "I've already got some ideas for the renovations."

"Yeah?" Gray leaned against the couch and put his hands behind his head. One corner of his mouth inched upward. "Still got that architect bug?"

Nick rubbed his eyes and gave a short nod. "I think it could work, but it could get complicated."

Gray's expression told him he knew exactly what that meant. "You really want to go to war against your old man, Coop?"

"If that's what it takes."

"It could get nasty."

"It's already nasty." He'd suffer more of his father's wrath that was certain. But it wasn't anything he couldn't handle, and it couldn't be any worse than what he'd already endured.

"Okay then." Gray pulled his arms behind his head and Nick heard his joints crack. He probably hadn't had a good workout in years. "So am I gonna have to see your ugly mug around here every day now or what?"

Nick laughed and walked the room, stopping by the photographs. "I don't know about every day. Some of us have to work."

"Yah. Poor you." Gray coughed and went back to the piano. "Where'd you go the last five years anyway? Lynnie told me you split the same summer I went to California. Nobody knew where you were."

"It's kind of a long story." Nick scratched his jaw, turned, and saw Gray watching him.

"Well, I figured. I've got one of those too."

Nick shook off the apprehension, found an odd comfort in this moment, talking to Gray again. "Maybe we can swap sometime."

His friend hiked up an eyebrow, played a couple of chords, and finally smiled. "I got all night, man."

Chapter Twenty-Two

Friday finally arrived. When Nick called at the beginning of the week, asking Lynette to dinner at the yacht club, at first she'd refused. But he could be very persuasive, and eventually she'd relented. A night out that didn't involve cooking or children might be just what she needed.

It wasn't a real date. At least that's what she kept telling herself.

She'd had second, third, and fourth thoughts already. Part of her said she was sailing beyond the boundaries, going into unchartered waters, and if she wasn't careful, she'd find herself flung upon the rocks.

A bigger part of her said that after all these years, she might still be holding on to some unresolved feelings where Nick Cooper was concerned and she needed to explore them.

~

Nick pushed up his tie, combed his hair, and braced his palms on the top of his dresser. His father had told him earlier that he'd canceled his plans for the evening and was staying home, much to Nick's surprise. Dad rarely missed social functions, which made Nick wonder how he was really faring with the treatments. Not that it would do any good to ask. He'd be waved off and the subject changed at once.

Nick made his way downstairs, stuck his head around the door of the living room. "Dad? I'm heading out." His father sat in a chair by the window, one hand clutching the top of his shirt. "Dad?" Nick crossed the room, took one look at his father's ashen face, and panicked. "Dad? What's wrong? What's going on?"

"I feel . . . I don't know." He set bleary eyes on Nick. "I don't feel very well, Nicholas."

Nick put a hand on Dad's forehead. "You're burning up. We should get you to the emergency room."

Dad groaned. "I don't need to go to the hospital." A cough rattled his entire body.

"Stay there. I'm getting help." Was Soraya even here? Nick raced through the house, gave up on finding the housekeeper, and grabbed his car keys. Like it or not, they were going to the hospital. Dad could ream him out later.

~

Lynette stood by the empty fireplace, her navy blue cocktail dress sticking to the back of her legs. David sprawled on the couch, pretending to read, but every now and then he glanced at her over the top of his glasses. Gray sat at the piano, playing the same chords over and over.

The front door slammed and Liz marched into the living room. "There's nobody next door. The place is dark except for a light in the hall."

"Try his cell again, Lynnie." David sat up and gave her a smile that she supposed was to make her feel better. It didn't.

"It just goes straight to voice mail." The excitement of an hour ago, when Liz finished doing her hair and forcing a touch of makeup on her, had long since faded. Now she just felt stupid.

"Maybe he meant next Friday." Gray played a little harder.

"He didn't." Lynette kicked off her shoes. Her eyes began to sting. "I guess something happened. I hope he's okay."

"You want me to beat him up for you?" Gray left the piano and came to stand in front of her. "Just because we're speaking again doesn't mean I won't punch his lights out."

"Gray." She willed her tears back but they fell anyway.

"Hey. None of that." Gray tipped her chin upward. "He's not worth it," he whispered.

She nodded and tried to control the suffocating emotions. "I know."

"Guys are scum, Lynnie." Liz attempted a quick hug. "The sooner you accept it, the better off you'll be."

"Not all guys." David joined their circle and put an arm around Lynette's shoulders. "You okay, Shortstop?"

"I'll be fine." She dabbed at her eyes and smiled for them. "It's not like this is the first time I've been stood up."

Except then, it hadn't been by Nick. In fact, he'd rescued her.

~

The clock in the hall ticked out the minutes. Another hour passed.

She refused to look at Liz, who had come home for the momentous occasion. Ryan pitched a baseball from hand to hand and kept staring at her. Every now and then he missed, and the ball thudded to the ground. Lynette wished they'd both stayed away. At least Gray had already left the house. He, Nick, and the rest of the band would be at the dance. Hopefully they'd be so into their music that they wouldn't notice if she never showed up.

Cecily hovered, glancing at her watch and sucking her teeth.

Dad shuffled over to Lynette, cleared his throat, and blinked at her through bleary eyes. He hadn't had a drink for a couple of hours— she had to give him credit for trying. But she knew as soon as this was over, he'd be heading into the study to talk it over with Johnny Walker.

"Sweetheart, I don't think he's coming." He held his arms open and she slipped into them.

Mark was a jerk anyway. She didn't know why she'd agreed to go to the homecoming dance with him. At fifteen, she'd never had a date. She didn't go all crazy after guys like other girls. But when Mark asked her, she got all tongue-tied and stupid and said yes.

"Well, I guess that's it, then. I'm going to sit outside a bit." She pecked Dad on the cheek and watched him wander off toward the kitchen.

Cecily gave her a long hug and a knowing look. "You gonna be okay, baby?" Lynette nodded, holding back tears.

"Lynnie . . ." Liz came forward, no doubt full of womanly advice that Lynette didn't want to hear.

"Leave her alone," Ryan growled. Lynette glanced his way and smiled her thanks, raised a hand, and slipped out the doors onto the patio. She sank into a comfortable wicker lounger, pulled a throw rug over her legs, listened to the sound of the sea, and allowed the tears to come.

Awhile later she startled and realized she'd fallen asleep. And she was no longer alone.

"Hey, Shortstop." Nick crouched by her chair, concern in his eyes. He leaned a little closer, smelling slightly of beer and that awesome cologne he wore.

"Hi, Nick." She didn't bother moving. "What time is it?"

"Just after one. You okay?"

"Sure." She smiled, but her wobbly voice betrayed her. To her embarrassment, her eyes filled again. "Where's Gray?"

Nick's brow furrowed. "He and Ryan went for a drive."

Lynette sat up and put her head in her hands. "Oh no." Poor Mark. The guy was toast.

"Hey." Nick raised an eyebrow, stern. "Don't feel sorry for him, Lynnie. He's getting what he deserves. Anyway, they won't really hurt him. Just shake him up a bit. I made them promise."

"I feel so dumb," she whispered. "I don't know why I thought that anyone would want to go with me in the first place."

"Enough of that." Nick took her hands and pulled her to her feet. "Let me see you." The beginnings of a smile started as he checked her out. "You picked the blue dress."

"Yep." She smoothed down the silky fabric. "Liz wasn't happy, but she got over it." Shopping with Liz was never fun. Actually, doing anything with Liz felt like enduring a month of detention.

She hated that Nick and Gray hardly ever came home from boarding school anymore. She'd been so glad when the dance committee had asked their band to play. They'd be off to college in the fall and then she'd probably never see them. But this weekend they were here, and for once, no girls tagged along.

Nick made her turn in a circle. "I like it."

His eyes sparkled like stars when he smiled. She could spend all her time just watching him and it wouldn't be enough.

Nick Cooper was six foot something of pure gorgeousness. Whenever she saw him now, Lynette found it impossible to keep her heart from thumping. She wouldn't deny she had a major crush, but it was her secret. If any of them found out, they'd never stop teasing her.

He abandoned his preppy clothes on gig nights, opting for black Ts and stone-washed jeans instead. His blond hair was a little on the long side and a hint of stubble on his jaw gave him a bad-boy look.

"You really like it?" She wished he still went to the same school as she did. Nick never would have stood her up. Not that he'd ever ask her to be his date, but she could always dream. "You're just being nice."

"Nope." He led her out into the middle of the patio, pulled her close, one hand around her waist, the other pressing her palm against his chest, and he began to hum.

"What are you doing?" Lynette couldn't stop a giggle as she tried to keep step with his slow movements.

"Dancing with you."

She still wasn't used to how low his voice had gotten. Or the way his soft laugh made her heart do multiple back flips. "Why?"

Nick hummed a few more bars, made a half turn, and stopped. "Because you're beautiful, Lynnie." He twirled a strand of her hair around his finger. "And beautiful girls were meant to be danced with." His dimple deepened with his wink.

"Thanks, Nick." She dared to give him a quick hug, then fled into the house.

~

"I'm going upstairs." Lynette left her siblings alone and went into hiding.

She checked on Dad, then tried to read but couldn't. Didn't want to paint either. The paintings she was doing for Evy were fine, but the other ones . . . Those were scaring her half to death.

Eventually she left her room to retrieve the dry cleaning from the car that she'd forgotten to bring in earlier. As she made her way toward Liz's room, she saw her sister at the door to their mother's bedroom.

Lynette stopped walking. "What are you doing, Liz?"

"Hey, Lynnie." Liz jiggled the door handle. "Did Nick call?"

"Not yet." She was more than worried, but wouldn't admit that.

"Sorry, hon." Liz tried the door again. "Why is this door locked?"

"I have your dry cleaning." Lynette clutched the plastic bags against her chest.

"Put it in my room. Why is this door locked?"

"Because it is." She needed to dump this stuff and get out of there, but she'd have to go past Liz. She needed to get her away from that door.

"But why? I asked Cecily about it this morning and she said she didn't know. That you'd told her she didn't need to go in there."

"That's right. And neither do you."

"Stop being ridiculous," Liz snapped. "I'll go in if I want. And I don't need your permission. Get the key."

"No."

Liz stared, pinched her lips together, and used the silent tactic. She adjusted the patterned blouse she wore over white pants and took a step forward. "What did you say?"

"I said no," Lynette half whispered, her breath catching. "You don't need to go in there."

"Who do you think you are lately?" Liz hissed. "You can't order me around, Lynette!"

"I'm not ordering you around. I'm just saying no." She moved at the same time as Liz, dropped the pile of clothes, and raced for the stairs, Liz screaming after her.

"Give me the key!" Liz chased her down and pulled on her arm. Her eyes blazed with a fury Lynette remembered well. "Where is it? What are you hiding in there?"

"Leave me alone!" Lynette broke free of her grasp and gulped air.

Gray and Victoria were in the living room and got to their feet. Lynette bolted for the front door. It was pushed open before she could reach it, and she ran headlong into David.

David stepped around her and put an arm on her shoulder. "Whoa, calm down. What's going on?"

"She's locked Mom's room and won't let me in there, that's what's going on!" Liz's normally pale cheeks blistered red.

Gray let out a whistle. Usually he was the first to jump in and take her side. But he just stood there, looking at her like she'd committed a mortal sin. "Did you hock all her jewelry or something?"

"Shut up, Gray." David took off his cap and wiped his brow. Humid night air swept through the house and he kicked the front door shut. "Lynette, why is the door locked, and why won't you let Liz in?"

They surrounded her, edging closer like the incoming tide. And she couldn't catch her breath. She inhaled and recognized the wheeze at once. Panic jumped her as she struggled for air.

"Because. I . . . don't want anyone . . . in there." She let it out in a rush and ignored the white spots dancing in front of her eyes. "It upsets Dad." Thick cables wrapped around her chest and squeezed. This wasn't happening.

"That's ridiculous. Dad doesn't know where he is half the time." Liz folded her arms and scowled. "Are you going to tell me you locked the art studio upstairs too? Because I can't get in there either."

"Yes . . . don't . . . go . . ." She cleared her throat, tried to breathe through her nose, tried to calm down, but it was already too late. Her enemy had returned and made its presence known by the asthmatic wheeze that slipped from her lips.

"Lynnie?" David's face got closer, his eyes worried. "Where's your inhaler, hon?"

"Purse. Up. My . . . room." She needed to sit, but couldn't make her legs work. David disappeared and she grabbed the nearest person, which was Gray.

"Holy crap, are you having an asthma attack? Do we need to call an ambulance?" Gray's eyes flashed concern, but the tremor in his voice confessed he was ready to bolt as soon as someone else took over.

"Lynnie, I'm sorry." Liz stood on the other side of her. "I didn't mean to upset you."

She tried to speak, but couldn't. The monster was sucking her dry, making it impossible to do anything but stand there and wait for the lights to go out.

"Move, Liz." Victoria stood in front of her, a blurry image she could barely focus on. "Lynnie, listen to me, breathe. Slowly. In. Out." She pushed her toward the couch in the living room.

"I . . . can't . . ."

"Yes, you can," Victoria commanded, and Lynette was helpless to argue. Victoria rubbed her back with slow, soothing motions. "Deep breaths. In. Out."

Her mother was always so good at calming her during the episodes. Memories stabbed, brought hot tears, and stamped out lucid thought. "My . . . mom. Want . . . my mom." She wheezed in again and the coughing started. All she could do was pray she wouldn't pass out.

"It's all right, hon." Victoria's worried expression vetoed her words. "You're going to be fine."

Gray sat on her other side and grasped her hand. "Hang in there, okay?"

David pounded back downstairs, inhaler in hand. "It's almost empty."

She took it from him anyway. He'd probably kill her when he found out how old it was, but hopefully there was some medicine left inside. She hadn't needed it in a long time.

After a minute, her chest tightened again and she shook her head. "Not working."

"Get her in the car." David was already searching for keys. "It'll be quicker than waiting for them to get here. Where are the keys?"

"No." She shook her head, desperate to form words. "No hospital."

"You have to, Lynnie," Gray insisted. "You're turning blue."

"Can't . . . afford."

"Seriously?" Liz rolled her eyes. "You can't breathe and you're worrying about being able to pay the bill? We should have come home a long time ago."

"Then . . . why . . . didn't you?" Lynette wheezed and wished she had breath to really speak her mind. She was in the mood for a good argument.

"Come on, let's get you into the car." David moved her toward the door.

"I've got her." Gray slid an arm around her waist and Lynette leaned on him, close to passing out, but something wasn't right.

"Dad—"

"Don't worry about your dad." Victoria hovered close, peering at her through anxious eyes. "I'll stay and keep an eye on him."

"Thanks." David opened the front door. "Okay, let's go. Lynette, don't pass out."

Chapter Twenty-Three

She passed out.

The awful smell of hospital cleaner tickled her nose and roused her from sleep. Lynette opened her eyes and got her bearings. She was on a bed, in a small cubicle, pale blue curtains drawn around her.

The emergency room.

She knew it well.

Her childhood was spent rushing here, it seemed, at least once a month. As she grew older, her asthma attacks lessened. The year her mother died they'd started again.

For a long time, she'd figured it was God punishing her. Punishing her for what, she didn't know. Or couldn't remember. The past few years she'd thought things were better. Thought she might get a free pass to forget what all this felt like.

Tears came quickly and she blinked them back, defeated.

The curtain pushed aside and David peered at her. "Hey. You okay?" He came in, reached for her hand. "You got yourself in such a state that once the Ventolin kicked in, you fell asleep."

"What time is it?" She struggled to sit up, but her brother put his hands on her shoulders.

"Take it easy." He fluffed up her pillows and ran a hand over her head. "You gave us quite a scare, kiddo."

Then it all flooded back. "The dinner. Nick . . ."

"Forget that, Lynnie." David narrowed his eyes. "Why didn't you tell me you don't have insurance?"

"Davy . . . I'm sorry." She let out her breath and swallowed, her throat sore. She'd never live up to their expectations.

"Well, we don't need to talk about it now." He didn't hide the worry in his eyes. "They want to admit you, just to be on the safe side. Don't panic. We'll look after Dad. You just think about yourself for a change."

"I don't want to stay here."

"I know. But it's just for tonight."

There was no arguing. They moved her upstairs into a private room. Lynette had no idea who would pay for it, but was too tired to care. Lack of sleep, stress, and emotional turmoil all ganged up and launched a vicious attack. She curled up, closed her eyes, and drifted off again.

When she woke, Nick sat in a chair beside her bed.

A navy sports coat was slung over the arm of the chair, sleeves of his white shirt rolled up, a gold-and-blue striped tie sitting askew around his neck.

"Hey, you." He gave her hand a squeeze, furrowed his brow.

"Well, at least I know you're alive." She pushed aside relief and pulled her hand from his.

Nick's smile disappeared. "Can I explain?"

"Explain what? I waited hours for you. You didn't call and you didn't answer your cell. I thought something must have happened." She spoke slowly, careful not to get her pressure up again, but her throat clogged anyway. "Eventually I figured you blew me off." She couldn't get the vision of him and Miranda Vanguard out of her head.

"Lynnie. I didn't blow you off. I'm so sorry." He reached for her hand again. "My dad got sick. He was almost passed out when I found him, right before I was about to leave. I had to get him to the hospital, and I had no time to call. When I finally got the chance, you didn't answer your cell. I guess you were already on your way here. I hated doing that to you. I swear. I'm really sorry."

All thoughts of Mindy left her at once. "Is your dad okay?"

Nick nodded. "He's okay. He's up on the third floor. They said it's a virus, so they want to keep him overnight until his fever goes down."

"I'm sorry." Lynette sighed, feeling horrible she'd ever doubted him. "I should have known there was an explanation. I just thought . . . It's stupid, but I was thinking about homecoming. Remember that night? I guess I figured I got stood up again."

He sat back and studied her, solemn. "Sheesh. I remember that. Your homecoming dance. It was so long ago, but . . ." Nick's dimple came out. "When I saw you that night, curled up, asleep in the chair, your face still a little red, I wished I'd gone with Ryan and Gray. I wanted to be the one to punch that guy's lights out."

Lynette turned her head so he wouldn't see her tears. "You were never the Rambo type."

"No. I guess not."

She pushed herself up and folded her arms across the blankets. "What's going on with us, Nick?" The hospital was quiet, except for the occasional squeak of rubber soles on linoleum when a nurse walked past her room. "What do you really want?"

He sat forward, moved a strand of hair off her face. "I thought you knew."

Lynette tried to clear the fog in her brain, tried to make sense of her thoughts. "I can't stop thinking about Mindy. And wondering if there's not more to it."

Quiet laughter snuck out of him as he shook his head. He reached for her hand again and warmed it between his. "All right. We'll talk about Mindy." Her name slid from his lips like it belonged there. But the discontent in his eyes said it didn't. Not anymore.

"We dated on and off for a few years. At one time, yeah, there was something. But it was superficial. And a long time ago. The past year she . . . well, she's been seeing someone her parents don't approve of. I'm her cover."

"You're what?"

His face darkened and he slid his tie a little farther down. "When she came up with the idea, I wasn't seeing anyone. I didn't see the harm; we ran in the same circles anyway. But her parents started getting antsy, thinking our pretend relationship is headed for the altar, and—"

"Nick, this is crazy!" *Crazy* wasn't a strong enough word. "You can't keep lying to these people; what are you thinking?"

"I've already told her she needs to come clean with them. And I've told her there's someone else I'd much rather be spending my time with."

New hope chased away her fears. "You know, there's something else I've been thinking about. Do you remember that Christmas you were home from college, the year I turned nineteen?" She watched his face for any sign of recognition.

"You mean the year Gray and I fought?"

"Yes. We went out, the three of us. He was determined to show me a good time on my birthday, if you recall Gray's definition of a good time."

A knowing grin hijacked his serious expression. "You probably haven't had a drink since."

"That was the last time I let Gray talk me into going anywhere with him." Lynette groaned at the memory.

They'd gone to a party at a friend's, had all consumed far too much; she was too young to be drinking anyway. Gray passed out somewhere, and she and Nick walked the beach to clear her head before he took her home. They talked for a long time. She told him things she'd never shared with anyone. Things that bothered her, things that made her happy, things she dreamed about.

But she couldn't tell him about the things that terrified her.

Still, a connection ran between them; sometimes it was like he had access to her diary. And then that night he'd done the unexpected.

Pulled her into his arms, stared at her a long time, and then, finally, he'd kissed her.

A gentle kiss. Her first. And one she'd never forgotten.

After he'd taken her home, she'd held tight to romantic hopes.

But a few days later he was gone.

"I remember—never mind. It was a long time ago." He probably didn't even remember it.

Nick got a little closer, his eyes glowing in the dim light. "It still seems like yesterday. I hadn't seen you for a while, and I just about fell out of my chair when you walked in the room. You weren't Gray's kid sister anymore. You were beautiful." He smoothed her unbrushed hair, ran a finger down the side of her face. The shiver his touch incited made her think she was going to need another round of antihistamine.

"I remember the way the moon lit your face when we walked along the beach. I remember all the stuff we talked about, how natural it felt. You told me you couldn't wait to get to college and become a teacher. You were so excited when you talked about the places you and Ryan were going to go, the kids you were going to see. You wanted to go on his next mission trip with him, remember? I envied you."

"Why?" Tears spilled onto her cheeks.

"Because you had goals. A dream. You knew what you wanted. Where you wanted to go. You had something you believed in."

"But it didn't happen, Nick. What good are dreams that don't come true?"

"They keep hope alive." His thumb made slow circles on the

top of her hand. "I wondered whether you'd remember anything the next day. I wanted to talk to you again, to tell you . . . things. But then Gray and I—well, you know the rest."

"Five years is a long time to hold a grudge, whatever it was you fought about. I hope you both realize that."

Nick nodded. "We're good now."

"I'm glad." A yawn crept up before she could stop it. As much as she wanted him to stay, sleep was descending. "I didn't realize how exhausted I was until I got in this bed."

"You've been running on empty for a while. You should rest. Are they letting you out tomorrow?"

"I hope so." Sort of. A night of peace and quiet without worrying about Dad was a welcome change.

"Good." Nick stood, leaned over her, and pulled the blankets snug around her shoulders. He stared for a long moment, his silence scaring her a little. "Want to know what I remember most about that night, Lynnie?" His nose almost touched hers, a small smile inching up the corners of his mouth.

"What?" She hardly dared breathe, because she knew he didn't have the slightest intention of answering her question with words. And when he pressed his lips to hers, ever so slightly, before applying gentle pressure that demanded a response, she knew her prayer had been heard.

He hadn't forgotten.

Nick straightened, giving a wink that made her want to hide under the blankets. "Is that what you remember too?"

"That sort of rings a bell." Lynette watched the light play in his eyes, afraid to believe it.

"Would you believe me if I told you I spent the last five years dreaming of doing that again?"

"Nope." She grinned and folded her arms across her chest. "But it was an admirable attempt at flattery."

"It's true." Somehow he managed to look dejected and

completely self-assured at the same time. "And that kiss in the park the other night? Exceeded those dreams big time."

"Nick." Lynette laughed and gave his hand a squeeze. "I kind of liked it too, if you must know."

He grew serious again. "I'm sorry I didn't tell you the whole story about me and Mindy. It was just so stupid. I should have ended it ages ago."

"Yes, you should have. And it definitely needs to end now, if you intend to take me out for dinner again. Or kiss me again."

"I know. And I do intend to take you out for dinner again. And kiss you again. Quite thoroughly. Just as soon as you're feeling up to it."

She flushed under his gaze. "You better get out of here before they kick you out."

"All right. I'm going." He studied her for a long, exquisite moment she didn't want to end. "I'll be here tomorrow."

"Okay, Nick." She let out a happy sigh and snuggled under the blankets again. "See you tomorrow."

After he left, just before she drifted off again, Lynette had the alarming thought that for the first time in a long time, she felt happy.

And she didn't quite know what to do with that.

Chapter Twenty-Four

G ray woke up drenched again, shaking, desperate to push off the cloying darkness that clouded his mind and tugged him back to places where he could forget everything. All it would take was a few hundred bucks, a couple of snorts, or a shot in the arm.

He pressed his fists to his forehead and shut his eyes.

No, no, no. He wouldn't, couldn't, go back down that road. It would kill him.

Literally.

Lynnie had scared him half to death, with that whole not-breathing episode on Friday night. The last time he'd seen her like that was after Mom's funeral. He hadn't known what to do then either. But she was home now and seemed back to normal. He wouldn't survive if anything happened to her.

Once daylight flooded his room, Gray forced himself out of bed and stood for a long time under the lukewarm shower, listening to the pipes screaming at him. It was better than listening to the screaming inside his head.

He needed to talk to someone.

Sunday. Dr. Miller might be on call. He couldn't remember. He could call his new AA sponsor, Doug. An older guy, reminded him way too much of Pops. If those options didn't pan out, he wasn't above hightailing it down to that church Lynnie toddled off to almost every week.

Pastors were supposed to help the afflicted.

Gray dressed, glanced around his bedroom, and tried to keep his mind on track. Maybe he'd take Pops for a walk on the beach later. He seemed to like their little adventures, and to his surprise, Gray found he enjoyed his father's company, even if he wasn't all there half the time.

He wandered down the hall on the second floor, peeked into rooms until he came to the one Victoria had been occupying. A suitcase lay open on the bed.

A thousand regrets launched, and he gripped the side of the door for support. "Tor?" He shuffled into the room, glanced around. No sign of her. Her musky perfume hung in the air, tapped at the rusted locks around his heart, and made a flagrant attempt at prying them loose.

She liked it here. He could tell. She'd started singing again.

But he'd known she'd leave eventually.

Three framed photographs sat on the chest of drawers by the window. They went everywhere with her. Gray stood in front of the dresser and stared at the images.

Her parents. Good people. They'd liked him at first. The photo was a few years old, before all the trouble started. A much younger Victoria stood between them, smiling, happy. And totally oblivious to the tractor-trailer load of pain headed her way.

The second photo was of him.

Gray let out his breath, not sure when he'd been that young and carefree. The first year they'd met, maybe. His hair was longer, and he'd had that awful goatee thing going on she'd quickly convinced him to get rid of. He sat at a piano, glancing over his shoulder at the photographer with a grin that said life was good.

And it had been.

Gray closed his eyes. Much as he was loathe to, he knew it was time to undo those locks that confined his memories and remember when it all began.

Gray played a few chords. Scribbled on the sheet music in front of him and tried again. They'd had their first gig the previous night. A small bar in LA, but the place was packed out. Neil was ecstatic, already on the phone booking more gigs. A record producer had been in the crowd. They were meeting with him later that afternoon.

Neil convinced the hotel manager to give Gray use of the piano in the ballroom for a couple of hours. They'd made mistakes last night. That couldn't happen again.

Gray concentrated on the music and tried not to think about what might come next.

The sound of someone clearing their throat stilled his fingers and forced his eyes upward. A young woman stood in the doorway, watching him.

Gray blinked as she came into the room. She was short, but walked with a self-assured air that told him to pay attention. Her jet-black hair hung straight, rested on slender shoulders, and framed a pale, perfect face. Luminous eyes the color of caramel looked him up and down. And then she smiled.

Holy Mother of Wonderful.

Gray sucked in a breath and steadied himself on the bench. "Do I know you?"

"Not yet." She came a little closer. "I hear you're on your way to becoming the next Springsteen. Thought I'd come see for myself."

He managed to get a grip as he checked her out. She was hotness to the tenth degree. Tight jeans, a well-fitting T-shirt, and Chuck Taylors. A bit too much makeup, but it didn't matter. She had the most beautiful smile he'd ever seen.

A grin tickled his lips. "You don't look old enough to know who Springsteen is."

Her laugh was even more enticing. "I'm from New Jersey. It's in the first-grade curriculum."

It was his turn to laugh. "How did you get in here?"

"My cousin is the concierge."

"I see." Gray pushed his arms high above his head and worked the kinks out of his neck. "So what can I do for you, Miss—?"

"Montgomery. Victoria." She came forward and stretched out a hand. "Actually, the question is, what can I do for you?"

"Really." Gray smiled and took her hand in his. The minute he touched her, electric fire filled his being. He let go and cleared his throat. "You should probably elaborate."

She nodded, folded her arms, and put on a businesslike expression. "You're going to need a manager."

"I have an agent."

"Yes. And Neil Downs is one of the best. Which tells me a lot about you. He's also extremely busy. He'll book your gigs, concerts, work out your deals, but he's not going to follow you around and remind you where you have to be when." She tapped a long red fingernail against her forearm. "He's not going to tell you that you could use a haircut or that your wardrobe could stand a complete overhaul."

He wanted to ask what she knew about his wardrobe but was having way too much fun counting the flecks of gold in her eyes.

"Are you listening to me, Mr. Carlisle?"

Gray pulled his feet up onto the bench and hugged his knees. "I'm hanging on your every word." He expected some reaction, but she stayed quiet. "Am I correct in assuming that you think you'd be perfect for the job? You want to be my . . . manager?" He almost laughed, but she was so serious he didn't dare.

"You could hire me on a trial basis. Three months. If it doesn't work out, no hard feelings."

Gray stood, rounded the piano, and leaned over it. "How old are you?" He'd just turned twenty-one, and she didn't look anywhere near that.

"Twenty-two."

"Lower."

Her cheeks lifted with her smile. "Nineteen. But I turn twenty next week."

Great. He sighed and played with his grad ring. "You're not in college?"

She niggled her bottom lip with her front teeth, her eyes never leaving his. "I'm not really interested in higher learning. Of the institutional kind."

Gray gave a low whistle. Oh, she was good. "Yeah. It didn't hold my interest either."

"I promise you, I know what I'm doing. I have references."

"From who? The parents of the kids you babysat for?" He let out a groan and shoved his fingers through his hair. "Nice to meet you, Miss Montgomery, but I'm kind of busy." He moved back to the piano bench and sat.

"Gray."

He closed his eyes. If he kept them shut long enough, she'd be gone and he wouldn't have to acknowledge what was going on here. What he'd known the moment she'd walked into the room.

A conversation he'd had with his mother years ago, when a girl he'd thought was "the one" had broken his heart, played in his memory.

"I know how you felt about her," Mom had said. "But she wasn't the girl for you. One day, when you're older, you'll meet her, the one. You'll know."

"How?" Gray asked.

"When you meet her, you'll feel it. Right here." She placed a hand against his chest. "She will speak to your soul."

"Puh-lease." He'd rolled his eyes and screwed up his nose. Mom was always so dramatic. But something inside him said to listen. And remember.

His mother had been right.

The way Victoria Montgomery spoke his name confirmed it.

Gray looked at her again. Cursed his mother's intuition and gave in. "Does anybody call you Tori?"

"Nope."

"Good. Well, Tori, you can start by getting me some decent coffee. I take it black. I think there's a coffee shop across the street. And grab me something to eat. But make it fast, I have an appointment this afternoon."

"At two." She whipped out a cell phone and punched the keys. "With Starsong Records. Which is why you're going to come with me, right now—don't give me that look. We're going to fix that hair of yours, get you some decent clothes, and find you a razor. And while we're doing all that, I'm going to give you a lesson in the finer art of saying please and thank you."

"Dang, girl." Gray's smile sizzled all the way down to his toes. What was he getting himself into?

"Let's go." She snapped her fingers and tipped her head toward the door. "We don't have all day."

Gray pushed to his feet, grabbed his jacket, and walked toward her. "Tori Montgomery, I think you're going to regret the day you walked in here and took over my life."

~

His hand shook as he reached for the third photograph.

Three years old, blond hair, blue eyes, and a cheeky grin.

Guilt and shame seized him.

"What are you doing in here?" Tori marched into the room lugging a laundry basket. She set it down on the bed and winged a couple of unspoken words his way through angry eyes.

He fumbled to put the picture back in place.

She hated when he touched her stuff.

"Sorry." He coughed and moved away from the dresser.

"Whatever." She began to sort her clothes. There were a lot of them. Gray picked up a black Van Halen shirt and attempted to fold it.

She allowed him to be helpful for all of two minutes.

"Give me that." Tori snatched a thin chemise from his fingers, balled it up, and threw it into her suitcase.

Gray sank onto the edge of the bed, his heart thundering. This couldn't be happening. Once again he found himself in a situation he had no control over.

Another mess he had no clue how to clean up.

She continued her frantic folding in stony silence, although it looked like she couldn't care less how the clothes ended up in the case, so long as they got there.

"Could we . . ." Gray stayed her hand and closed his fingers around her thin wrist. Her pulse pounded through her skin and reached right through him.

"Could we what, Gray?" Those amazing eyes nailed him, challenged him, and dared him to admit his sins.

He shook his head and let her go. "When are you leaving?"

"I'm catching the ferry. I'll get a bus back to New Jersey. Should be home for supper."

"You talk to your folks?"

"Yes." She yanked clothes off hangers, threw them into her case, stalked the room, and began to gather her belongings.

"And they're okay with you coming back?"

"They're okay with it. They know I've been clean the past two years. I promised them I'd still get counseling. I'll get a job. They . . . they said they're willing to give me a second chance." Her voice got muffled, like it did whenever she was working to shove down her emotions. The past couple of days, since she'd voiced her intentions to go, he could barely stand to listen to her.

"Would it make a difference if I told you I was sorry?"

She turned, clutched a photograph to her chest, and took slow steps toward him. He didn't have to ask which one she held.

"Sorry for what, Gray?" she whispered. "Sorry that you seduced me, slept with me, got me pregnant—then told me you could never love me like I deserve—that we could never have a future together? What—exactly—are you sorry for?"

Gray lowered his eyes and pressed his fingers into his legs. "All of the above." He looked up and found her watching him.

Tears shimmered in her eyes. She closed the gap between them and held out the photograph. "If you want it."

"Thanks." His throat burned as he stared at the silver-framed image of the daughter he would never know. "She's lucky she has you."

"She barely knows me. A few visits here and there don't measure up to being a real mom." Tori's sigh was thick with regret. "You know I wasn't in any shape to be a mother when she was born. I'm not so sure I am now. My folks are the only parents she's known. What if she doesn't like me? What if I . . . mess up again?"

"You won't." He stood, put the picture on the bed, pulled her against him, and let her bury her face against his chest.

After a while, she looked up at him with a sheepish smile and tried to step out of his embrace. He held tight.

Gray studied her face, wanting to commit everything about her to memory. In a few hours she'd be gone. "Why did you stay?"

"What?" Her eyes widened.

"With me." He let his fingers run along the side of her jaw, across her full lips, and down the slender neck he'd been secretly admiring for way too long. "After everything I put you through, everything that happened, why didn't you just leave? You could have worked things out with your parents. Got your life together back there. Been with Tess all this time . . . but you didn't. You came back to me."

She pressed her lips together. "I knew Tess was happy. Safe. The truth is, I was scared. I've lived this life so long, on the road, with the band, and you. I didn't know how to leave and start over.

I believed Tess was better off without me, that my going home would only confuse her. And you needed me." Tori lifted a thin eyebrow and showed him the smile he knew he'd never get over. "I'm a little masochistic, I admit."

"A little?"

"Okay, a lot." Thick, wet lashes came down over eyes. Her hair was getting longer, no more spikes, just gorgeous dark curls that framed her face and hid her expression from his scrutiny. "But I don't believe that anymore. I need to go home, Gray. I've wasted too much time already. I need to be with my daughter."

Our daughter.

Neither one would say it.

Gray let her go and reached into his back pocket for his wallet. Pulled out the wad of cash he'd withdrawn from the bank the day before and took her hand in his. "Here. It's not what I owe you, but I think my checks are bouncing."

She snapped her head up, stared at him, the cash, and then him again. Her mouth hardened into a thin line. "That's not why I stayed."

God help him, she was tearing his heart out.

"Just take it, Tor. Take it for her."

"Fine." She took the bills and shoved them into the pocket of her jeans. "Are we done then? I need to get packed."

The self-preservationist returned.

Gray gave a reluctant smile. "Can I drive you to the ferry?"

"Lynnie's going to."

"Oh." He folded his arms across his chest and quelled the urge to cough. A shudder grabbed hold and shook him anyway.

"You okay?"

"Sure." As okay as he could be watching his entire life walk out the door. "I . . . um, don't have your number."

"You don't know my cell number? You only called me a million times a day."

"I mean your address." He scratched his jaw and tapped a bare foot against the rug. "I might want to send you chocolates or something."

"Chocolates?" She laughed and placed the last pile of clothes inside the beat-up case. The green canvas was covered with stickers and emblems and flags of all the countries they'd toured the last few years. She yanked on the zipper, maneuvering it around, closing her life up and hauling it away, out of his. "Gray, when have you ever seen me eat a piece of chocolate?"

"First time for everything?"

"No." She dropped the suitcase to the floor, scanned the room, then came to stand before him. Her eyes were too bright again.

Gray reached for her hands and threaded his fingers through hers. "What am I going to do without you?"

"I have no idea." She sniffed, put on a brave smile, and gave his hands a squeeze. "I've left Lynnie all my recipes. I know you don't like those shakes, but they're really good for you. And I don't want you to skip any meetings. I know the first two weren't exactly your cup of java, but stick it out, Gray. Promise me?"

"Yeah, okay." He'd promise her the world if he believed he could follow through. "Will you . . ." He blinked moisture and cursed inwardly. He was too close to losing it now, but it didn't matter anymore. "Will you tell her . . . tell Tess . . . about me?"

"Gray." Tori placed a soft hand against his cheek, her lower lip trembling. "What do you want me to tell her?"

"I don't know." He could hardly get words out. His shoulders began to shake. "Tell her . . . tell her that her daddy loves her. Very much." He muted her reply as he drew her into his embrace, buried his face against her hair, and lost the battle to pull it together.

She drew back first, rested her hands against his chest, and waited. "Okay?"

"Don't leave."

"I have to. It's time. You know as well as I do. It's time for you to get rid of all the junk you're still carrying around. Find some peace out of all this. Find yourself again. The person you used to be before you left this place." She ran a finger down his nose. "I've seen a bit of that guy the past few weeks. I kind of like him. He's still in here somewhere." Tori tapped her fingers against his chest. "Maybe one day he'll come see me."

"What about us? Where does this leave us?"

An errant tear escaped and slowly slipped down her face. "I think we need to figure out our own lives first. Then we can figure out if there should be an us."

"You'll always be too good for me, Victoria Montgomery."

"I might have heard that before." Her eyes twinkled in a snatch of time, before the sadness returned. "Take care of yourself, Gray Carlisle."

"Wait." Gray pulled her back into his arms, met her eyes, and prayed she would see everything he couldn't say. There would be no promises made, none given. But he needed her to know he wasn't giving up without a fight. Needed her to know exactly what she meant to him.

Just needed her.

He placed his hands around her face, ignored the way her eyes widened as she tried to pull back, and brought his lips down on hers.

In that instant he knew exactly what he was letting go.

Her initial protest died a quick death as she molded to him, threaded her fingers through his hair, and allowed him to deepen the kiss that exploded into a moment of exquisite pleasure.

"Gray." She pushed him back, confused. A slow smile started, followed by a throaty laugh that hinted of defeat. "You always did have lousy timing."

"Still leaving?" He tried to sound hopeful even as he watched her slip into her black pumps and pull on a denim jacket.

"Don't work too hard around here. I'd hate for you to put your back out or anything."

He released a sigh, wanting to relive the moment but knowing she'd probably kick him if he tried. "Nah. I plan to make Cooper do all the heavy lifting."

Tori checked her watch. "He's a nice guy. I'm glad you're friends again."

"Yeah. Me too."

"Gray?" She shifted, uneasy again. "Don't call me, okay? Not right away."

"Tor . . ." He moved closer, but she held up a hand.

"Please. Don't make it any harder."

Gray let out his breath and squeezed his eyes shut. "I know it's way too late for this, but . . . I do care. In my own whacked-out way. I'm sorry it's just not . . ."

Tori slung her purse over her shoulder and gripped the handle of her suitcase. "You're right, Gray. It's just not."

Chapter Twenty-Five

Dad sat in the front seat, arms crossed over his seat belt. They'd been parked outside Dr. Miller's office for ten minutes already. Lynette only had the morning off, and Mondays were crazy, the kids still worked up from the weekend.

"Come on, Dad." Lynette leaned forward and put a hand on his shoulder. David had driven; she, Gray, and Liz sat in back. "You know Dr. Miller. He's not going to hurt you."

"You said we were getting ice cream."

"Oh, for Pete's sake," Liz grumbled. Lynette shot her a fierce glare. Her sister rolled her eyes and pushed Gray's shoulder. "Get out. It's boiling in here."

When it was just the three of them in the car, David turned to Dad. "Know what I thought of the other day? That time you and I went sailing and got caught in a storm coming home."

"Came out of nowhere." Dad gave a sudden chuckle. "You were scared out of your little mind."

"I was only ten." David glanced back at Lynette, surprised.

"Thought you were going to jump right out of the boat."

"Yeah. I wanted to." David smiled. "And what did you tell me?"

Dad sighed. "I don't know. Something stupid."

"You said after every storm comes the calm. But that I had to learn to sail through the storms so I'd never take the calm for granted."

"Right. Stupid." Dad harrumphed.

"Dad, we're here for you," David said. "Whatever's going on, we'll get through it together. But we need to see Dr. Miller to find out what it is."

Silence thickened the already stifling air. Lynette wiped her eyes and waited.

"Know what it is," Dad whispered. "Saw it on Dr. Oz. That old timer's thing."

"Well." David's sigh was heavy. "If that's our storm, we'll sail it."

"Can we still get ice cream?" Dad unbuckled his belt.

"As much as you want."

The five of them stood at the entrance to the building, huddled close.

Dad took the first step. "Come on, then. I don't suppose that doctor wants to wait forever."

~

Nick scanned the letter David had thrown on his desk the minute he'd walked into his office Monday afternoon. They'd filed their application with the zoning board and it had been rejected. Almost immediately.

Anthony Cooper had played his first hand.

"What is this all about?" David's eyes blazed. "It's our house. We can do what we want with it."

"Not exactly." Nick undid the top button of his shirt, feeling warm. "As I explained, in order for you to convert Wyldewood from a single-dwelling home into a guesthouse, you need approval from the zoning board. If other residents in the area don't like the idea, they're free to file a complaint."

"Which they've all done." David sank back against his chair and glared at Nick. "This is your father's doing."

"Probably."

"What can we do?"

"Talk to the board commissioner. File an appeal."

"We don't have time for that."

Nick put his hands behind his head. "I know the BC. Bryan Johns is a decent man. I'll talk to him. While I'm at it, I'll have a chat with the neighbors as well. But we can't do any major renovations on the house until we're approved."

"This is absurd. It's almost August. Do we just sit around and twiddle our thumbs?"

"No." Nick worked to keep frustration from his voice. "We can still do improvements on the interior. Work on refurbishing the floors. Painting. That sort of thing. It's not ideal, but at least we can get going on the rooms that aren't going to change structurally."

"Fine." David's irritation bounced off the walls. Nick couldn't blame him, but their hands were tied.

"How's your dad?" Nick asked.

"Well, we finally got him to the doctor this morning. Lynnie tell you?"

"Knew you were going. Haven't talked to her yet today." Nick planned to go over to the house tonight.

"She'll fill you in. But he's as bizarre as ever." A smile chased off David's frown. "He's suddenly remembered how to paint."

"Really?" That was interesting. "Does he still have it?"

"I wouldn't have a clue." David laughed and checked his watch. "You'd have to ask Lynnie about that. She's the only other artist in the family."

Nick inhaled and almost asked David to repeat himself. He'd forgotten. "That's right. She was pretty good. Does she still paint?"

"I guess so. Spends a lot of time up in the art studio anyway. How's *your* dad?"

Nick sighed. "Sick. But still causing trouble, obviously. I'm sorry about this, David."

"We'll get through." David rose and extended a hand. "I'm

heading over to the mainland for a couple days to see my wife. I think things are finally on the upswing."

Nick stood and they shook hands. "I'm pleased to hear it. Good luck."

"Thanks. Let me know how it goes with the board commissioner. Drop by the house when you can. Gray needs a kick in the backside. He's been messed up since Victoria left. I'm worried."

"Will do." Nick watched David leave, then he stood, grabbed the letter, and marched down the hall.

His father sat behind his desk, flicking through the *Wall Street Journal*.

"Working hard, Dad?"

"Hello, Nicholas." He barely glanced up. "How's David?"

Nick tugged on his tie and walked around the spacious office. The shelves were filled with books, journals, and photographs of his father with officials and celebrities. Not a single one of him. Never had been.

"Did you need something?"

Nick turned and met his father's blunt stare. Dad's hair was sporting a few more strands of gray these days. Shadows circled his eyes. His normally tanned skin was sallow.

Nick got right to the point, waving the letter. "Why are you so determined to stop the Carlisles from turning Wyldewood into a guesthouse?"

"Me?" He drummed his fingers on the desk and looked contrite. "It's not just me. Everyone in the neighborhood is against the idea."

"But they wouldn't be against knocking the house down and putting up a hotel?"

Dad shrugged, a thin smile appearing. "I guess we'll never know."

"This is the only chance they have of holding on to their home."

"Where would they get the money for those kinds of renovations, Nicholas? Is the singer footing the bill?"

Nick glanced at his shoes. "They have investors."

"Investors? Fascinating." His father gave a hacking cough that took up all space in the room. "So help me, Nicholas, if you're spending your inheritance on that monstrosity of a house—"

"Dad?" Nick didn't like the shade of his father's cheeks. He went for water and handed him a glass.

After a couple of swallows, Dad's eyes were steely again. "If you want to throw your money away, I can't stop you. They'll have to appeal the board's decision."

Nick yanked off his tie and prayed for patience. None came. "I really don't know how we're related." He watched a slight hint of aggravation flicker across his father's face.

Dad stood and placed his palms on the desk. "I see whose side you're on."

"This isn't about sides. It's about what's right."

"Because you know so much about that."

Nick faced the window, the start of a migraine pinching his neck. "You'll never get over that, will you? Never believe I wasn't at fault."

"I don't think it matters what I believe."

"I'm with the Carlisles on this, Dad. We'll appeal."

"You're making a grave mistake."

"Interesting analogy." Nick managed a tight smile. "I think the mistakes have already been made. Wouldn't you agree?"

Fury flashed across his father's face but he tamped it. Drew his lips together and tipped his head toward the door. "Get out."

~

Cecily was wiping down the counter top when Nick strode into the kitchen at Wyldewood that evening. "Hey, gorgeous. Did I miss dinner?"

"Don't you gorgeous me, Nicholas Cooper." But her dark

cheeks got rounder. "There are enough leftovers to feed the rest of the island. Nobody around here wants to eat nowadays."

"Where's Lynnie?"

"Babysitting. I'm staying late, until she gets home."

"Oh." He masked his disappointment and took a seat. "Nobody else is here?" Nick's stomach began to growl as she made him a plate. "Heard David's gone for a few days. What about Liz?"

"Gone too." Cecily set a plate of food before him. "That's all I got to say about that."

"She's a grown woman, Cecily."

"Crazy's what she is." Her sigh was deep. "I don't think things are right with that boyfriend of hers. If you ask me, he's trouble. The worst kind. But I guess she'll have to figure it out for herself." She began to empty the dishwasher. "Well, she'll be back by the end of the week. Or so she says."

"Hope so." Nick stabbed a piece of chicken with unnecessary force. "Lynnie needs the help."

Drake came into the kitchen, the dogs bounding after him. "Hello, Nicholas."

"Sir." Nick gauged his facial expression to see which way the winds were blowing and returned the familiar smile.

"It's a great day for a sail, my boy!" Drake slapped him on the back and eyed his food. "Now, that looks good. Is it dinnertime already?"

Cecily fixed Drake with a withering glare. "You had your dinner, Mr. Carlisle. You told me it tasted like rotten tomatoes."

"Nonsense, woman!" Drake plopped down on the other side of the banquet and pounded on the table. "Get me a plate. I'm starving."

"You could say please."

He curled a strand of gray hair around his finger and somehow looked charming. "Please?"

Cecily pursed her lips. "Fine, then."

"Sweet." Drake grinned and Nick stared.

"I'll sweet you." Cecily served Drake and cleaned up while they ate.

Nick inhaled his meal. Good home cooking. So much better than that gourmet garbage his father insisted Soraya make for them. "Where's Gray?" He grabbed a paper napkin from the holder and wiped his mouth.

"Out again. You know that boy and his shenanigans." Drake cocked an eyebrow. "Didn't your parents ground you, Nicholas? What are you doing over here?"

Cecily's eyes clouded over. "Come on, Mr. Carlisle. You want to watch *Judge Judy*?" She untied her apron. "Gray's upstairs in his room. Said he had a headache."

She took Drake's arm and ushered him out of the kitchen. When she returned she took a seat opposite Nick. "That boy's been miserable since Victoria left. Lynette's convinced there was something going on between them, although they both swore there wasn't. Did he say anything to you?"

Nick chugged from his can of soda and tried to avoid Cecily's eyes. "You know guys. We don't talk much."

She narrowed her eyes and leaned in. "Do you know that your jaw twitches ever so slightly when you're lying?"

Nick didn't doubt it. "Maybe I'll go talk to him."

"Maybe you should talk to me."

"Ce-ce." Nick enjoyed her aggravated expression. "I can't."

"You do know something!" Her eyebrows came together as she tried to stare him down.

"Not gonna work. Not this time."

Her stern look slipped and she let out a laugh. "All right. Is there anything I can do?"

"Yeah." He stood and took his dishes over to the sink, then turned back to her. "Pray."

"Huh." Cecily gave him a skewed look. "Guess sometimes you got more sense than I give you credit for."

Nick left the kitchen and headed upstairs. A minute later he ran downstairs. Cecily and Drake were in the den watching television. "Did Gray come through here?"

"No." She put her book down and stood. "He's not in his room?"

"Nope. Nowhere upstairs." Nick marched to the front door, flung it open, and confirmed his suspicions. "He took my Jeep."

"Lord, have mercy." Cecily stared out into the dark night. "How?"

"I left the keys in it." Gray always ragged him about the bad habit. Tonight it had worked in his favor.

"Where would he have gone?"

"I have a pretty good idea." He hoped he was wrong, but he probably wasn't.

"Not to see Victoria?" Cecily's eyes widened and she looked even more concerned.

"No. I don't think so. I think he went to see another friend." Nick wished he could calm her down, but nothing he said would help. "Can I borrow your car?"

Chapter Twenty-Six

"Heads up, Lynnie." Jed stuck his head around the kitchen door. "Your brother just walked in."

"What?" Lynette whirled from her position at the grill, spatula in hand. "Which one?"

"Gray."

"No." Bacon sizzled on the wide griddle in front of her. She turned down the heat and stepped forward. Gray was here. In a bar.

Jed eyed her carefully, waiting. "You wanna go talk to him?"

"I can't." She turned back to the burgers and flipped them one by one. Put the crispy strips of bacon onto a plate. Dumped a pile of chopped onions and mushrooms onto the blackened grill and watched them sizzle. "Don't serve him, Jed."

His whispered curse floated around the noisy kitchen. "I don't have a reason not to, hon. Sorry. If you're that concerned, get on out there and send him home."

Lynette bit her lip. Fumes from the onions stung her eyes, but they were watering anyway. "I don't want him to know I work here." She glanced over her shoulder. "Please, Jed. Don't say anything."

"You are one weird chick. You know that, right?"

"Hagerman, you in there? You want me to help myself or what?" Gray's bellow sailed through from the bar and Lynette jerked her head toward the door.

"Go. And keep your mouth shut!"

Lynette finished the burgers and slid them across the counter to Lila. She peeked through the opening of the window and tried to get a glimpse of her brother.

Jed's big head was in the way. Her heart started a slow rumba. If she went out there and confronted Gray, he'd make her quit. And the money she was making enabled her to keep up her stock of art supplies. Her paintings were selling. She couldn't quit now.

"Please don't drink," she whispered. "Please, God, don't let him drink."

~

Gray glared at the two drinks on the counter. The tall mug of beer was losing its froth. The whiskey chaser sat beside it, mocking, daring him to get it over with.

Jed's eyes were on him again, burning a hole through his conscience. He was using the old stare-at-'em-till-the-guilt-kicks-in technique. But if he didn't stop soon, Gray was going to ram a fist into his face.

A group of kids, high schoolers from the looks of it, sat at a nearby table. They were staring at him too. If the place hadn't been practically pitch-dark already, Gray would have put on his shades.

Soon, a couple of the girls hovered near his stool. "Excuse me?"

Gray sighed inwardly, found his signature smile, and swiveled to face them.

"Omigosh! It is!" They squealed, did a little jig, looked at each other through wide eyes, and then looked back at him. "It is you, right? Gray Carlisle?"

"In the flesh."

Jed snorted and Gray pitched him a glare when the girls went fishing in their purses. Between the two of them, they came up with paper and a pen and managed to ask for his autograph between giggles.

"I just love your last song," one of them gushed. "You know, the one that came out before you OD'd and went to rehab."

Gray scribbled his name, handed back the paper, and felt his gut twist. "That OD thing was a rumor."

"Oh." They rolled their eyes simultaneously and he wondered if they'd practiced that. "Well. You should write a new song. They keep playing that old one, over and over and—"

"It's in the Top 40, stupid!" her friend chimed in.

Gray's spine tingled and he sat a little straighter. "Top 40?"

"Well, duh." More eye rolling. "So, are you writing new stuff?"

Gray smiled again and watched them practically melt into pink little puddles of Juicy Couture. "Ladies, not only am I going to write a new song, I'm going to write a whole album. And I'm going to dedicate the first track to you. What are your names?"

"Omigosh! I'm Jessica." Girl number one almost passed out. Her friend poked her in the ribs, clearly far more mature.

"And I'm Ashley."

Gray's laughter caused another round of giggles. Then he put on the sternest expression he could manage and nodded toward Jed. "It was nice to meet you, girls. Now, if you and your friends over there are smart, you'll call it a night before Jed here decides to card you. He's got Nantucket PD on speed dial."

After the doors slammed behind the group, Jed dissolved into side-splitting laughter.

"Dang, you're a piece of work, Carlisle." Jed mopped down the top of the bar.

"That's what I hear." Gray poked a finger into the vanishing foam in his beer and stuck it in his mouth. The taste was bitter on his tongue. He waited for the familiar desire to snake around him and force him into downing the whole thing.

It didn't come.

A small fire of excitement lit. Top 40. They were still playing his stuff. Which meant he wasn't quite floating facedown in the water. Which meant he'd still be getting royalties. Which meant a chance to start over.

Maybe.

He pulled his phone from his pocket and punched a number. He couldn't wait to tell Tori. But then he remembered. His eyes smarted at his knee-jerk reaction, and he canceled the call.

The bar doors banged open, letting in a whistle of wind, a blast of salty air, and Nick.

"Oh, goody. The cavalry has arrived." Gray tried out an eye roll of his own.

Nick hopped onto the stool next to his. He saw the evidence and set a steely gaze on Jed. "You served him?"

"Hey, man." Jed held up both hands with a look of chagrin. "This is a bar, not a freakin' AA meeting. He's age of majority."

"Not that it would have stopped you if I wasn't." Gray ducked as Jed's dish towel snapped perilously close to his face.

Nick checked him out, squinting his eyes. "How much have you had?"

Gray sighed and wished he hadn't decided to quit smoking at this particular time in his life. "You don't look like my father."

"Relax, Cooper, he's not drinking them," Jed growled. "He's playing with them."

"What?"

Coop looked so confused that Gray couldn't help laughing. He pushed the two offending objects toward Jed. "Toss 'em. I'll have a Coke, please."

"Make it two," Nick added.

"And I could use a burger. I skipped dinner."

"I'll have some fries." Nick jogged Gray's arm with his elbow. "You took my Jeep, you jerk."

"Told you not to leave the keys in it. Serves you right." Gray coughed and jumped off the stool. "How'd you get here?"

"Borrowed Cecily's car." Nick took out his phone and called

the house to let her know he'd found Gray. Gray noted Nick didn't tell Cecily where.

They slid into a booth and gave Jed a hard time while he worked.

About ten minutes later a bell dinged from inside the kitchen and Jed returned with the food. Gray couldn't remember ever being served so quickly in here.

"Glad I found you." Nick bit into a fry. "I sure didn't feel like driving to Jersey tonight."

Gray rubbed his face and let out a breath. "That wasn't one of my options." Suddenly he wasn't hungry anymore. And he wanted those drinks back.

"Eat something." Nick pushed his plate back toward him. "You look like you just got sprung from Alcatraz."

"Thanks. You're as cheerful as a Hallmark card." But he bit into his burger anyway. Once the food hit his stomach, he started feeling a little better. "Hey, did you see those kids before you came in?"

"Those kids who shouldn't have been in here, yeah." He glanced at Jed. "What about them?" Nick chugged his Coke and twirled a fry in a mound of ketchup.

"They said my stuff's playing on the radio."

Nick chewed. "I heard you this morning. Twice. My secretary is nuts over you, by the way. If you ever feel like stopping into the bank and giving her a heart attack, I'd appreciate it."

"You do have a way with the ladies, Coop." Gray sat back, letting his stomach rest a moment. "I didn't know. I mean . . . I thought with rehab and all . . ."

Nick shrugged and continued to inhale his basket of fries. "You're still the hometown boy, Gray. So you screwed up. Happens all the time. People get over it."

"You think I could have another chance at this gig?"

Nick sat back, seemed to mull the question over. "I think the only one around here who doesn't believe that is you."

"Well, if it's true, if I start earning money again . . . Lynnie's idea might just be doable." He grinned at the thought of telling her.

Nick rolled his eyes. "You're that good, huh?"

"I'm amazing." Gray puffed out his chest, then dropped his smile. "You won't tell Lynnie you found me here, right?"

"Nah." Nick sat in silence for a long moment that inched into awkward. "I think you should tell the family, you know, about Tori and . . . your daughter."

He sighed and rubbed his jaw. "Yeah. I know. I just . . . I don't know what to say. It's not like I'm ever going to be part of Tess's life."

"Why not?"

Gray scowled, rolled up a sleeve, and displayed the history written on his arms. "Take a wild guess." Nick blanched, but didn't look away.

"People change, Gray. You can get through this. You're already well on your way."

"Yeah." He held his thumb and forefinger together so they were almost touching. "Coming this close to smashing a whiskey chaser down my throat means I'm about ready to babysit."

Nick shrugged. "You're going to have bad days. You might even take that drink one day, but that doesn't mean you're a failure. Or that you shouldn't keep trying. Aren't they worth that to you?"

"Thank you, Dr. Phil." Gray slammed his head against the wooden bench and flinched. "Even if I was ready, it's too late. Tori and I are done."

"Don't bet on it." Nick angled his head the way he did when his brain was working overtime. "She's put up with you this long. That tells me she's either completely certifiable or she's in love with you."

"Can't be one without the other." Gray picked sesame seeds off what was left of his bun. Warmth ignited that fire of hope again. Maybe one of these days he'd let it burn.

"What're you doing tomorrow?" Nick wore that look that usually meant trouble.

"Thought I'd go for a facial at the spa. Why?"

"Want you to come sailing. You look like you could do with some fresh air."

Gray erupted into laughter. "Are you kidding me, Cooper? I haven't been on a boat in years."

"Just like riding a bike, Gray."

"You're actually not kidding." Gray fished his straw out of his empty glass and aimed it at Nick's chest. "Well, I guess drowning might be better than OD'ing my way out of here. Okay. But hey, do something for me too."

"What's that?"

Gray sat back and allowed a smile. "I'm going to work on a new album. And I want you to write it with me."

Chapter Twenty-Seven

Nick and Gray had stayed for two hours, eating, talking, and being thoroughly annoying. What was worse, they were too far away for her to hear any of their conversation. Lynette had begged Jed to kick them out, but he took perverse pleasure in her torture. She'd tried to flee through the back door, but the lock was still jammed. Jed needed to fix that before the fire marshal's inspection. By the time they got up to leave, the kitchen was spotless.

Jed opened his mouth, but Lynette shut him down with one look. She picked up a tray and went to clear Gray and Nick's table. She saw the cell phone sitting on the table at the same time that Nick strode through the doors.

"Jed, I forgot my—" He stopped midstride and stared.

Lynette had nowhere to run. No story would explain why she stood there wearing a white apron, carrying a serving tray. She put down the tray and reached for the phone.

"Looking for this?"

"Yeah." He blinked a couple times, ran a hand over his head, looked at her and Jed, but didn't move. "What's going on?"

"Closing time." Jed was trying to help, but the annoyance simmering in Nick's eyes said that wasn't the answer he wanted.

She put his phone down on the table, picked up plates and

glasses, and set them on the tray. Shifted her hand under it, pushed up, and headed for the kitchen.

Then Nick moved. Like he'd suddenly remembered how to run track.

"Don't go anywhere, Lynette." He pulled the tray from her hands and shook his head. "Are you seriously working here?"

"Don't know about seriously, but she's working here, yep." Jed let out the belly laugh Lynette had grown surprisingly fond of, but tonight it didn't work its charm.

"Nick. Just take your phone and leave. And please don't tell Gray."

"This is insane," Nick muttered, looking like he'd been hit in the head with the boom. "Are you trying to put yourself back in the hospital?"

"An honest day's work never killed anybody."

"In this place?" His voice jumped a couple of notches.

"It's fine. Quit yelling." She tried to push past him but he wasn't budging.

"You can't work here. This is a—"

Jed's cough rumbled around them. "A very fine establishment that any law-abiding citizen should be honored to find employment in. Especially given the current economic conditions of the country."

"Hagerman . . ."

"All right. I get it." Jed headed in the direction of the kitchen. "Lynnie, may I just remind you that you are loved and appreciated. I'll up your salary by a dollar but that's as high as I can go."

"Thanks, Jed." She sent him a grin, then glared at Nick. "Are you done?"

"No, but you are." He set the tray down on a nearby table. "*This* is your babysitting job? You've been lying to everyone so you can come work in a bar?" His eyes blazed under the flickering overhead light. "The money can't be that good."

"No. I've been babysitting too. It all helps, Nick." She pulled at her ponytail and stared at a puddle on the floor. Hopefully it was just water. "And you're not in a position to talk about lying."

"What?" He looked incredulous. Mortally wounded. "You're seriously going to throw that in my face?"

"Oh, stop overreacting." She moved past him and returned to clearing the table. "Look, David's out of work. Liz gives all her money to that wacko boyfriend to invest for her, and Gray—"

"Gray is about to get severely ticked off." Her brother stood in the doorway, mirroring the I-don't-believe-this look Nick wore a few minutes ago. "Please tell me I'm hallucinating."

"Thought you were in the car," Nick said.

Gray rubbed a hand over his face. "Lynette, what? What am I seeing here?"

"I could ask you the same thing," she retorted before she could stop herself.

Her brother flushed but crossed his arms. "I didn't have anything."

"I know. Jed told me."

Gray scowled. "So what are you doing in here, wearing that?"

"Working, obviously. And we're closed. So leave. Both of you." She picked up the tray and tried to duck past them but was intercepted by two pairs of blue eyes shooting blazing arrows at her.

Gray took the tray from her and slammed it down on top of the bar. A glass rolled off and hit the floor and shattered. Jed yelled from somewhere in back.

"Gray! Seriously?" Lynette pulled at her apron, wound her hands together to keep them from making contact with his face. "Please. Could you both get out and leave me alone?"

"Nope. You don't need this job." Gray took two steps around her and undid the top of her apron, pulled it off her, and tossed it to Nick. "Go get your stuff."

~

Lynette stormed through the house and out to the garden with the dogs. She marched across the damp lawn, took deep breaths, prayed, and tried to quell her anger. Eventually she walked back up to the patio. Took a puff of Ventolin and waited for her breathing to slow. She was still too angry to sit. She paced up and down, stopping when Nick stepped outside.

"I don't want to talk to you." She put her back to him and walked onto the lawn again. The dark sky was clear, about a million stars out. Normally she would have appreciated the beauty of the evening, but tonight her thoughts ran wild.

"Cecily says she'll see you tomorrow."

"Fine."

"Why did you take that job?" Nick came up behind her. "You can't carry all this on your own. It's time you stopped trying."

Lynette whirled to face him. "For once, Nicholas, mind your own business!" She stomped past him and went back up the stairs.

"Lynnie, wait." He grabbed her wrist and made her look at him. "What's going on here? Talk to me."

Lynette sat on the low wall of the patio. Finally she tried to put her jumbled thoughts into words. "You and Gray had no right to march in there and make demands like that! Thinking you can make me quit. Taking on that job was my decision. And when I quit, that will be my decision too. Not yours."

Nick sat beside her, a safe enough distance away. He stayed quiet a minute, then scrubbed a hand down his face. "Can I say something?"

"I'm sure you can. And will." She pulled her arms tight across her chest and refused to look at him. His low chuckle weakened her resolve to stay mad and she snuck a glance at him. Nick smiled and tucked a flyaway strand of hair behind her ear.

"I'm sorry. We acted like idiots."

"You think?"

"Look, I know you're worried about the house, about your dad, but I'm worried about you." He moved a little closer until he sat right next to her. "We all are."

"I'm fine."

Nick sighed, placed two fingers beneath her chin, and forced her to meet his gaze. "Are you? When's the last time you got a full night's sleep?"

"I don't know." Unwanted tears burned and she blinked them away. "Why is it so wrong for me to want to help?"

"It's not wrong." His smile set her pulse racing again. "But you're doing too much. The money will be there for the renovations, Lynnie. You don't need that job. Didn't you hear anything Gray said? He told me he talked to you on the way home."

She pulled her hair out of its ponytail and ran her fingers through it. Maybe she would quit. Part of her would be glad to never smell a French fry again. "He doesn't know for sure if he'll get that money. And what if your investor friend decides they're not interested? What if we don't get the building permit? What if—"

Nick put an arm around her shoulders. "What if you stop thinking the worst and have a little faith? Isn't that what you keep telling the rest of us?"

She gave up and rested her head against him, her anger finally dissipating. Exhaustion hit hard. "I just get scared sometimes. The house, my dad . . . We're looking at long-term health care down the road. Where's money for that going to come from?"

"You guys took him to the doctor's today, right? How'd that go?"

Lynette sat up and pressed her palms against her knees. It was what they were all expecting, but it terrified her just the same. "It's definitely Alzheimer's." The awful word prodded her and made the future more frightening.

"Oh, Lynnie." Nick pulled her close again. "I'm sorry."

Tears left trails on her cheeks. "I was still hoping he'd say it was just old age."

"So what's the plan?"

"The others think we should carry on. See if we can do the B&B thing. We'll manage Dad here as long as we can, but—" She sighed and swiped at her cheeks. "He'll have to go into a nursing home eventually."

Nick smoothed down her hair and rested his head against hers. "How are you really doing?"

"Trying not to fall apart, I guess." She ran a finger over the strap of his watch "It's horrible, seeing him change. All those wonderful memories, everything he knew . . . just disappearing. I can't sleep thinking about it. And when I do sleep, those dreams won't leave me alone."

Nick swiveled to look at her. "You're still having them?"

She stared at his earnest expression through the darkness. Nick was the only one she'd trust with this. Yet somehow the right words wouldn't come. "I don't know what to think. I kept hoping they'd go away. That they didn't mean anything."

"What do you think they mean?"

She shrugged. It was silly really, believing her mother was trying to tell her something from beyond the grave. But God could be. "Sometimes I wonder if they're not dreams at all, but things I know. The things I can't remember."

The wind moved across the patio and played a tune on the chimes. Crickets caught the rhythm and sent their song into the night. Lynette tried to enjoy the peaceful sounds of summer, but her mind would not still.

Nick rubbed her arm as she gave a shiver. "Maybe you should see someone, you know? Talk to a professional about what you're going through?"

"Like a shrink?" She laughed, pushing hair out of her eyes. "You think I'm nuts?" Not that she could blame him. Lately she'd been thinking the same.

"No. I didn't say that." His eyes softened and he leaned back again, enveloping her in a comforting embrace. "But sometimes it helps to talk things out."

"Maybe." She wound her fingers through his. "I thought if I could remember that day, things would make sense. But now, I'm not so sure I want to know. Does that sound weird?"

He shook his head. "No, I get it. I won't say I know what you're going through, but I do know what it's like living with hard memories. Memories you can't shake, no matter how much you want to get rid of them."

Something in his tone made her sit up. "What are you talking about?"

Nick stood and began to pace, hands thrust into his pockets. "There's something that happened . . . something I want you to know." He positioned himself across from her, his serious expression shadowed by the soft glow of the hanging light above them. "When I was at Princeton, I was involved in an incident. It's haunted me for a long time."

"Okay." Lynette couldn't imagine what he was going to say, but the pain that marred his face almost made her wish he wouldn't tell her.

Nick took a breath. "It happened the year Gray and I fought, after the Christmas break. The swim team—we were all together at a party—some of the guys got pretty drunk." He looked at his shoes. "I was looking for the bathroom, heard some noise in one of the bedrooms, some yelling, a girl screaming, so I went to see what was going on. There were about four guys, and they were forcing her . . . forcing themselves on her. She was trying to fight them off, but the party was pretty crazy . . . nobody would have heard. I didn't know what to do; I just stood there." He let his breath out in a rush. "I don't think I really believed what I was seeing. I tried to stop it, but one of the guys lit into me, threw me back into the hall, and slammed the door. By the time I was able to call the police, it was too late."

Lynette wrapped her arms around him. "That's awful. What happened?"

"She was in bad shape. The guys said I was involved, and it was my word against theirs. We were all brought up on charges. My father went ballistic. I swore to him I had nothing to do with it. Eventually the girl told the cops I had no part in it. My name was cleared, but my reputation was tied up with the rest of the scumbags. My dad convinced me to transfer to Oxford, spend some time over in England, start fresh. So I left. But the guilt of that night has stayed with me."

Lynette drew back and shook her head. "It wasn't your fault, Nick. Don't carry that guilt anymore. It doesn't belong to you."

"Lynnie." Nick rested his forehead against hers and sighed. It was the saddest sound she'd ever heard. "I've tried to let it go. I know I had nothing to do with it, but I should have been able to stop it. In some ways I felt like I committed the crime myself. And my father . . . I don't know. I knew he never quite believed me."

"Well, I believe you." She met his eyes and shook her head. "You're one of the good guys, Nicholas Cooper. I've always known that."

"Thank you." He stared at her for a long moment that made her heart beat a little faster. "Lynnie . . . I'm falling in love with you," he whispered.

Tears stung as she allowed the words to wind their way into her heart.

"Is that okay with you?"

Lynette nodded and lost herself in his smile. The moment his lips came down on hers, all other thoughts melted away. Lynette slid her arms around his neck, and allowed herself the luxury of a few moments of absolute contentment in his arms.

Nick stepped back first. "Everything will work out, Lynnie."

Lynette let out a tired sigh. "When I'm with you, I actually believe that."

He kissed the tip of her nose and pulled her against him. "Good. Because I'm not going anywhere."

Lynette leaned against the rise and fall of his chest as they watched the night sky in silence. The moon threw shadows around them and waves crashed against the rocks as they did every night. But this was no ordinary night.

Nick Cooper, the boy she'd loved for most of her life, actually loved her back. The astounding thought overrode doubt and fear and any nightmares that still dared to haunt her dreams.

Whatever came next, she'd survive it.

Because if Nick loved her . . .

That changed everything.

Chapter Twenty-Eight

Lynette tidied up the art studio Saturday evening. She'd take her latest painting to Evy Monday morning before work. Didn't want to look at the others she'd stacked in the corner and covered with a sheet. As long as nobody else ever saw them, she could just pretend it hadn't happened.

If it was true, if that last scene she'd painted was the memory that had eluded her all these years . . . She shivered.

Enough. Hopefully she'd sleep tonight and try to forget about it. She didn't have a clue what time it was now, but the heaviness of her lids said it had to be late. The predicted storm had rolled in about an hour ago. Rain pelted the windows and wind howled around the house.

Gray and Nick spent all day on the water, grilled steaks, and then passed out watching a movie. She presumed they were still where she'd left them after dinner.

The sound of yelling floated up the stairs. Had to be the television.

Lynette lowered into the rocker, too tired to get to her own room. Summer was slipping by so fast. Much as she wanted to savor having everyone home, dark shadows were crowding out her joy. Her siblings all carried a different kind of pain. While she longed to share her faith—and encourage them in their own faith—doubt stopped her. How could she talk to them about putting their faith in God when she was having difficulty doing it herself?

Sleepless nights were starting to take a toll.

She closed her eyes and gave up fighting the memories.

~

Lynette huddled in bed and waited for the noise to die down. Her parents were home from the party—she'd heard them come in a while ago—but they'd stayed down in the kitchen. The yelling stopped. A glass crashed to the floor. A few moments later the house had grown silent, so she pulled on her robe and slippers and crept downstairs.

Mom was in the kitchen, curled in the corner of the banquet. Her hair was swept high on her head, thick blond curls falling around her face. She wore the bright green silky dress with the Chinese pattern that Lynette loved.

"Mom?"

Her face was redder than normal, her eyes a little puffy. Lynette bit her lip and grabbed the bottle on the table beside her as she walked past. Went to the kitchen sink and tipped what was left down the drain.

"How dare you!" Her mother scrambled to her feet, slipped, and fell. Slowly she crept toward her on her hands and knees, an odd smile perched on her lips. "Why'd you do that, baby?" She struggled to stand and lurched forward. They'd gone over to the Coopers for dinner. Lynette stayed home, went to bed at her regular time, and fell into a deep sleep. Until they'd woken her with all the yelling and throwing stuff.

"You're drunk, Mom. You don't need any more." The stink of the rum wound around her, shot up her nose, and made her eyes sting.

"You don't know what drunk is," Mom slurred, trying to walk in her high heels. "You're only eleven. Unless of course you've been having parties of your own with those wild boys."

Lynette shook her head. "No. I . . . don't do that." The last time Gray had come home for the weekend, he and Nick got into Dad's whiskey. She doubted her brother could sit comfortably yet.

"That's good, darling." The fire in Mom's eyes dimmed and Lynette's pulse slowed.

"Where's Daddy?"

Mom pulled pins from her hair and shook out her long tresses. She gave a nervous laugh. "He went to bed. Got in one of those moods."

So he was drunker than she was.

Lynette swiped a hand across her nose. "You should go to bed too."

"I will. I just . . ." Mom sighed and met Lynette's eyes. "Nick's home for the weekend."

"So?" She hated the way her heart did that weird flutter at the thought of Nick Cooper. He was just a dumb boy.

"I don't think he likes being away at school very much." Mom breathed out a sigh that said she just didn't understand. Lynette was used to hearing it these days. "I can't imagine why. This is only their first year. At least Gray likes it."

"Gray hates it." He'd told her so his last visit home.

"Nonsense, darling." She laughed. "Gray would have told me if he was unhappy."

Lynette shuffled her feet and stared at her fuzzy pink slippers. The only reason her brother didn't say anything to Mom and Dad was because he thought being there was better than being here.

Some days Lynette had to agree.

"They're all gone. All my babies, up and gone." Mom played with her hair, sounding sad. Ryan started boarding school the year before, and this year Gray went. "All except you, Lynnie. You don't want to go away to school, do you?"

"I don't know." She shrugged, not really sure what the right answer was. "Do you want me to?"

"Of course I don't. I'm sorry I yelled at you." Mom's eyes filled with tears. "You were right to throw that away. I've had enough. I just . . . Sometimes it makes things better, you know?"

Lynette didn't know. Didn't ever want to know. "Sure, Mom."

When had Mom changed? Lynette missed the way things used to be. The way she could cuddle up in bed with her late at night or early in the morning, sharing all her secrets and dreams. Mom had been more like a best friend, someone she couldn't wait to spend time with. Now . . . she was somebody else. Someplace else.

The wind whined and rattled the roof of the house and shook the windows. Lightning slashed across the sky before a rumble of thunder. They both jumped.

Then the lights went out.

"Well, that's just wonderful. Get the candles, Lynnie." Laughter trembled on her mother's tongue. She was close enough to touch, close enough for Lynette to put her arms around, hug her tight, and tell her it was all going to be okay.

But on nights like these, Lynette didn't know if it was.

~

The slamming of the front door jolted her out of the past. Lynette frowned and crossed the room. Nick wouldn't be so careless. He knew her father was sleeping. She locked the studio door and ran down the stairs. And then she heard it. Almost as though she'd conjured up the sounds from her imagination.

Crying and yelling.

Gray's voice getting louder, then Nick joining in.

Lynette ran downstairs and made it to the doors of the living room just as Nick came through them. "What's going on?"

"Lynnie. We thought you'd gone to bed." Nick pulled her into a brief hug. "It's Liz. I'll be right back."

"Liz?" Lynette went into the room, took one look at her sister, and clapped a hand to her mouth. "What happened?"

Liz's face was bruised, one eye completely closed, her lip cut and bleeding. Lynette tried not to stare. Gray flung open the front door, letting the dogs out. Their barking echoed back through the house and Liz gave a low moan. Gray called them in and shut the door, bolted both locks, and swore. Loudly.

"Gray—" Lynette began, but the look on her brother's face convinced her his outburst was warranted.

"He didn't follow me. I told you." Liz could barely talk through her swollen lips. Lynette tried to process what was happening, unable to move. Nick came back with a washcloth.

"Here's some ice. Go sit down." He took Liz by the arm and led her back into the living room. Lynette sat next to her sister while Nick applied the cloth to Liz's swollen face.

"Who did this to you?" She must have been mugged or attacked, or worse.

"Who do you think?" Gray spat the words, pacing the room like a lion waiting for its kill. "I told you, Liz, the dude's insane. But you don't listen to me. Are you happy now?"

"Gray." Nick's voice held a clear warning that Gray had the good sense to heed.

"Your boyfriend did this?" Lynette took Liz's hand in hers, but Liz pulled away and wouldn't look at her.

"He was drunk," she whispered. "He . . . loves me."

"Do not make excuses for him!" Gray thundered. He stormed toward them, eyes blazing. "Look at yourself, Elizabeth! Is this what you call love? If it is, you've got a pretty warped idea of the concept."

"Like you would know?" Her sister wiped her eyes. "I don't need this. I never should have come back here." Liz pushed off the couch, stalked out of the room, and a minute later an upstairs door slammed.

Lynette stared at Nick and Gray. "What do we do now?"

"Well, she won't let us call the cops. So I say we wait until the goon shows his face and then we crack his skull wide open."

"Gray, please." Lynette shuddered at her brother's acrid tone. "I meant about Liz. Is she going to be all right?"

Gray inhaled and rocked on his bare feet. "When is Liz ever not all right?"

"Apparently now." Lynette stood, headed for the door. "I'll go talk to her."

She went to the kitchen first and made tea. After fixing Liz a mug, Lynette went upstairs and knocked softly on her sister's bedroom door.

"Liz?"

"What do you want?" Liz stretched out on her bed, one arm flung across her face. Diggory lay across the end of the bed, Jasper on the floor. They watched Lynette through mournful eyes.

"I made you tea. Milk, no sugar." She put the peace offering on the bedside table and glanced around the bare room. The light beige walls blended perfectly with green curtains that had never been removed. A comfortable recliner sat in one corner, but the walls were void of paintings and photographs, the room unused, untouched really, for years.

Only the double bed, mahogany dresser, and the desk by the window remained, a lone Tiffany lamp to keep it company. Liz had spent hours holed away up here, doing homework and studying for her SATs. Anything less than a 4.0 average was not acceptable. She was sent to boarding school at fourteen on the recommendation of the local school's principal who felt Liz needed a more challenging environment.

She'd only returned to them for holidays. And probably only because she had to.

The summer before she went off to Harvard, Liz commandeered Lynette to come help clean out her room. She couldn't remember where they'd put the boxes containing Liz's childhood. Probably up in the attic with all the other stuff Mom could never throw away. By the time they finished, it was almost as though her sister had never lived here. She'd often wondered if that had been Liz's intention.

Lynette spotted the ratty-looking teddy bear, holding pride of place in the middle of Liz's dresser. She'd put him back in here when she heard Liz was coming home. A smile touched her lips as she picked up the only remnant of Elizabeth Carlisle's former life.

~

Lynette hovered by the door and watched as Liz and Mom packed the last of her things into a big green metal trunk. Liz was leaving for boarding school that afternoon. And her sister was actually happy about it.

Mom, hair tied in a messy ponytail, wiped her hands down her madras capris and gave a long sigh. "Are you sure this is what you want, Elizabeth?"

"Mother." Liz rolled her eyes, put her hands on Mom's shoulders. "If you ask me that one more time, I'm going to scream."

"It's not home, you know." Mom tucked a strand of Liz's thick blond hair behind her ear. "They have all kinds of rules. They'll make you study all the time."

"And scrub the toilets. With your bare hands." Lynette trailed into the room, ducking as her sister tried to smack her one. She stuck out her tongue and grinned. "Well, I'm just warning you. David says they make him eat bread and water and pig slop at his school."

"David's full of it." Liz smiled anyway, turned, and lifted the quilt on her bed to check underneath it. "Oops. What are you doing down there?" She dragged a dust-covered teddy bear out from under the bed and pulled away the cobwebs. "Hello, Ringo."

Lynette chewed on a torn fingernail and tried not to notice the tears in her mom's eyes.

"Do you want me to pack him, sweetheart?" Mom asked. "You've already got a few stuffed animals in there, you know."

Liz pushed her shoulders back and walked toward Lynette. "Will you take care of him while I'm gone, Shortstop?"

Lynette pushed her hands deep into the pockets of her denim overalls and shrugged. Her fingers curled around the pretty shell she'd found on the beach that morning. She didn't know why, but she suddenly felt like crying. "I guess. If you want."

"Here, then." Liz held out her old teddy bear, and Lynette grabbed him quick before her sister changed her mind. "And take off that awful cap." She tossed the Red Sox cap to Mom and pushed her fingers through Lynette's mess of tangles. "You know you'd be pretty if you just took a little care. You've got to remember to brush your hair or you'll get horrible rattails. You're not one of the boys. You know that, right?"

"Sure." She pretty much was, but she didn't want to argue with Liz. Not today.

"I got you something." She produced the shell and handed it to Liz. "If you put it to your ear, you can hear the ocean. It'll remind you of home."

"Thanks, Lynnie." Liz's voice cracked a bit and her cheeks got red.

"Do you really want to go away and leave us?" There was no worse punishment in her mind. Lynette couldn't imagine a day away from Wyldewood.

Liz bubbled with an excitement Lynette didn't understand. "I'm not leaving you, silly. I'll be back for some weekends. And holidays, of course. And we'll have all summer together."

"We can go over to Boston anytime, hon. They'll let us visit," Mom added. She didn't fake enthusiasm very well.

"Sure." Lynette sniffed and bit down on her lip. A little kid would just bust up right about now, but she was almost ten. And she wasn't a sissy.

"Will you write to me?" Liz seemed a lot taller this summer— prettier and thinner. She would probably end up being one of those models David and Ryan drooled over, move to Italy, and never come home.

"Yeah. But my paintings are better."

"Send me some then."

"Okay." Lynette blinked. Her face felt hot all of a sudden. And next thing she knew her eyes were wet.

And so were Liz's.

Her sister drew her into a hug, held her a minute, then pushed back, smiling through her tears. "You better not let the boys catch you like this."

"Don't tell." She rubbed her eyes and tried to stop her shoulders from shaking.

"I won't." Liz shook her head, solemn again. Mom put her arms around them both and kissed their wet cheeks. Lynette huddled close to them and wished somehow she could stop the world from changing.

~

Lynette hugged Ringo and listened to Liz's muffled sobs. The storm raged outside, but it was no match for the turmoil inside. She mustered courage, sat on the edge of Liz's bed, and placed the worn bear on her sister's chest.

Liz sniffed, sat up against the mound of pillows at the top of her bed. She picked up the old bear and folded her arms across him. "You can say it, you know."

"Say what?" Lynette looked away, stroked the dog's soft ears, and listened to the wind pitch against the shutters. She couldn't look at the bruises.

"That I got what I deserved."

Lynette forced her eyes to connect with Liz's. "Why would you even think that?"

"Because it's true. He told me he loved me. I was stupid enough to believe him. I believed him every time he said he was sorry. Believed he'd never do it again."

"Liz." Lynette grasped her sister's hand and blinked back tears. "Nobody deserves to get beaten. I wouldn't wish this on you."

"I wouldn't blame you if you did." She picked off a few stray cobwebs wound around the old bear's head. "I haven't exactly been the best sister in the world."

Lynette couldn't really argue with that. So she shrugged and tried on a tiny smile. "I suppose we could be closer."

Hollow laughter stuck in Liz's throat. "Don't you ever get mad, Lynnie?"

"What should I be mad about?" She longed to scale the wall around her sister's heart, but it was too high. No matter how good things were, with Liz, there was always something to gripe about. The Great Complainer, Dad used to call her. *"There she goes again, oy."*

Liz dabbed at her cheek with the washcloth. "You're such a Pollyanna. It makes the rest of us look bad."

"Sorry." Lynette grinned at her sister's frustration. Then she grew serious. "So this isn't the first time he's hurt you?"

Silence forced her to listen to the storm. Lynette shuddered and pushed away the memory.

"No. But it will be the last." The spoken words sang with victory.

"Will you go back to New York?"

"I don't know." She tossed Ringo from one hand to the other. "The apartment is Laurence's. I'll have to go get my stuff. I might look for a new job. Maybe even work from here for a while, until I decide if I want to stay with the company."

"He works there too?" Lynette didn't remember the details. She'd only met the man once, about a year ago when her sister dropped in unannounced for a brief visit.

"Sweetie, he's the CEO."

"Oy." The word slipped out. She twisted her hands together and debated her next move. But then Liz began to laugh.

"Oy vey." Her sister made a sound that landed somewhere between hilarity and despair.

Lynette moved a little closer and put her arm around Liz's shoulder. "It can only get better, right?"

Liz gave a long sigh, sat up, and wiped her eyes. "Right. Que sera, sera."

Mom sang that song to death—until they ran from the room whenever she started humming it. But no truer words were written.

Whatever will be, will be.

Lynette waited a moment, then unclasped the chain from around her neck and held it toward Liz.

"What's this?" Liz examined the small key warily.

"The key to Mom's room." There was no use fighting the inevitable.

Not anymore.

Her sister stared at it, silent. She was quiet for a full minute. "What have you been hiding in there?"

Lynette sighed. "You'll see."

"What does that mean?"

"It means . . ." Lynette ignored her fear. "I can't remember things, Liz. But I think I need to. I'm tired of hiding from the truth."

"What things?" Her sister's eyes got rounder, filled with fear. "What truth? Are you talking about when Mom died?"

"Yes." She whispered the words, desperate to get this done.

Liz put her hands on her shoulders and held her gaze. "Lynnie, what are you telling me? You . . . don't remember . . . anything?"

"I didn't. But now . . ." How to explain the unexplainable. "I was there, Liz. When Mom died. I know that. But I can't remember anything about that day. I don't know what happened."

The truth lurked in her nightmares, danced in the dreams that disturbed her sleep.

Somewhere in the recesses of her mind, memories hid. Memories so full with bitter ache that she'd buried them way down deep and out of reach. Left them alone, undisturbed for years.

But like it or not, they'd started to claw their way to the surface. And sooner or later, they would become real.

Chapter Twenty-Nine

Nick closed the door to his room the next morning and walked down the hall. He'd spent the night in one of the vacant rooms at Wyldewood, but it had been quiet. Not that he'd slept much. He woke with every noise, thinking any minute Liz's boyfriend might tear down the front door. And the fact that Lynette's room was just a few doors away from where he was trying to sleep hadn't exactly lulled him into deep slumber. He'd crept home before the sun rose and grabbed a couple more hours of rest.

Lynette.

Just thinking about her made him grin. He sure hadn't come back here looking for romance. And he certainly hadn't expected to be slayed at the knees the minute he set eyes on her. But Nick recognized the feeling.

Happiness was within reach. So close now he could almost touch it. Yet there was still so much sorrow. So much of the past left between them.

Lynnie's lack of memory troubled him most. Some of the things she said scared him. Pushed him toward truths he didn't want to think about, much less face.

What had she seen the day her mother died?

What did she really know?

One day they'd have to talk about the things he'd attempted to banish from his mind. One day he might be able to face the trans-gressions of their parents without bitterness and shame. Today the thought still made him ill.

If Lynette didn't know, what right did he have to tell her?

But he suspected she did. He'd seen too many ghosts in her eyes the past few weeks.

And lately he'd had this awful feeling that she knew more than all of them.

"Nicholas? So nice of you to join us for breakfast," his father said in a sardonic tone. Nick drew in a breath and turned around. When he entered the room, his heart jumped.

Maurice Vanguard sat with his father at the long mahogany table. His wife, Cheri, sat opposite him, and next to her sat Mindy. The two men were dressed for the golf course, while Cheri and Mindy both wore Lily Pulitzer and matching anxious expressions.

"Hey." Nick raised a hand and tried to act casual. "Didn't know you guys were on the island."

All three stared at him like he was next in line at the firing range. As their target.

"Where, pray tell, have you been?" Dad's eyes were ice chips.

Nick almost ducked, frantically trying to get his brain to work. "Next door. They . . . uh, had some problems. I was helping."

"All night?"

"How nice of you." Mindy smiled and dabbed at her lips with a linen napkin. "I don't suppose, in all your neighborliness, that you bothered to check your messages?"

Nick fished his cell phone out of the pocket of his jeans and pressed a couple of buttons. "Dead."

"Sit down." His father jerked his head toward an empty chair.

Nick obeyed, trepidation crawling up his spine. Dad had said something earlier in the week about the Vanguards coming on the weekend. He'd totally forgotten. After spending all day sailing, he'd just wanted to crash. Then Liz showed up and all hell broke loose.

Soraya served him a plate of steaming eggs, bacon, and sausage with a side of hash browns and roasted tomato. Nick's mouth began to water, and for a moment he forgot his present company as he shoveled food into his mouth and gulped coffee.

"Lord, Nicholas." Dad slapped a newspaper onto the table and pushed his chair back. "When you've finished making a spectacle of yourself, come into the living room. We need to talk."

Nick tried not to choke on a bite of sausage. He and Gray were going to work on some music today. "Um, kinda busy," he mumbled between bites, lowering his gaze to avoid his father's blistering glare. He reached for the coffee and poured himself a refill.

"You'll get unbusy. Don't take too long in here." The two men strode out of the room.

"Come, Miranda." Cheri excused herself, leaving behind a haze of perfume that made his eyes sting. Mindy shot him a look he couldn't read, then scurried after her mother.

Nick leaned back in his chair and ran a hand down his face. The hurriedly eaten food settled in his stomach and he downed a glass of orange juice. If they planned to haul him in for questioning about Mindy's relationship with Horse, he'd cheer. Life probably wouldn't be easy for Mindy for a while, but her parents would get over it. Eventually.

Nick finished his coffee, waited a few more minutes before joining them.

His father wasn't sitting. He was pacing. Maurice was doing the same on the other side of the room. Cheri and Mindy sat on opposite ends of a pale yellow couch, looking like they'd just been told Saks was shutting its doors.

Nick flopped onto a leather recliner and folded his arms. He steadied his gaze on Mindy and felt his pulse kick up a notch.

Her eyes brimmed with unshed tears, her normally flawless face sporting a scarlet hue.

"All right." His father stood ramrod straight. "You're one of the first to know this, but Maurice is going to be running in the next presidential election."

"Okay." Nick mustered a smile for the senator. "Congratulations, sir." God help America.

Maurice nodded. Nick studied his father and tried to figure out his thoughts. As always, it proved impossible.

Dad smoothed his hair, his eyes still fixed on Nick. "This isn't the best news in the world, but we'll deal with it. If we start arrangements now, I don't see why a Labor Day ceremony couldn't happen."

"Agreed." Maurice cleared his throat. "You know, I hoped for a little more respect, Nicholas. I know I'm old-fashioned and set in my ways, but—"

"Darling, you're terribly old-fashioned." Nervous laughter came from the direction of the couch. Mindy's mother's smile threatened to undo her latest boost of Botox. "Young people these days don't think like we do. Just consider yourself fortunate that they will actually be married before the baby comes. I know at least three young women Miranda's age who are raising children alone."

The words *married* and *baby* bounced against his brain. Indigestion burned upward, threatening to evict his hastily eaten breakfast. "What . . . what's going on?"

Mindy made a small choking sound. "They found out," she whispered. Two tears rolled down her cheeks. Cheri moved to her side and took her daughter's hand.

"Found out what?" His palms grew damp. The back of his throat was on fire. If they didn't quit staring at him, he was going to say something really stupid. Or puke on the rug.

"We don't blame you, Nick. I know Maurice can be a little intimidating. Mindy said you were waiting for the right time to speak to us, but she was so upset yesterday . . . Well, I suppose I forced it out of her."

"*I* was waiting for the right time? For . . . ?" His stomach began to roll and he gripped the sides of the chair. "Mindy?" A million thoughts raced through his brain. Not one of them good.

"I told them about the baby, Nick." She wouldn't look at him.

Nick slid his feet to the floor and put his hands on his knees. Light flashed in front of his eyes. "Baby?"

"I suppose congratulations are in order," Dad said drolly. Nick watched in disbelief as he strode to stand before him and stuck out a hand. "Guess I'll live to see my grandchildren after all. Assuming I don't pop off in the next few months."

His father's comment seemed to lighten the mood, but the real meaning behind it slammed into Nick with the force of a linebacker. He sat motionless as his father slugged him on the back and then went to shake hands with Maurice. Cheri started prattling about wedding gowns and flowers.

They were opening champagne.

Suddenly Nick saw the rest of his life laid out before him. He slowly got to his feet and walked to where Mindy sat. Her eyes begged him into silence. But he shook his head. It was time he stopped running from the truth.

All of it.

"You're pregnant?" It didn't surprise him. What surprised him, what hurt, was that she was willing to throw him under the bus in order to protect herself.

"Nick, please. Don't do this."

"Are you kidding me?" No, no, no. He wouldn't let her suck him in again.

"I'm sorry," she whispered, fresh tears falling. "They just assumed, and I . . . I didn't know what to say."

"You didn't know what to say? I'll tell you what to say!"

"Is everything all right?" Mindy's mother hovered, concern shining in her eyes.

"No, everything is not all right." He blew out a breath, fought for calm, and raised his hands in surrender, ignoring Mindy's desperate look. "Sorry. I can't do this anymore, Mindy. I'm not doing it. Tell them the truth. Now."

"Nicholas, what are you talking about?" His father moved closer, his brows inching together.

They all stared at Mindy, waiting. For a moment, Nick felt sorry for her. But not sorry enough to continue the charade. He should never have agreed to it in the first place.

"It's not Nick's baby." Mindy faced them bravely, her voice shaky, but she lifted her head and met Nick's eyes with a faint smile.

"Don't even tell me . . ." Maurice swore, Cheri shushed him, and Mindy started to cry.

Nick had been around the Vanguards enough to know how this would go down.

Mindy would come clean, Maurice would have a fit, and Cheri would run interference, trying to soothe the stormy seas, eventually they would all calm down, and life would return to normal. And Mindy might even get to marry Horse.

He backed away and left the room, relief flooding through him.

Outside on the patio, the sun spread warmth across the flag-stones and Nick sank into a chair. It was over. He'd been an idiot to let it go on this long, and yes, he felt badly for Mindy, having to face her parents and admit to all the lies, but that wasn't his problem.

Not anymore.

The French doors opened and closed, and he heard the scrape of a chair being pulled up beside him. Dad sank into it and stared at him in disbelief.

"Are you seriously going to tell me you've been letting that ridiculous girl use you as her pretend boyfriend all these months?"

Nick tipped his face toward the sun. "I didn't see the harm in the beginning. You know how Mindy is. But I let it go on too long."

"I'll say." Dad let out a long whistle. "Well, Maurice is not happy, I can tell you that."

"I didn't figure he would be. He'll get over it."

"When hell freezes over, maybe. What were you thinking? This could have been disastrous. Sometimes I wonder about you, Nicholas. Why do you have such a need to be everybody's hero?"

Nick closed his eyes. "Do I? I don't think I do, not really. I just like knowing people are happy. What's wrong with that?"

"I suppose the Carlisle girl is now on your list of people you'd like to keep happy?"

They'd had this conversation and he was in no mood to rehash it. "I'm not doing this with you."

"Oh, simmer down." Dad waved a hand. "Do what you will. If she makes you happy, bully for you. But remember, I need you to be available the next couple weeks for board meetings. We'll be in New York a few nights, and you'll have to go back and forth a bit. So if you've made plans, cancel them."

"I hadn't forgotten." Well, he sort of had. He'd wanted to take Lynette out for dinner, start spending more time with her, just the two of them. "I'll be there." He stood to leave, and Dad cleared his throat.

"Why didn't you just tell the truth weeks ago?"

Nick met his father's gaze and held it. "Would you have believed me?" He waited a moment, hoping for the answer he knew he wouldn't get.

His dad shrugged. "I don't suppose it matters now, does it?"

Nick shook his head. "No, Dad. I don't suppose it does."

Chapter Thirty

He'd survived another week without talking to Tori. And it was killing him.

Gray sat at the piano Sunday morning, erased the last few notes on the sheet music, blinked and rubbed his eyes. He played a couple of chords and tried to urge the song out. The sun streamed into the living room, threatening to turn the place into an inferno by midday. He pulled at his T-shirt and pushed up off the bench. If he was sticking around, now might be a good time to invest in some air-conditioning.

He checked his cell phone again as he walked through to the kitchen. Neil had finally gotten back to him. Gray's fans were clamoring, and the record company had softened. They wanted a new contract, wanted him back in the studio before Thanksgiving. And his agent was forwarding a few checks to Nantucket. Gray hadn't asked how much. Didn't want to appear too desperate.

Gray hadn't shared the news with the family yet, still mulling it over. He wanted the music back, more than anything. But he'd definitely be making some changes to his lifestyle. But it was more than he'd hoped for. Perhaps Lynnie was right about God hearing their prayers.

The house was quiet with Lynnie at church, David somewhere outside, and Pops settled in the den in front of the television. He assumed Liz was still asleep, didn't blame her with what she'd had to deal with lately. Gray put down his phone and went about making some coffee.

He found his stash of Starbucks in the depths of the cupboard and added grounds and water to the coffeemaker. He should also invest in a Keurig for the house.

Liz came into the kitchen as he fixed his first cup. "Well, if it isn't my darling sister. Coffee?"

"Is it caffeinated?" Her bruises were starting to fade, but the bitterness in her eyes burned brighter than ever.

"The real deal." She took the mug with trembling hands. "You okay?" She looked like she hadn't slept at all, still wearing a baggy white T-shirt and checkered pajama pants that looked suspiciously like the ones he couldn't find. "Hey, are those—"

"Gray, where's David?" Liz glanced around the room a little cautiously.

"Probably outside cutting down a tree or something. Do you know what time he gets up? It's indecent. There should be a law."

"Is anyone else around?"

"Nope. Lynnie's at church and Dad's watching TV."

"Okay." Liz dragged her fingers through her hair and niggled her bottom lip. "Go get David. I need to show you guys something. Come up to Mom's room when you find him."

"Mom's room?"

"Don't ask. Just do as I say."

"Liz, I'm in the middle of writing." He took another sip of coffee and hesitated. The way she eyed him made him uncomfortable. "What the heck is wrong with you?"

Tears stood in her eyes. "Just go get David."

A few minutes later Gray glared at Liz's back as she marched toward their mother's bedroom, annoyed to be wasting valuable writing time on her drama. "What are you going to do, kick the door down?"

"That might actually be worth seeing," David added, and the two of them smacked palms.

"Grow up." Liz shook her head and held up a small gold key.

"Where'd you get that?" Gray moved toward her, already uneasy.

"Oh, keep your shirt on. Lynnie gave it to me last weekend." She faced them again. "I came in here on Monday. I've been trying to figure this out all week. But I don't know what to think." Liz unlocked the door and looked back at them. "Prepare yourselves."

Gray checked the time. "This better be good, Liz. I really need to get back to work."

As soon as he stepped into the room, Gray felt the blood drain from his head.

Writing would wait.

"What the—" David shoved past him and patrolled the room in silence.

Gray followed a few paces behind.

If he'd walked in here a few months ago, this would have been much easier to explain. But today he was sober as a schoolboy, and the sight left him dumbfounded.

Everything in his mother's room was exactly how it had been the day she died.

Exactly how it had looked twelve years ago.

Liz wiped her eyes and stared at them. "I'm not crazy, right? You are seeing what I'm seeing?"

"Oh wow." David slumped into a nearby chaise lounge and pinched the bridge of his nose.

Gray worked his jaw, his eyes stinging as he picked up a china statue on his mother's dresser. The little ballet dancer in shades of blue and gray—far more than he could afford at the time, but Liz insisted and went halves with him—Mom's Christmas present the year before her death.

There were the crystal animals Lynnie gave her every year.

Dogs, cats, unicorns, and the turtle Ryan thought she needed to add to the collection. An array of perfume bottles sat in a semi-circle beside the mahogany jewelry box Pops surprised her with one anniversary.

Framed photographs of all of them from birth to the last family portrait, everybody pressed and neat and tidy for once. And smiling. Even her hairbrush sat in place next to the sterling silver hand mirror they'd all looked into at some point and shared secrets with.

The funeral had been held the last weekend in June. He'd just turned fourteen, and all he remembered was the heat and being smothered by people he didn't really know wanting to comfort him. Pulled into big perfumed bosoms, slammed against suits that smelled like mothballs.

He couldn't recall much of the service, who was there, who wasn't. He, Nick, and Ryan snuck out of the house later while everyone was still milling around. Nick produced a few beers from somewhere, and they sat on the beach drinking, playing cards, and pretending nothing was wrong.

Afterward, with Pops in no shape to do anything and Lynnie staring out to sea half the day, the rest of them took on the task of emptying the master bedroom. Their father had moved into his own room down the hall long before that summer. None of them knew whether packing up Mom's stuff was the right thing, but somehow it seemed appropriate.

They were only able to work a few hours a day because of their summer jobs and because it hurt too much. The pain was searing, their loss unspeakable. But, by the end of August, before they all headed back to school, this room had been empty.

Gray sank onto the edge of the soft four-poster bed. "Lynnie."

"You don't think Dad did it?" David seemed skeptical, but Gray shook his head.

"No." Somehow, deep in his gut, he knew this was Lynnie's handiwork. Even the bed was made. He squeezed his eyes shut as the scent of his mother's perfume whispered to him through the glaring silence. "Looks like Pops isn't the only one who's nuts around here."

"Gray!" David snapped, eyes flashing with unusual anger.

Gray rolled his shoulders and groaned. "Okay, sheesh. I'm an idiot. You know I say stupid things when I can't think straight."

"Which would be all the time," Liz sighed, still looking rattled. "I've been too freaked out to really go through things, and I haven't said anything to Lynnie yet; she's hardly been home all week anyway. With Nick away, she's babysitting a lot. But I wonder . . ." She went to the dresser and began pulling out drawers. Gray watched, wanting to tell her to stop, but unable to form the words. Liz finally ceased her rampant rummaging and turned around.

In her hands she held a thin leather-bound journal.

"Fair game?" She raised an eyebrow, her jaw set in a way that told him she'd already made up her mind.

"No, Liz." David went to where she stood and tried to snatch it, but she moved too quickly. "It's Mom's diary. It's private."

"But it might tell us more about what went on before she died, Davy. Don't you want to know?"

David stared at her wide-eyed, like he was about to fall off the edge of a cliff into the pit of insanity.

"I want to know." The quiet proclamation slipped from Gray's lips before he could stop it. He looked up to see David and Liz eyeing him carefully.

"Gray . . . I don't think we should do this. For a lot of reasons." David's warning landed hard, but Gray shrugged it off.

"Relax. I'm not going to down a bottle of Jack or call my ex-dealer. Whatever is in that book, if anything, needs to be dealt with. Take a look around, big brother. Don't you want to know why we've suddenly stepped into the Twilight Zone?"

If they were ever going to be free from the past, they needed to exhume it.

"Read it, Liz." David sat forward and put his head in his hands.

The past few weeks were taking their toll. Gray had seen his oldest brother plunge himself into the repairs and restoration of the house like he was on some mission from God to save the world. Maybe it was more a mission to save himself.

Gray knew all about those.

Liz crossed the room and sat on the chaise lounge by the window.

Gray's head started to hurt.

Chances were good that their mother hadn't written about the affair in that book.

Nothing that would give away the secret he, Nick, and David had kept from the rest of them. Gray put a hand over his eyes and waited.

About ten minutes later, Liz's gasp told him he was wrong. "No! It's not true!" The book hit the floor with the force of an engine backfiring. Gray watched his sister curl over her knees and dissolve into tears that morphed into sobs.

David moved first and crouched beside her. "Liz . . ." His voice shook, his eyes bleary as he put an arm around Liz's shoulders. "I'm sorry. It's okay."

She lifted her head. Her trained eyes only had to look once. "You knew?" She ran a hand down her face and sat back. "You too, Gray?"

Gray sat on the edge of the bed and tried not to inhale. The atmosphere, the smell of the room, it was as though Mom had been in here just that morning. He crossed the large suite and pushed up the window, letting fresh air flood in.

"I've known for the past five years. Nick told me." Gray sat again, staring at her tear-stained cheeks. "That's why we fought that Christmas. I didn't believe him. Refused to believe him. So I . . ." He swallowed and studied the worn rug beneath his feet. "I kicked him out of my life."

"Gray came to see me that New Year's." David sank to the floor and pushed his legs out in front of him. "Told me Nick's story. I didn't know whether there was any truth to it, although I kind of had my suspicions, but we agreed to keep it between us. When I ran into Nick a few weeks back, I asked him about it and he told me everything. How he'd found them . . ."

Liz held up a hand. "Nick was just a kid."

"He was old enough, Liz. It went on for a few years." David rasped out the words. "Maybe even up until she died."

"It's just so hard to believe. Yet, in a way, it's not." Liz leaned over and picked up the journal again. "I remember now . . . things . . ." She skimmed pages for a while and they sat in silence.

Gray clenched his fists and watched the tips of his knuckles grow white. Had Lynnie known all along? How long ago had she put this room back together? Had she found the diary and discovered the truth that way?

There were too many unanswered questions. He couldn't think straight. He concentrated on the floor and prayed Liz wouldn't start reading aloud.

She did.

I couldn't possibly love him. Not the way I love Drake. That's different. But Anthony is so . . . consuming. He seems to take possession of me without saying a word. I'm drawn to him . . . Oh, I know it makes no sense. I hate myself for it. But Drake spends all his time up in that studio, half drunk and painting. It's like he barely sees me anymore. Like he doesn't want to see me. Anthony on the other hand . . . God help me, I know it's wrong—

Liz swore and shook her head, her eyes growing hard. "I thought I'd seen and heard pretty much everything. You never expect it in your own family. Okay, June 25, here we go."

"Liz, don't." Gray jerked his head up, tried to focus on her, but his vision blurred. He swiped a hand across his face and squared his shoulders. "No more."

Suddenly he was back at The Longshoreman, staring down those drinks. Wanting them so bad he could taste it, yet knowing with everything in him it would be the worst mistake he could make.

"I'm not stopping now," Liz retorted, even though her voice trembled. "You said you wanted to know what happened."

"I'm not sure it matters anymore." It wasn't the right answer, wasn't the answer she wanted to hear, but it was the only one he could give. "All this time I've been trying to put myself in her place. Trying to justify it. I remember Mom and Dad fought a lot. Pops could be a pretty mean drunk."

"No." David drew up his knees and folded his arms around them. "Yes, he and Mom fought, and he said stuff—they both did—but he was never physically abusive. She was the light of his life."

"We don't know what went on behind closed doors." Gray looked around, shivered. "We don't know what went on in this room."

Liz started to cry again. She probably hadn't cried this much in years. David braced his hands on the floor and dropped his chin to his chest.

Gray looked out the window and watched the sun duck behind a mass of white clouds. A shutter banged against the side of the house and made him jump. He closed his eyes and muttered a prayer that he hoped might make it past the ceiling. It was impossible to make sense of the situation. He wasn't even sure God could. But if there was ever a time he needed direction, wisdom, any help from above, it was now.

"Do you guys think Lynnie knew? About Mom and . . . Coop's dad?" He had to ask, though the thought made him want to hurl.

That his sister might have carried this secret around with her all these years—buried it so deep that she no longer remembered . . .

"I don't know what to think anymore." David's voice was low and barely audible. "Read the rest, Liz."

"I can't." She tossed it his way. It landed near his feet, and David reached for it and flipped it open.

June 25. I'm not sure how much time I have before this all comes out. I went to see Anthony today. Took Lynnie with me, stupid thing to do. I didn't want him to start anything, so I thought if she was there, at least out in the car, things would be okay. I told him it was over, that I wouldn't see him again. He yelled a lot and followed me out to the car. I'm not sure what she heard. I drove around the island a couple of times and she didn't say one word. Even refused ice cream. As soon as we came home she ran to her room and slammed the door.

Drake knows. I'm sure of it. The look in his eyes today, that silent, seething anger. He's gone now, but he'll be back. There's a storm coming. It's already raining.

He's going to confront me soon. Or he'll light into Anthony. Or both. I've known this was coming for a while now. It's probably best if I just leave, get away for a bit. Not sure how I'll live without—

David cleared his throat and sat in silence for a minute. Gray watched two tears spill from his brother's eyes and slip down his cheeks.

Without my darlings. I love them so much, even though they think I'm pretty dumb most of the time. They're the best kids in the world and I don't deserve them. I don't want to hurt them. Or Nicholas. This is such a mess . . .

"That's it?" Liz squeaked.

"That's it." David tossed the book back to her and shook his head.

It was even worse than he'd imagined, when he allowed his mind to go there. Gray fiddled with the strap of his watch and thought about Nick. Knowing for years without saying a word. In his own way, he'd been trying to protect them from this. Trying to do the right thing, as usual. But who'd been looking out for him? What kind of pain had he endured, knowing the kind of man his father really was?

Gray pushed to his feet and wandered around the room, trying to make sense of it all.

The room.

The past.

The truth.

"Mom and Cooper's dad had an affair," he finally said. "That much we do know. What we don't know for sure is who did this." He gave a wide sweep of his arm. "And why."

"Obviously it was Lynnie." Liz seemed to have recovered. Her business tone was back. "Why else would she have pitched such a fit when I wanted to come in here?"

"It could have been Dad," David suggested. "Who knows where his mind is these days."

Liz shook her head. "I don't think he'd have the wherewithal to do this. It had to have been Lynnie."

"Why do you think she finally gave you the key?" Gray watched his sister tear up again.

"Maybe she wanted us to know." Liz sucked in air and wiped her cheeks. "If she knew about Mom and Anthony Cooper, and she's been keeping that secret all this time . . ." She raised her hands and let them fall. "She told me she doesn't remember things. Specifically, she can't remember anything about the day Mom died. I think Lynnie saw what happened. I think she's the only one who can tell us whether Mom's death really was an accident."

Gray didn't hear the footsteps at the door until it was too late.

Pops stood in the doorway, staring at the three of them, eyes wide, mouth open.

Chapter Thirty-One

David scrambled to his feet. Liz blanched and, for once, had nothing to say.

Gray tried praying again.

"Oh." The word fell from his father's lips like one of David's decimated trees, thudding through the silence. Something flashed across the plains of his face as he entered the room—recognition? shock?—Gray couldn't tell. Pops's eyes remained vacant as ever.

Nobody spoke as they watched him wander the room.

He stopped at the dresser and picked up the hairbrush and started that slow humming he'd taken to doing of late. Turned it over in his hand and gently placed it back down again. He fiddled with a couple of the ornaments and then turned around to face them, a funny sort of smile on his face. "I can't remember why I came in here."

Liz moved first. Put an arm around his shoulder, leaned in, and kissed his weathered cheek. "It's okay, Dad. We were just going downstairs anyway. Would you like some tea?"

"Tea?" The disturbed look left him and he smiled. "Yes. Lovely. But . . . Oh, that's it!" He smacked a hand to his forehead. "Can anybody tell me why there is a little black boy running around the house?"

"Dude." Gray didn't know whether to laugh or cry.

Drake Carlisle had managed to pull off his final retreat into insanity at just the right moment.

Pops's timing was always perfect.

"A what?" Liz also sounded on the verge of laughter as she caught Gray's eye, her eyebrows shooting skyward.

"A child. Tiny. Very dark." Pops shook his head in annoyance. "He's tearing around the place screaming like a banshee. What's he doing here?"

"No idea, Dad." David rounded him on the other side and squeezed his shoulder, his face marred with pain he couldn't voice.

"Oh." He shrugged and gave that lopsided smile Gray was getting used to. "Well, perhaps we should offer him tea?"

"Sure, Pops." Gray couldn't help grinning despite the ache in his chest. The humor faded a minute later when a small child raced into the room and ran circles around them, punching the air with his fist.

"Jambo!"

"There he is!" Pops lunged, but the kid was too fast and sped out of the room quicker than he'd come in.

"Jambo!" The kid's raucous yell reverberated down the hall.

"What just happened?" David scratched his chin, a bemused smile twitching his lips.

"I don't have the slightest idea." Liz stalked to the door and looked into the hall. The dogs were barking, the kid still yelling, and the astonishment on Pops's face was more than Gray could take.

Laughter erupted like Mount Vesuvius. His dad joined in, even though he probably didn't know what he was laughing at.

"This is an insane asylum!" Liz glared at him. "Grayson, I don't see anything remotely funny about this. And who was that child?"

"Hey! Anybody home?" A familiar voice rumbled up the stairs.

Gray stopped laughing. Liz's austere expression fled, chased away by a smile.

David let out a low whistle. "Well, it's about freakin' time."

A moment later Ryan marched into the room, holding the little boy by the hand.

"Hey, guys!" Their brother hugged Liz first, clapped his arms around David, and embraced Pops and Gray. Ryan was so caught up in greeting them that he didn't appear to notice anything amiss in the room. Or that Liz's face was all banged up and she was still in her pajamas.

Gray crouched by the small boy. "Hi, little dude. What's your name?"

"Isaiah." Big brown eyes stared up at him, his earlier exuberance gone in the presence of so many adults.

"Cool name." Gray smiled and held out a hand. "I'm Gray."

Isaiah nodded and smacked his palm. "Like the color?"

"Guess so."

"I am seven. How old are you?"

"A lot older than seven." Gray chuckled and moved off as Ryan patted the boy on the shoulder.

"Isaiah, Gray is my brother. And that's my other brother, David. And this is my sister, Liz. And my dad, Mister Drake."

"I am pleased to meet you all." A huge smile split Isaiah's face as he went to each of them in turn and solemnly shook hands. "I say *Jambo*! It means hello in my language."

"Jambo!" Pops clapped his hands together, his eyes twinkling as he smiled at the boy he'd been ready to paddle moments earlier.

"Man, I almost forgot!" Ryan pointed at David. "Your wife's downstairs with the kids. I couldn't get through on the house phone to tell you all I was coming, so I called your house. Isaiah and I stayed with Josslyn last night, and she decided to come with me."

"Decided that all on her own, did she?" David gave their brother a knowing look.

Ryan's eyes sparkled and he held up his hands. "God works in mysterious ways, brother. Go on, we'll talk later."

David sped out of the room like his feet were on fire.

Gray's mouth threatened mutiny with a smile. If he hadn't been on the verge of a nervous breakdown, he might have allowed it to spread.

This was all too much.

He caught Liz's eye and indicated the door. She got the hint and somehow managed to sound nonthreatening as she invited Isaiah downstairs for a snack and took Pops along too.

Gray watched them go, then set his gaze on Ryan.

Only older than Gray by two years, he and Ryan had always been close. But after Mom's death, the last few years of high school pushed them in different directions. Ryan took up with a group called Young Life and started yammering on about Jesus and getting saved. Suddenly he was all about Bible studies, bake sales, and car washes. And Gray wasn't.

Nobody was shocked when Ryan chose to go into ministry. He took a post at a small church in Virginia for a while, but soon the call of Africa got too loud, and he moved over there to work full-time. Gray tried to keep in touch, but as his life got crazy, it was easier not to.

"It's been awhile." Ryan pulled him into another firm embrace. "I've missed you, brother."

"You too, man." Gray nodded, his throat thick. They'd always called Ryan Stringbean, but now Gray would tag him Quarterback. But the extra bulk suited him. His dark hair was on the longish side and curled around his neck, his face covered in a few days' stubble. He looked so much like Pops it was a little freaky. "How've you been, Ry?"

"Good. Can't complain. And you?" His look said he knew exactly how Gray had been, but his smile was genuine and somehow reassuring, putting a little light into what had turned into a rather dark day.

"I'll be okay." Gray believed that sometimes. Right now he wasn't totally convinced. "Who's the kid?"

Ryan grinned and scratched his chin. "He's mine."

Gray widened his eyes. "Uh, Ry, hate to break it to you, man, but there isn't a whole lot of family resemblance there."

"No?" His brother laughed, shrugged out of his lightweight coat, and tossed it over one arm. "Isaiah's family was killed two years ago, and he ended up in the orphanage where I work. We got pretty close and I . . . well, I decided to adopt him."

"You did, huh? Don't suppose you've got a wife you're not telling us about either?"

"No." Ryan looked away, finally scanning the room. "No wife." He inhaled sharply and let his breath out again. "Uh, Gray?"

"Yeah, I know."

"Didn't we . . . ?"

"We did."

Ryan moved around in slow motion, taking it all in. Checked out the items on the dresser, the clothes in the closet, even checked out the bathroom. At last he sank onto the edge of the bed and stared up at Gray. "What's going on?"

Gray cracked his knuckles and tried to come up with words that wouldn't give Ryan cause to question his sobriety. There were none. "We're not exactly sure. Lynnie had the room locked up. Liz finally got her to give the key over, and we found this . . . just today. We're still trying to figure it out."

"Lynnie did this?" Ryan pulled a hand down his face and muttered incomprehensible words.

"We think so. We don't know why. Liz seems to think she's got some repressed memory or something, that she knows what really happened the day Mom died."

Ryan's eyes clouded over, his jaw working double-time. "Oh, Lord in heaven. Gray, where is she?"

"She was at church. But now . . ." Gray checked his watch. It was early afternoon. "Babysitting." The sound of children's laughter floated up the stairs. "She'll be back tonight." His head began to thrum and the old familiar tug started. This would all be so much easier with a little something to get him through . . .

He squelched the thought and studied Ryan again. "Before

we go downstairs, there's something else you need to know. Well, actually a few things. I just don't know exactly where to start."

"Okay." Ryan lifted his hands and let them fall into his lap. "Start at the beginning."

~

Ryan took all the news rather well. Said he'd had his suspicions about Mom and Mr. Cooper all along, just never voiced them. And as Gray expected, he treated Pops like nothing was wrong, showing more tact and respect than any of them, with the exception of Lynnie.

After Gray helped with the bags and got them all settled in rooms upstairs, they sat in the kitchen while Josslyn foraged through the cupboards looking for something to give the kids. Lynette had asked him to go to the grocery store yesterday, but he'd forgotten. Liz scanned the day's paper and drank wine. The fruity aroma singed his nostrils and put more unwanted thoughts into his head.

Gray sat as far from her as he could and looked on as Ryan and Isaiah had Dad absorbed in photos of Africa. Zebras, giraffes, elephants, the village where they lived . . . Gray tried to pay attention, but his eyes kept moving toward the two towheads on David's lap.

Brandon and Bethie clamored over their father, vying for his attention. He hadn't stopped cuddling them since they'd arrived. And if the kiss between him and Josslyn that Gray happened to walk in on was any indication, things were definitely better between them.

Gray's heart twisted again. The twins were about a year younger than Tess. Her cousins. Their thick blond hair and big blue eyes reminded him of her big time. Forced him to acknowledge all he'd missed out on. He wouldn't swear to it, but he thought they might share the same grin.

Not that he would know.

The moment Victoria had tearfully told him she was pregnant, he'd mentally disconnected. Told her he didn't want any part of it. He wasn't ready to be a father and never would be. He'd seen his daughter once, the day after she was born, in the hospital, before he'd left on a six-month tour.

Much to his surprise, Tori joined him a month later, still messed up and under the misguided impression that they actually had a future. He'd made it clear where he stood.

If he couldn't love his daughter, he certainly couldn't love her mother.

The lie had been good, served its purpose, but it was one he no longer believed.

"Gray?" David was staring at him a little warily. "You okay, man?"

"Sure." Gray cleared his throat and studied the scratched tabletop. Noticed his hands shaking.

They all noticed.

Liz scooted out of her seat and filled a glass with water. She patted his shoulder as she handed it to him. "It's been a rough day, huh?"

"Yeah." His throat was so jammed with emotion it was difficult to talk. Liz removed her glass of wine and shot him a look of apology.

Ryan put a hand on his arm and gave him a smile that didn't need words.

"Is spaghetti okay for dinner?" Josslyn asked. "There doesn't appear to be much else."

"Sure, why not." It was all they seemed to eat around here. "Just don't put garlic in it," Gray muttered, his eyes starting to burn. He pushed out of his seat. "I gotta get some air."

Gray sat on an old weathered bench on the back patio and tossed his phone between his hands. He should call Nick, but he didn't know what to say. And he was in New York anyway, busy with his father. The last thing Coop needed right now was more to worry about.

The only person he really wanted to talk to had made it perfectly clear that she didn't want to talk to him.

"Gray?" Ryan stepped outside. "Everything all right?"

Gray shrugged and put down the phone.

Ryan wandered across the patio and glanced toward the tennis court. "The place is a mess."

"No kidding. None of us had any idea things were this bad. I don't know how Lynnie coped this long." Gray stretched his legs out and accepted the guilt. "I can't stand to think about what she went through all this time, trying to deal with Pops on top of it."

"I didn't go overboard to keep in touch either." His brother backed up and perched on the wall opposite him. He played with a thin leather band around his wrist, his eyes fixed on Gray. "I had a feeling something was wrong awhile back. Her letters changed. She seemed almost too happy. It was weird. And then she stopped writing. I would have come sooner, but it took ages to get all the paperwork done for Isaiah's passport."

"You never got her letter about the house?"

"What letter?" Ryan shook his head. "I just knew I needed to come home. I prayed a lot about it, and felt like God was telling me to get back here as quickly as possible."

Gray let out a whistle. "Well, okay." He hadn't gone into detail earlier, more concerned with telling Ryan about Pops and the stuff about Mom and Coop's dad, so he filled him in on their financial affairs and where they were with the house situation. "Lynnie seems set on the idea of doing the guesthouse thing, but after today—seeing Mom's room like that—who knows what Lynnie's dealing with. It might be better if we sell."

"Sell." Ryan looked around, his face masked with sorrow. Gray knew what he was seeing. Years of memories, love, and laughter flowed through every part of this place. He'd fought the feeling for a while, but it grew stronger each day.

"It's hard to imagine not having Wyldewood, Gray."

"I know. But if Lynnie— Well, I'm not sure what she's going to be able to handle."

"We have to talk to her, see what this is all about, right?"

Gray nodded. "I know. But I'm not looking forward to it."

Ryan crossed one leg over the other, his eyes filled with fresh concern. "So what's going on with you? I know what I've heard and read, but I'd like to hear it from you."

Ryan listened while Gray talked. He teared up when Gray succumbed to a mysterious prodding at his heart and told him about Tess. Eventually his brother released a deep sigh and came to sit beside him on the bench. Put an arm around Gray's shoulders and squeezed. "You're going to be okay."

Gray swiped a hand across his eyes and gave a shaky laugh. "Don't be so sure, preacher man. Some days I think I'm this close to losing it."

"You're stronger than that, Gray. Even if you don't think you are. I saw it in your eyes when you talked about them, about Victoria and Tess. You can do this. Do it for them."

"What if they don't want me?"

Ryan laughed and mussed Gray's hair. "Then I guess the rest of us are stuck with you."

Gray pushed him off but couldn't stop a smile. "Thanks, Ry. Hey, I haven't told anyone yet, about Tess, okay?"

"No problem. Whenever you're ready. I'll be praying for you, bro."

Gray met his brother's eyes and allowed the weight of his words to wedge into that empty spot in his soul. "I've been doing a bit of that myself lately." He wound his thumbs around each other. "Not sure God can take a first-class loser like me, but Lynnie says He'll listen to anyone."

Ryan's chuckle filled the porch and made Gray feel better. "Lynnie's right. Keep talking to Him, Gray. Hey, I need to go check on Isaiah." He reached for the cell phone on the bench and handed it to Gray. "Why don't you do what you came out here to do?"

Chapter Thirty-Two

Gray sat alone in silence for a while, finally gave up the fight, and hit the keys. Pressed Send and waited. A moment later his phone beeped. Tori's picture lit up the screen and he checked the message.

Thought I told you not to call.

He grinned and tapped out a reply. You never said anything about texting.

Gray kept his eyes on the screen as minutes ticked by. Nothing. Great. He'd screwed up again. Then her ringtone blared from his cell and made him jump. "Walking on Sunshine." Gray smiled, put the phone to his ear, and tried not to sound desperate. "Hey."

"Hey, yourself." She sounded cheerful, but wary. His heart flipped just the same. "You all right?"

He'd missed her voice. Missed her. His eyes began to water and he swiped at his cheeks. "No, not really."

"Talk to me." Her reticent sigh made him wonder what he was doing, but slowly the words tumbled out. She let him talk without interrupting.

"So that's where things are at," he finished. "We've got to talk to Lynnie about everything. I just don't know what to say. I feel sick over the whole thing. But I, um . . ." Gray swore and stared at his feet. "I'm not going to do anything stupid, Tor. I'll be okay."

It was a promise. Somehow he would make it through this night. If that meant getting Ryan and David to tie him to a chair and sit on him, so be it.

"Of course you will." She actually seemed convinced. "But call Doug. He's your sponsor. He'll be there for you. I know you believe you can do this on your own, but—"

"I don't. Not anymore. I think I need all the help I can get."

"Okay. Well, good." She got quiet. "I believe in you, Gray."

"Yeah." She always had. He rubbed the stubble on his chin and tried to picture her face. "I don't know if you've talked to Neil recently but—"

"He called." Tori cleared her throat. "It's good, huh? You'll be back in the game in no time."

"Maybe, yeah." He'd been giving some serious thought as to what he wanted his life to look like from this point on and the revelations were startling.

"Guess this means you'll be going back on tour soon?"

"I'm not planning on it." A breeze floated up from the water but didn't really soothe him. His heart was in too much turmoil.

"You're not?" Did she sound hopeful or was that wishful thinking?

"No." He'd made up his mind a few days ago. "I don't want to go back to that life. Things are going to look a little different this time around. No tours right now. I'll be doing some studio time, though. Maybe in New York."

"Not LA?"

"Nope. Think I'll stay closer to home."

"I see." Her pause was a bit too long for his liking. "Well, that's good, I guess, if that's what you want."

"Yeah." His heart jumped as he heard a little voice in the background asking Tori who she was talking to.

"Just a friend, hon. His name is Gray."

That wasn't the answer he was hoping for, but what did he

expect? He clenched his jaw and watched the dogs race across the lawn after a sea gull. The sun was a ball of fire, slowly inching down toward the inky blue line of the horizon. "Can I talk to her?"

"Excuse me?"

He imagined the look on Tori's face. Horror, disgust, maybe contempt—all of which he deserved. Gray sniffed and rubbed his eyes. "I asked if I could talk to her. I'd like to talk to my daughter."

"Gray." Tori rarely cried, but he thought he heard her voice catch just a bit. She stayed quiet a long time. "Are you sure?"

Gray made up his mind and inhaled. "Yes."

For a while he thought she might have hung up. Then the phone crackled.

"Hello?" A shy, sweet little voice came down the line and captured his heart without even trying.

"Hi, Tess." Gray smiled through his tears. "How are you?"

"Good." Her breathy voice rendered him motionless. "Know what? Mommy's making spisgetties. Is my favorite."

"Yeah? That's what I'm having too." Gray registered the overwhelming urge to wrap his arms around this child he barely knew. His child. Before he could assimilate to what was happening, the world as he knew it changed.

"An I . . . an I have lettuce! With the pink sauce. Do you gots to have lettuce too?"

"I don't know. Maybe." He grinned and shook his head, wishing he could see her face. "You don't like salad?"

"Sometimes I likes it. But *no* carrots. I'm 'lerrgic."

Gray began to laugh, warm hearty laughter that flooded through him, shoved off reality, and convinced him there were indeed better times ahead. "Me too, how 'bout that?"

"You're funny." Her giggle made him realize how much he'd already missed.

"Yeah, I guess I am." He floundered for words, wondering what appropriate conversation with a three-year-old looked like.

"I likes your voice," Tess whispered. "Do you wanna come over to my house? I gots swings. An a BIG slide! Wanna come?"

"I would, Tess." He bit down on his lip. "I'd like that a lot."

"When? Tomorrow?"

"Tomorrow?" More laughter slipped out of him. "Probably not tomorrow. Soon. I'll ask your mom, okay?"

"Okay. Mommy says I gotta go. So, bye."

"Oh, okay. Bye, Tess."

"Gray?" Tori was back, sounding a little unsure. "Are you still there?"

"Yes." He leaned against the back of the bench and reveled in the moment. "Thank you."

"She's a bit of a chatterbox. Kind of like someone I know." Tori's sudden laughter charged through him, bringing new energy, warmth, and hope.

"Yeah? You think I talk too much, Tor?" Clouds moved in from the west, turning the sky dark and threatening.

"Sometimes." She hesitated. "Gray, you sound so . . . I don't know. Different. Are you really doing all right, I mean outside of what happened today?"

"Sure." He knew she wasn't buying it, but it was the best he could do. "How's it going there? Are you okay? Do you need anything?"

Her sigh was long and a little sad. "No, thanks. It's going okay. I got a job at a plant nursery during the day, close by the house. I like it, it's fun. And I haven't killed anything yet. My mom looks after Tess. And I . . . well, don't laugh, but I signed up for some night classes."

"That's awesome. What are you taking?"

"Oh, just first year stuff right now. Some English and math. I think I might want to be a lawyer."

"Seriously?" Gray wasn't surprised. She'd make a good one. "Well, you can't have too many of those in one family."

"In whose family?"

Talk about a Freudian slip. He niggled his bottom lip and willed his brain to come up with something smart to cover up that remark, but suddenly all he could think was that he'd finally figured out what he wanted.

He just didn't know how to tell her.

"I don't know. Forget it. So, you . . . seeing anyone?" It had been a few weeks, after all, and with the way he'd been acting, it wouldn't surprise him.

"What kind of stupid question is that?"

"Well, I—"

"First of all, when would I have time? Second, why would I be remotely interested in starting a relationship with anyone when I'm just getting to know my daughter, and third— Why are you laughing?"

"Sorry." Gray tried to control his mirth. "I'm just really glad to hear that. I mean, that you aren't seeing anyone."

"You are?" The question confirmed what a jerk he'd been.

"Tor?"

"What do you want, Gray?"

Time stilled. If she'd asked him yesterday, even a few hours ago, he'd have a different answer. But over the course of the afternoon, and through the last few minutes of his life, things had come into focus. The only thing he wasn't sure of was what her response would be.

"A second chance." He'd always liked to live a little dangerously.

That was exactly what he wanted.

He wanted to be with her. And Tess.

Wanted it more than anything.

"Are you still there, Victoria?"

"Yes." Her trembling voice barely reached above a whisper.

"Are you crying?"

"Maybe."

"Gonna stop anytime soon?"

She sniffed and gave a long sigh. "You are *such* an idiot."

"Yep. I think I've finally clued in to that, but thanks for the reminder." Jasper wandered up and laid his big head on Gray's knee. Gray scratched the dog behind his ears. "You have no idea how much I miss you."

"I might have some idea. You're not starving to death, are you? Or eating junk that you shouldn't be?"

"Who me?" He wouldn't tell her about all the burgers and fries he'd been scarfing down lately. "Spinach shakes every day."

"Liar."

He laughed. "Okay. No shakes. But I've been going to all my meetings, and Nick is making sure I stay on the straight and narrow. Can't get anything past him."

"Good to hear. Well. It's dinnertime. I should probably go. Do you want to call me—us—again?"

"Are you sure?" He pulled air into his lungs and prayed harder than he'd ever done in his life.

"As long as you are."

His smile felt good. "I am. I'm one hundred percent sure." Gray knew the road to recovery would still be long, but he was even more determined now. He'd kick this. For her. For them. "Can I ask you something?"

"You will anyway."

Her sudden laughter pulled him from the dark shadows he'd been hiding behind and made him chuckle. "Well, I don't have to."

"Oh, go on, now you've got my curiosity piqued."

His voice retreated. Gray cleared his throat a couple of times and wrestled with the right words. Nerves pelted the pit of his stomach.

"I don't have all night, Mr. Carlisle."

Dang, she was sexy when she got annoyed. "Okay, don't have a cow. Well, the thing is, I was thinking that I . . . well . . . um . . ."

"Puke it up, Gray."

"I was wondering if I could come see you. See Tess." He blurted out the words and wondered if she'd be able to decipher them.

Another long silence threatened to break him.

"Can I think about it?"

Air rushed from his lungs and disappointment dampened hope. "Sure." A light rain began to fall and the wind picked up, throwing drops against his cheeks.

"I mean, she's just getting used to having me around and I . . . I need to figure out what to tell her, and whether you . . . Did you just say sure?"

"I think so?"

"You're not going to argue with me or threaten to take me to court if I don't let you see her?"

"Why would I do that?"

She gave a short laugh. "Because a few months ago that's exactly what you would have done."

The truth galled him, but he faced it and nodded. "You're right. I'm sorry."

"I know you are."

"I'm sorry for all of it." Gray leaned forward and drew in a deep breath.

They said confession was good for the soul. He'd beg to differ.

It was raking his heart across hot coals.

"I'm sorry for walking out on you when you told me about Tess. Sorry for shutting you out. For not seeing her. I know how much I hurt you. I'm not going to pretend none of that happened. But I really want to start over with you. Would you maybe . . . just consider it?" Please, God, a miracle right about now would be real sweet.

She made a sound he couldn't decipher. Gray closed his eyes and waited for her to hang up. "Tor?"

"I'm thinking."

Relief washed over him like an unexpected wave and almost sent him to his knees. "I want to be there for you, for Tess. I want to be her father." He smiled even though his eyes burned and his throat hurt. "Please believe that."

"You can't change your mind, Gray." Her voice was low and full. "If I let you into her life, you can't walk away again. Do you understand what you're asking me?"

"Yes. I do." He tapped a foot and willed his body to stop trembling. "I've had a lot of time to think, Tor. I know what I want."

She let out her breath in a muffled cry. "Gray. I want to trust you, but it's hard, you know?"

"I know." And he hated himself for it. "We could maybe start with dinner. Lunch. Go to a park or something? I mean, you know, if you decide you want to see me. And if you'll let me see Tess. Because I'd really like to see her. And you." Nothing like a little groveling to get the point across. Gray smacked his palm to his forehead.

"Okay, I get it, Gray. I'll let you know." He heard Tess calling her in the background. "It was good to talk. I'm glad you called."

"Actually, you called me."

She laughed. "I'm hanging up now. Tell everyone I said hi." She paused, sniffed again. "Gray?"

"Yeah?"

"Remember when we met and you said I'd live to regret the day I walked in and took over your life?"

Guilt punched his gut and Gray made a fist against the pain. "Yeah, I remember." Like it was yesterday.

"You were wrong. I have no regrets."

He sucked in air and sat in a downpour of gratitude.

Disbelief, amazement, and love flooded his heart. This was unlike anything he'd ever felt in all the time they'd been together. This was real, here, now.

His.

He'd spent years chasing down all the wrong things when the most wonderful thing in the world had been right there beside him the whole time.

And he'd let her go.

He wasn't about to make the same mistake twice.

"I love you, Victoria Montgomery. Just so you know."

She breathed into the phone a moment and then sighed. "I kind of figured you did."

"And?"

Sweet laughter infiltrated the darkest parts of his soul and he fell in love all over again.

"I love you too, Gray. Although most days I don't have the slightest idea why."

"Give me a second chance and I'll help you figure it out."

She laughed again. "I'll think about that. Call me in a couple of days."

They hung up, and for the first time in a long time, even despite the turmoil of the day, Gray felt completely at peace.

Chapter Thirty-Three

Lynette walked through the house early Sunday evening, the dogs at her heels, glad to be home. Tyler and his little sister had worn her out this afternoon. All she wanted to do was crawl into bed, but she probably needed to make dinner. And feed the dogs. Liz didn't know her way around the kitchen, and if she left it to Gray or David, they'd be having peanut butter on toast.

And sooner or later, there would be questions. Because by now, Liz would have gone into Mom's room and discovered her secret. Lynette had been waiting all week for her sister to say something, but she'd been strangely quiet.

The noise reached her first. Children's voices. She shook her head. Lack of sleep was getting to her. She entered the kitchen, blinked a couple of times at the number of people in the room, then let out a shriek as Ryan stepped toward her and swept her into a bear hug.

"You're back!" Lynette gripped his shoulders and stared, just to make sure she wasn't dreaming. Time had treated him well. He was tanned, fit, and healthy, but sadness stood in his eyes. They must have told him about Dad. She sighed and gave him another hug. "I'm so glad you're home."

Her brother introduced her to Isaiah, and then she turned her attention to David's family. She hugged Josslyn and the kids, loving the cheeky grins on their little faces. The last time she'd seen them, they'd just learned to walk. Now they were talking up a storm and charming her with wide smiles and eyes full of mischief. David was beaming, no sign of the strain on his face she'd grown accustomed to of late.

"You look great, Lynnie. What's it been, a year or something? You really need to come over and visit us more often." Josslyn bustled around, already right at home.

Lynette hadn't spent much time with her sister-in-law; it would be nice to get to know her better. "I will. Just . . . things have been busy around here."

She wanted to be happy—the whole family here together under one roof. That hadn't happened since . . . the year Mom died. Her chest tightened again and she pressed back sudden tears.

If only she could throw off the darkness shadowing her.

"Come, sit." Ryan ushered her to the banquet and she squeezed in beside Isaiah and Dad. Josslyn had dinner under control. David set the table in the dining room; even Liz helped by throwing together a salad. Gray fed the dogs.

Lynette offered to help, but nobody would hear of it. So she sat and listened to Isaiah's recounting of his long plane journey that brought him to the place he'd dreamed of since he was a little boy. America.

Later, Gray caught her eye across the dining room table as Ryan said the blessing. She tried to smile, but tears flooded her eyes, exhaustion winning. After dinner Josslyn took the twins and Isaiah upstairs to bathe and get ready for bed. Lynette got Dad settled, then she went back to the kitchen to help clean up.

Gray kept glancing her way, like he wanted to say something, dropping things and making strange noises in his throat.

"Gray, what's wrong with you?" His eyes were clear, but she didn't like the way his hands shook when he reached for the next plate to dry.

He stopped what he was doing and faced her. "Nothing."

"Well, you're acting weirder than normal," she muttered, then yanked the plug from the sink and watched water swirl down the drain.

"Coffee's ready." Liz sent Gray an exasperated look Lynette didn't understand.

"Come on, Lynnie, let's go sit down." David took her arm and led her out to the patio, despite her protests. She had to work tomorrow. All she wanted to do was go upstairs and try to get some sleep. But apparently her siblings had other ideas.

If they'd changed their minds about the house . . .

Lynette refused coffee, pushed aside fear, and faced them down. "If this is about the house, I thought we'd decided. Just because Ryan's back, that doesn't give you the right to pull the rug out from under me!" She hardly recognized the shrill voice that shot from her. Her brothers and Liz stared at her in clear surprise.

David spoke first. "It's not about the house, Shortstop."

Gray stared across the lawn. Ryan sat quietly beside her, his presence a comfort. Liz tapped her shoes on the floor in fast rhythm.

Lynette met Liz's eyes and knew. "You want to talk to me about Mom's room."

Liz nodded, silently studying her as though she half expected her to start speaking in some foreign tongue.

Ryan took Lynette's hand and gave it a gentle squeeze. "Did you put Mom's room back together like that, Lynnie?"

"I did." She could hardly get the words out. She wished Nick were here. He didn't think she was crazy. But he was still in New York.

"Can you tell us why?"

She took a moment to steady her breathing, collect her scattered thoughts, and finally faced her family. "I did it because I thought it would help. I can't remember what happened that day, the day Mom died. For years I tried not to think about it, told myself it didn't matter. But the past few months, I've been having these dreams. I know it sounds crazy, but it's like Mom is trying to tell me something. And I just have this weird feeling that it's about what really happened that day."

David drew in a shaky breath, his eyes misty. "So you put the room back together thinking it would jog your memory?"

"I hoped it would." She tried to smile, almost laughed at herself. "The boxes were all there, in her closet. At first I thought the idea was nuts, and it scared me that I was even considering it. But then, once I started, in a way it was like getting part of Mom back." She did laugh then. "I know how it looks. That's why I locked the room. I figured if Cecily went in there, saw it all put back together, she'd think I'd gone off the deep end. But it helped me. I'd go in there some evenings and just remember her, remember how things were, how much fun we all had together. But then the dreams started and I got scared, so I stopped."

"Can you tell us about the dreams?" Ryan asked, his soft voice stirring more emotion. Lynette nodded and slowly recounted as much as she could.

"So what exactly *do* you remember about the day, Lynnie?" Liz sat forward, intent on drawing blood from a stone.

"I've told you. Nothing really." Lynette rubbed her face and sighed. "I remember the bad storm. Lightning. Thunder. That's it. Something about stairs. A staircase. I don't know. The only thing I vaguely remember . . . is being in a closet."

"You were hiding in Mom's closet," David said. "That's where I found you."

Liz cleared her throat. "When you put all Mom's stuff back, did you see a book? A small, brown journal?"

Lynette stared at Liz and shook her head. "I don't think so. I just put stuff back where I thought it might have been. I didn't really go through it. Why?"

"So you don't remember anything about Mom and—"

"You know what, Liz?" Gray got to his feet too quickly. "I don't think it matters. Does it, Shortstop? I mean, whether you know what happened or not, it's not going to bring Mom back, right? Maybe it's better that you don't remember anything."

"Maybe." Lynette wanted to agree. Wanted to keep the past at bay, silent and locked away, where the things she knew couldn't hurt her.

But the last few days her memories had started to take on a life of their own, grown stronger, more insistent. What she'd remembered most recently disturbed her deeply. She'd gone somewhere with her mother, couldn't remember why or where, but she did remember feeling angry. Betrayed.

~

You can talk yourself into anything, Lynette. You have the most vivid imagination, and one of these days it's going to get you into trouble." Mom was really mad. Her voice shook and her eyes glowed with angry tears.

Lynette folded her arms, looked out the window, and watched the rain. Thunder rolled in the distance. Her heart hammered against her chest and she was starting to have trouble breathing. That would just make Mom angrier. She hated it when Lynette's asthma attacked. Said it scared her too much, made her feel helpless. "I'm not making it up. I know what I heard. I'm going to tell Dad."

"No!" Mom shrieked and marched across her bedroom, grabbed Lynette's arm, and forced her to turn around. "Don't you dare, young lady! I'm warning you—"

"Why, Mom?" She pulled air into her lungs and let out a small cry. "Why did you have to go out there today? Why was Nick's dad so mad at you?"

"He wasn't, honey." Mom didn't sound convinced and she quickly looked away. Then she took a deep breath, put her hands around

Lynette's face, and kissed her forehead. "Please, sweetheart, believe me. It was nothing. Nothing at all for you to worry about. I promise."

~

Lynette shook her head, unable to stop her tears. Gray stared at her, his forehead creasing.

"What, Lynnie?"

"I . . ." She put a hand over her mouth, inhaled, and stared at her brother. "Mom lied, Gray," she whispered. "I think she lied to all of us."

"What does that mean?" Liz's tone grew more insistent, and Lynette shrank against Ryan, trembling a little.

"I don't know. I wish I did, but I don't."

"It's okay. That's enough for tonight." Her brother put an arm around her and held tight.

"But—" Liz began to sputter.

"It doesn't matter, Liz," Ryan said sharply. "Let's just drop it, okay?"

"Drop it?" Liz's eyes flared. "But she hasn't told us anything!"

"There isn't anything more to tell." Lynette shook Ryan off and got to her feet. "If you're done with your interrogation, I'm going to bed." She swept her gaze over them and fought the terror that tried to drag her down.

Gray was right. It was better to leave the past untouched.

Because if they knew, if what she thought she knew was really true, they'd never get over it.

Chapter Thirty-Four

Gray stood in the middle of the pool, knee-deep in muck, and watched Liz march across the back lawn toward him, arms swinging.

He'd kept busy the last week, since they'd talked to Lynnie, still kicking himself over that conversation. He hated that she'd gotten so upset. That was the last thing he'd wanted. He tried not to think about what she might be hiding from them. After her outburst on the patio Sunday night, they decided the best course of action, for the moment anyway, was to let her be.

But her behavior since then worried him. She'd retreated into a silent presence, coming and going without saying much. It was unnerving. Reminded him way too much of the days after Mom's death. And what was that about Mom lying to them? Did she know about the affair after all?

He fished out another pile of rotten leaves and dumped them onto the huge collection near Liz's feet.

"Hey, watch it!" She skipped back and shook a stray leaf off her shoe. "Gross, that stinks. You know this is going to take you forever. We should just hire somebody to clean it out."

"I'm used to dealing with crap." Gray shot her a grin and wiped sweat off his brow. The sun beat down on his bare back and reminded him he hadn't thought about sunscreen that morning.

"You're burning."

"Yeah, I figured." He slopped through the sludge to the shallow end and hopped out. Kicked out of his rubber boots and peeled off the heavy-duty gloves, tossing them to the grass. "You didn't bring me a drink? I'm dying out here."

"You just said you were fine."

"Never mind. What's up?"

Liz lifted her Gucci sunglasses and stared at him with a quizzical expression. "Did you know Lynnie has been painting?"

Gray rubbed his nose. There was a bit of water left in the bottle he'd brought out earlier and he downed the warm liquid. It tasted like plastic. He shuddered and spat onto the pile of decaying dross. "Painting what? The living room?"

"Gray." Liz pursed her lips. "Painting like Dad, you idiot. Except she's better than Dad."

"Nobody's better than Dad." Gray reached for a towel and rubbed his face. "Pops was a genius. You know if we could talk her into selling his stuff we'd probably make a fortune."

"You're not listening to me." Liz smoothed back her hair and stepped closer. "I saw her putting some paintings into the car yesterday morning. At first I thought that's exactly what she was doing—selling Dad's stuff. But she left the studio unlocked. I think she's selling her own paintings. You should see them."

"Get out." Disbelief tried to win him over, but an old memory tapped him on the shoulder. Lynnie, winning prizes at school. Entering her artwork in competitions. Mom telling them her baby girl would be famous one day, just like their father. "Okay. This I gotta see."

~

Gray sat on the beach later that Friday and watched Lynnie and Josslyn build a sandcastle with the twins and Isaiah. Lynnie had taken the afternoon off, to spend time with the family, she'd said.

They were all tiptoeing around her like one wrong word would cause her to break into a million pieces.

He'd seen her stuff. Liz was right. She was good. Really good.

So why was she hiding it? Or if Liz's suspicions were correct and she was selling her work, why not tell them?

Gray frowned under the sun's glare. Poor Lynnie. She'd do anything for anyone, anytime, no questions asked. It wasn't fair that she should be the one to carry so much pain.

"Land ho, Grayson!" Dad sauntered past, Ryan at his side, David on the other. He pointed up to the house with a wide flourish. "Did I ever tell you boys I was once a pirate?"

His heart squeezed at Ryan's good-natured laugh. They all shared a smile and kept Pops moving. Gray lay back and closed his eyes. He couldn't envision the future without Pops. As much as they'd butted heads, Gray loved his father. He hadn't respected him all that much in later years, when the drinking got bad, but now he knew the power of addiction firsthand. He wished his dad could know Gray was trying, doing his best to break the cycle.

But maybe in his way, someplace in the depths of his confusion, Pops did.

Gray held on to the thought and found comfort in it.

His cell buzzed and he groaned, found it in his shorts pocket, and held it to his ear. "You are disturbing the peace. This better be good." Nick's laugh made Gray sit up in a hurry. "Cooper! Finally. Where the heck are you, man?"

"Still in New York. Last meeting this afternoon. Why do you keep calling me?"

"Have you talked to Lynnie?" Gray dug his toes in the warm sand and watched the waves.

"I spoke to her this morning. Why?"

"How did she sound to you?"

Nick laughed again. "Real good."

"Shut up, Coop." Gray groaned. "She didn't sound weird or say anything was wrong?"

"No. She sounded fine."

"I don't think she is." Gray shifted so he could see his sister. "There's some stuff going on, man. She won't really talk to any of us, long story. I figured maybe she'd talked to you. Has she said anything about, uh . . ." He didn't even know where to begin.

"About what? What's going on over there?" Now Nick sounded worried.

Gray picked up a handful of sand and let it trail through his fingers. Maybe the fewer people freaking out right now, the better. "Forget it. Just get in touch once you're home."

"Gray—"

"No, man, forget I said anything. We'll talk when you get back."

"Well, okay. I'll be back as soon as I can," Nick said. "Tonight, hopefully, but it might be late. I'll come by tomorrow."

"Actually, I'm headed to Jersey tomorrow." The thought sent his pulse racing. Tomorrow he was going to meet his daughter.

"Serious? That's awesome, dude."

"Yeah, it is kind of." Tori said Tess hadn't stopped talking about him since their phone conversation, and that if he really wanted them in his life, he'd better come meet Tess.

"I'll call Lynnie again later," Nick promised. "Stay cool, bro. Have a great time."

"Will do. Keep me posted from this end." Gray clicked off and tried to ignore the churning in his gut as he watched Lynnie wander away from Josslyn and the children, down the beach alone.

~

Nick breathed a sigh of relief as the board meeting ended and he pushed his chair back. Men and women filtered past him, some stopping to say a few words.

He waited until he was out in the hall to check his messages. Nothing more from Gray. Lynnie assured him everything was okay, so he wasn't sure what Gray was worried about. Probably nervous about his visit to see Tori and Tess.

"Nicholas." His father caught up too quickly. "Everything all right?"

"Fine." Nick nodded to Maurice as he passed, but was unable to produce a smile. Truth be told, he was still pretty angry with Mindy for trying to pin her pregnancy on him. But she'd apologized, too many times, and from the sounds of it, she'd managed to convince her father that Horse wasn't such a bad guy. The wedding she really wanted wouldn't be so out of reach after all. He had to hand it to her, Miranda Vanguard always landed on her feet.

Evy McIntyre had called him three times, which was weird. She usually e-mailed when new paintings were in.

His father clapped him on the shoulder. "Good job in there. You did your homework. I was impressed."

"Uh-huh." Nick scanned his messages, his pulse picking up.

"You want to grab an early dinner before you head home?"

"What?" Nick wasn't sure he'd heard right. "With you?"

Dad frowned, then a rare smile lifted his lips. "Is the idea so aberrant?"

"Uh. Actually, yes." Nick grinned and put his phone away. "But okay. As long as you're paying."

Later, Nick settled into the backseat of a cab that smelled like sardines and called Evy back.

"Well, it's about time."

"I was in meetings."

"Are you on the island?" She lacked her usual cheery tone.

Nick cranked the window down as the car stopped in traffic. "No, I'm in New York. Headed back to Nantucket now."

"Good. Come and see me when you get in, Nicholas."

"It might be late. I'll come by tomorrow."

"No. Tonight. It's urgent."

Nick sighed and leaned against the seat. Sweat slid down his back and he ripped off his tie. "Okay. Do you mind telling me what this is about?"

"I'll tell you when you get here. See you soon." She clicked off and left him listening to the Soca music coming from the cab's radio.

~

Nick arrived home a little before nine that night, changed, and headed into town. He let his gaze veer as he drove past Wyldewood. He'd see Lynnie tomorrow. It was too late now; she'd said she was going to try to get to bed early. When he arrived at the gallery, he found the door open, Evy waiting for him.

"Hello, dear. Good flight?" She greeted him like an old friend, which Nick supposed by now was appropriate.

"A little rough. They said we've got some nasty weather coming."

New paintings hung on the walls. He walked across the room to check them out. Verity's, but not quite as good as the last he'd bought. They were happy scenes. Christmas in Nantucket, the houses decorated with red ribbon and garland, a light snow falling as a horse and carriage making its way down the cobblestones of Main Street. The other, another beach scene, similar to the ones she'd done before. Both pieces lacked the passion and mysterious feel that drew him to her paintings in the first place.

"Nicholas."

The way Evy spoke his name made him turn in a hurry. She crooked a finger and headed for the back of the gallery, but not without locking the front door first.

"What's going on?"

Evy led him into a long storage room and backed up against

a table. She took off her glasses and wiped her eyes. "I probably should have done this awhile ago."

"Okay." Nick wondered at her stricken expression.

"It's about Lynette."

"Lynette Carlisle?" Things were getting stranger by the second. "Do you know Lynnie?"

"Yes." Evy nodded and cleared her throat. "Have you talked to her recently?"

"Sure. Why?"

"How does she sound to you?"

"Uh." Why was everyone asking him that? Nick rubbed his jaw and shrugged. "Fine, I guess." He had no idea the extent of Evy's relationship with her, so wouldn't share Gray's thoughts.

Evy shook her head. "Those paintings you've been buying? They're hers."

"What?" Nick reeled and gripped the nearest chair. It took him a minute to process the information. "Lynnie is Verity?"

"I'm afraid so." Evy twisted her hands together, her face creased with concern.

Nick leaned forward. "Start talking, Evy."

Evy sighed and nodded. "I met her last year at a friend's house. We hit it off, and eventually she showed me her work. I had an awful time convincing her to start selling it. She didn't want to call attention to herself. Didn't want to ride on her father's coattails, yada, yada."

"That sounds like Lynnie." Nick smiled before he could stop himself. "Why didn't you say anything? I told you we were friends."

"Yes. But I made her a promise. I didn't have any reason not to keep her secret up until now. I know the two of you are close, she's confided in me, you see, and—"

"Evy, get on with it."

She sighed and moved around the long table. "Lynnie came in the other day with those paintings you saw outside. And there was another one. I'm pretty sure she didn't mean to bring it, but somehow it landed here, and . . . well, see for yourself." She pulled off a white cloth and revealed an unframed canvas.

Nick moved closer, unsteady on his feet.

The painting came to life, told the truth in living color.

Dared him to deny it.

Dark muted colors screamed at him, forced him to acknowledge thoughts he'd been pushing out of his head for too many years.

The woman at the bottom of the stairs lay curled as if in slumber, her long blond hair covering her face. Only on closer inspection did he see the trail of blood seeping around her head. The house was clearly Wyldewood, the old ships clock on the wall a perfect match to the one that still hung there.

He needed a few minutes to comprehend what he was looking at. "She signed it." He stared at the small signature at the bottom of the painting.

Verity.

Truth.

Evy slid up beside him, put a hand on his shoulder. "Why are you in this painting, Nicholas?" She pointed to the man standing at the top of the stairs, a look of sheer horror on his face. But it wasn't hard to miss the coldness in his eyes.

Nick swallowed and tried to ignore the hammering of his heart. He placed his hands down on the table in front of him, closed his eyes, and waited for the room to stop spinning. "That's not me. It's my father."

Chapter Thirty-Five

Storm clouds rolled across the dawn sky as thunder rumbled over the ocean. Rain began to fall in heavy drops, pelting his back. Nick yanked up the zipper of his slicker and banged on the front door again. He breathed a sigh of relief when it finally opened, but then stared in surprise. "Ryan?" Lynnie had told him her brother was back, but he'd forgotten.

Lynette's brother frowned, scratched his chin, and then a smile lit his face. "Hello, Nick." He looked back over his shoulder. "Why are you banging the door down at this time of the morning? You're going to wake everyone."

Nick hadn't checked his watch. All he'd thought about was getting here as soon as possible. It had been far too late last night to come over so he'd waited until daybreak. And with the storm chasing him he hadn't wasted any time. "Sorry. Is Lynnie home?"

Ryan blocked the doorway. "No. She was off yesterday, but spent the night in town. Babysitting. Said the mom had an emergency."

"Are you sure?" Nick crossed the front porch and peered in the window. "She didn't say anything to me yesterday about babysitting."

Ryan shrugged. "Must have come up after you spoke. She left around suppertime last night. What's going on?"

"Can I come inside? I need to take a look at the art studio."

"Are you serious?" He widened his eyes. "Nick, what is this about?"

"I can't explain right now, but it's important." Nick raised a hand as David came up behind Ryan, bewildered and sleepy-eyed. "David, thank God . . . maybe you'll listen to me."

"What are you doing here, Cooper? It's barely seven a.m."

Ryan yawned and crossed his arms. "Says he needs to go up to the studio."

"Please." Nick shuddered as thunder inched closer and the sky got darker. "I think Lynnie's in trouble."

David gave a quick nod and they let him in, following him up the stairs until he reached the third floor. "It's locked." He jiggled the handle as if to prove the point.

"Move." Ryan pulled him out of the way and in one swift kick, the old door flew open. Nick stared. Preacher or not, he wouldn't want to take him on.

He scanned the room and finally found what he was looking for hidden in a dark corner, covered with an old horsehair blanket. He pulled back the blanket to uncover what he hoped he wouldn't find, but somehow knew he would.

"Here." He pointed to several paintings propped up against the far wall, almost identical to the one Evy had shown him.

Ryan crouched in front of them. "Oh, you've got to be kidding me."

David stood next to his brother and gave a low whistle. "Liz told me Lynnie was painting again. I'm guessing she didn't see these." He backed up, faced Nick with a stricken look. "How did you know?"

"Evy McIntyre from the gallery in town called me." Nick told them everything. "Apparently Lynnie's been selling her paintings to her. One of these was left with a few other . . . normal ones."

"She's been trying to remember." David rifled through the hidden artwork, pulling out sketches and half-finished paintings—all the same horrifying scenario in various stages. "All this time . . ." He ran a hand down his face and Nick listened, astounded, as David filled him in on the events of the last few days. "She must have been there. Seen the whole thing. Once the ambulance left, I found her. She was hiding in the closet in Mom's bedroom." He sniffed, his words thick with sorrow. "I never thought—afterward we never asked her what she saw." He peered closer and looked back at Nick. "That's—"

"My father." Nick nodded, replaying the facts over and over in his mind. Rain pulsed against the roof and lightning lit up the room. Thunderstorms were predicted for the whole weekend. His stomach turned inside out. "Are you positive Lynnie's babysitting?"

David and Ryan exchanged a worried glance. "Where else would she be?"

~

The swish and squeak of the car's windshield wipers were getting on his nerves. Nick spent all day scouring the island but came up empty. As soon as Liz called to tell him she'd spoken to Tyler's mom and Lynette hadn't been babysitting, his heart kicked into high gear. She wasn't with Cecily. Wasn't with Joanne. Wasn't anywhere.

They'd spread out, but so far nobody had spotted her. The sky remained dark and menacing, the winds fierce, the rain unyielding.

Nick drove on past Brant Point and tried to imagine where she might have gone. He'd checked in a couple of times with Evy but she hadn't heard from her either. And Gray was in New Jersey, going crazy and texting all of them every five minutes for news.

Nick doubled back past Jetties Beach again, but it was deserted. As it should be. Nobody in their right mind would be out in this weather. He drove on. Darkness descended as he crossed the moors and crested the hill; his eyes began to droop. No point in getting into an accident. Reluctantly he swung left and veered down the long drive that would take him to the place he hoped to call home one day.

The thought of getting through the night without knowing Lynnie was all right terrified him. He'd call David again and see what they wanted to do. She had to be somewhere.

Nick pulled up to the front of the beach cottage and smothered a yawn. Something different caught his eye. A car was parked on the other side of the cottage. And then he saw her.

He almost cried with relief at the sight of the drenched figure standing on the path, staring at the house.

A warning as loud as the evening cannon at the yacht club sounded through him the moment he'd spotted her. Instinct told him why she was here. Why he'd been the one to find her.

And why he wanted to put the Jeep in reverse and peel out of there before she even knew he'd arrived.

But she had his heart now. There would be no going back.

Nick reached for his cell and called David. "I've found her." He gave the address and hung up, debating his next move.

She turned in slow motion, her face pale, ghostlike in the harsh headlights, soaking wet and shivering.

He shut off the engine and got out, hesitating when she backed up as he got closer, eyes wide and full of fear. "Lynnie? It's me. It's okay. Everything's okay."

Nothing was okay.

He took slow steps toward her and prayed she'd stay where she was. "Hey." He reached her, put his hands on her cold shoulders. "What are you doing out here?"

Bloodshot eyes stared through him as rain pelted them from all sides. "What is this place, Nick?" She sounded tired, looked scared and confused.

"You're soaked through. Let's get you inside." He pulled his slicker up and over her head and guided her toward the stairs. For all he knew, she'd been here all night.

She stiffened and started to tremble. "I can't go in there."

"Lynnie. It's okay." He really needed to stop saying that. "This is my place."

"Your place?" She ducked away from him and backed up against the door. "No. It's . . . his." She twisted her hands and walked across the small porch. Fear held her face captive. "I've been looking all over for it. I couldn't remember where it was . . . but we . . . came here. My mother brought me. And he . . . he was here." She took huge gulps of air, her face so pale now that Nick put one hand on his cell phone.

"This was my grandparents' cottage, Lynnie." He worked to keep his voice level. "Before they built the Cooperage. My grandfather willed it to me. I'm going to renovate it. I can show you the plans if you'd like, inside." He had to get her out of the rain, out of the storm.

"Your father was here that day," she whispered. "My mother told me to stay in the car while she went to talk to him. They were yelling." Thunder and lightning cracked through the air and she let out a small cry. Nick got to her before she fled, fumbled with the key, and somehow maneuvered her through the door.

The warmth of the house and the sweet scent of the pine walls didn't provide the usual comfort. Another round of thunder made her jump again. Nick pulled her into his arms and held her trembling frame. "Shh. It's just the storm. You're safe here, I promise."

She pushed him away, clasped her arms, and took on that vacant expression again, glancing around as though the ghosts from the past would appear any minute. "They had an affair. Your father and my mother. I . . . I'd forgotten." She ripped her fingers through her wet tangled hair and looked straight at him. "How could I forget that?"

"Because it wasn't worth remembering." He shrugged off his coat, tugged at his damp shirt, and wished for the right words for this moment. The moment he'd been dreading for days. "I'm sorry, Lynnie. I wish it'd never happened." Nick watched her come back to him, watched her eyes widen, register his words and prepared himself.

"You knew?"

He hesitated and fought the urge to go to her. Her stunned expression told him it wasn't a good idea.

"Answer me! Did you know?" She gripped the back of her neck and glared so fiercely that he was left with little choice.

"Yes." The admission, once said, allowed a certain sense of relief.

Water dripped down the side of his face and fell off his chin. Nick gauged the glint in her eyes and got it over with. "I've known since I was a kid. I didn't tell anyone, not for years. And I never wanted you to know."

"No." She let out a strangled cry and sank to her knees. "Of course you didn't. Because none of you ever believed I could handle anything. Right? Poor little scatterbrained Lynnie. Did you think it was better to lie?"

Nick squeezed his eyes shut for a brief moment. How would they survive this?

"I never lied about it, Lynnie. I just didn't tell you what I knew."

She didn't reply. Just sat there, hunched over her knees.

He went to the closet for towels, returned to find her standing in the living room, staring at the collection of paintings he'd amassed over the last few months.

"Nick?" Lynette spun around, new confusion creased her face. "Why are these here?"

He pulled in a sharp breath and took slow steps toward her, holding out a towel. She didn't take it.

"Why are my paintings in this house?" Lynette marched across the room and began tossing them aside, one by one.

Nick ran to her and took her by the arm. "Stop it, Lynnie! Stop."

She whirled to face him. "You bailed me out, didn't you? Like always! I thought I was actually selling them to people who liked my art! But it was just you. You were paying Evy for them? All that money! I suppose you never wanted me to know about this either?"

Nick shook his head, hating the desperation in her eyes. "No, Lynnie, you're wrong. I bought the paintings because I liked them. I didn't know you were the artist until last night, I swear."

She put down the painting she held. Carefully.

She believed him.

"I wanted to tell you." Lynette shook her head and shuddered. "But I didn't want anyone to know I was painting." Her voice pitched desperately. "All this time I think I knew. About them. Your father and my mother. I was painting . . . other ones . . . to try to remember."

"I know." He wouldn't tell her he'd seen them, didn't want to upset her further, and he didn't like the fear in her eyes. Nerves threatened to turn his insides out any second. "You need to calm down, sweetheart. Just take a breath." Her breathing was growing tight and he didn't see this ending well.

"I hate them!" Lynette picked up the painting and hurled it toward the fireplace, her cry of anguish splitting through the room. The wood frame splintered and scattered across the old Persian rug. "I hate them for what they did! How could they?" She faced him again with a beseeching look that split his heart into pieces like the splinters on the rug. "And all this time, you knew? How could you even face me, knowing what your father did? Knowing how much my dad loved her? Here I was, thanking God for bringing you back into my life. Thanking Him for bringing us together!"

"Lynnie." Nick sighed, tears stinging. "I didn't know what to do. Maybe it was wrong not to tell you. But I only wanted to protect you."

"Yes, you always do!" She kicked at another painting and sent it flying. The wind howled against the windows of the house as the front door flew open. Ryan, David, and Liz raced inside, followed by Cecily. Nick held up a hand for them to stay where they were.

Lynette focused on him, not even acknowledging the others. "You lied to me, Nick. Just like your father lied. Just like my mother lied. They all lied! And he—" She paced the room, her eyes as wild as the weather. Nick watched her face change, the past grabbing hold once more.

Her breathing started to get shallow, raspy, and all Nick could think about was getting her out of here, but he couldn't move. He needed to allow this to play out.

Needed to let her remember.

"What happened that day, Lynnie? Can you tell me?"

She nodded, keeping her glassy-eyed gaze on him. "He followed us back to the house. I wanted to tell my father we had come here, but my mother got so angry that I . . . I ran away. I hid in her closet. And then I heard yelling. I thought it was my dad but . . . it wasn't. It was yours. Your father was in the house. In our house." She took a deep wheezing breath. "In my mother's room. I was so scared. I didn't know what to do. I knew I should go out, make them stop, but I couldn't move. I was terrified." Sobs wracked her and she knelt on the floor again, buried her face in her hands. "And then I heard her scream."

"Lynnie, don't . . ." Liz. Speaking softly, coming a little closer.

Lynette looked their way and shook her head. She stared at Nick like he was the only one in the room. The only one she wanted to hurt. "Somehow I forced myself out to the landing. And then I saw her . . . my mother . . . facedown at the bottom of the stairs. My dad was kneeling beside her, yelling and screaming and crying." She trained tear-filled eyes on him. "Your father was at the top of the stairs. Just standing there. He turned, saw me, and I ran back into the closet. But I knew she was dead." Lynette's wail was long and gut-wrenching—a sound that would haunt him forever.

Cecily was the first to break out of the trance they all appeared to be in. In a minute she had Lynette cradled in her arms, rocking her and saying the same thing over and over again. "Oh, baby. Oh, baby. Oh, baby."

The others soon surrounded her, covering her with comforting words Nick knew he could never come up with. She pushed them aside and nailed him once more, her eyes piercing his. "All this time I couldn't remember. They told us it was an accident and everyone secretly blamed my dad. But it wasn't my dad at all, Nick. It was yours."

~

Nick refused to leave the hospital. They wouldn't let him up to her room for fear of setting her off again. So he sat in the waiting room, exhausted and filled with fear for what the future might now bring.

He saw them leaving. David, Liz, and Ryan, arms around each other as they walked to the front doors, battle-weary soldiers returning home after losing the war.

Nick got to his feet. "David!"

They stopped walking. David shook his head, his face unreadable. "Why are you still here?"

Nick crossed his arms and scowled at the stupid question. "How is she?"

"She's asleep," David said. "They've sedated her. They want to keep her a few days. You don't need to be here, Nick. Go home." His eyes grew wet and he sighed. "Maybe we were wrong. Maybe we should have told her."

Nick shrugged. "I don't know. I didn't know she was there, though, that day. I didn't know that she saw . . . David, I had no idea that my dad—"

"It doesn't matter now. What matters is Lynnie, and getting her through this. But I think it's best if you just keep your distance for now. Until we see how she's coping. I'm sorry."

Nick watched in disbelief as David and Liz headed outside.

Ryan walked to where Nick stood and put a hand on his shoulder. "She's okay, Nick. They want to monitor her for the next few days. Memory repression can occur in stages. Personally, I don't think anything else is going to come out, but . . . who knows." He shrugged, his bleary eyes giving away exhaustion. "We're all tired. Go home and get some rest. There's nothing you can do here."

Nick pulled at his collar, his heart thudding uncomfortably. "Ryan, I need to know what you guys are thinking—about what Lynnie said happened. Will you go to the police with this?" The thought had been hounding him the past few hours.

Were he in their position, he wasn't sure what he'd do.

"Nick." The barest of smiles crossed Ryan's face. "What would be the point? Lynnie didn't actually see it. Unless your father confesses, we won't know for sure. And it won't bring my mother back."

Nick let out his breath, his eyes burning.

Cecily's words the day Gray came home wound around him.

"Grace, Nicholas."

Grace.

Ryan glanced toward the doors where David and Liz waited, then looked back at him. "Lynette and I talked quite a bit this past week. She told me about your dad's illness. I'm sorry."

"Thanks." That they didn't want to string his father up was hard to comprehend. If he was guilty . . . Nick didn't know what to think. What to believe. "Maybe he's getting what he deserves."

Ryan studied him for a long while. "Maybe you could give him what he doesn't."

Nick shrugged and looked away.

Forgiveness.

That would be about as easy as scouring Everest in a blizzard.

Chapter Thirty-Six

Nick sat outside his house for a while. He pulled off his raincoat and let out his breath. He'd been holding on to all this for so long, now that it was out, he figured he'd be relieved. But that sick feeling still plagued him, and worsened each time he thought about Lynnie's painting and what it could mean.

He needed the truth from his father.

Nick found him in the den watching the late-night news. "Dad? Can we talk?"

Dad switched off the set and waved him in.

Nick lowered himself onto the couch. He studied the lines on his father's face. His skin was sallow, his normal healthy glow almost gone.

"Where on earth have you been? I thought you said you were coming back to the island yesterday, but you were nowhere to be found when I arrived this morning. I've been worried."

Nick kind of doubted that, but appreciated the effort. "Sorry. I got back last night. I've been with the Carlisles. There've been some . . . developments." He pushed his head back against the cushions, not sure how to say it. Best to just put it out there. "Dad?"

"What?"

"Did you kill Diana Carlisle?"

His father jerked in the chair like he'd been zapped with a bolt of electricity. "Excuse me?"

Nick lifted his hands. "I need to know."

"Why the devil would you ask me that now, after all these years?"

"Because Lynette Carlisle thinks you did. And I'm not so sure I don't believe her."

A shudder ripped through Nick.

The truth was, he was afraid to hear the answer. Afraid to hear his suspicions confirmed. Afraid to hear his father finally admit it.

Anthony went to the bar and fixed himself a drink. Nick noticed the limp in his stride. Dressed in jogging pants and a light T-shirt, his weight loss was obvious.

"I'm dying, Nicholas." He sat, breathed out a ragged sigh. "The cancer is in my liver. Spreading into bone. They told me I have a couple of months, maybe more, maybe less." He took a gulp of the amber liquid, his cheeks pinking. "We should probably start talking to the lawyers. I want to get things squared away, while I can."

"Dad?" Nick's pulse accelerated with every word, acid twisting his stomach.

"Nick. I didn't kill her." He put his glass down and rubbed his hand over his eyes. They were wet. "Did I love her? Yes. Did I know it was wrong? Yes. God help me. After your mother left, I pursued Diana. I wanted a future with her. She wouldn't leave Drake."

He lowered his head. "I went to their house that day to get her to change her mind. We were arguing. I went after her . . . Her foot slipped at the top of the stairs. I tried to catch her . . ." Tears crept over the hollow crevasses of his cheeks. "It was an accident." His father's gaze was steady, unwavering. "An awful accident. But that's what happened. I'd say you could ask Drake, but . . ."

Nick sat straighter. "Drake was there?"

"He came around the corner just before she fell. Tried to catch her too . . ." A strangled sob caught in his father's throat. "He told the police it was an accident."

Nick swallowed hard, memories jarring, taunting. "You guys were pretty good friends, weren't you?"

"Until I crossed the line, yes." Dad ran a finger around the rim of his glass. "He could have ruined me that night. It would have been his word against mine. But he didn't. Even then, he . . . showed me grace." He shook his head. "All these years I've blamed Drake for my own sins. I thought if I could get rid of that house, I'd finally be free of the memories. Make him pay for being the one she loved more. But he's already paid that price. From what I've heard . . . they thought he did it, didn't they? Those kids thought their father was responsible for their mother's death."

"Maybe." Nick let out his breath. All the fight in him fled with the fear in his father's voice. "Lynnie was the only one who knew you were there."

"Let her think what she likes." His father closed his eyes for a moment. "I may as well have killed Diana."

"I knew about the affair. I kept quiet because I thought it was my duty to protect you."

Dad sat silent for a long, painful moment. "I got it all wrong, Nicholas." Harsh laughter caught in his throat. "Your mother said I'd regret the choices I made. She was right." He stood and walked to the mantel.

The few family photographs Nick's mother had left behind sat there. Nick never looked at them.

She'd given him a choice when she'd left. Come and live with her, what she wanted, or make his primary home with his father.

Nick chose to stay here.

Chose to stay with a man he was never quite sure cared either way. He wondered now whether that choice had been some sort of self-inflicted punishment or whether he hadn't wanted to leave the family next door.

Dad reached for a silver-framed image with a trembling hand.

Nick's eyes filled as he caught a glimpse of it. The two of them on a rare fishing trip together. He must have been about nine or ten. He held up his catch, grinning from ear to ear, while Dad stood beside him, one arm around his shoulder, pride in his eyes.

"That was a fun day." Dad faced him, his face sagging. "I've done a lot of things in my life that I'm not proud of. But you . . . you're different, Nicholas. Maybe I resented that a little. You always saw the good in people; always had this relentless desire to do the right thing. And you still do. I admire that now." Dad put the picture back in place. "So I want to apologize for everything, while I still can."

"Dad." Nick raised a hand. He wasn't ready for this.

"Hear me out." Anthony coughed, rocked on his heels, and tossed him a timid smile. "My own father was never one to show emotion. He had a list of expectations that stretched from here to Florida and I did my best to meet every one of them. Everything I accomplished, I did for him. So he would be proud of me. Tell me how great I was." His mouth pulled tight and he uttered a low curse. "He never did. Up until the day he died, I never knew how he really felt about me. And I repeated the pattern with you. I knew I was doing it. Hated myself for it, but I didn't know any other way."

He took slow steps until he came to stand in front of Nick. "I hope that one day you'll forgive me for that. Forgive me for my failures. I may not say it, or show it, but I'm proud of you, son. I really am."

Nick sat very still and let the words sink in. Thought about grace again, and what his life might look like, were he to truly embrace it. Finally, he nodded. "I forgive you, Dad. And maybe it's not too late. Maybe we can start over."

"Bah." Dad waved a hand with a short laugh. "Don't expect miracles, Nicholas. It's too late for me. But you . . . I know you hate that job at the bank. You're only there because I asked you to come back. I know you've always wanted to do something else. Architecture, right?"

"Yeah. A long time ago," Nick admitted, his throat thick. "Doesn't matter now."

"Yes, it does. We'll find someone else to fill your position." Dad sat forward. "If you still want to, go back to school. Study what you wanted to in the first place. Make the choices that will satisfy you, son. Live the life you want. Not the one you think I expected."

"Dad—"

"No. I want you to promise me. After I'm gone, you'll follow your dreams."

Nick blinked. Never could he have imagined sitting here having this conversation with his father.

"And marry that girl next door too. If you love her."

He almost missed the wink Dad shot him, but caught it in time and smiled wide. "I do."

"Well then." Dad sat back, looking more at peace than Nick had ever seen him. "That's settled."

"Dad? Would you be up to taking a trip?" The idea came out of nowhere. Suddenly he knew time was short. And he very much wanted to know his father. "We could rent a private yacht, hire a crew. You wouldn't have to do anything. We'll go anywhere you want. I can take some time off. Leave Tucker Watts in charge."

"Mercy." Dad downed his drink in one gulp.

Chapter Thirty-Seven

Nick waited two long weeks until they gave him the okay to go over to Wyldewood. With updates from Cecily and Evy, he kept up with Lynnie's progress. He'd called her, but she hadn't answered her cell. He wasn't sure she really wanted to see him, but he and Dad were leaving in a couple of days.

He needed to say good-bye.

Gray answered the door, disheveled in shorts, a dirty polo, and bare feet, holding a little girl with curly blond hair and familiar blue eyes.

"Hey." Nick spoke first.

"'Bout time you showed up." Gray's grin came out of hiding.

Nick looked at his feet a minute. "I'm sorry, man. It was a mess. I should have told her in the beginning."

"You weren't the only one who knew."

Nick's lips curled upward. "So, we're good?"

Gray's nod said it all. "We're good."

Apprehension slid away and Nick knew no matter what came next, he'd survive it.

"So. This is Tess." Gray rubbed the little girl's back as she gave a yawn.

"Hi, Tess." Nick chuckled as she buried her head against Gray's shoulder. "You're not shy, are you?"

"Nah. She's pretending. Give her two minutes. Come on in. Everyone else is down on the beach. We just got up from our nap."

"Nice." Nick followed Gray through the house. "So . . . you gonna marry that girl, dude?"

"Coop." Gray laughed and kissed Tess on the head. "That would be rather conventional of me, wouldn't it?" He stopped walking and turned to Nick. "I'm still working on getting my life back, but yeah. And when I do, I'll need a best man."

Nick put a hand on Gray's shoulder. "I'd be honored."

"Cool. Just take it easy with the speech." He lowered his voice and winked. "Tori's parents are just starting to like me again."

"Okay." Laughter felt good. "I'm really happy for you, man."

Gray threw him his classic bad-boy grin. "Wouldn't want to do it without you, Coop."

They clasped hands and Nick allowed the memories to take one final bow.

It was time to move on.

As they walked through the house, Gray peered through one of the long windows in the dining room. "Lynnie must have come up."

Nick's gaze went to the window and his lungs almost bailed on him.

Lynette sat on the bench, head bent over a book. The breeze played with her hair and the wind chimes conjured up a lifetime of memories and a bucketful of feeling, ready to spill over and wash away all the grime and grit of the grisly scenes his mind kept replaying.

If only he'd let it.

He rocked on his heels, suddenly nervous. "Um . . . maybe I should—"

Gray rolled his eyes and opened the back door. "Lynnie, someone to see you."

~

Lynette knew Nick would come eventually.

She looked up as he approached, unable to stop a smile. "Nick."

"Hi, Lynnie." Hesitation lurked in his gaze. "How are you?"

"You mean aside from being a little north of normal?"

Nick's grin came and went. "I hear normal is highly overrated."

"You might be right." The hospital stay was the worst. Meeting with the doctors, rehashing it all. But now the memories brought clarity instead of confusion. And the future didn't seem so far out of reach. "Thanks for the flowers." Every few days a new arrangement arrived. "Want to sit?" She put her book down, shifted to make room for him.

Nick settled beside her and draped one arm across the back of the bench. His eyes searched her face, maybe wanting to make sure no more ghosts sat on her shoulders and kept her up at night.

"Did you meet Tess?"

"Yeah. Quite a surprise, huh?"

She laughed at his expression. "Nothing Gray does surprises me anymore. I'm just glad he's finally decided to be a dad. He's awesome with her."

"I saw."

"How's your father, Nick?"

"He's hanging in there." Nick studied his knees, and when he looked up again, his eyes were a bit too bright. "The doctors say they've done all they can. It probably won't be much longer, months at best. We've had some good talks the last few days. We're taking a trip. He's always wanted to sail the Mediterranean. We've got a boat and a crew. A doctor buddy of his is coming along. Leaving next week. I . . . would have come to see you before now, Lynnie, but they thought, I mean, I didn't know . . ."

"You didn't know if I'd want to see you." She remembered her anger that night, finding out that Nick had known about the affair and kept it from her. But then she'd discovered David and Gray knew as well. "I needed some time to process everything.

I know that you wanted to be here, I knew you were thinking about me."

"You didn't take my calls."

"Nick. I'm sorry. My doctor thought, given the circumstances, it was better that way. But you're here now."

"I was really worried. But I get it." He smiled then, and she felt better. "You look amazing, though. Your hair is shorter, right?"

"A little." She enjoyed Nick's obvious pleasure as he took in her new look. Liz practically dragged her to the hair salon, but once it was done, she liked it. "I figured it was time for a change. And it's only been two weeks since you've seen me. But thanks. I'm feeling good." She fiddled with the ring on her finger. "I'm glad for you, Nick, that you're getting to spend some time with your dad. I hope it's everything you want and more. You'll always have those memories."

"Yeah. Better late than never." Nick stretched out his legs. "Oh, and get this. He wants me to go back to school. Become an architect."

Lynette captured the joy in his eyes and felt it herself. "That's wonderful! It's what you always wanted. You'll do it, won't you?"

"Probably. Those details can be worked out later. But, yeah. It's good."

"It is. I'm excited for you."

"Did you ever think about going back to college?" Nick asked, giving the smile she'd missed so much. "Getting your teaching degree? I mean, once things with your dad settle down, and the house . . . We could go together."

Together. More laughter slipped out and she relished it. "Well, I can't say I've thought about it lately, but it's an interesting idea." She clasped her hands and got on with it. "Actually, I'm going away too."

"You are? Where?" His eyes were wide, perhaps a hint of regret tagging along.

So Gray hadn't told him.

"I'm going back to Africa with Ryan. Gray bought me a ticket. My doctor thinks it's a good idea for me to get away. Just for a while."

"What about your dad?"

Lynette pushed her hair out of her eyes and nodded. She was learning to accept that aspect of her life as well. "He'll be looked after. David and Josslyn are talking about maybe moving here, getting a fresh start. Josslyn could apply for a teaching job at the high school. I think David really wants to oversee the renovations and help look after Dad. I'm not sure what Liz is planning to do. I'm not sure she knows." Tears pricked her eyes but she let them come. Avoiding the truth was a thing of the past. "He'll get to the point where he won't know if I'm here or not."

"I'm sorry, Lynnie."

She nodded, stood, and moved around the porch, picking deadheads off the potted geraniums and roses. When she trusted her ability to speak again, she turned around.

"Evy's coming over next week, to go through Dad's paintings with us. She'll start brokering them and hopefully they'll do well. We're all pretty upbeat about the renovations and running the B&B, but you know, things don't always go according to plan. If for some reason we end up having to sell the house, then we will." She could say it now. Hear the truth without it hurting. "I realize now that it wasn't so much about saving Wyldewood. It wasn't the memories of the past I was desperate to hold on to, it was the past itself. The things I couldn't remember. Things I knew and didn't want to face."

Nick clasped his hands behind his head. "Should I have told you the truth, Lynnie? About our parents?"

"It doesn't matter." She shrugged, understanding the conflict. "I don't blame you, Nick. You thought you were doing the right thing." She'd had time to think, to pray, to process, to forgive.

"And I think I needed to remember, to understand the truth of what happened, on my own."

God had not abandoned her, even though at times she'd felt like it. He'd been there all along, guiding her, pointing her toward the doors she needed to walk through.

Now all she had to do was sort through her feelings for Nick.

She turned toward the sea. Nick's steps came closer.

"Did Gray tell you I talked to my father?" He stood so close their arms touched. "About what happened the day your mom died?"

"Yes. And I believe it was just an accident." Lynette shifted to look at him. "I don't want it to be something that comes between us. I hope we'll always be friends, Nick."

"Friends?" Questions crossed his face, furrowed his brow. Questions she wasn't sure she wanted to answer yet, but knew he would give her little choice, and she owed him that much.

"Let's go sit over there." She picked her way across the lawn and positioned herself on the wall, facing the ocean. Nick joined her and they watched the waves in silence.

"Gray and I used to do this all the time."

"Yeah, me too." Nick picked a small shell from the wall and tossed it toward the water. "Except he always tried to push me off." They fell quiet.

Eventually she swiveled, swung her legs around, and planted them firmly on the grass. The windows of the house seemed to smile at her, gleaming in the sun. She could almost see the shadows on the steps, coming and going. But they didn't haunt her anymore.

Nick got up, paced the perimeter of the wall, then walked back to where she sat. "What are you thinking?"

"I'm not sure you want to know."

He sat beside her again and put a hand over hers. "I always want to know what you're thinking."

She studied his face, wanting, wishing, but knowing the difference now between hope and reality. "I'm thinking that you're a wonderful friend. I'm lucky you cared enough about me to want to protect me, to help me. But you don't have to anymore."

"Lynnie, I don't think you understand." He sat forward, squeezed her hand. "Don't you know how I feel about you?"

"Nick." She'd tried to prepare for this conversation. Tried to steel herself for what she knew was best, but now, looking at him, having him so close . . . she wasn't sure she could do it. "I think . . . perhaps it's best we leave all that alone. For now." Her heart was in for a long recuperation. She stood, needing to put some space between them.

"Wait. What are you saying?" Nick was beside her in an instant. He took her hands and held tight. Beyond the questions in his eyes might have been something that spoke of connection, of kinship, of a bond neither of them could deny. Maybe even real love. He'd said as much. She'd wanted to believe it. Still wanted to.

But now she needed more. Needed to find out who she really was.

Needed not to rely on old safety nets.

And Nick had always been one of them.

"I'm saying I want to take this time, Nick, for me."

"Okay, good." His smile didn't last. "But then?"

"Then we'll see."

He shook his head, like he could make her take the words back. "Please don't kick me out of your life, Lynnie. I don't think I could stand it."

"I'm not kicking you out of my life. How could I? You've been in it too long for that."

"But you're saying good-bye, making it sound like it's forever."

"Not forever, Nick. Just for now."

"So, when you get back we can—"

"Nick." She pulled her hands from his, folded her arms. "I need you to be patient with me."

"Okay." He took a few steps back, exhaled. "But . . . I thought you . . . I'd hoped . . . you loved me."

Lynette couldn't look at him and answer the question. Couldn't lie either. So she watched an ant trek across the top of her foot and said nothing.

Nick pressed his fingers under her chin. "Lynnie, look at me."

"Please don't, Nick." Tears blurred her vision.

"Do you love me?" A knowing grin curled his lips. "It's a simple question, Shortstop."

"Of course I do. I always have, Nick." The confession brought a smile. "Is that really news to you?"

Nick's hands slid upward until they cradled her face. "I needed to hear you say it."

She allowed hope to infiltrate her heart once more. "I'm going to miss you."

"Probably not as much as I'll miss you." One finger traced over her trembling lips, and then he gently pressed his own against them. Any protest she might have made died in her throat as she molded against him, put her arms around his neck, and allowed him to kiss her for a long while.

Eventually he pulled away, stared at her, satisfaction lighting his face. "I love you, Lynette Carlisle."

Happiness she couldn't comprehend—and wondered what she'd done to deserve—filled her with new anticipation of what life might be like from now on. "Are you sure?"

"I am." He ran his hands over her hair, truth standing in his eyes. "Maybe you can't accept it right now, but there it is." His fingers burned into her skin while his words burned into her heart. "I know we have things to work out, things to work on, but I want to, Lynnie. I want you to be part of my life. You already are."

"I think I've wanted this too long to really believe it," she admitted with a laugh. "I'll give you a minute to change your mind."

He quickly shook his head. "Not gonna happen. I love you. I love the way you smile, laugh, and talk to me. I love the sound of your voice. I know that I miss you when you're not with me, and

I spend way too much time thinking about seeing you again. And I know that if I have to spend the rest of my life without you, it'll be as worthless as those magnets on the fridge your mother used to collect."

He brushed the tears from her cheeks. "So you can go off to Africa for as long as you want, but I'll be right here waiting for you when you get back. And I'll still love you." He drew back ever so slightly, watching, waiting. "Do you have anything to say?"

"You'll really wait for me?"

"For as long as it takes." He laughed, slipped his arms around her, and held tight. "I do love you, Lynnie, now and forever. And that's the truth. Verity."

She shivered in the wind, met his dancing eyes, and allowed his words to settle into her heart.

Truth.

It was all she'd ever wanted, asked for, prayed for.

Truth that had the power to blast through thick concrete walls that secrets and deceit hid behind. Truth that overshadowed lies, spoke of grace, mercy, and forgiveness. Truth that brought revelation and healing.

And kicked open the door to a wide and wonderful world of endless and exciting possibility.

"What do you say, Miss Carlisle? Will you let me be part of your future?"

"I couldn't imagine it without you." She put her arms around him again and pulled him close. "Whatever comes next, Nick, we'll face it together. And I'll love you the rest of my life."

"So this is what happiness feels like." He pressed his forehead to hers and sighed deeply.

"I think so," Lynette whispered. "I want this forever."

"Done." They stood in the wonder of the moment, both smiling through tears. And then at last, Nick brought his lips to hers one more time and sealed that promise with a kiss.

Discussion Questions

1. In *The Things We Knew*, Lynette's attachment to Wyldewood, the house she grew up in, is very strong. Why do you think she feels this way? Have you ever felt so attached to a particular home or place?

2. Change is often unavoidable. In *The Things We Knew*, Lynette's life is changing dramatically, and she's doing her best to keep up. Have there been times in your life when everything seemed to be changing too fast and you just wanted it to stop? How did you handle it?

3. Which character/s in *The Things We Knew* did you relate to most and why?

4. At the beginning of the story, Nick is conflicted over his feelings for Lynette, and his attachment to the Carlisle family. Do you think he made the right decision in not telling Lynette the truth about what he knew?

5. What do you think you might do if you were in Nick's position, knowing that the secret you keep might do irreparable damage to so many people you care about?

6. Grace is a prevalent theme throughout the story. It's often the most difficult thing to do, show another person grace, especially when you think they don't deserve it. Have you ever been in a situation where you chose grace over

judgment? How did that make you feel? Have you been on the receiving end of somebody extending grace to you?

7. Estrangement and fractured family relationships are common in our communities, but so difficult to navigate. What do you think the Carlisle siblings might have done differently to stay closer during their turbulent childhood years? Why do you think they all chose to go their separate ways?

8. Was there a particular scene or chapter in the story that resonated with you? Why?

9. Gray's life choices have led him to a place of no return. How hard do you think returning home to his family, knowing all his failures, would be?

10. Were you challenged in any way by this story? Would you recommend it to others? Why or why not?

Acknowledgments

Once upon a time, I decided to become a writer. And then I discovered how hard it was. But something made me do it anyway. Still, it's not an easy road. I told God I was quitting a bunch of times. You'd think I'd learn not to argue with Him. I never win. And He is faithful.

The birth of this particular book baby did not happen by chance. It was a long journey of stopping and starting, and God brought more than a few folks into the mix to encourage me and push the process along.

As always, my fabulous agent and friend, Rachelle Gardner—who never gave up, never let me quit, and always told me the dream was within reach—I don't have the words to fully express my heart. Thank-you isn't enough. I wouldn't be celebrating this book without your tireless spirit and endless encouragement, and I'm delighted to share this moment with you! You, the Books & Such team, and all the Bookies are true treasures. Thanks must also go to Mick Silva, the first editor to lay eyes on this story and tell me it was good, then show me how to make it even better. Yes, you said this would happen. I believe you now.

To my publishing family at HCCP—I'm still astounded that I have the privilege of working with you! Thank you for making this author's dream a reality, and loving this story as much as I do. Becky Monds and Natalie Hanneman, your fine editing skills created an even more compelling story—thank you! Daisy, Karli, Kristen, and the rest of the amazing team at Thomas Nelson who work so hard to give the world great books—thank you so much for all you do.

All the wonderful writers within ACFW—your constant encouragement and teaching over the years has been incredible. It's something special when you can look around a room and find a few hundred like-minded individuals just as crazy as you are. Special thanks go to a few—Beth Vogt, you're my anchor, truly. Thank you for knowing what to say and when to say it, and how to pray. I'm so grateful for our first meeting and the amazing friendship birthed from that moment. Katie Ganshert—girl you inspire me, always. Jennifer Major—thanks for keeping it real and making me laugh, even when I don't want to. My Spice Girls, you're a blast and I love you. All you amazing people who've been so patient, kind, and loving—you know who you are, and I couldn't do this without your support.

To my wonderful friends at home—LeeAnne, for never giving up on this dream of mine; Cathy K, thanks for reading and letting Nick have your Jeep TJ! Debbie, Karla, Debi, and so many others; my church family for praying and standing in the gap for me, I love doing life with you.

My precious family—Dad and Vivian, I'm so thrilled to celebrate these moments with you. My sister Pam and US family, I'm so grateful for you. And all the Canadian crew, thanks for taking the journey with me.

My awesome and talented kids, Sarah, and Chris, and your loves—Randy and Deni—you all continue to leave me awestruck and amazed by everything you do; I love you so much. Thanks for keeping me laughing.

And to save the best for last—my incredible husband, Stephen. Your love and encouragement and never-ending support every step of the way keeps me going. Thank you for all you do to help make this dream of mine a reality and for sharing it with me. I'm so grateful for our amazing life and love. I would be lost without you.

> *"Now to Him who is able to do far more abundantly beyond all that we ask or think, according to the power that works within us, to Him be the glory in the church and in Christ Jesus to all generations, forever and ever. Amen."*
> —Ephesians 3:20–21 NASB

About the Author

Catherine West writes stories of hope and healing from her island home in Bermuda. When she's not at the computer working on her next story, you can find her taking her Border Collie for long walks on the beach or tending to her roses and orchids. She and her husband have two grown children.

~

Visit her online at catherinejwest.com
Facebook: CatherineJWest
Twitter: @cathwest